The shining splendor of our Zebra Lovegram logo on the cover of this book reflects the glittering [illegible] of the story inside. Look for the Zebr[illegible] [illegible]r you buy a historical roma[illegible] [illegible]ntees the very best in qual[illegible]

PRAISE [illegible]

"All the emotions y[illegible] [illegible] dose of earthy sexuality make t[illegible] reading."

—[illegible]*ezvous* of CARESS OF FIRE

"Martha Hix always shows her talent for writing Westerns, and CARESS OF FIRE is no exception. I look forward to the rest of the McLoughlin Clan series."

—*Inside Romance*

HUNGRY FOR LOVE

"I told you—don't look at me that way," Charity demanded, pulling at her handcuffs. "I'm not some entrée at a starving man's feast."

"Perhaps you'd like to think you're not," said Hawk. He blew at the steaming spoonful of stew, then offered it to Charity. "You see, I am also a person of powerful hungers."

"Tell me, Hawk. Are you planning to have your way with me before you try to extort money from my family?"

"Eat your stew."

But the moment he placed the spoon at her lips, she turned. The motion sent his arm on a downward path. The spoon fell to the pillow and Hawk's hand landed on her breast.

Charity clasped the bed rails and Hawk watched as a conflict of emotions stormed across her face. He murmured her name as if in a chant.

"You *are* going to have your way with me," she whispered.

"Don't you want me to?" He moved closer. Her lips parted. He knew it was to make some scathing remark, but his mouth descended on her first. She tasted sweet. *Wah'Kon-Tah!* His hunger surprised him. Always he'd gotten a thrill from bringing down wild beasts. This woman was the wildest and most beautiful of them all, and he meant to send the bow of lust straight into her. . . .

THE FIERY PASSION, EARTHY SENSUALITY,
AND THRILLING ADVENTURES OF
THE MCLOUGHLIN CLAN
CONTINUE IN THESE OTHER MARTHA HIX
TITLES, PUBLISHED BY ZEBRA BOOKS:

Now Available:

BOOK I, CARESS OF FIRE

by Martha Hix

Lisette Keller was determined to leave Texas and pursue her dream of opening a millenery shop in Chicago—but first she had to find a way to get there. If she could persuade handsome rancher Gil McLoughlin to hire her as a cook on his cattle drive to Abilene, she'd be well on her way. To Gil, a cattle drive was no place for any woman. But the headstrong rancher was soon not only agreeing to take her on as cook, but also vowing to take her in his powerful embrace. The long hard Chisholm Trail lay ahead, with many a starry night beneath the Texas sky, and Gil meant to savor Lisette's sensuous beauty and velvety kisses . . . all the way to Kansas!

Coming in August 1993:

BOOK III, WILD SIERRA ROGUE

by Martha Hix

Sparks flew when the dark and devilish Rafe Delgado teamed with prim short-tempered Margaret McLoughlin, triplet daughter of Lisette and Gil, on an expedition into Mexico's dangerous, bandit-filled Copper Canyon. Margaret was determined to see her mother safely retrieved from Mexico and brought back to the states, even if she did have to spend time with the infuriating rake, whose only dubious virtue was carnal charisma. Rake knew Margaret disapproved of his roguish ways, but he still meant to have her in his bed. The problem was, Rafe had always been able to love 'em and leave 'em before, and now, after sampling Margaret's sweet offerings, he wanted to claim her as his alone forever.

MARTHA HIX

Lone Star Loving

ZEBRA BOOKS
KENSINGTON PUBLISHING CORP.

SPECIAL THANKS to Jacqueline Masten of Fredericksburg, Texas

ZEBRA BOOKS

are published by

Kensington Publishing Corp.
475 Park Avenue South
New York, NY 10016

First Printing: January, 1993

Printed in the United States of America

*To my little angel
of crippled wing*

Chapter One

Charity McLoughlin was, as usual, in a mess of her own making.

Unloved by her family, disowned by them, she had no choice but to turn to a female acquaintance for help. Not a penny lined her brocade clutch as she hurried through the crowded, torch-lit streets of Laredo, a town lying along the Rio Grande, a town more Mexican than Texan. Nothing—and certainly not lack of funds—would stop her from fleeing this place. *Nothing.*

Chances were, Maria Sara Montaña could be of assistance in helping Charity escape from so much as a smell that would remind her of south Texas and its riotous neighbor across the border. More important, the *mexicana* might help her avoid having to face her crime of the previous month.

But where was her friend? On this, the evening of the sixteenth of September, 1889, Charity had looked everywhere, including the main plaza, from where speeches droned on lauding Mexican independence, mingling with mariachi music.

A voice from the past echoed in her mind: "Stay

put, and the world will find ye." Charity chose to disregard that bit of great-grandmotherly advice. If she stayed put, the world might indeed find her—the world being the long arms of the law!

Best to keep searching for Maria Sara.

Clothed in a simple calico dress, Charity sidestepped a pushcart piled high with tequila bottles, and made her way to the center of town again. All at once, firecrackers popped and a covey of pigeons flew from the belfry of St. Augustine Church. Roman candles went airborne to dazzle the night with red, white, and spring green.

This was no night for Charity to appreciate such a display; the fireworks jarred her already frayed nerves. She nearly stumbled at the spectacle.

Just then, a trio of brown-skinned drunks shoved into her path, and in his zeal the heftiest one shouted, *"Viva México!"* His elbow slammed into her ribs, shoving her into a table that collapsed with a thud, echoing her prospects for a bright future.

She landed on the broken table, its pile of round tortillas plopping atop her bosom and trailing down on to her skirts. *Great, just great,* she thought. As the trio continued on their merry way without so much as a backward glance, Charity muttered snidely, "Stand back, ladies, and let the gentlemen pass by."

The tortilla vendor, a toothless woman dressed in rags, fired off a round of protests over her destroyed property. Charity, under her breath, spat a swear word of the caliber that would have sent her mother rushing for the nearest cake of lye soap, had she been on the premises of her parents' ranch in central Texas.

What else could go wrong?

From behind a strand of waist-length dark hair

that had fallen to block the view of one eye, Charity spied a tall man approach the vendor and hand over a small stack of bills.

"This should take care of the damages," he said, the deep tone of his voice gripping Charity's attention. "Now, why don't you go and enjoy the fiesta, ma'am?"

"Ah, yes. I will drink to good fortune," the peasant said, smacking her crinkled lips and stabbing the bills into her skirt pocket. She grabbed the walking stick that rested against the nearby adobe building and hobbled off in the direction of the plaza.

"Thank you," Charity said to the stranger as she brushed the wayward hair from her face, trying to get a good look at her benefactor. Who was he? Why had he spent money on her behalf? Good Samaritans didn't appear in the night. Had the *world* found her? Surely not! But she warned herself not to be too trusting.

He extended a large hand that Charity ignored. "Are you hurt?" he asked.

It was then that she noticed two things. The street was practically deserted, the revelers no doubt gathered to hear the garrulous speeches. And clouds had passed over the full moon, allowing Charity to make the following observation about her rescuer: the man was big.

Even taller than her kinsmen. Probably no more than thirty—though it was hard to tell since a Stetson shadowed his features. He wore a fringed jacket that accentuated expansive shoulders. She lowered her gaze to buckskin britches that hugged narrow hips and cupped a formidable region no decent woman—not even a godforsaken one, for that matter!—ought to notice.

And there was something about him, something that bespoke authority. *Heavens, what if he's a Texas Ranger out to arrest me?* she worried. *Don't be ridiculous.* Ian Blyer had threatened to go to the authorities, but he did grant a few days' grace.

She must not assume this kind stranger posed any threat.

"I asked if you're hurt." The stranger thumbed the brim of his Stetson, raising it a fraction of an inch up his forehead. "Are you?"

She couldn't help but chuckle nervously. It "hurt" to be sprawled on the ground so absurdly. Then again, she had mastered the art of presenting herself in a bad light.

After slapping a tortilla off her bodice and dislodging a piece of broken table from her behind, she raised up on an elbow. "I find it amazing that people always ask if someone is hurt at a time like this," she said. "If nothing else, we're talking bruised pride here."

"Excuse me for asking."

"Why did you . . . ?" she began, then stopped to rearrange her skirt, since what was probably a lecherous ogle seemed welded to an unladylike display of legs that, in the silvery moonlight, appeared even whiter than usual. "Why did you give that woman money to leave me alone?"

"You were in trouble. I saw fit to help." He bent to crouch back on his booted heels, one forearm resting on his thigh. "Anything wrong with that?"

Suspicions spurred higher, she asked, "Who are you?"

"Hawk."

Hawk. *Are you as magnificent as your namesake?* It was difficult to tell. Yet from the formidable proportions apparent even in the dark, she sensed the name fit the man.

Unlike how the name "Charity" fit her. How many times had Papa chided her for not living up to it? Not to mention her esteemed family name?

Trying to scan Hawk's shadowed features, she said, "I don't know you."

"You do now."

"But you didn't know *me.*"

"Wrong. You're Charity McLoughlin of Fredericksburg. Daughter of United States Senator Gil McLoughlin, who happens to be one of the most successful cattlemen in Texas. And you're in"—in one smooth move Hawk stood to tower above her—"You're in a lot of trouble, lady."

He had to be a Ranger! How could she escape—quickly? He looked as if he could run up Mount Olympus without losing his breath, and muscles she never knew existed were throbbing as a result of her fall. Somehow, she had to outwit him.

Recovering the empty clutch that had fallen amid the scattered tortillas, Charity began an ungraceful climb to her feet. The man still towered above her, for his height topped her five-eight by seven or eight inches.

"Thank you, Mister Hawk, for helping me," she said, her eyes level with the lower part of his throat. "But I cannot repay you, not at the moment. You see, my purse was stolen just this morning, and I find myself financially compromised."

What a lie. On the purse score, anyway. At the moment, though, she would have sold out the other two of her triplet sisters in order to keep her freedom. Desperation had a way of doing that to a person.

"Stolen purse, you say?" His tone of voice and stance expressed skepticism. "What's that in your hand?"

"I own more than one handbag. And believe me, this one is empty." *Unless you want to count one shredded handkerchief.* "Don't worry. I'll make restitution as soon as possible."

"Money isn't what I'm after."

In her estimation, her hide and getting it behind bars figured prominently in his desires. *Think again, Mister.* Never would she prove a sitting duck for some bird-of-prey Texas Ranger.

Unwilling to go on conjecture alone, though, she inquired, "You're a lawman, aren't you?"

"The law is my profession."

A good enough answer. He *had* to be a member of the state police force. Hearing a disturbance down the street, Charity got an idea. Taking a step around Hawk, she craned her neck toward the street corner. Three drunks passed by, waving bottles and singing off-key. They were the same louts who had knocked her to the ground.

"There he is!" She jabbed a finger in the air. "That's the one! That's the one who stole my purse! The fat one!" Hands waving frantically now, she implored the Ranger to act. "Help me, Mister Hawk! That man must be arrested!"

Thank God this one was gullible. The moment Hawk wheeled to rush the drunk, Charity disregarded the protest of her abused body. She whirled around, grabbed a broken leg from the table, swung it with all her might, and hit the Ranger on the side of his head.

Stetson flying and releasing straight long raven-black hair he fell with a thud, facedown on the cobbled street. Facedown and lifeless.

Charity's conscience reared as her eyes widened on the inert form. Her heart jumped into her throat. "Oh, Lord, I've killed you! I'm sorry, Mister Hawk! So sorry."

Now the authorities would add murder to her inadvertent crime of acting as go-between for the ring that had smuggled Texas silver into Mexico.

Now she'd murdered someone's son. Perhaps someone's husband. Couldn't she do anything right? Why couldn't she have just stunned him?

Emitting a groan, the Ranger moved his hand.

Charity breathed a sigh of relief at that sign of life, then took flight. In the interest of time, she had to abandon any thought of finding Maria Sara.

Moments later, Charity had returned to the squalid lodging she'd rented the previous May and was throwing a change of clothes into her valise. She had to get out of town, even if that meant walking. Which appeared to be her sole option.

To a master horsewoman, walking was an indignity. But when she had parted ways with her family, her papa hadn't allowed her prized and adored Andalusian mare to accompany the mad exodus. *Now isn't the time for caterwauling about Papa or Thunder Cloud!* she thought.

A soft knock brought her out of her dark reflections.

"Charity?" a female voice called through the open

doorway. "What's going on? What is wrong?"

She turned to face the exotically beautiful Maria Sara Montaña. "Everything. But I've no time to talk."

The blonde of twenty-two—petite, serene, ladylike, all the things Charity was not—stared at the open valise and rushed into the room. "Where are you going?"

"Away. Far away. I don't know where, but I've got to hurry." Charity fastened the valise. "Ian caught me burying the smuggling loot." When asked what he'd done with the money, she replied, "He handed it over to the Rangers. Said he'd found it."

"Madre de Dios!"

"He says if I don't marry him, he'll change his story and turn me in to the law."

Maria Sara eyed the tiny room and its layers of expensive dresses, bustles, and finery, bought when Charity had been an accepted member of the wealthy McLoughlin clan. Clothing that Charity had been unable to sell, even at a fraction of their value, thanks to Blyer intervention.

Eyes as blue as Charity's and filled with sympathy settled on the busy form. "How will you leave? The train won't depart until tomorrow. You cannot rush off into the dark of night."

Dark of night. The very words frightened her, but she had no choice. "I must. I whacked a Texas Ranger with a table leg."

"Then, the police have found out about—?"

"I've no time for explanations. Hawk knows who I am, and he'll be here to arrest me. I know he will. As soon as he gets his wits about him."

Shaking her head of upswept hair, Maria Sara sat down on the bed. *"Pobrecita,* trouble does seem to find you." She lifted a finger to her throat thoughtfully. "Don't you think the best course would be to find yourself an attorney?"

"I've thought of that a thousand times since I discovered what I'd done for the Gonzáles gang."

What a fool she'd been, getting duped into their scheme. Adriano Gonzáles led her to believe he offered employment, a decent way to earn a living. And she'd needed a job, since Ian Blyer and his influential father had warned respectable firms and citizens against hiring her. Even work as a washerwoman had been denied her.

"Charity, what about my idea? What about a lawyer?"

"Yes, I need one. But how would I pay?"

"You could ask your mother. Or your great-grandmother."

Pain, icy and sharp, lodged in Charity's veins. "My mother stands by whatever my father says, and Maiz . . ." She swallowed. *Neither one has done so much as drop me a postcard.*

"What about your brother?"

"Angus? He's but a child. Thirteen."

"You have two sisters."

Charity glanced at the clock that sat on the battered bureau. Fifteen long minutes had passed since she had left the Ranger on the street. She set the valise on the floor. "Maria Sara, I've got to go."

"How can I help?"

Charity hesitated. The young *mexicana's* financial situation wasn't much better than hers, given that she had a young son to support on a meager salary. As friends, though, each had always helped the other.

Charity's problems—at least those associated with

south Texas—had started the previous May, when she'd arrived in Laredo to marry the son of a local Anglo politician. After Ian Blyer proved to be a scoundrel interested only in getting his mitts on McLoughlin money, Maria Sara Montaña had flown to her aid with an offer of friendship.

Leaning toward her, Maria Sara repeated her question.

"If you have any money, would you loan me some?" Charity asked.

"Of course," the brothel singer replied. "And, for once, I do have some cash. The patrons were generous with their tips last night."

There was an odd lilt to that dulcet voice. Charity reasoned it stemmed from wounded pride. A couple of years ago, the proud *mexicana* was turned off the family estate after admitting she carried a bastard. Finances had forced her to accept a job in a house of ill repute. Finances and some crumb of a father, who'd abandoned his child and his obligations.

The singer emptied her purse and extended a wad of bills. "Take it."

As Charity placed a kiss of gratitude on her friend's smooth cheek, she had a fleeting thought of how much she missed her sisters, even though as children the three had been at odds more than not. Sisters were like that, Charity supposed. *At least my sisters love me. They're the only ones in the family who feel that way.*

It had been too long since she'd seen Olga and Margaret. Both were far away, each living respectable lives, neither aware of Charity's break with their parents and great-grandmother, unless one of the elder McLoughlins had informed the better two of the triplets. A likely situation. Charity had been too ashamed to tell them anything herself.

But if Margaret or Olga knew—

"I will miss you, *amiga,*" Maria Sara whispered, patting Charity's arm. "May God go with you."

"Thank you." She turned to leave. "I'll miss you, too."

"Charity . . . before you go. What about Ian?"

"Let him eat cake."

"Don't take him lightly. Ian will be furious when he finds you've left here." Two ticks of the clock. "He's ruthless when crossed."

Not replying, Charity rushed from the room and started down the stairs leading to a darkened back street of Laredo. Her foot had no more than touched the ground before a big hand grabbed her forearm. In the wink of an eye, she was forced to drop her valise, her arms were brought together in front of her, and a set of iron manacles—even more insistent than a predator's talons—was clamped on her wrists.

Hawk had captured her.

Chapter Two

"Damn you!" Charity screamed as the Ranger slapped the handcuffs on her wrists. Realizing the gravity of her situation, she tried to plead with him. "I didn't mean to do wrong. Please leave me alone."

She might as well have saved her breath, yet she hoped against hope Maria Sara would hear her, would rush to her aid. But no one appeared on the dark, deserted street.

The Ranger—wearing his now-battered Stetson—gave no verbal response to her continued shouts, not until after he'd grabbed her valise and clutch bag, tucked them under his arm, and began dragging her by the elbow toward the corner, where a buckboard and team were waiting. "Get in," he ordered.

"No," Charity replied adamantly.

He tossed Charity's valise in the wagon bed; without another word, he yanked her off her feet and deposited her onto the seat.

"I don't cotton to anyone resisting arrest," he growled, dusting his hands. Swinging up beside her, he turned his face her way. "You're going to answer to the law, lady."

Defeat. As a buzzard did carrion, defeat ate at Charity; she wilted on the spring seat. She wouldn't cry, though, refusing to show her vulnerability. Never had Charity allowed anyone that much purchase into her soul. Never. Not even her favorite sister, Margaret.

She straightened her back stoically. "All right. I'll go along peacefully," she relented.

A funny, medicinal smell drifted to her nose; she disregarded it to eye her antagonist. The full moon afforded some light, but his face was hidden by the battered western hat, making it impossible to distinguish his features. It was easy to see he was big; it was just as easy to figure he could overpower her, especially with her hands tied.

Flying in the face of her usual luck, she said, "My name will be cleared, you wait and see."

"What you need is a good lawyer."

"No, Mister Hawk, I don't." Bravado was this, but bravado was all Charity McLoughlin had left. "The truth will set me free."

"Yeah. Right."

He picked up the reins, set the buckboard in motion, and the two rode in silence through the streets of Laredo, silence that was shattered when the wagon veered off in the opposite direction from the city jail.

"Don't you know left from right? You've turned the wrong way." Charity's voice lowered. "Where are we going?"

He snapped the reins over the team.

Watching as they passed by the muted lights of huts lining the outskirts of town, she repeated her question.

"Giddyup," was his only reply.

By now they had cleared the edge of Laredo, and Charity realized there was something very, very wrong. What *was* going on? Who *was* this man?

If only she could get a good look at his face, perhaps she might get a clue. If only she had something to go on, something beyond the active imagination that had gotten her into hot water time after time.

"Take off your hat," she demanded.

"You don't give the orders."

Oooh! "All right." *I'll teach him.* "Why don't you take off your hat so that I might be allowed to see if you're as ugly as I think you are."

All he did was chuckle.

Quite unamused, the shackles heavy, she said, "You know me, and you said I must face the law. You let me believe you're a lawman. Yet you didn't take me to jail. Who are you?"

"I'm called Hawk."

"I know that. But it's just a name. A hawk is nothing to me but a mean-eyed bird with sharp, nasty talons." Well, hawks were regal. Under the moonlight she watched as he moved a leg slightly, the faint light outlining the strength of long, long limbs not at all birdlike.

"Mister Hawk, where are you taking me?"

"To your deliverance."

"I beg your pardon?"

"You heard me."

"Why did you let me think you were taking me to jail?"

"I am Hawk. That's all you need to know."

She begged to differ. But arguing became secondary to the fear that crawled up her spine. Fear as cold as the manacles stiffening her wrists. If this Hawk were a Ranger or a sheriff or whatever, he would admit it, wouldn't he? His vague answer spoke for itself.

He was not the law.

Undoubtedly, he was outside of it.

Wasn't this a fine kettle of fish?

She said, "If you're one of Adriano Gonzáles's men, I—"

"I am not."

Small comfort. "You're not a lawman. You weren't a partner of Adriano's. What does that leave, Mister Hawk?"

As she somehow expected, he didn't reply.

The wooden seat hard against her backside, she tried to make some sense of his identity; the conclusion drawn did nothing to settle her nerves. Several times she'd read newspaper accounts of persons from prominent families being seized, then ransomed to their loved ones. Especially if the booty didn't materialize, they were sometimes never seen again. Alive, anyway.

It wasn't a publicized fact that the McLoughlins wouldn't give a red cent for their wayward daughter's return. But Charity knew they wouldn't.

Her only chance was to escape.

She glanced at the man beside her. He seemed intent upon driving the team, nothing more. *Think,*

Charity. Think. Since he'd been unconscious once tonight, surely he was in a weakened condition. What about trying to hit him again? Should she try to push him off the seat and beneath the rolling wagon wheels?

Neither option sounded as if success was written into it.

Continued inquiry seemed the best course. "Mister Hawk—"

"Just call me Hawk."

"Hawk. Ah, um, I've deduced something. You've kidnapped me. Am I right or wrong?"

"I've taken you away."

Just minutes ago, she'd wanted to be away from Laredo. And riding beat walking, but . . . "Deliverance was how you put it—a peculiar choice of word. Doesn't it imply that you're taking me to my freedom?"

"Could happen, provided events fall in the right order."

His vague answer settled in the abacus of her brain—rarely a reliable tool, but all she had to work with. "Kidnapping is a hanging offense. You'll pay for your folly, Mister Hawk."

"You talk too much."

Too many times she'd been told what a blabbermouth she was. Too many times it had been pointed out that she was less than worthy to open her mouth. Nonetheless, she'd never learned to keep that mouth shut.

"Don't you think I have a right to say whatever I please, especially if it might shake some sense into your noggin?"

"You're much too argumentative. You'd never sway a jury with your words." Hawk tapped the reins. "And a jury, lady, is just what you would've faced, if I hadn't come to your rescue. Matter of fact, your pretty head would soon be resting on a jail cot, if not for—"

"Rescue?" she repeated, ignoring the last part of his statement. She didn't give a hoot how he knew about her law troubles. Ian knew; probably a lot of people hereabouts knew her for a smuggler. "Since when have rescue and kidnap been synonymous?"

"Be quiet."

"In no way, form, or fashion!" When he shrugged, she made a huge demand of herself: patience. "There's something you need to know. If you think to extort money from my father, think again—I'm worthless to him."

"Perhaps you underestimate your worth."

For a moment she didn't say a word. If only what he said were true. *If only.* Wait a minute. Could it be possible . . . ? Had her father sent this man to collect her? She warned herself not to live in a dream world. Gil McLoughlin would never budge from his parting words: "If you leave this house, Daughter, and go running after that Blyer man, I'll consider you dead." Papa wasn't one for idle threats.

"Even a black sheep has its value," Hawk said.

"Not in the McLoughlin flock."

Given her lack of alternatives, she knew she had to act quickly. That's all there was to it. She leaned slowly to the side, bracing one foot on the floorboard. She raised her arms discreetly, and then quickly reared up, meaning to bring the manacles down on his temple. But she was no match for Hawk. In less than a heartbeat, he had dropped the reins, feinted her blow, and grabbed her arms. The wagon wobbled. The horses picked up speed. Charity fought him.

"Dammit, woman, be still or you'll get us both killed!"

She kicked frantically at his muscled body, tried to elbow him off the seat. Not succeeding with either course of action, she leaned to bite his shoulder.

She tasted buckskin, and the warm scent of man filled her nostrils. "Ouch!" she heard him shout as he flinched. "Hellcat, be still or I'll—"

His grip on her loosened, and such an advantage was put to good use—she slapped her iron-clad wrists against his throat. The next thing she realized, he had tossed her across his lap, and her head was swinging from the moving buckboard. Her hair nearly touched the ground, and her fright rose to a pitch—she'd be the one to get tangled in a wagon wheel!

It figured.

When good luck was passed out, it must have missed the dunce's corner—where Charity had to have been banished.

Right then Hawk pulled her hair up, and reached over to grab something from the floorboard, something that turned out to be a white cloth. Before pressing the wet cloth over her nose, he said with a growl, "I'd hoped it wouldn't come to this."

A sharp smell poleaxed her; she attempted to

avert her head. What . . . ? What was . . . ? She felt the fight leave her, felt herself drifting off to sleep. Her last thought was, *The louse has drugged me.*

Chapter Three

Rendering Charity insensible had been Sam Washburn's idea.

David Fierce Hawk hadn't liked the suggestion the day before, when the doctor had concocted the evil brew, and Hawk didn't like the idea one whit better tonight. Not when he shut the hellcat up, not as he drove to the prearranged hideout located a few miles east of Laredo. And the idea of drugging her didn't sit any better now, now that he and Sam had leashed her in the two-room shack and left her to sleep off the chloroform's effects.

Nevertheless, Hawk had taken the jar and rag with him that morning upon leaving the doctor's hermitage. He had heard too many tales about the wildest, most undisciplined of the McLoughlin triplets not to play it safe. And it was a good thing he had, since as it turned out Charity McLoughlin hadn't gone along peaceably.

At least she'd fallen for the lawman trick, which she, herself, had planted in Hawk's mind; it was consistent with the handcuffs he'd thought of himself. Getting her aboard the wagon had proved easy enough.

Brute strength, Sam's medicine, and the trappings bartered from a Uvalde lawman did have their advantages.

Right now, in the dark of midnight, as Hawk settled a boot heel on Sam Washburn's rickety corral rail while watching the hideaway's only door to the outside world, he rubbed the lump on his head and the bruise on his throat, then gave thought to the bite mark on his shoulder.

What a hellcat.

It was doubtful he'd have even gotten the opportunity to use the chloroform, had she known his true purposes in kidnapping her. As he'd been alerted, she would have fought to the death—clawing and spitting until the end—rather than go with him.

Better she should think he was out to ransom her, that he was a kidnapper interested only in dirty recompense.

She'd learn the truth soon enough.

"Reckon she knows who you are?" asked Sam.

"I doubt it. I've been told she'd recognize my full name, but . . ."

"You gonna tell her?"

"No. I was warned she'd be set against returning to the fold, and from what I've gathered, that is the case. I can't let her make that connection." He cast an eye at his old friend from Fort Smith, who was swilling from a flask of rye whiskey. "Shouldn't have been this way, Sam. Figured when

I met Charity McLoughlin, it would be on her turf. At some fancy ball . . . with violins playing. Or somesuch."

A white man with a red man's way of thinking, Sam chuckled. "Your lawyering in Washington was a bad influence, my Osage friend. You went soft in the heart."

Hawk pushed away from the corral railing and straightened. "Better check on the woman," he said, inhaling the clean, dry smell of south Texas. Lacking the beauty of the high plains, this was a flat, harsh land, swept by drought and dotted with chaparral and cactus; it would be a difficult place to hide in. But he would find a way to keep out of the paths of well-meaning strangers who might come to a kidnapped woman's aid. "She may be sick, once she wakes up."

"Another sign of your soft heart. Never thought I'd see the day you'd turn sap." Sam tapped the flask into his back pocket, then ran long fingers through his crop of gray hair. "Look at you, Fierce Hawk of the Osage. Worrying over a white woman, dressed as a paleface—"

"I draw less attention, wearing the raiment of their kind."

Sam chuckled dryly. "You may not know it, but you've turned into a paleface. Your speech, your mannerisms. And in a dozen other ways that I doubt you're aware of."

Hawk crossed his arms and tucked his fingers under his armpits. Was Sam's assessment correct?

"I suppose you aren't alone in doing such," said

the grizzled physician of fifty winters. "Many of your people have taken the white man's habits."

"The times forced us into it." A sour note curdled Hawk's tone. "In Washington I behaved as a white man. As you know, that was the expected conduct for an advocate of Indian rights. If one wanted to be taken seriously."

Hawk knew the older man needed no reminders of acceptable behavior, that which was dictated by the white race; in siding with a renegade Kiowa in a dispute with the army, Sam Washburn—a mountain man whose brilliance with a scalpel had earned him a degree from a prestigious school—had lost his medical practice in Arkansas.

Under the full moon Sam scrutinized Hawk. "It's been difficult for us both, life. I've suffered for siding with the red man. And you're out of place in both worlds."

"Sam—"

"Had you been born in the previous century, or even earlier in this one, you could've gone with your instincts. You could have ridden the plains, free as the wind, your bow and arrow at the ready. You would have been a warrior with a war. And you would've been a good warrior."

But now, in 1889, Hawk had nothing to fight for.

"Since you're more white than Osage—"

"I don't accept my mixed heritage."

"Accept it, Hawk. Accept it. You're more than halfway there already. You've got an advantage. Your white blood near-about overrode your Indian strain. Most folks figure you're white. Or no more than a white man with a native ancestor somewhere in the family tree."

"You know it needles me when I'm mistaken for something I am not."

"But you are what you are. Be as white as you can. Be the white man's attorney. And make use of the legacy from your paleface grandmother in Maryland. You'll be well-served, since there's no future for your people." On a dry note, Sam added, "And your money is the great equalizer."

All of that might have been good advice, but Hawk would rather have been born a century earlier. "Your suggestions are unacceptable."

"Then you're a fool, my friend." Sam glanced at the sky; moonlight highlighted his prominent nose when he lowered his intense scrutiny. "The Indian culture has been dying since ole Christopher Columbus first set foot on American soil."

It had taken hundreds of years for Europeans to subdue the natives. Now, that task was on the road to completion. It left a bitter taste in Hawk's mouth, especially as Sam was echoing advice given him by the land-baron senator from Texas, Gil McLoughlin of Fredericksburg.

Hawk took his own look at the moon. It was the same moon shining over the Osage reservation, up in the Territory. What were his mother and father doing now? Had the corn crop been brought in? What about Amy? Had his sister delivered her baby yet? He shook off sentimental thoughts, replacing them with angry ones. He thought about how, without a shot being fired, the Territory Indians had stood by passively and allowed the land rush of the previous April.

By May first the council elders had sent a communiqué to Washington ordering Hawk to cease his demands for fair play. He severed his ties with his Osage brethren that same afternoon. At least one thing was accomplished before his leaving. Congress granted the Osage nation sovereign rights to their latest reservation. But how long would that last?

"Will you marry the woman, now that you've captured her?" Sam inquired.

Shaken out of his gloom, Hawk grinned. His thoughts went back to that day in 1869 when he had told the lovely German woman Lisette McLoughlin, then carrying her triplets, that he meant to take her daughter as his own. "It was a boy's decision, my intentions to marry a McLoughlin daughter."

"Yep, but I've heard you talk about it since you were knee-high to a grasshopper. And here lately, you still . . ."

Hawk laughed. "I'd be lying if I said I haven't given it a thought or two." *Or a thousand.* "But you know what's going on in my life. I've no business with a wife. Especially one as wild and felonious as Charity McLoughlin." Another chuckle. "You should have seen her earlier this evening—she's the image of her father. Obstinate as a Missouri mule."

"That so? Seems to me, I recall you never had

anything against women more mulish than your own self."

Hawk cleared his throat. Best to shut up. He didn't hanker to discuss the lustful thoughts he'd been entertaining from the first moment he'd laid eyes on Charity McLoughlin.

Settling an elbow on the corral rail, Sam cocked his head. "Why'd you want one of them in the first place?"

"I figured the daughters would be as good as the mother." Lisette, a pretty blonde who had accompanied her husband on a cattle drive through the territory, had said the right words to bolster Hawk's youthful vanity. And she had set him on the road to education. Back then—and now—she was a damned good woman.

"In my mind," he said to Sam, "I always figured any daughter of that good lady would be smart and brave and compassionate. A woman who'd fight at her man's side, rather than against him. Like her mother. Like a good Indian woman. Perhaps she is. But I'm thinking Charity isn't."

"Good or no-good, she's a fine-looking gal. I myself always liked 'em like that, tall and brunette and top-heavy." Sam hitched up his pants. "If I were a young buck like you—"

"I don't have anything against her looks."

"Then what about one of the sisters? You said you heard the three ladies look just the same. Maybe one of the other two would be more to your liking."

"Even if I were interested, which I am *not,* one

is married and the other attends a university back East."

"Okay. Don't marry any of them."

"I won't."

"I doubt their father would allow it, anyway."

"Right."

Were he salivating for the love of Charity, Hawk supposed he'd have the fight of his life with Gil McLoughlin. But as it was, he wasn't panting for wedlock. Bedding Charity was a different matter.

The sound of horses neighing in the corral diverted Sam's attention. "Think I'll take a walk," he said. Maybe give the girls a goodbye pat, seeing's how you'll be taking them tomorrow."

Half listening, Hawk nodded. Yes, come morning, he'd hitch up the elderly mares for the trip to Miss Charity McLoughlin's destiny.

An image formed. He saw the woman he'd been following for days, who was now sleeping just yards away. She was all the things Sam had mentioned admiring in looks. And more. Her eyes—the contrast of those blue, blue irises to her sable-dark mass of waves—could neither be ignored nor forgotten.

But she was trouble.

It hadn't taken much investigating to discover she'd fallen in with the notorious Adriano Gonzáles and his bandits. Several of them had died at the hands of John Hughes and his Rangers upon being ambushed near Shafter, but somehow Charity had escaped with her life. Hawk grimaced. A woman ought to behave, ought to be above reproach.

And though the law wasn't yet aware of Charity's complicity in the smuggling, Hawk was sure that was only a matter of time.

Charity McLoughlin needed a damned good lawyer.

David Fierce Hawk was a damned good lawyer.

But he had to get his life in order, perhaps by setting up a law practice in Texas's capital at Austin. Back in Washington, in the wake of recalling their meeting in '69, Gil McLoughlin had suggested the Austin move. "Success in Texas will mean playing up your white blood," Hawk had been advised. Such a proposal had and did sit like a tomahawk in his gut. Yet, at loose ends after the fiasco of the previous spring's land rush, Hawk had been curious enough to travel to Texas and seek the rancher-solon out.

A week of indecision ensued.

On a horseback ride across the vast Four Aces Ranch, McLoughlin had asked, "Will you make your home in Austin?"

"I've got to give it more thought."

"If not Austin, what then?"

"Time will tell."

But what were his options? There just weren't that many wars left to wage for an Osage in these times.

He eyed McLoughlin, seeing silver-winged black hair and an air of confidence etching a sun-dried face. Hawk grinned. "Maybe I do have an idea or two," he joked. "Maybe I'll just find me some nice white woman and wage war with her. Where did you say those unmarried daughters of yours are right now? Margaret, for instance."

A look crossed McLoughlin's face much akin to that of an Apache with a thorn in his toe—black fury. "I respect you, David Fierce Hawk," he replied with a note of restraint in his voice. "I think you're one helluva lawyer, and you're a damned fine man, but don't overstep your bounds."

Bounds? More like racial lines, Hawk thought.

Hawk set his mount into a prance to circle in front of McLoughlin. "All right, forget Margaret. What about the other one? Charity. You said yourself she's been a hellion since the day she was born." Spunky had always had its allure to Hawk. "I could take her off your hands."

"Do as you please." McLoughlin tugged on the reins and kicked his mount. "As far as I'm concerned, that one is dead and buried."

Hawk knew Lisette stood by her husband's decision over their black-sheep daughter, though he had seen sadness in her expression. A damned sorrowful situation. Catching up with the senator, Hawk said, "She couldn't be all that bad, your girl."

"Dammit, don't concern yourself with my family. And don't interfere, either."

On that August morning, Hawk had laughed heartily. The senator might claim to have buried a daughter, but blood ran thicker than family feuds.

And if red were to mix with McLoughlin white . . .

"No need to worry yourself," he called after the departing McLoughlin. "I'll keep my britches buttoned where your girls are concerned." *Maybe.*

What he hankered for was a good look at one of those girls promised to him back in '69. Then, on the eve of his leaving the Four Aces to visit Sam Washburn, Maisie McLoughlin had set Hawk on his current course.

"Bring the lass home," she had said, appealing to what she knew to be Hawk's affection for her, a ninety-year-old Scotswoman who pined for a wayward great-granddaughter. She'd also piqued his curiosity.

"But keep yer hands to yerself," the feisty woman—old as the plains and skinny as a rail—had demanded. "Bring my great-granddaughter back in the condition ye find her. A virgin."

"What if she's not?"

Fires jumped and blazed in the aged blue eyes; she shook an arthritic finger. "The lass may be a lotta things, but ye'll not be finding her loose. So don't ye be poking at her maidenhead."

As for the "lass," Hawk had been wondering what it would be like to mate with a McLoughlin daughter since he'd obtained the medicine of manhood. He made no promises to her great-grandmother.

The Old One started jabbering about how she had lost weight and sleep over the "tarnished angel running off t' wed that Blyer peacock."

Recalling her parents' banishment of their daughter, Hawk asked, "If you want my help, I need some answers. Do Lisette and McLoughlin hate her simply because she's a runaway?"

"They doona hate her! They love the lass. But she is"—the Old One dabbed at her eyes—"hard to love. She has done her best to drive us all mad. Running off to marry that peacock was the last straw."

"I was under the impression they aren't married." Hawk crossed his arms. "And I'm no magician. I can't make a virgin out of a married woman."

"She ain't wed! Her father alerted every county clerk in the state t' watch for an application for a marriage license. There hasna been any. Now, get riding, lad! I'm wanting me lass at home."

Hawk packed his bag. The Old One gave him one last instruction as he was riding away. " 'Twon't be easy, lad, bringing her home. She's a stubborn wench. Scare sense int' her if need be. And she'll be needing it."

"Scare sense into her?"

"Ye're an Indian, ye know what t' do."

"Ma'am, my people are the peaceful sort. With a bow and arrow I'm considered a fine hunter, but I'm not a marksman with a gun. And I am *not* trained in scare tactics."

"Ye'll think of something."

That had been Fredericksburg; this was the aftermath of Laredo. His curiosity had been appeased. As for keeping her virginity intact, there was a good chance Charity was no flower of purity, given that she'd run off after that Blyer character, then had taken up with Gonzáles and his lot, which spoke chapters about her nature.

Spunky might have its allure, but an outlaw woman went against the grain of a man who fought for right, not wrong.

Anyway, the Old One would get her descendant to an attorney. Hawk squinted at the stars before he strode into the physician's shack. All he had to do was get Charity to the powwow point in Uvalde, then escort the two women to the Four Aces Ranch.

Then Hawk would be done with her.

Chapter Four

A minute or so after vowing to be done with Charity McLoughlin posthaste, Hawk entered the sleeping room that was lined with the paraphernalia of medical science. But his eyes didn't linger on the stoppered bottles, nor the shelves of medical books, nor the instruments of Sam's trade.

Hawk eyed his captive. A lantern cast a soft glow over her shapely form. Her hands shackled to the rungs of an iron bedstead, she lay dressed atop a worn quilt. Her skirts had worked their way up to her knees, displaying worn velvet slippers and curvaceous legs.

"Not bad," he murmured to himself. "For a hellcat."

His gaze moved upward. Wavy hair, long and luxurious, cascaded across her shoulders and down to her nipped waist, and his fingers strummed the air in a rhythm suddenly and irrationally impatient to twine through those locks. His glance settled on cheeks tinged with roses, then on a lush mouth opened slightly as if in invitation. His head moved downward.

Back off. She's trouble you don't need.

Were the situation different, though—if Charity were a different sort, or if he were nothing more than a kidnapper out for his own gain—Hawk would crawl in bed with her and find out just how much was spunk and how much was bluster.

He grew hard just thinking about it.

Hard and hot.

Gulping a couple of drafts of air to ease his engorged lower region, Hawk shucked the fringed jacket, leaving his torso clad in a cotton shirt. He felt somewhat relieved. He turned from the sleeping woman; when he did, he heard the bedclothes rustle.

"You dirty, low-down polecat," he heard her mutter.

Keeping his eyes on the door and his back to Charity, he stopped his retreat. "You've awakened."

"Brilliant deduction."

"Are you feeling all right?"

"What a question. Of course I'm not all right."

From the venom spewing from her tongue, Hawk figured the chloroform hadn't upset her stomach.

The iron posts protested as she tried to get free. "Unlock these blasted shackles," she ordered.

"Are you hungry?"

"I said unlock these manacles!"

"Not a good idea. But I am willing to feed you some dinner, Miss Charity McLoughlin. There's a pot of venison stew simmering. Sure you wouldn't like a bit of supper?"

Silence descended; it didn't take glancing over his shoulder to know she was skewering him with a look of loathing.

He decided to get the rules of the warpath straight. "Charity, you are my captive. And I give the orders. You can make it easy on yourself. Or you can make things difficult. Take your pick. Now, I'm not going to unlock the handcuffs. Understand? But I am willing to feed you, and I suspect you may be hungry, so do you want the stew, or not?"

He wondered what would win out, her hunger or her defiance.

"I . . . I do."

"Good girl."

He quit the room.

Those turquoise eyes were half closed, yet the anger in them was full-blown when Hawk carried a bowl of stew into the sleeping room. "Charity, I'll have to prop you up with a few pillows," he said, "or you'll strangle on your meal."

"You're ever so kind," she said sarcastically.

"Raise up."

He placed a couple of pillows behind her, catching a whiff of rose water blended with the musky scent of woman as he did so. He felt the rush of her breath against his shoulder at the same moment that strands of her hair brushed against his mouth. And the collective effect—

"You're smothering me, you big ox."

He reared back to sit on the bed's edge.

She was watching him, denouncement written in her oval face. Rebuke that turned to pure curiosity. Her brow quirked as she looked him up and down. "Do much wood chopping?"

"Beg pardon?"

"I asked if you're a woodchopper. With brawn like yours, you must spend a hefty amount of time swinging an ax. Then again . . ." She paused to continue her assessment. "Your skin isn't quite white and I see traces of savage in your features. Perhaps axes don't interest you at all. Perhaps you swing war clubs. You're an Indian, aren't you?"

"I am," he answered, giving her credit for her astuteness.

Sam had been right. Not many pegged him as Indian, especially not when he was garbed in white trappings. Hawk took it as a compliment that Charity had made such a swift and accurate appraisal of his ancestry.

Complacent, he smiled. "Earlier, you wondered if I was as ugly as you expected. Do you think Indians are ugly?"

"If you're fishing for a compliment, think again. If you were as handsome as John Wilkes Booth—Lucifer, burn his soul—I wouldn't tell you." She eyed the knife thonged to his thigh, swallowed, then nervously moistened her upper lip. "Going to scalp me before this is all over?"

He'd heard more than his share of comments like that in his twenty-seven winters. Such affronts were especially bad when he'd attended law school in Maryland. But his mother's relatives had pulled strings to get their "heathen" relative enrolled, and Hawk had wanted a law degree bad enough to suffer the indignities. By becoming an attorney, he had concluded that he could help his people in these days of reservations and government agents.

Thus, he had become inured to prejudice. But it was a good ways to Uvalde, and he could do without her insults.

Hawk said, "Not all Indians are out to scalp women."

Despite her superior airs, her mouth bowed sensuously, and Hawk read something in her expression. The hellcat eyed him as a man. Color be damned. Maybe she wasn't as much her father's daughter as he had first supposed.

"I'm not interested in scalping you," he said. "Not unless I have to."

"Don't gawk, redskin. It's rude. If you're going to feed me, do it."

He reached for the bowl. Raising the filled spoon to her lips, he watched as she devoured the portion, then another and another. "Charity, how long has it been since you've eaten?"

Her throat worked as she swallowed. Her eyes closed, a dense fringe of black lashes rested against her fair skin. "It seems as if forever. I've got a powerful hunger."

The huskiness in her voice and his own powerful hungers broke his resolve to leave her be. To hell with misgivings. To hell with any disapproving McLoughlin. In the matter of man and woman, it was nobody's business but their own.

Furthermore, he would enjoy it, conquering this tarnished angel. It might take using the Old One's scare-tactic suggestion, Indian or otherwise, but Hawk wasn't above using any means to get what he wanted.

"I told you—don't look at me that way," Charity demanded. "I'm not some entrée at a starving man's feast."

"Perhaps you'd like to think you're not." Captivated by eyes that were like turquoise before sun and time had mellowed the hue to green, he went for another spoonful of the fragrant stew, ate it himself, then blew to cool another. "You see, I, too, am a person of powerful hungers."

Before she accepted the offering, she asked, "Tell me, Hawk. Are you planning to rape me before you try to extort money from my family?"

"Eat your stew."

But the moment he placed the spoon at her lips, she turned not only her head but also a shoulder. The motion sent his arm on a downward path, the spoon falling to the pillow. His hand landed on her breast; his fingers curled around the heavy mound.

It was soft, sweet. And he felt the nipple harden beneath the pad of his thumb. Charity clasped the bed rails even tighter. Scanning the conflict of emotions written across her face, he murmured her name as if in a chant.

"You *are* going to have your way with me," she whispered.

"Don't you want me to?"

Her eyes narrowed. "If I let you do your dirty deed, will you set me free?"

"It wouldn't be a dirty deed." He stroked the calico-covered, hardened crest. She squirmed on the bed. And he felt a quiver that he knew she was trying to hide. He moved closer, combing his fingers through the thick hair at her temples. "I think anything between the two of us would be nothing but good."

"I know your wife would be thrilled to hear that."

"I don't have a wife."

Her lips parted, and he knew it was to make some scathing remark, but he angled his head, his mouth descending on hers to restrain the comment. She tasted the way he knew she would, warm and sweet, and his tongue worked its way inside.

She could have bitten him, but she didn't. She could have kicked him. She didn't. There were a lot of ways Miss Charity McLoughlin could have fought him, and Hawk wondered why she didn't. He didn't mull over her lack of fight for long.

His hands skimmed her arms, settling at the sides of her breasts, and his shaft throbbed in his britches. *Wah'Kon-Tah!* The reality of Charity was sweeter than any youthful fantasy. His hunger surprised Hawk, and he realized no woman had ever excited him this way. Perhaps because she *was* so wild and untamed and unpredictable . . .

Always he'd gotten a thrill from bringing down

wild beasts, and this woman was the wildest and most beautiful of beasts. He meant to send the bow of lust straight into her.

He whispered her name, once and then again. His fingers becoming acquainted with the feel of her throat, her earlobe, the rich texture of her hair, he murmured in his native language, "Maybe I'll never take you home. Maybe I'll keep you with me. Forever."

One of her legs moved across the back of his thigh as she whispered against the edge of his lips, "Hawk, won't you let me put my arms around you?"

"No."

"That doesn't seem fair." Her voice, soaked in the richness of warm thick cream, spread through him. "Unbind me, Hawk."

"Don't ask that of me. Don't . . ."

"I *am* asking."

Those huge blue eyes beseeched him; he felt his resolve weaken. He knew it was foolish. He shouldn't trust her. Yet he wanted their lovemaking to be everything it ought to be.

His fingers reached for the key.

Chapter Five

"Gotcha!"

Charity's unfettered fingers immediately went for the bowl of stew. Once more she had outwitted Hawk; the hot contents slashed his left cheek.

He shouted something—probably some Indian curse—and grabbed his face. Charity put all her strength into a mighty heave that sent him tumbling to the hovel's dirt floor. Despite her aches and pains of earlier that night, she bounded out of bed and was halfway to the door before he'd grabbed her waist and hauled her to his washboard stomach. Her shoulder blades thudded against a wall of chest.

"All right, hellcat," he growled in her ear, his breath disturbing her hair. "We won't be sleeping together tonight. But you aren't getting away—"

"I'd rather die than sleep with a red devil!" she exclaimed.

Yet her words were false. Maybe the tumultuous emotions raging inside of her had something to do with the fantasy of a particular red man whom she'd never laid eyes on—*Good gravy, don't be thinking about that one!*

When this savage had stroked her, this bronze, rugged, handsome man, he'd dashed her guard momentarily; she'd let herself become aroused, foolish enough to dream about a different situation, one where they would have wanted each other for each other. A lunatic's conception, given the situation.

But all Charity McLoughlin wanted in life was to be loved *for herself.* Always, she'd been judged on her headlong ways. Or for the family fortune no longer at her disposal.

"Let me go!" she insisted, and he pushed her away, yet his fingers fastened around her wrist; he swung her to face him. Eyeing her foe, she forced her lip into a curl. "I cringe at the mere thought of being your squaw."

"You weren't cringing a few minutes ago."

"I most certainly was."

"You most certainly were not." Above eyes brown like rich cocoa trimmed with cream, his straight black brows elevated. "I think you're as lusty as I am, hellcat angel."

"A lie!" She tried to free her wrist; more pressure met her efforts. He turned his head to profile, presenting a rather hawklike and proud nose. "You disgust me," she said.

She despised lies and liars, though she had been less than honest tonight. She had not cringed at his touch. And Hawk certainly didn't disgust her. There was enough of her mother in her not to be against someone because of their ancestry. Nonetheless, the only defense she had against her own torrential emotions was a sharp tongue. "I would never be a squaw to you or to anyone of your ilk."

Again he faced her, and the look on his long, sculpted face taunted her. "Let's clear up a misconception. Number one, the white man's word 'squaw' degrades women of my breed. Don't ever use that word again. Second, in your kind's parlance, 'squaw' implies lifelong companion." His fingers squeezed Charity's wrist with enough power to elicit from her a wince. "I'd never have you for wife," he said.

She blinked. "Th-this is my l-lucky day." A curious stab of pain knifed her breast, though she couldn't imagine why his denunciation had hurt her. Matching his cruel expression, she said, "Next you'll be telling me 'papoose' is a bad word."

His expression softened. " 'Child' is never a bad word. Children are loved above anything in my culture."

Not a bad culture, his, Charity thought. "If you had a papoose, wouldn't it be ashamed to know its father is an outlaw?"

"If you had a papoose, wouldn't it be ashamed to know its mother is a shrew? A shrew *and* an outlaw?"

Despite herself, she fought the urge to laugh aloud at the absurdity of their situation. While his words had been as uncharitable as hers, his eyes had lit up in amusement. "Boy howdy, wouldn't a child be in a mess if it had the bad luck to have us as parents?" *Good gravy.* Why was she carrying on this way with her *kidnapper?* "We'll save humanity a bad seed, since you'll never, ever touch me."

"Wrong."

"If you think so, you're in for another think."

"I don't think. I act." He yanked her to him, pulling her wrist high on his chest. Beneath her fingers she felt the rapid beat of his heart and the stove-hot heat of his chest. His scent, manly and kissed by all outdoors, enveloped her as he bent to whisper against her ear, "I mean to have you. Temporarily. And you won't regret it."

"Have you no conscience? There could be a child."

"*Wah'Kon-Tah* would never rain such bad spirit."

She attempted to put some distance between them. "You hold much faith in yourself and your . . . whatever you called it."

"Red devils have a way of doing that."

Since he had a comeback for everything she said, Charity was beginning to think she wouldn't have the last word. A disturbing notion. "You're well-spoken for a heathen. Some white missionary must have taken pity on you at some point."

His mouth captivated her, with its white teeth and full lips, but suddenly those lips were set in a thin line."Lady, don't put my temper to the test."

"Likewise."

“Get some rest,” he said in exasperation, and shoved her onto the bed.

The lumpy mattress, ill-covered by the worn quilt, bit her spine. As he clamped one of the manacles on her wrist again, she kicked his thigh and pummeled his upper arm with her free fist. Talon-strong fingers grabbed her hand, and he had a rope looped around that wrist as well as the bed rail in no time.

Her chest heaving, she spit out, “May hell take you. If you intend to wrest money from my father, Hawk, have at it. You’ll know soon enough that your efforts are in vain. As fruitless as those of your kind when they tried to keep whites from their manifest destiny. You’ll fail. And in the meantime, I’ll make your life a living hell. I’ve got twenty years of experience along those lines. Ask any McLoughlin.”

“Get yourself pulled together before sunrise.” He rose to his full height, staring down at her almost murderously. “We leave at dawn. As I said before, you can make this as easy or as difficult as you want it.”

“Go to hell.”

“You have a harlot’s mouth.”

“You seemed to like it a few minutes ago.” *Good gravy, don’t give him any encouragement!*

“Your submissive lips, not your sharp tongue.”

Gads, her lips had been *submissive!* She drilled Hawk with a look of defiance. “Perhaps I was too free with my favors. It won’t happen again. You may have kidnapped me, but I demand respect.

You *will* keep your hands to yourself. Understood?"

Without a word or a gesture of acknowledgment, he quit the room, dropping the hide door in his wake and leaving her with her thoughts. *Thoughts?* They would be better categorized as fantasies.

It was as if she were a girl again. The same sort of scene happened countless times. Each occurred at home, at the Four Aces Ranch. A specific incident stood out. The triplets must have been seven at the time. Their brother Angus had just progressed to baby steps. And they had recently moved into the grand home Papa had built for Mutti.

Papa's delay in returning from one of his cattle drives to Kansas left a pall on the Christmas Eve festivities.

In deference to their mother's heritage, a tree had been brought into the great hall. The scent of cedar permeated the room, along with beeswax candles and bows of holly. Mutti—as the triplets called their mother in the German language she was set on teaching them—fastened candles on the tree. Their great-grandmother sat in her rocker and complained about all the fuss.

"Lass," Maisie had said to Lisette, "ye'll be burning the house down with all those candles. And if we'll not be reduced t' ashes, yer bairns will be learning t' play with fire."

Lisette's blue eyes sparkled. "Hush," she said in the accent of her fatherland, and gave a look of love to her husband's grandmother.

Righteous indignation, mingled with love, met that adoration. "Sometimes I wonder aboot yer ways. Such as the time ye promised a daughter t' that Indian lad up in the territory."

Charity's ears pricked up, and she abandoned the wooden puzzle that had kept her occupied since supper. Her sisters stopped stringing popcorn to look at each other, then at Charity. Over and again, the triplets had heard this tale. And they had always been interested in it. Well, Margaret wasn't all that interested; she reverted to stringing.

Lisette placed a candle on a cedar bough. "I didn't *promise* a daughter to David Fierce Hawk."

Small fists covering their mouths, Olga and Charity giggled. Olga then reached for little Angus, who cuddled against his sweet sister. Charity, never one to keep her mouth shut, implored, "Tell us more about the Osage boy, Mutti."

"Shut up, triplet." Margaret pushed the needle through a kernel of popped corn. "You talk too much."

"Do not!"

"Yes, you do."

Charity wanted to cry; she loved Margaret and longed for her approval. But instead of crying, she balled her fist, boxed Margaret's shoulder, and hissed through a half-grown-in front tooth, "I hope you catch smallpox and die, like Aunt Monika did."

This sent Margaret crying. And Charity felt awful, for her mother went white. Uncle Adolf's wife hadn't been the only one to die last spring. So had Charity's three-year-old brother, Gilliegorm. Yet she couldn't bring herself to apologize to either her mother or her sister.

"Charity, you aren't very nice," Olga interjected.

"I'm nicer than you are." She forced a smirk at her nearsighted sister. "And at least I can see out of my two eyes!"

"Girls, hush." Collected, Lisette moved over to the table that held a punch bowl of spiked eggnog, then filled a cup that she handed to Maisie. She received a pat on the hand and a smile in return. "Fierce Hawk is a splendid Indian boy. I use the word Indian loosely, since his mother is white. And his father's mother is half white. That makes him one-fourth Indian, doesn't it?"

The brainiest of the triplets, now fully recovered from her bawling fit, piped up. "It does."

"Thank you, Margaret. I'm pleased you studied your sums."

Charity shrank a bit at her mother's remark. Everybody in the whole world knew that Charity McLoughlin was stupid at sums. But she wished her mother would say something nice about her.

Lisette settled into a chair and tucked her long legs beneath her. Sipping eggnog, she said to Maisie, "I wonder what's happened to Fierce Hawk. Gil hasn't encountered the Osage tribe since our trip to Kansas in '69."

" 'Tis too bad ye havena made the trip again, lass."

"I've small children, Maisie."

"But I wooud be happy t' look out for them."

"I know, dear one, but Gil says this is his last trip as trail boss. We're set for life, he wants to spend more time with the family, and he's looking to explore political possi—"

"We don't wanna hear about any old cattle drives," Charity broke in. "We wanna hear about Fierce Hawk."

Olga pleaded, "Oh, Mutti, do tell us."

"All right." Lisette smiled. "Fierce Hawk was such an interesting boy. I'll wager he's learned to read by now."

"I like to read."

"Oh, Charity, shut your trap." Margaret took a sip of fruit juice. "You never let anyone else do the talking."

Olga's weak eyes tried to focus on their mother. "Mutti, what about the part where he wanted to marry your daughter?"

Lisette scoffed. "Those were the words of the moment. I'm sure he's forgotten them by now."

"He wouldn't forget them. He's an Indian. And Indians are good for their word. You said so, Mutti."

"You don't know anything, triplet." Margaret popped a piece of popcorn into her mouth.

"Thank the Lord, Indian days are coming t' an end," Maisie commented, lowering her cup. "Ye may be fond of those Osage people, Lisette, but I'm thinking no Indian is t' be trusted."

"You've been listening to too many of Gil's stories of the old days," Lisette replied. "This is 1876. Times are changing."

"Lass, how can ye be forgetting your own sister died at Comanche hands?"

"That was a long time ago. Indians will no longer be a menace, once the government has finished relocating them to reservations."

"Was Cactus Blossom a menace?" Olga asked.

Three sets of girlish eyes waited for Lisette's reply, but Charity was the one to speak. "Let's don't talk about her."

It made her mother cry, mention of her dead friend. Charity didn't like it when her mother cried. Always, she wanted to put her arms around Mutti's shoulders, but each time she balked. Everyone would think her silly. "Let's talk about what Saint Nicholas is going to bring us."

"You won't get anything," Margaret pointed out. "You haven't been good."

Hurt, and afraid her sister spoke the truth, Charity picked up Angus's rubber ball and threw it at her sister's smug face.

"Charity!" At the same moment the ball missed its mark, Lisette wagged a finger. "That is more than enough. If you don't behave, you're going straight to bed."

Withdrawing into the safe world of her fancies, Charity turned back to her puzzle, trying to fit Illinois into the United States map . . . and she wondered about Fierce Hawk. Did he really mean to marry one of the triplets? She hoped he'd pick her.

"I doona like eggnog." Maisie stopped rocking and set her cup aside. "How aboot a cup of cocoa?"

"I'll fix it." When Charity jumped to stand, a loud crash and splintering of glass accompanied her.

Margaret gasped. "Look, triplet, you broke the popcorn bowl!"

The crystal dish had belonged to Mutti's mother, and had been hand-carried all the way from the old country, from the hamlet of Dillenburg in the province of Nassau-Hesse. From the look on Mutti's face, Charity knew she had committed a grievous wrong. Why couldn't she do anything right?

"Sit down, Charity. Cook will get the cocoa." Lisette bent to gather the shards; her voice held exasperation. "Why can you never be still?"

"Such a prize oughta be kept outta a bairn's reach. And ye should be recalling she is a sweet lass. Headstrong, I'll be granting, but . . ."

"You've made Mutti cry," Olga informed her sister.

Defeated at last, the hapless triplet tucked her chin on her chest and uttered in a small voice, "I'm sorry."

Charity rushed toward the staircase leading to the sleeping wing. Halfway up the stairs she heard Maisie say something in her defense. *Maiz is never mean, at least to me.*

In fact, she was usually a partner in warming milk for Dutch chocolate. It was even better when the Keller boys were staying over, since the cousins liked cocoa almost as much as Charity did. Cousin Karl, though, had a way of scaring her. He teased her about Easter fires that kept Comanches away from the area. Charity wished Karl wouldn't scare her like that.

She also wished that Fierce Hawk would make a grand entrance some night, with all the glory of Saint Nicholas. Fierce Hawk would stroll past the better of the McLoughlin girls, and he would stop in front of Charity. "You're the one I choose," he would say.

Olga and Margaret would beg for his attention. He wouldn't be swayed. He'd laugh at the others. Fierce Hawk wouldn't shout at Charity. He'd think she was as pretty as Margaret and Olga. "You're smart and clever," he'd say as they made mud pies together. And, most of all, he would like Charity for Charity.

Maybe it wouldn't be so awful to go live on a reservation north of the Red River.

Gee, she wished she knew what Fierce Hawk looked like.

It was on that Christmas Eve that Charity decided to wed the Osage boy. And she waited years for him, though she never told a soul about her decision. She didn't dare. She knew her papa wouldn't allow one of his daughters to marry a redskin, which only added to Fierce Hawk's allure.

But Fierce Hawk never materialized.

As the years passed and the family divided its time between Texas and Washington, the arguments between Charity and Margaret grew less and less.

Margaret became more patient with age, and more compassionate as she saw how Charity was shuffled to the rear because of her impetuous behavior; they formed a sisterly alliance.

Margaret stayed closer to Olga, nevertheless. At seventeen, the demure Olga had married the highborn son of the Spanish ambassador to the United States, had gone away with her husband to live in his homeland. The Countess of Granada's letters divulged a wellspring of details to the naive sisters, giving advice on married love and proper behavior both in and out of the marital bed.

By that time, though, college was in the offing for the unmarried triplets. Charity demanded to be sent to the same university as Margaret, and Papa and Mutti had agreed. But the dean of the college had expelled Charity upon catching her puffing on the one and only cigarette of her life. Then Ian Blyer had come along, and his silver-tongued lies had made her cast aside her girlish dreams of tom-toms and wigwams and a black-haired savage.

It's time I stopped dreaming of happily ever after.

This pragmatic thought thrust Charity into the present. Hers was a despicable situation. This wasn't some Indian village turned Valhalla.Nor was it Paris or Madrid, Charity's favorite cities. This was some hovel in south Texas that Hawk had—

Hawk?

A crazy notion filled her head. Could Hawk and Fierce Hawk be one and the same? she wondered as she huddled—as much as her shackled hands would allow—into the bed. Of course, her abductor held no resemblance to the Indian of her many dreams.

Fierce Hawk was a hero.

Hawk was surely an outlaw.

Fierce Hawk had reached for respectability in white society and had gotten it. In a letter penned last spring, Mutti had said he was now an attorney and lobbyist in Washington, dedicated to serving his people. In her mind—she still wasn't good in sums—Charity couldn't quite equate the Fierce Hawk of her dreams with the gentleman he had turned out to be.

But she knew one thing for certain. David Fierce Hawk wouldn't lower himself to abduction. That was a savage's game.

Sunlight was streaming through a crack in the single, oiled-paper window when the redskin entered the room again. Immediately, Charity noticed the blotch of fiery scarlet that covered his left cheekbone, evidence of their struggle. Good gravy, she'd hurt him! She gawked at the purple bruise at his throat, plus the red outline of her teeth on his wide, wide shoulder. She immediately squelched any feelings of remorse.

Instead, she glared at Hawk. "Have you forgotten something? Where are your feathers and war paint?"

Today he'd dressed as one of his kind. Gone was the Stetson; a leather strap banded his head of straight hair that trailed to his shoulders. Hair black as a raven's wing. He wasn't wearing a shirt, but a silver pendant studded with turquoise dangled on his smooth, hairless chest. She swallowed, perusing the prominent veins exposed on his strong arms. Once more he wore buckskin britches, but these were Indian style; a breechclout covered his private parts. Again, a long knife was strapped to his thigh.

Charity hadn't realized that an Indian, not even Fierce Hawk, could be so attractive and virile and—*Wait.* No doubt his mode of attire sent a silent warning: behave or be scalped.

Had Fierce Hawk ever scalped a woman? This was, Charity decided, one of her more ridiculous thoughts. David Fierce Hawk, Esquire, wore cravat and spats and walked the halls of Congress.

And why start with the comparisons again? Yet . . . Hawk's shoulders were as wide as she'd imagined Fierce Hawk's to be. Okay, she admired his height, for she was too tall for most men. Hawk was even more dashing and ruggedly handsome than the Indian of her dreams—look at that set to his mouth, look at those piercing dark eyes, take a gander at the way he moved—surely the similarity between Hawk and Fierce Hawk was purely semantic.

"It's daylight," he said. "We leave."

"No thank you. I'm not going anywhere with you," she replied brashly. "As soon as you unlock me from this bed, I *will* fight you to the death—yours or mine—for my freedom."

His brown eyes dissolved to the hue of dark chocolate. His stance grew immediately predatory. He reached for his knife and twisted it in the air. "If anyone dies, it will be you."

A tad uneasy, she lifted her chin. "You don't scare me, dressing in that get-up and waving that knife." He remained unimpressed; she aimed to pacify him. "As kind as you were last night, feeding me and all, I'm thinking you're nicer than you'd have me believe. You're no typical Indian."

"What do you know about my kind?" he asked irritably.

"Nothing. I've seen a few renegades, but I wouldn't know a typical Indian from a buffalo. Anyway"—she swallowed as he brandished the knife anew—"y-you seem nice enough. And good men don't carve up ladies."

"I am *not* a good man." He took a threatening step in her direction. "The savage in me is capable of anything."

Chapter Six

Hawk took another menacing step toward her, his shins butting the mattress edge. Swift as the blink of an eye, he brought the knife's tip within a hair of the skin at her jugular. "If you die in the fight, be warned. You asked for it."

Gads!

Charity's shoulder blades pressed to the bed; a shiver ran through her limbs; her teeth chattered in the heat of the September morning. She hadn't expected Hawk to ignore her taunt about fighting to the death, spoken only moments earlier, so she knew she shouldn't be surprised at his comeback. But she was shocked to realize how much she wanted to live.

She, who had no future, who had nothing to live for.

Was there no justice in the world? This Indian held her destiny, like Atlas gripped the earthly globe. And her hands were tied, while Hawk's gripped a knife.

She shut her eyes tightly.

Here she was, kidnapped.

Probably to be raped.

Possibly to be scalped.

Most likely her carcass would provide a feast for buzzards.

If there was any consolation, it was that no McLoughlin money would ever line Hawk's breech-clout, whether she lived or died.

Pull yourself together. Daring not so much as a swallow, not with the tip of his knife at her throat, Charity felt certain that *if* her life was spared, Hawk wouldn't be foolish enough to give her another advantage. She must back down from her incensed remarks, or he might see fit to do no telling what.

She managed the sweetest smile possible.

"Uh, um, Hawk . . . maybe I was a bit hasty." Each syllable brought her throat in contact with the knife. "I, uh, g-goodness. Would you put that knife away, please? Maybe an apology is in order."

As she groveled, he rolled his eyes and shook his head. "Damned fool disagreeable woman."

She stopped herself from telling him how disagreeable she found him. Now wasn't the time to trade insults.

"I-I've never been malleable. I can't help that. P-please don't kill me."

The knife eased away from her throat. Thank her lucky stars! Maybe, after all, she did have at least *one* shining in the heavens.

She didn't say another word as Hawk sheathed the knife and unshackled her hands from the bed-stead. He was quick to replace the manacles on her wrists again. On her feet, she wobbled, both from a night of sleeping in an uncomfortable position and from her aches and pains suffered from falling on that table. Hawk offered no assistance.

Neither did the ugly toad of perhaps fifty who called himself Sam, who looked as if he embraced the liquor bottle as a babe did its mother's breast. She didn't wish to be helped along. She stood outside, her wrists tied, and shuffled her feet in boredom while the dastardly duo went about the business of ransom-seeking.

Hawk rolled a water barrel to the wagon's side, hoisting the oaken cask with ease up and onto the conveyance, as if it weighed no more than a feather pillow. His accomplice grabbed and loaded the stacks of provisions already assembled—a pile of blankets, a wooden box, a knapsack, her belongings. Charity's attention moved to the horses.

You'd think any kidnapper worth his salt would buy a proper team! These two didn't look as if they could make it to the water trough much less all the way to Gillespie County. The poor things—a piebald and a gray—ought to be pastured, so elderly were they.

"I've never had much use for anyone who doesn't respect horseflesh," she commented, cringing. *Keep your mouth shut.* Neither man imparted any sort of acknowledgement, and Charity sighed in relief. She took another gander at the mares. *Hmm.* If they couldn't make it to Fredericksburg . . . Maybe it wouldn't be so terrible if they *were* to keel over.

"Fixed you some more food," Sam said to Hawk, handing him a basket. "Best wishes to you, boy."

Hawk smiled. "Thanks, my friend." Deigning no more than a sidelong glance in her direction, he ordered Charity to get in the wagon.

It was on the tip of her tongue to ask how the heck he expected her to climb into that buckboard, trussed as she was. She clamped her lips. She did have her pride. She managed to get herself seated in the wagon, even if her climb lacked grace.

As they traveled north and then east from the hovel of her captivity on the sweltering day—the team demonstrating more fitness than her earlier assessment—she kept quiet.

Three times, Hawk stopped and offered to escort her into the bushes for a nature call. Each time she demurred; she'd rather pop her bladder than allow him to help her with her pantaloons. And she was too proud to let Hawk hand-feed her again. So she went hungry. All day.

She spent those hours in silent suffering, the wagon pitching as its wheels hit ruts in the ungiving, parched land known as brush country. Her thoughts focused on all that was behind her, her family, Maria Sara. Dear Maria Sara, she had sacrificed her pay for what turned out to be a useless cause: Charity's freedom. *I'll repay her, somehow,* she thought.

But how was that going to come about? Charity decided not to fret over the future. Not yet. Her first priority had to be winning her freedom from Hawk.

Just before sundown, he stopped the wagon to make camp alongside a dry creekbed. Charity, uncomfortable in a dozen ways, sat fidgeting while he tended to the two nags, made a fire, and put together a pot of coffee. The heaven-scented liquid brewing, she watched as he stretched his arms high above his head, the fading sun catching the blue in his black hair, catching the play of powerful arm and chest muscles.

Something warm and intoxicating, not altogether foreign to her after the previous night, wound through her at the sight of him. A man so robustly fine-looking shouldn't have to lower himself to extortion. The world ought to be falling at his feet.

Yet the world didn't cater to Indians. Society scoffed at him and his kind, and a feeling of sympathy suddenly flooded through Charity for all the prejudice Hawk had endured. What was she thinking of? He had kidnapped her, for goodness' sake! Besides, it wasn't her fault Indians hadn't received a decent shake in society.

On moccasined feet, as the sun's final rays reflected on his silver, turquoise-studded pendant, Hawk walked toward her. Unaccustomed to seeing a necklace adorning a man's neck, she nonetheless found it—and him!—wildly intriguing. There had never been any accounting for her judgment.

Whether it was wise or not, she wondered about him. Who was he, really? Where did he come from? She didn't know Indians; in fact, she'd never been on speaking terms with one in her life, and Hawk seemed so different from the stories she'd heard of his kind.

"Hungry?" he asked and motioned to the box of provisions.

"No, I'm not. Thank you."

"Thinking to starve yourself?" Quizzically, he examined her features. "You haven't done much talking today."

She spoke the words her papa had longed to hear: "I've nothing to say."

He chuckled. "I rather miss your sharp tongue."

When she didn't reply he shrugged, then went over to the fire pit. He skewered a piece of beef, brought from Sam's smokehouse, and staked it over the cookfire. The meat sizzled over dancing flames, and the aroma made her mouth water. Yet it was something other than an empty belly that finally felled her pride.

As he poured a cup of coffee, she looked at the ground and admitted, "Hawk, I . . . I've got to r-relieve myself."

"All right." He set the cup aside and walked over to her. Taking her elbow, he helped her to her feet. "There's a mesquite tree on the other side of the wagon."

"I don't want you pulling down my underclothes." If she ever got her dratted pantaloons off, she'd leave them off. She had enough fetters already not to let one more constraint impede future trips to the bushes—on her own! "Furthermore, I don't want you watching me."

"You have no choice. I won't unlock the manacles."

She stopped in her tracks. "Then forget I asked for a decent turn from you."

"I'll think of something." Staring downward, he frowned. The motion drew brackets around his mouth. His fingertip fiddled with the turquoise charm swinging from its silver chain. Within a couple of seconds he was unlocking one of Charity's iron handcuffs. His grip firm so she wouldn't get any ideas about escaping, he clamped the one loose cuff around the thin tree trunk.

"Now," he said, "you may do as you please."

Then you won't mind if I kick where Olga says it hurts a man? Beneath that breechclout, in this instance.

He turned and strode toward the wagon.

It took quite a one-handed effort to get her skirts up and her pantaloons down, but Charity did it. And when she had finished with her nature call, she flung the dratted pantaloons to the slight wind and waited for Hawk to retrieve her.

Twilight darkened to night. She heard the chirping of a thousand crickets and the hoot of an owl. Something howled in the distance. Hawk, she couldn't see. No doubt he was tending his supper fire, the scent of which wafted to her nose. She waited several minutes for his return, waiting in vain.

She began to get uneasy. The aroma of burning wood and sizzling beef waned. What if Hawk had left? Well, he hadn't taken the wagon, yet he seemed capable of walking from here to California. Since she'd been hideous to him—and he liked his captives docile!—why should she wonder why he might desert her?

Dark fear arose, blacker than what she felt to be an uncertain fate at the hands of an enigmatic kidnapper. Abandonment. Once, when she was nine, she'd gotten separated from her family on a trip to San Antonio. It was the next morning before Papa and Mutti found her. After she had spent the most terrifying night of her life.

And tonight—tonight she was chained to a tree. She might never see Paris again.

Chapter Seven

"Hawk? Hawk, where are you!"

"I'm right here."

Charity jumped at the sound from behind her. Turning, she asked, "Where were you?" Then it all fell into place, here in the dark after twilight, in the wilds of Texas brush country. She pointed an accusing finger at Hawk. "You rat, you were watching me."

"Guilty. I had to keep an eye on you."

"Am I not allowed even the most basic of privacies?"

He crossed over to the tree, unlocking her from it. This time he kept one end of the iron bracelet in his hand. "We will eat now."

"Will you allow me to feed myself?"

"Perhaps."

And he did, after they had returned to camp and he had warned her against making any quick moves. It was a small enough concession; she made no attempt to flee, not that she could have if she wanted to, still unnerved by the long wait for Hawk at the tree.

She sat on her ankles in front of the fire. It took all her strength of will not to fall on the food as if she were a famished mongrel being tossed steak bones. No food had ever tasted better than the spit-roasted beef, the canned beans, the black and strong coffee. For dessert, Hawk presented her with a handful of dried figs. Delicious.

Stretched out on the ground, propped up on his elbow, and smoking a cigarette, he watched her. "Did you enjoy your meal?"

"I've had better."

"A beautiful woman like you, spoiled by her rich family, yes, I imagine you have."

It wasn't a compliment; it was criticism. Yet few men had called her beautiful—they had too often been put off by her caustic tongue—and her cheeks went hot. She barely realized she spoke when she uttered, "My sisters are the beauties in the family."

"Aren't the three of you identical?"

"So they say. But how do you know about Olga and Margaret?"

"Competent kidnappers do their research. I found out you sisters look exactly alike . . . except for a slight deviation in the shade of your eyes." Past a curl of smoke, he winked. "Now tell me—what makes you think you're not as pretty as they are?"

Maisie had said she was pretty. "Ye're bonny as heather on the banks of the Loch Ness," she'd said over and over, "and there's a grand beauty t' ye, down deep." Even Maisie had thrown up her arms and given a gasp of exasperation when Charity had packed her clothes for the trip to Ian.

Oh, Maiz, I miss you.

"Charity . . . ? What about your sisters?"

"Everyone comments on their looks. 'Olga is so lovely in her serenity.' 'That Margaret, she's as smart as she is beautiful.' People say those things all the time."

"What do they say about you?"

" 'Why can't she keep her mouth shut?' "

Tossing back his head, he laughed.

Offended, Charity said, "You don't have to agree with them!"

"Don't put words in my mouth, angel. I'm not agreeing with other people at all. The way I figure it, a man would never be bored around you." He grew serious and tossed his cigarette into the fire. "And I think you're highly clever. I've got the bruises to prove it. Furthermore, you *are* beautiful. I've never seen such beautiful hair. Or eyes. And you haven't got a feature to be ashamed of."

Embarrassed at his praise, she ducked her chin and popped another fig into her mouth.

From the corner of her eye, she watched as he reached for his cup of coffee. If the situation were different—if he wasn't holding her for ransom and no telling what else—she might have been tempted to remark on his appeal.

Curious about his motives, she asked, "Why are

you in such desperate straits that you need to extort money?"

Shaking his head, he glanced toward the heavens. "Never gives up, does she?" he muttered, then shifted his position and sat Indian-style.

All sprawl-kneed like he was, how could Charity not gawk at him? Her eyes lowered to the soft breechclout draping between his legs. She would have to have been blind as Olga not to notice how the supple buckskin highlighted his hard male planes. Oh my, Charity's face felt flushed, almost as if she had a fever.

Gads!

Gulping, she pulled herself together and back to conversation. "You don't have to lower yourself to criminal means, Hawk. You could get a job. Why, as strong as you are, I'll bet you'd make an excellent blacksmith."

"Think I'm pretty strong?" A look of hawk-got-the-prey spanned his longish face of high cheekbones and sensuous lips.

"Of course you're strong." *And handsome.* She tried to divert her attention from the purely physical. "Can you read and write?"

"We'd better sleep now," he said and poured coffee grounds into the fire.

Poor thing. He was illiterate. And she had embarrassed him, she figured. That was why his face had turned to the night's shadows. "Sleep is a good idea," she said, eager to change the subject. "If you don't mind, I'll take the wagon bed."

"I mind. You'll sleep beside me. Right here on the ground."

"I can't sleep on the ground," was her indignant reply. "I've never slept on the ground and I don't intend to start now."

"The grasses are soft, spoiled rich girl. And we've plenty of blankets. You won't suffer."

Why argue the "spoiled rich girl" part? She had been spoiled, she had been rich, although, at barely twenty, she was no longer a girl. Rich, spoiled, broke, or desperate, she was what she was, so why try to disabuse his notions? "But I will suffer," she protested. "I'm aching all over."

"Did you hurt yourself?"

"Of course I did." She liked what she heard in his deep, sonorous voice. "Last night, when I fell, I hurt, why, just about every bone in my body." This was a bit much; she had no grievous injuries, after all. But she did enjoy seeing the look of concern on his face. "Remember?"

"Why didn't you say something earlier?"

"I'm saying it now."

His visual canvass went from her head to her toes and back again. "Do you have cuts that need tending?"

"I don't think so."

"I'd better take a look. You could get sick from an untended wound."

"Would it matter if I got sick?" She laughed nervously. "Oh wait a minute, I forgot—of course it would matter. You need me for the booty."

"Right. Only for the ransom."

"I've got to give you some credit, Hawk. I'm glad you didn't lie." *Like Ian had.* "Liars are the scum of the earth in my estimation."

Hawk smiled a tight, enigmatic smile. "I'm glad something about me pleases you. Now, lie down."

Ye lie down with dogs, ye get fleas. How many times had Maisie said that to Charity? *Don't be thinking about her.* "Hawk, I will *not* sleep with you."

"I said, you'll have the soft grasses and plenty of blankets. You won't suffer."

Whining a bit—it had sometimes worked with her family—she pointed out, "But, Hawk, I've always been a restless sleeper." She eyed the suspended end of the manacle. "I'll be uncomfortable with my wrists tied together. Will you please leave this the way it is? I promise I won't run off."

He studied her for a minute, then casually picked up his knife to run a thumb down its edge. "You'll sleep on the ground. And you'll sleep with your wrists together. End of discussion."

A scathing remark was on the tip of her tongue, but she quelled it. She wanted to live to see morning's light. So, once more the dangling manacle was locked to her free wrist.

Afterward, he placed blankets near the dying fire, then pulled her down to the pallet. Yanking one of the covers over his bare shoulders, he turned his back. Within moments, she heard the soft cadence of his sleeping breath.

She was restless. The ground was wet from dew;

it soaked the covers. Gusts of night air feasted on her flesh. Her teeth chattered; she shivered. And this was no soft mattress. The ground was uneven and somewhat rocky, and all of it dug into her arms, her back, her hips, her legs. A bundle of misery—that's what she was.

For hours she listened to distant creatures on the prowl and howl. And she must have counted a million stars. Then she recalled Hawk's kiss of the night before . . .

Over and again, she made the cumbersome effort to roll and toss.

"Be still," Hawk grumbled in his sleep.

"But I'm uncomfortable."

She heard him sigh in exasperation. "You'll get used to the Indian way of sleeping," he said.

"Get used to? How long do you intend to keep me?"

"Till after your family pays the ransom."

"When . . . ? Have you approached them about it?"

"Your papa will know soon enough."

"Oh."

She had to admit that she'd been holding on to the hope that Hawk's was some bizarre scheme hatched by Papa to bring her back into the fold. Not so. She blinked her suddenly burning eyes. How silly, harboring such a desire. Even if Papa were pining for the sight of her, he wouldn't have sent an Indian to pluck her from the streets of Laredo!

"I . . . I've told you. He won't pay." Hurt

clutched at her chest. "What will you do with me then?"

Hawk sighed again, rolled to face her, then pulled her to him. He raised himself up to slant his lips over hers. "It all depends," he murmured before stealing a kiss that lingered and lingered.

Charity wanted to protest. At first. But his mouth made magic on hers. The brush of his hair against her collar elicited a shiver of excitement within her. His hands, oh, such warmth. Her own crossed hands were caught between her breasts and his chest, and her fingers flexed over his silver pendant . . . settling on the smooth, wall-strong planes of his naked flesh.

It was wicked, the passion she felt. Olga would be shocked! But she had never sought her sister's approval, so why worry about it now? Besides, making love with a savage brought back her daydreams of old. Daydreams of Fierce Hawk. But Hawk wasn't her Osage brave. Here and now, it didn't matter. Hawk was Hawk. And, dear providence, these magical hands, these blazing lips . . .

She forgot how uncomfortable she had been just moments before.

When Hawk finally released her to stare into her eyes, he said, "I want you, sweet Charity."

"I know." She felt the physical indication of his need, hard at her thigh. Somehow a modicum of sense overtook her."But I . . . Oh, Hawk, don't do this to me."

"Why? Because you don't want me?"

What did she want, besides her freedom? At the

moment, she had no idea. But she knew that everything flowing hot through her body shouted for this man. Yet . . . While she had done many horrid things in her life, and while her reputation lacked a lady's credibility, she believed in keeping herself pure for marriage. The man for her would be motivated by love and acceptance, not greed, and they would learn about man-woman things at the same time.

Olga—and Mutti and Maisie—would be proud.

Marriage? What was wrong with her? Her prospects were dim. Even if she got free of Hawk, she still had to answer to the law, and smuggling was a hanging offense.

Don't think about it. She wasn't swinging from a rope, not yet.

"Don't you want me?" Hawk repeated and traced his finger down her jaw to her throat.

Her attention riveted to his touch and her body's response, she didn't think answering was possible. She swallowed hard and breathed deeply. "I know nothing about you. Except for a name. And for all I know, you could be making it up."

"I'm not."

"What other names do you have? Is Hawk your first or last name?"

"I'm an Indian, remember? We aren't named as you whites."

"Where are you from? All the Indians hereabouts—except for a few renegades, of course—live on reservations."

"My people consider me a renegade."

"Who are your people?" She thought of all the tribes still talked about in Fredericksburg. "Are you part Comanche? Kickapoo? Apache?" She studied him. "You are most certainly part white. There are certain elements of your features that don't look as Indian as the renegades I've seen."

"I am all Indian."

Her tongue rested for a moment, but her curiosity did not subside. "Tell me about yourself."

"Charity, I've taken you for ransom. You'll not be getting a life story that you could turn over to the law."

She wiggled away from him. "Then don't expect to have carnal knowledge of me."

He chuckled. "Is that the ticket to 'carnal knowledge' of you? Just a few vital elements to my wicked life? I could tell you many things about me. But how would you know if they're true?"

Picking up on his method of ending conversations, she ordered, "Oh, go to sleep."

His hand trailed along the column of her throat, his thumbnail moving upward to outline the curve of her lower lip. The intensity of his gaze took Charity aback . . . yet she felt her passions building anew.

"Love me to sleep, Hellcat Angel."

Chapter Eight

Like a child tempted with a bonbon, Charity yearned to surrender to Hawk's plea of loving him to sleep. With his fingers cupping and kneading her breast, with his leg nudging between hers, she felt wholly weak of will. What would Olga do at a time like this? "I'd never consent to anything of the sort."

"Don't say things you don't mean."

"I—I mean it," she squeaked, barely noticing as the campfire popped and died.

One hand moved to scoot her skirts up, and Hawk's fingers stroked the crook of her knee. "What did it take for Ian Blyer to get between your legs?"

Who? It took a moment to recall just exactly who Ian Blyer was, for she could hardly breathe, much less think, with Hawk caressing her the way he was. "Uh, oh, my g-goodness. He never asked for anything more than a kiss. He's too much of a gentleman."

"Gentleman-fool, if you ask me," Hawk whispered low in his throat. "A man would have to be a fool not to want all you can give."

His praise, base though it was, excited her, and she smiled. No man had ever acted as if she was driving him wild before.

Hawk's fingers pressed into her thigh. "Would you have given more . . . if Blyer had asked?"

"No."

"Somehow I think you speak the truth." He was silent for a moment before he asked, "Has anyone ever had you?"

"No."

Hawk muttered some sort of something, probably an Indian oath. He tossed to his back and ran a palm down his face. "I suppose I ought to be glad."

"Meaning?"

"It means I ought to keep my hands off you."

"Ought to? Are you forgetting last night? I asked you to respect my virtue."

She thought about her actions. A lady wouldn't have given him so much as a kiss, much less liberties over her flesh. Her kinswomen had advised as much. Well, no one had ever called Charity a lady, but . . . "You will treat me like a lady."

"Charity, has anyone *ever* gotten the last word with you?"

"Don't criticize me." Good gravy, why did she take *this* opportunity to gaze upon male perfection limned in the moonlight? Mmm, she liked what she saw. "I don't like you criticizing me."

"Sweetness, I—"

"Hellcats aren't sweet."

"Sometimes you are." He turned his head toward her; her breath stopped at the starlit sight of brown eyes and a hawkish yet soft expression. Before he stared at the sky again, he said, "Such as a few minutes ago, when we were kissing."

"We're getting off the subject of respect." Had her wrists been free, she would have gotten to her feet and parked her hands on her hips. "I want to know something. Since you seem to have no intention of honoring my request for respect, exactly when are you planning to ravish me?"

"That sounds like an invitation."

"It's rude to twist words." She sighed and maneuvered to face him. "Please tell me what your plans are."

"There may be ravishing, though I don't think much of the term. Lovemaking, I'd call it."

"One doesn't make love to someone whom one plans to k-kill . . . does one?"

"Kill?" He chuckled, the motion crinkling the corners of his eyes. "Charity, it never was, and never will be, my intention to take your life."

"Really?"

"Really." He punched the rolled blanket that served as a pillow. "Now go to sleep."

She grinned. What a relief! He wasn't going to divest her of her scalp. Actually, she'd pretty much come to that conclusion during dinner. All he wanted was loot, and lovemaking. Of course he would be foiled in both cases.

Be that as it may, this kidnapping had turned out nicely; his absconding with her, a blessing in disguise. Laredo was at least two days in the distance. And each day put more miles between herself and her crime—not to mention Ian Blyer. Plus, she would have time to consider exactly how she would avoid Papa, and how she'd get out of the legal mess she was in.

She had been in worse situations.

But what would she do, once she was free of this one? Paris seemed a good choice. She had always loved the City of Lights. And there was Madrid. Charity had fallen in love with Spain on a trip to visit Olga and Leonardo. Paris or Madrid, she could make a new start.

She chose not to fret about how she would get passage across the Atlantic, or about how she would make a living once there. Those were problems better settled another time—such as when she got her freedom.

Life, all of a sudden, appeared rosy.

Benevolence coursed through her. "Hawk . . . I'm changing my mind about you. You're going to think I'm crazy, but I like you. There's something infinitely strong and trustworthy about you. Isn't that peculiar, my thinking? You do hold me against my will, after all. But, isn't it strange, I can't imagine giving myself to anyone but you. That's really very peculiar, I think. You see, I have an aversion to men interested in my papa's money. I wish we could have met under different circumstances. Do you think me much too bold to admit such a thing?"

No reply met her admissions. None except for . . . Why, of all the nerve! He was snoring to beat the band.

* * *

Charity had been missing three days, and Ian Blyer was at his wit's end. Perspiration slid down his spine; his hand chopped the air in a gesture of frustration. He'd thought the angles were covered: keeping her from employment, then holding her crime over her head. He had thought.

Where was she? How had the chit managed to flee Laredo?

"Sit down, Ianito. You make me uneasy."

Ignoring the conspirator he'd summoned an hour ago, Ian paced the worn rug of his father's town house. He stopped when Maria Sara Montaña asked, "With your gambling losses high, why didn't you keep the smuggling money to pay your debts?"

"I took the biggest gamble of all. I gambled that Charity would turn to me in her desperation. Then I would have control of the McLoughlin fortune."

The bells of St. Augustine Church pealed through the balcony's open doors; the calls of a street peddlar floated up to the second floor; the dankness of the muddy Rio Grande filled his nostrils. "Charity could have been my ticket out of here," he lamented.

"You cut a pathetic figure," Maria Sara snickered. "I almost pity you."

He would have been outraged at her remarks if he didn't himself believe that they were true. In every way he had botched his grand plans of becoming as rich as a sheikh of Araby. He must get himself under control. "Charity *will* be my ticket out of Laredo."

"You have seen many schemes fall by the wayside. I would think that experience might have taught you to give up your futile quests."

"Futile? I think not." Refusing to ponder past failures, Ian sneered at the petite blonde who was seated in a wing chair near the cold fireplace. "Yes, Charity is estranged from the rich McLoughlins, and, yes, her father has no use for me, but—"

"I imagine Senator McLoughlin would delight in seeing you muck out his stables. And I would rejoice to see you thus employed."

"Muck out barns? I think not. McLoughlin will change, once the marriage vows are exchanged. I couldn't be that wrong about family loyalty."

And the father would share his wealth with an earnest son-in-law. Ian Blyer intended to act humble, hard-working, God-fearing for as long as it took to get control over land and cash. This didn't mean he didn't love Charity in his own way, even though she didn't accept his feelings. When she had arrived in Laredo, he had been upset by his father and had said some regrettable things about money. But Charity wouldn't listen to his apologies.

"I shouldn't have to chase after what was promised under an April moon: Charity's hand in wedlock."

"I am pleased she got away."

Surely he hadn't heard right. "I believe you wish me no good."

Maria Sara lifted a shaking hand to smooth wisps of dark blond hair from her nape. Running his hand through his own dark blond hair, he heard her pained voice. "Wish you no good? What about what you've done? Why do you say frank things in front of me? You should know they hurt—"

"You know volumes about me—why shouldn't I be candid?"

"You know why."

Choosing not to contemplate what had been, Ian halted at the balcony's doorway to concentrate on what might have been.

Charity should have been Mrs. Blyer by now. After all, he came from a good family—financially strapped, but good. The Blyer name meant something in this part of the country, and his father served in the state senate. Granted, that wasn't as august as being a U.S. senator from the great state of Texas, as Charity's father was, but the Blyers didn't want for respectability. Besides, what about the personal element?

He, Ian Blyer, was the handsomest man in Texas. The Baylor College annual for 1885 had named him such, and no woman in her right mind wouldn't agree. To reassure himself, Ian stopped in front of a large mirror that graced one wall of the sitting room. He saw thick, wavy hair in a tawny, fair shade, green eyes that were roofed by expressive eyebrows, a nose of patrician proportions, a clefted chin, a rogue's mouth. He smiled, and was rewarded with a flash of perfect teeth.

For years he had meant to cash in on his looks.

But, blast it, so far he had been thwarted. He had even failed at his one attempt at larceny. Yet all wasn't lost, not if he was careful. And diligent.

Eyeing Maria Sara's reflection in the looking glass, he asked, "Where in blue blazes has Charity gone?"

The woman shrugged. "I have no idea."

Images formed in Ian Blyer's mind, horrifying thoughts of being stuck in Laredo forever. His patience grew taut as a bowstring. "I gave you money—before she left—to keep me informed. You haven't."

"That is correct."

Maria Sara's look of superiority, of defiance, ran a sword through his composure. Foiled again! Ian rushed the chair where she sat, and shook her shoulders. "You're keeping something from me. And I won't have that, you understand. I won't!"

"Remove your hands."

He slapped her, his palm hard and flat against her cheek. Her head snapped back; the mark of his hand burst on her face.

"Tell the truth—where is Charity?"

Maria Sara straightened her shoulders. "I love seeing you this way, Ianito. You've finally had your comeuppance. Charity is gone, and there's nothing you can do about it."

Desperate, he would have gladly killed the smirking little witch—baggage long grown weighty—but if he took her life, he still wouldn't know what happened to his ticket to riches. "You took my money for information, yet you stall in the carry-through. What does that say about you, Maria Sara?"

"That I have no integrity. At least when it comes to choosing between honoring my commitment to you and my friendship with Charity."

"Then you *do* know what happened to her!"

"Even if I knew for certain, I wouldn't share it with you." Maria Sara rose from the chair. The tiny woman looked up at him with a satisfied expression. "And I won't return your money."

Earlier that week, the day before Charity had disappeared, he had sold family heirlooms to get Maria Sara's information. His mother's ruby brooch, his father's gold watch, the faded Aubusson that had graced the dining room tiles. Ian had sold them for a song, and turned the money over in good faith. Yet Charity had slipped through his fingers, Maria Sara was withholding information, and his debts were piling up.

Desperation rising, he reached for the pistol hidden in his breast pocket, then forced the barrel against Maria Sara's temple. "Tell me, or you won't live long enough to trick me again."

Surprise marked her Latin features before her eyes went wide with fear; her insolence receded like the ebb of a storm tide. "Don't kill me. Remember, I have a babe."

"I care nothing for your child."

"But Jaime is your son!"

Ian asked the first question that rushed to his mind. "You haven't said anything about that to Charity, I trust?"

"I haven't." Swallowing, Maria Sara stared at the

hand holding the pistol. "Will you leave your son without a mother's love?"

"You don't love him any more than I do." Ian pulled back the hammer. "I care nothing for a spawn of greaser trash."

Maria Sara's body shivered beneath him. "Don't shoot me," she pleaded. "I'll tell you. She . . . I saw Charity in her apartment, and she said a Texas Ranger was after her."

"That's a lie. No Ranger was after her."

"She believed there was. And someone took her away. I saw a man herd her to a buckboard, then force her into it." Her brows drawn together, Maria Sara chewed her bottom lip. "I did not go to her aid. I thought she had been apprehended for smuggling and that I had best stay out of it."

In the hands of a brute unknown to decent society, no telling what had happened to Charity, Ian fretted. "What did he look like?"

"I don't know. It was night."

"You know, you despicable And you'll tell me. Or I'll scatter your brains all over this room."

"I . . . I-I'm not certain of the man's description. He was tall, wide-shouldered, slim-hipped. A large man. I doubt he's old. He didn't move as one of advanced years."

"Him. The big one," Ian surmised aloud. Word had reached him that a towering stranger had been asking questions around town and hadn't been seen since Charity's disappearance. Why hadn't he made the connection? *You fool!* "Why did he take her?"

"I know not," Maria Sara replied; Ian knew Maria Sara well enough to know she spoke the truth. "She—she thought he was the law."

Cursed Jesus. He had paid good money for nothing, for Ian had no idea what the stranger's motives might be.

"Get out of here," he ordered his lover of old, then replaced the pistol in his pocket to make a wide, slashing motion with his hand. "But I expect you to keep me informed."

"Yes, Ianito. I will. I promise."

And he took her for her word. Trouble was, it proved worthless. When Ian called on Maria Sara the next afternoon, he found her apartment cleared of personal items. She and her brat were gone. And it didn't take much research to find out that the pair had departed on the morning train, headed east.

To hell with Maria Sara. And the boy. He must rescue Charity.

It took a couple of days to form a plan and summon his flunky. It took Ian Blyer and Señor Grande less than an hour to saddle their horses and get on her trail.

Once she was in his hands, Charity would see the light and agree to become Mrs. Blyer. It was only a question of time.

Chapter Nine

"We're traveling in circles."

So, Charity had seen through his ruse. Admiring her perception, Hawk glanced at the clouded sky of late afternoon. Yes, he was taking a circuitous route to Uvalde. The powwow with the Old One was planned for the first of October; he had plenty of time to get Charity there, this being the twenty-first of September. And, addlepated though the route might be—and even though her crossness had once more surfaced after her sweet talk had failed to get him to unlock the manacles—he was enjoying his time with the hellcat.

"Why, Hawk? Why are we going in circles?"

"Do you realize most of your sentences start with 'why'?"

"Don't criticize me. I've warned you."

"A thousand times." Taking the reins in one hand, he eased five fingers atop her dress-covered thigh. "Sorry, angel."

"I am not your angel," she protested and gave a manacled swat to his hand.

He knew she'd push him away. She had done it a

dozen times. But each time he made an attempt, he got a second or two to enjoy the feel of her, which had to last until his next bold move. Since their first night by the campfire, she hadn't allowed him any more liberties.

"Hawk . . ." Her mane of dark hair fell forward as she laced her fingers. "Couldn't you . . . ? It's like this. You won't get any money out of Papa, so why don't you set me free?"

"Right here in the middle of nowhere?"

She licked her lips. "Well, uh, you could find a town."

"Charity, you disappoint me. You think I'd give up my booty?" He pulled in the reins. "Looks like a good stopping place. Let's make camp for the night."

"Could I have a bath?"

"No."

"Please?"

"No."

"Hawk, we've been traveling for days in the same clothes. Frankly, you're beginning to smell a bit rank. I must, too."

"We can't spare the water. The barrel's half empty."

"Half full," she corrected. "There's plenty enough for at least a sponge bath."

"I might consider it." Baths had their appeal, especially when he took a sidelong look at womanly attributes he would enjoy giving a good laving. "You wash me and I'll wash you. How about it?"

"You don't smell *that* bad."

* * *

On the heels of Charity's evaluation of his aroma, Hawk made camp, took care of the team, and trapped a rabbit for dinner. After he had loosened one end of her handcuffs, Charity went about the business of nature. Afterward, she sulked on a knee-high rock.

He squatted Indian-style by the fire. "Time to eat."

She huffed over to seat herself opposite him. Her spirits didn't pick up as they ate, which got to him. He wondered if maybe he ought to tell her the truth.

No.

He knew she was distraught over her father disowning her because of that Blyer character, and if he said, "I'm taking you home," he'd have more trouble on his hands than if a whole village of Kiowa braves were to attack.

But he could do one thing to make her journey more comfortable. He had concluded something; she was scared of being in the wilds alone at night. This gave him a certain sense of security. Yet he knew he wouldn't be able to close his eyes tonight if he liberated her from those cuffs.

"Charity . . ." One elbow braced on a spread knee, he stared at her petulant face. "I might take the handcuffs off you. *If* I have your assurance you won't run away."

Lights reflected from the flames danced in her eyes. "Oh, Hawk, I won't run. I promise!"

Jubilant, she hopped to her feet and rushed around the campfire to bend down and throw her arms around his neck; the swinging end of her restraints caught his shoulder blade. She didn't smell bad at all.

He was tempted to take advantage of the situation, yet the honorable part of him got the better of Hawk's libido.

"Unless you want the heat, don't touch the fire," he said. Beneath his hands, she tensed, and he warned, "It wouldn't take much for me to toss you to the ground and have your delectable legs spread before you know what's happening."

She stood. "That's all you think about, isn't it?"

"Just about."

Returning to her place at the far side of the fire, she picked up her coffee cup. "It's a nice night, considering all these clouds. Balmy, if you ask me. Oh, how nice it would be if you were to change into a new set of clothes—you do have a change, don't you? And I'd feel so much fresher if I could get out of this calico. I have clean things in my valise. Of course, I would *demand* privacy for my bath."

Here we go again. Getting to his moccasined feet, he approached her. "Charity, don't you ever think about the two of us . . . together?"

Her head turned to the grazing horses, then she stared at her hands. "Of course I do. How could I not? What with you trying to touch me all the time, how could my thoughts be on, say, needlepoint?"

"Do you like needlepoint?"

"I like anything that uses my hands."

Staring at the lovely shape of her fingers and knowing they were as soft as they looked, he murmured, "You could use your hands on me."

"No!"

"Why not? Because I'm a red devil?"

"Red devil? No, that has nothing to do with it." Amusement playing in her eyes, she admitted, "Actually, I lied that night at Sam's house. I have nothing against black-haired warriors."

Surprised and delighted, Hawk grinned. "If that's the case . . . Don't you find me attractive, Charity?"

It was as if he could see into her soul when she gazed up into his eyes. "I find you wildly attractive. My body is in a state of chaos at the very thought of you. And you may be my only chance at"—she blushed—"being with a man. I may pay with my life for getting mixed up with Adriano." She swallowed; her fingers curled into her palms. "But don't you see? You've taken me prisoner. *Prisoner.* That's an awful feeling."

Now that he thought about it, he had to agree. When he was making his plans and collecting the accoutrements of a kidnapper, he hadn't given much consideration to how Charity would feel about having her freedom of choice wrenched away.

"Is being held captive the only thing you have against me? If you knew you could trust me, then would you take me into your . . . heart?"

The loose part of her manacle slapped against her bosom as she covered her face with a hand. "This has nothing to do with heart. This has everything to do with lust. We have that between us. But if I ever lay with a man, it will be because he is special. Because we respect each other for each other. And—absolutely!—not because he's after Papa's money."

"Admirable values."

"All I have left is my sense of integrity."

The honesty in her expression was something to behold, and Hawk regarded her with respect. *Wah'Kon-Tah* be praised, they were halfway to bed already, with all the respect he had for her right now! And Hawk certainly had no need for Gil McLoughlin's money.

"Do you find anything to admire about me?" he asked, regretting his words immediately. He wasn't looking for praise, yet somehow he coveted her approval.

"As I said, I like your honesty." Her unfettered hand swept her loose hair from her cheek to expose more of her forthright and compelling face. "Nothing said is a *lot* better than even the smallest of a lie between two people who trust each other."

"You trust me?"

"Crazy though it may be, but I find an integrity to you."

Her beguiling honesty gave him pause. Jesus, Lord of the paleface. For the first time, Hawk considered what she would think, once she found out about the web of lies he had concocted to get her back to the Four Aces. *You'd better stick to the truth, as much as you can.*

A gust of wind rearranged her hair. Blowing a dark tress out of her face again, she added, "I may like your honesty, Hawk, but don't be getting ideas I'm not curious about you."

"Curiosity works two ways." He leaned to take her hand in his. "I'd like to know what was so special about that Blyer character that you would give up your family for him."

"Who can explain why one person falls for another? At least, I can't. All I know is I was mad for Ian." Hawk watched her swallow as she said this, and the hurt she'd experienced was a visible thing. "He disappointed me so deeply."

"Do you still love him?" Hawk waited with bated breath for her answer. If she loved Blyer, then—it would change everything. Hawk didn't want everything to change. He ached for Charity to yearn for him, and him alone. "Do you still love Blyer?"

"I was attracted to his flash and dash, and to the adventure of doing something outlandish and forbidden. It was nothing more than a mere crush."

Relieved, Hawk said, "You paid a high price for it."

"And I regret it. Since it tore me away from . . ."

"Do you want to make peace with your family?"

She shook her head with vehemence. "Papa and the others are through with me, and I'll never beg for forgiveness. Anyway, I don't want to. I simply want to get on with my life, and make something of it."

He understood her feelings; he had them himself. His rift with the Osage, and especially with his father, Iron Eagle, cut to the quick. Would he ever see his mother and Amy again? If he did, it would be on his own terms.

Satisfied with his decision, he glanced at Charity. Such a sad angel was she. "I've heard you have an elderly kinswoman. I can't imagine such a woman not wanting you within reach."

"Maiz made her choice."

"She's that cold?" Hawk knew otherwise.

"Maiz? Oh, heavens no. She is anything but. Always, she was my chief ally. And I love her above anyone else on the face of this earth. Well, except for Margaret."

Hawk studied the glistening eyes, the dropped chin, the pain in Charity's admission. "You feel as if no one loves you, yet you speak warmly of two in your family. Those odds aren't bad."

Charity imparted a look of irritation. "You're taking the McLoughlins' side."

"I might not if I understood more about the situation."

"Then I'd like to set you straight. When I was a baby, my father pegged me a defiant troublemaker. That's why he named me Charity, so I might 'think before I act.' A strike against me from the beginning. He and my mother gravitated toward the darlings of their daughters. I was shuffled aside. It got worse after Angus came along. I am the unwanted McLoughlin."

"And the more unwanted you felt, the more you tried for attention."

"I . . . I suppose by getting their attention by whatever means, even if it was the negative sort, I had what I wanted. Their attention. But I pushed them past their limits."

Hawk touched her jaw, and he felt the shivers of hurt wracking her body. "No one ought to feel so estranged from family. There's a chance your parents don't understand you, but I bet they love you, crippled wing and all."

"You are wrong."

It was pitiable, the confidence she lacked. Hawk decided that if she ever learned to believe in her abilities and in her potential, then the sky would be her limit. "Beneath your prickly surface, there's a spirit to you. It cries out for understanding. You're an angel who's fallen from grace and has broken a wing. Each time you try to spread your wings, you fall again. With each fall . . . the angel cries."

Hawk saw a struggle in her eyes. When she dragged her gaze from his, she whispered, "You . . . you say these heavenly things, but you are a pagan."

"No. *Wah'Kon-Tah* guides me. God is everywhere."

"You believe in the spirit of angels?"

"Yes."

Unnerved, and perhaps pleased, she labored to stand. "I—I need a moment alone. I think I'll brush my hair." She glided over to her valise and took out a brush. Her back to Hawk, she ran the bristles through those long, long locks. As she had from her family, as she had from Ian Blyer and from the crime she stood accused of committing, she was attempting to distance herself from simple truths.

I need to face life's truths, she decided.

When she repacked the brush, Charity returned to the fire and lay down beside Hawk. He wondered what she would say. For several minutes, she said nothing. Hawk somewhat regretted trying to delve too deeply into her soul. And if the truth be known, he'd gotten out of the spiritualistic mood anyway. Upon watching her groom her hair, her entirely *human* presence had roused an altogether masculine reaction in Hawk.

Finally, looking over at him with eyes full of turquoise hardness, she announced, "You're wrong about me. I'm no angel, fallen or otherwise. And I never cry."

While he disagreed, Hawk kept his mouth shut.

"Will you promise I won't have to see my father when you talk to him about the ransom?"

It was on the tip of his tongue to strike a deal, but Hawk collected his devious and lusty thoughts. "I promise not to make you face your father."

This had never been Hawk's plan anyway. His intent centered on returning her to the Old One, then letting the entire McLoughlin clan settle their differences in the way they saw fit. Which remained a sensible plan. But with all the bad medicine between them, what would the others think about that smuggling business? There would be another strike against Charity.

Concerned, Hawk mused aloud. "It seems strange, your tying in with one such as Adriano Gonzáles. What happened?"

"I'll tell you on one condition. That you explain how you know about it."

Hawk nodded. "When I got to Laredo, I asked around. A fellow across the border in Nuevo Laredo was in need of some money, so he had a lot to say. I followed up on it."

"Who was he?"

"Señor Grande is all I know."

"Big man," she uttered with a twist of her lips. "Rufino Saldana. That evil worm had a nerve saying anything bad about me. He's the one who introduced me to Adriano."

"Charity, I've made good on my word, now make good on yours. How did you get mixed up with Gonzáles and his men?"

"I was hungry. I'd sold everything I owned that was worth selling, and I had no option but to find work. Adriano offered me employment, that's all. Or at least I thought that was all. It turned out that I wasn't bringing Cuban cigars into Texas, as I had been told. I was carrying cigar boxes of money to the silver-smuggling go-betweens in Shafter."

"You didn't *know* what you were doing?"

Earnestness in her voice as well as her expression, she riveted her gaze to his searching eyes. "I didn't know until after the fact, when the rangers showed up in Shafter. God help me, Hawk, I was horrified, finding out I'd committed a felony."

He believed her.

All along he'd thought her halo tarnished.

His respect for her gave it an extra polishing.

Moreover, he worried about her. It was a damned good thing the Old One had sent for her. No telling what would have happened if her kinswoman hadn't loved her enough to send a kidnapper to Laredo. An angel like this needed a lot of protection. Not to mention top-caliber legal aid. *You could take care of her, in and out of court.*

He could protect her forever, perhaps, if she ever wanted him in the ever-after sort of way. But even if he made her understand that he wasn't interested in extortion, and certainly not in "Papa's money," David Fierce Hawk was in no position to take a wife.

There was that law practice in Austin yet to be settled on. And he had his own dragons to slay. Of course, he was hot for Charity, but a man shouldn't let his future rise from something that had risen in lust. Forever was a long, long time.

"Let me get those manacles off you," Hawk said. "Then I'd best see after the horses."

Hawk returned to the campfire shortly thereafter. Charity lay asleep on her side, her freed hands making a pillow for her head. Easing down on the pallet of blankets, Hawk placed a gentlemanly kiss on her forehead.

With no intention of sleeping—he had to make certain her word was good—he let his mind drift. His chest heaved as he stifled a chuckle, recalling her words about black-haired warriors. Reared in Texas, where prejudice flowed thick and wide, she didn't hold his race against him. *You're one remarkable woman, Charity McLoughlin.* Remarkable and adorable—in a mind-boggling sort of way. Maybe it wouldn't be so terrible, a lifetime with her.

He patted her arm, brushed a strand of long hair over her shoulder. His heart thudded, for her womanly being was all over and through him. And he wanted more. He reached for the hem of her calico, his palms working up a curvaceous leg to stop at her unclothed, womanly mound. *Wah'Kon-Tah,* she felt good! Better than anything he had ever touched before. And she grew wet beneath his questing fingers.

She fidgeted in her sleep, issuing a mew of approval.

His lips played across hers. He moved his breech-clout aside, his shaft rearing and demanding surcease. *Behave.*

What was he thinking of? He didn't know for certain if he wanted her for a lifetime. Matters needed sorting. Once they reached Uvalde, after she'd learned he was no ransom-minded rogue, then they could go from there; he hoped the place they were led to had a future to it. In that light he needed to treat her with all respect, which meant—for *now!*—he must leave her virginity intact.

Pitching away from her, exhaling in need and frustration, he willed himself not to think of the warm, sweet, voluptuous body lying so near yet so far. It must have been a good ten minutes before he got control. He yawned. And his eyelids grew heavier and heavier.

He awoke to sunlight.

His angel had flown the coop.

Chapter Ten

With all haste she reached the Four Aces Ranch. It had been a tiring trip by train and stagecoach for Maria Sara Montaña and her son. On this sweltering morning—as she toted the exhausted, irritable Jaime up the steep rosebush-lined carriageway that led to the two-story limestone mansion with its tall columns—she hoped against hope that Charity would meet her at the door.

She also hoped to be forgiven for not having been honest about where the money she had lent Charity had come from. She had taken it from Ian Blyer because she had felt it her due; she had parted with it because Charity was a friend in need.

She prayed the *gringa* had somehow escaped from whatever danger had befallen her. If that hadn't happened, Maria Sara could at least alert the family that one of their own was in peril.

In the beginning Maria Sara had viewed Charity McLoughlin as nothing but a threat. The green-eyed monster had swept through her, for Ian was

Charity's for the taking. She brushed away a tear that had rolled down her cheek. Ian had been the one to demand she ingratiate herself with his new love; she'd fought against offering the woman friendship. But in spite of her jealousy, she'd come to like the willful girl. And Charity was the only person in her life ever to prove loyal and true.

Jaime whined, drawing her attention to the burden in her arms. "Silence, *chico.*" She dug in her pocket for a piece of candy, then popped it into her young child's mouth. "You are much like your father. Greedy. Let us hope you don't become even more like him, avid for blood."

She shuddered. For years she'd clung to the belief that Ianito would return to her and give her the respectability she craved. But after his threat of murder, she realized there was no chance for her. It was then she had vowed revenge.

By now she had topped the steps leading up to the vast McLoughlin home. Her knuckles rapped on the mahogany door.

Charity didn't answer the summons, as she had hoped. A servant escorted Maria Sara and her toddler into an expansive and cool salon, where but one McLoughlin received them.

"Sit down, lass," Charity's great-grandmother ordered after Maria Sara had introduced herself. "Take the settee." She motioned to a sofa in the latest Victorian style. "It will be comfortable for ye and yer wee lad."

Taking a seat and settling the now quiet Jaime to her shoulder, Maria Sara eyed the lovely room, all velvets and rich woods with a fireplace dominating one wall that rose two stories in height. Her eyes settled on Maisie McLoughlin. The elderly lady—spry for seventy, much less ninety—sat straight and tall in an old-fashioned rocker out of place amidst the manse's splendor.

Not wanting to appear overly awed by the surroundings, Maria Sara launched into her story of Charity's abduction by dark of night, the treacherousness of Ian Blyer, and of an offer of employment gone awry.

"I feared she'd come t' no good with Blyer." The rocker squeaked as the matriarch leaned forward. "Always, Charity has tried t' set herself apart from her sisters by willfulness and impetuousness."

"She thinks none of you care for her."

"Considering the hell that was aboot when she left this house, it wouldna be hard for that impression t' stay with her." The Scotswoman clicked her tongue. "But what's done is done."

"We've got to find her," Maria Sara implored. "She needs help. Right away. Señor Blyer—"

"Is no threat." A thin hand waved dismissively, and an amused gleam replaced the melancholy cast of the old woman's Wedgwood-hued eyes. "That peacock will be getting his tail feathers plucked if he keeps scratching round our Charity. Doona be worrying aboot an abduction. She's in good hands. *I* sent the Indian after her."

Indian? Maria Sara blanched. When she found her voice, she said, "Far be it from me to question your reasons."

"Ye've every right. Not many wooud put herself out t' make a journey such as yours, just t' see after a friend's well-being." The *vieja* paused. "Let me answer the query I see in yer eyes—pretty, they are, by the way."

But Charity's great-grandmother had no desire to expound upon Maria Sara's attributes."For four months," she explained, "I have been waiting for my stubborn grandson t' come t' his senses, but he hasna. So, I decided t' take matters int' my own hands. Trouble was, I couldna think of a way. Charity left here angry with me as well as with her maither and faither. I dinna figure she'd be too happy if I went after her. Besides, I'm not as young as I used t' be, and 'tis, as ye know, quite a trip betwixt Fredericksburg and Laredo."

Maria Sara glanced at her squirming son. How well she knew the ardors of travel.

"He looks t' be a lively one," the elderly woman commented when Jaime twisted in his mother's arms and emitted a scream of protest at the bonds of her fingers. A smug look on her wrinkled face, the McLoughlin matriarch put the rocker in motion. "Our Charity may be presenting us with a babe in the course of time. Through wedlock, of course! That Fierce Hawk looks as if he's virile enough."

"I take it you sent him after her with matchmaking in mind."

"Aye. He is a good catch. Fierce Hawk is more white than red. He's educated. His grandmaither in Maryland left him a sizable estate, which he doesna even need, since he's a lawyer by profession."

Perhaps it wasn't such a bad idea, Maria Sara decided, the *vieja* sending a lawyer to Laredo.

By now Jaime had squirmed out of his mother's arms. He grabbed for a candy dish that his mother impatiently pushed out of his reach. He lunged; she swatted his hand. Naturally, he filled the rafters of the high-ceilinged room with his protests.

"Come here, lad. Granny has something for ye."

The *vieja* dug in her pocket, pulled out a brass ring of keys, and dangled them. Jaime took the bait, was across the room in no time, and was rattling the keys himself. He smiled at the old lady and received a rustle to his tawny head of hair.

"There's a good lad."

For the first time in days, his mother thought, he was being a "good lad." The old lady worked magic on the tired *chico*. When he plopped down at her feet to play with the ersatz toy, she rang a bell that rested atop the marble-topped table beside her rocking chair. Almost immediately, a servant appeared and was ordered to "bring the wee lad a nice cup of cocoa."

"You aren't worried about the smuggling trouble?" Maria Sara asked, eager to get back to Charity's predicament.

On a shake of her silvered head, the *vieja* swept Jaime into her arms and began to rock him. The servant reappeared with the cocoa mug, and the elderly lady deftly put the lip to his eager mouth.

"We will be getting our Charity out of trouble. Money talks. And she'll have Fierce Hawk on her side too."

"You seem quite certain they'll make a match."

"I am. I doona have t' be telling ye Charity is headstrong. She needs a man who'll not quail at her tongue. They'll be making a match, or I'm not Maisie McLoughlin."

"And you're certain her parents will approve?"

"My grandchildren will be approving." Such confidence defied the old woman's disquieted expression. "Lisette right away. My grandson, eventually."

"Where are they, by the way?"

"On their way home from Washington. Senate is in session, ye see, but I've sent a telegram. 'Trouble with Angus.' Angus is Charity's braither, but ye probably know that," she explained. "Lisette and Gilliegorm will be here in a matter of days."

These calm guarantees eased Maria Sara's anxiety over Charity's dilemma. Now she could think about her own. Survival and security. And she must find a lover. Soon.

She didn't worry that Ian Blyer would come after her. She knew his mind was on Charity; he didn't care enough about "greaser trash" to waste his time on her and Jaime.

But his time would come, and he'd pay for his transgressions. Someway, somehow, he would be punished for his victimization of both her and Charity. In her own case the victim had turned from an innocent girl into a woman with an unquenchable need for sexual gratification. Maria

Sara realized she was a lost soul. Her only chance for redemption was to help Charity.

"This is a fine, bonny lad ye have."

"You wouldn't think him thus if you'd traveled with the scamp," Maria Sara replied in exasperation. "He tripped the conductor, kept passengers from their naps, and yanked feathers from a matron's hat. All within an hour of our boarding."

She met the *vieja's* amused laughter with a grimace; she didn't see anything humorous about her son's behavior.

The old woman's eyes sparkled. "I remember a train trip from Chicago with three wee lasses. Younger than yer Jaime, they were. And under my care, so their parents might enjoy a belated honeymoon in their own private car. The lasses cried and cried—'twas lucky we dinna get put off the train!"

Money did have its privileges.

Maria Sara quit the settee. "We must take our leave now," she said.

"Ye dinna arrive by conveyance, so I'll be assuming ye'll be needing the loan of a carriage."

"A ride into town would be very much appreciated. Our things are at the stage stop, and—"

"What will ye be doing after ye get t' Fredericksburg? Are ye off t' Laredo again?"

"Actually, I had hoped to find employment in town."

"Señora—"

"S-señorita," Maria Sara corrected instinctively, then could have bitten her tongue, for undoubtedly condemnation would meet her slip of the tongue. It did not. While she now lived a sordid existence, Maria Sara was adamant about keeping up appearances.

"Señorita Montaña, wooud ye be of a mind t' stand an old woman's company? And can ye sew a straight seam? I want t' hire ye. There's no one round here t' chat with—the grandchildren and their bairns are away more than they're here—and me wardrobe could use some improvement. Will ye stay here at the Four Aces?"

"I would be honored and pleased. Thank you for offering." Maria Sara dropped a curtsy. "You'll find me a hard worker."

"Ye'd better be, 'cause I doona waste coin on laggards. "Charity's great-grandmother gave one firm nod to her head to punctuate her statement. "Lisette bought me bolt after bolt of material for new· frocks, but that wasna all she bought. Ye'll be finding a new treadle Singer in the solarium. Do ye think ye can be learning t' peddle that contraption?"

Warming to the subject, Maria Sara smiled. "I saw one in an advertisement when I was expecting Jaime. Since then, I've imagined my hands on one—a thousand times."

The *vieja* winked again. "I am betting our Charity will be happy as a clam when she gets an eyeful of ye."

"I hope that happens soon," Maria Sara replied frankly. "And I hope her happiness is as you imagine it'll be. Over Fierce Hawk."

"Doona be worrying. Nature will take care of those two. Fierce Hawk will be scaring sense int' her."

The old Scotswoman's suggestion of scare tactics?

Bah!

When he got his hands on Charity, he was going to wring her neck. Hawk *would* find her. He'd been on her trail since daybreak. The sun was now high. His eyes swept the ground. She had left a trail that even the dumbest Indian could have followed, even a gullible fool who'd made this trip but once, on his way to collect a conniving little hellcat misnamed Charity.

It wasn't that she had made a getaway—such was to be expected, or should have been—nor was it that she'd taken anything with her that had Hawk in an uproar. It was what she had left, and how she had left them, that made him stop to grit his teeth and shake his fists at the sky, and not for the first time that day.

Oh, how satisfying it would be, tightening his talons around that swanlike neck!

Going north and then east, he followed a narrow creek, the San Lorenzo. It took him less than a half day to catch sight of her. She was bathing in the stream, humming, as if she hadn't a care in the world.

Arms crossed over his chest, Hawk slunk up behind her. He was too angry to take his fill of her wet-petticoat-clad form, though he wasn't completely unaware of her alabaster skin and the perfection of her form. The last thing he wanted was to get between her legs. No, that was the second last thing. The last thing he would ever want? Marital chains binding him to this spoiled, devious brat.

"Afternoon," he said with a restrained growl, which made her jump.

She whirled around and covered her pert, thinly veiled breasts with the wet calico dress. "You."

"Yes, me," he said through clenched teeth. Dropping his arms from his chest, he tightened his fingers. "You were expecting a knight in shining armor?"

"Actually, one did come along." Brazen as she pleased, Charity motioned to the left. "A nice man. He's a *sheriff,* and he'll be back any moment now—he gave me privacy for my bath, you see." She took a sidestep toward the creek bank. "Better run along before he arrests you."

"You'll have to come up with a better one than that. Stay right where you are," he ordered as she took another step. "You and I have unfinished business."

"We do not."

"Oh, yeah? What about the horses? Nice of you to show horseflesh so much respect." He watched her face turn red, which gave him some satisfaction at least. "Where is the key?"

"Key? What key?"

"Don't act the innocent, it doesn't fit you."

To his amazement, she merely smiled at him. Advancing on her, he molded his fingers around an imaginary form. "Charity McLoughlin, I'm going to wring your neck for handcuffing those poor dumb horses together."

Chapter Eleven

He looked like he'd eaten bullets for breakfast.

"You might as well have cut those horses' throats. They'll die like that." Hawk stood, wrists raised to do battle, while his dark eyes fired at her from the creek bank. "Damn you to whatever hell you fear."

His words hurt her more than his fists ever could.

Charity plopped down in the water. A jagged rock caught her in the posterior. She wanted to scream. And not from the sharp pain, either. Dismayed over yet another harebrained scheme gone awry and chagrined at being recaptured, she muttered her own "Damn."

Before dawn, it had seemed a good idea, shackling the team together to keep Hawk from driving the buckboard after her. In the dark, and fearing what might befall her before dawn, she'd been in a dither to get away. But now, in the light of midday and the harsh glare of her captor's eyes, she realized the stupidity of her actions.

She might have known an Indian wouldn't track someone by wagon. And she should have realized that leaving horseflesh stranded on the prairie was just as murderous as Hawk had charged. She would never have done such a thing had she been thinking straight.

Was there any silver lining to this cloud? None she could see. Well, maybe one.

Despite his being a kidnapper, and in spite of his claim to be capable of any savagery, and belying the look of fury in his aquiline face, Hawk, she felt, was a decent sort of fellow. The previous night he had instilled trust in her, to the point that she'd had second thoughts about escaping. His greedy bid for Papa's money just hadn't seemed that important under the stars, and she'd gotten the impression that his mind could be changed. Shortly thereafter, when he had roused her from sleep with his delving fingers . . .

Well, last night was last night.

"Get out of that water," he demanded.

"No, thank you."

"Get out and get dressed." The glint in his eyes became even more feral as Hawk marched toward her. *"Now!"*

Charity gulped and huddled. "Don't touch me," she squeaked when he swooped down and plucked her, like a wren of broken wing, from the stream. "Vulture, get your claws off me!"

"Be informed—vultures feast on hellcats."

She fell to her back as he thrust her upon the bank. "You . . . you promised not to kill me."

"All promises are off."

Towering above her, Hawk planted a long, buckskin-clad leg at each side of her waist. Her eyes made the lengthy journey from his spread calves past the knife strapped to his thigh. The breech-clout billowed from his waist, giving her a very shadowed view of the arch difference between a man and a woman. She supposed he'd be considered well-endowed, even if she had nothing to gauge her opinion, never having seen a man's equipment before. She trembled, and it wasn't from the threat of bodily harm.

"Gotten an eyeful, you wanton hussy?" he taunted, leaning to cut off the paltry view.

Her line of sight traveled upward, seizing on bronzed skin and silver before settling on his unforgiving face. My, Hawk was a handsome predator.

"Is this where you scalp me?" she asked quietly.

"I ought to." He jabbed a finger in her direction. "But I don't want any reminder of *you* cluttering up my lodge."

Gads, she couldn't even get a man to scalp her. *I guess I really, really ought to think about reforming.* On that thought, she laughed.

"You think it's funny, leaving dumb animals—"

"I'm not laughing about what I did. I'm laughing at myself." She rubbed her eyes with one hand. "I'm thinking I should be left at the nearest lunatic asylum."

Palms on his knees, Hawk angled downward. The silver pendant as well as his black hair swung in the air. "What makes you think you'll live long enough to see so much as a proper building?"

"You said you wouldn't scalp me."

"I said nothing about not wringing your neck."

She lifted a brow at Hawk's enraged expression and stole another look at the perfection of his brawny chest and muscled, veined arms. "I know you're a bit angry, but must you hover so?"

"Shut up." The order hissed past his clamped teeth.

Her eyes flitted along the sculpted lines of his taut lips. Something hot blazed through her. Her thoughts surprised her. *I want him to kiss me; I want all his fury to abandon itself to passion.* She wanted to be ravaged, right here at creekside.

Good gravy!

When she had bathed, she must have scrubbed away whatever was left of her brain.

There was but one thing to do. Get a grip on reason. Back in Sam's hovel, Hawk had warned her of his savagery. While she doubted he'd make good on his threat, she decided she'd best play it safe.

Her voice softer than usual, she asked, "Would you still want to wring my neck . . . if I were to say I was sorry?"

"Try me."

"I'm sorry."

He straightened, then hoisted himself away from her. From a distance of a yard or so, he faced the stream and said, "You're an abomination of a woman."

"I . . . I never claimed to be otherwise." She gulped, then rolled to her bare feet. "Last night, though, you said nice things about me."

"Lies to get between your legs."

You're fibbing. "I am sorry about the horses. I

would *not* have hurt horseflesh deliberately." She coerced a smile as he faced her anew, and saw some of his anger vanishing. "I bet my virginity you've done something to make it easier on the team."

His lips the thinnest she had ever seen them, he reached for her valise and tossed it at her feet. "Get dressed. And give me the key. We've got to rescue the horses."

She hurried. Abandoning the wet calico dress, she pulled a gingham one over her head, then pushed her feet into last year's velvet slippers. Finger-combing her hair, she chewed her lip. "Uh, Hawk, there's a problem. You see, I, uh, um, well, I've l-lost the key. Actually, I threw it away."

"Why am I not surprised?" he fumed.

By late afternoon there was still no trace of the missing item. A dozen times, as they combed the trail she had taken that morning, Hawk impressed upon her the importance of remembering where she had tossed the key over her shoulder. A dozen times Charity had hefted her shoulders in uncertainty.

His eyes to the ground, and within a quarter mile of the beleaguered team, Hawk still searched the dried grasses. He sidestepped prickly pears and scrub brush; he disturbed jackrabbits, armadillos, and a nest of rattlesnakes. The key, he didn't find.

"We've missed it, Hawk. It was hours after dawn that I threw it away. And I was certainly well past this area."

He muttered some kind of something, probably

another Indian curse word. Dusting his hands, he said in English, "I give up. We'd better get back, before dark falls."

He stomped onward; she followed, trying to match his long strides. When they reached the campsite Charity ground to a halt and brought her hand to her mouth to stifle a giggle.

Hawk wheeled around once more. "What's—You're *laughing?* You featherbrain, don't you have an ounce of shame?"

"I . . . I guess not."

Not able to contain herself any longer, Charity laughed long and hard. The horses sure were a sight. No better than nags, the two were shackled together, one's foreleg to the other's hind leg. They leaned in to each other. The piebald's tail whisked across its partner's forelocks. The gray's mouth twisted comically, then curled back to display a pink tongue and overlong yellow teeth receded from black gums; it had a woebegone expression in its eyes, a look that beat any puppy's for pitiful—and, why, adorable.

Her line of sight shifted. Indeed, as she had suspected, a pile of dried grass and buckets of water were set below each horse's muzzle. "I guess I'm not in danger of losing my virginity."

"You got that right. Very right."

"Well, I know you're a bit peeved," she said, ignoring his harsh tone. She hadn't expected him to be courtly about the day's events, for heaven's sake. But . . . "You know, Hawk, you really are something. I'd say . . . gallant."

He looked at her as if she had gone daft. "Gallant?"

"Yes." As she stepped closer, an armadillo rushed across her toes, and she jumped nervously. "I'm glad you found me. I was scared alone."

"You didn't look all that scared in your bath."

"I had to do something to keep myself occupied until you showed up."

Doing another about-face, he said, "Now is not a good time to butter up to me, Charity McLoughlin."

All right, her timing was poor. They could talk later. And shame beset Charity again. How were they going to get the handcuffs off the horses?

"You got a hairpin in that valise of yours?" Hawk asked.

She did not, so he tried to come up with another method of picking the lock. A quill from the headdress he had stored in the buckboard snapped in the cylinder, as did a stick. A fork proved no use. Neither did the ax, since each time Hawk meant to swing it between the chains, the gray bucked and chaos erupted.

"Shoot the chains apart."

"And tempt true chaos? Think again, Charity McLoughlin. I'm not a sharpshooter, I'm a law—I'm a *law-abiding* man." He talked as fast as a snake-oil salesman. "A somewhat law-abiding man, except for the ransom deal."

She got the impression he'd stumbled over the word "law." It almost sounded as if he were starting to say lawyer. Of all the crazy things! Hawk was no officer of the courts. In her scattered brain, she must have been looking to mix him up with the heroic Fierce Hawk, whose aim could probably sharpen a knife's edge from a distance of thirty feet.

Hawk, a forefinger roofing his upper lip, stomped back and forth in front of the gray; she observed, "I'm surprised you can't shoot. Guess you make up for it with tomahawks and"—she eyed the weapon strapped to his thigh—"knives."

"Exactly."

Suddenly a shot rang out, startling them both.

It came from the rise to their left.

The gray horse reared and screamed, catching pistol fire in the side, then fell against the piebald. Hawk, his knife raised, rushed in the sniper's direction. Charity ran for cover. Another shot rang out. Crimson exploded into the air as the piebald horse took fire in its head.

A man, pistol leveled, stepped into sight.

Ian Blyer.

"My God," Blyer said after Hawk's knife caught his hat and set it flying to the ground, "you've been abducted by an Indian!" He aimed his pistol. "I will avenge your honor, dear one!"

Charity screamed, "No! Don't shoot."

Another shot rang out, striking Hawk in the shoulder and stopping his direct charge. Hawk clutched his wound.

Charity was grabbed from behind. The stench of chilies and body odor surrounded her; she was hauled back against a bulky form. *"Hola."*

She recognized the voice and the smell. Rufino Saldino. Señor Grande of Nuevo Laredo. Manager of the Pappagallo whorehouse. Now obviously in cahoots with Ian Blyer.

Disgust coursing through her, Charity shivered. She hadn't thought of either cur in days. How naive she'd been to think she'd seen the last of them.

Grande's meaty hand clenched her upper arm as he shoved her in Ian's direction.

"Let her go," Hawk shouted, marching toward them.

"You don't give the orders, Injun." Ian brandished the revolver. "Take one more step, and I will shoot again!"

Hawk stopped in his tracks.

Ian's mouth formed itself into a tight smile as he held out an arm to Charity. "Dear one, thank God, I've rescued you. Do come to me."

Charity sized up the situation. Here was her chance to get free of Hawk. Yet it was all she could do not to laugh at the farce her life had become. The Indian would rend her pride by ransoming her to Papa; Ian betrayed both God and the devil.

She glanced at Hawk. From the look in his eyes, she knew he didn't trust her not to fly to Ian. Charity stood right where she was.

Chapter Twelve

"Fräulein."

Stooped over her sewing, Maria Sara quit treadling the Singer to eye Charity's cousin. Karl Keller, a sturdy cattleman of twenty-seven, filled the solarium's doorway. The last rays of afternoon sun filtered through the room's many windows to highlight the man's gold hair, combed neatly behind his ears.

And they were nice ears, she noticed, neither too large nor too small against a face square in dimensions. Sunshine also emphasized the flush on Karl's cheekbones. Maria Sara got the disturbing feeling, as she had the first time she'd met him at the McLoughlin estate, that she'd seen him somewhere before.

Ridiculous.

Turning his tan Stetson around in his hands, Karl shuffled his booted feet. "Oma said I should take you to town."

Oma. Maria Sara had learned the word meant "grandmother" in the predominate language of this part of Texas. It seemed everyone save for Angus called Maisie McLoughlin the German equivalent of grandmother. Maria Sara had also taken to calling the *vieja* that particular term of endearment.

But what was the take-you-to-town contract? Apparently Oma was up to her matchmaking tricks again. Even from a distance. Yesterday, the old woman had departed the Four Aces in a carriage fit for an empress, her destination a rendezvous in Uvalde with Charity and the Indian called Fierce Hawk.

"Are you ready?" asked the *alemán* rancher.

Maria Sara snipped a thread from a taffeta skirt. "It's too late in the day for such a journey, Señor Keller."

The room fell silent, the only sound being that of a mockingbird outside the solarium. Until Maria Sara heard a swallowing. A very human swallowing.

"Oma said I must take you to town. Tonight." While he'd been born in Texas, Karl Keller's accent paid homage to the Kellers's German fatherland. "We must honor Oma's wishes."

Maria Sara eyed his face, which reddened to a deeper shade of scarlet. His Adam's apple bobbed. She knew him to be shy. It must have taken a huge effort on his part to go this far with Oma's schemes. Touching. But how could she put a stop to his efforts without hurting the man? She needed the fire of such men as Ianito and his brief successor, El Aguila. *Don't think about either one.*

"Señor Keller—"

"Most folks call me Karl."

"Karl, I am quite busy." She pressed her palm on her handiwork. "Oma expects her new wardrobe to be completed before she returns from Uvalde, and I must not drag my feet."

"Ja. I understand." On the toe of his boot, he turned toward the door. Yet he didn't quit. One hand moving to the top of the door facing him, he stood firm. Stammering, he said, "There is a dance this evening at the Vereinskirche. Oma said you must dance."

Pushing the sewing chair back, Maria Sara got to her feet and stepped toward the blond giant. She had to look up at him, way up. Strangely, surprisingly, it felt good to look up to so much strength. Karl Keller abounded with it.

Yet . . .

She knew well the hurt that man could bring woman.

"I'm not interested in dancing, *gracias.* And, besides, I have a son to take care of."

"Graciella watches over the boy."

Her blush matched Karl's, hers in shame. How easy it had become to accept the trappings of wealth such as she had known at her girlhood home in Vera Cruz. Yes, the servant Graciella had taken charge of Jaime, and Maria Sara felt perhaps too grateful for the respite. Too often she viewed the child in the light of his father, and this, she knew, was both monstrous and regrettable. A child shouldn't pay for his father's sins.

She bent her head. How could a mother at the same time both love and hate the child of her body?

"Fraülein Maria Sara, will you dance with me tonight?"

Her eyes traveled up to Karl's open gaze. "Until your cousin Charity reaches here and I know she is all right, I cannot think of merrymaking. Another time, perchance."

"Another time," Karl echoed.

He exited the solarium, and Maria Sara suddenly felt bereft. Karl Keller was not only appealing, he seemed solid as a rock. He didn't drink liquor, nor did he behave crudely. He didn't dip snuff, like so many of the Four Aces cowboys did. Furthermore, he was no mere cowhand. Karl owned a nearby farm-turned-ranch, which he had bought from his lame father who lived in San Antonio in retirement. His toil with land and cattle could only be described as diligent. Yet it was obvious he had no fire in his loins.

Besides, she was living at the Four Aces primarily to sew frocks for Oma, not to have affairs with McLoughlin kin. While she'd been hunting for a lover or two, a voice from the past echoed in her mind. It was as if Sister Estrella of the convent school were saying, "Decent men are for decent women, like Charity!"

Oh, Charity, how are you?

Charity and Hawk could have been better.

Now, as the half moon hovered high in the sky and the campfire Señor Grande had made lit up the night, Charity stole a glance at Hawk. He, too, had his hands tied behind him. He, too, sat on the hard ground with one shoulder resting against a wagon wheel.

Ian's shot had but grazed Hawk's other shoulder, and the bleeding had stopped an hour ago. Charity knew he had to be in pain, though his stoic expression revealed nothing. She felt awful.

Her eyes turned to the carcasses of the horses. Her heart ached. Thankfully, the team's suffering had been short-lived. And they were still alive, she and Hawk; Charity was glad for that.

Ian, a wine bottle stolen from the buckboard tucked under his arm, ranted at Grande, "I cannot believe that she wouldn't be overjoyed that I've rescued her. She chose a dirty Indian over the handsomest man in Texas!"

"Maybe, señor, he have a long tongue and he know how to use it."

Ian whirled around, pointing a finger first at Charity, then at Hawk. "Is that true? Has he soiled you?"

She shook her head. "No. Never."

Yet Ian rushed forth to kick Hawk's side. Not so much as a sigh passed the Indian's throat, much less a yowl of pain. He imparted a withering look at his tormentor, nonetheless.

Ian hastened to Charity. Standing over her, he brushed the side of his hair with the heel of his hand. "You had better be telling the truth," he sneered, "or I will kill you, dearest. As soon as your father's fortune is in my control."

"You'd really have a hard time keeping your mitts on Papa's money if my blood stains them."

His brows furrowed; he laughed in a way that made her wonder what she had ever seen in the man. "What's come over me?" he said deliriously. "How could I even think . . . ? You would've scratched his eyes out, were he to try to touch you. You would never choose a red bastard over me."

"I'd choose the devil over you, Ian Blyer."

"How dare you say that!"

His hand arced through the air, finding its target, Charity's cheek. Pain exploded in her face; she saw Hawk struggling to come to her rescue. Surprisingly quick of motion in spite of his cumbersome form, Grande charged Hawk and held him back with a booted foot pressing into his wound. Blood oozed over the toe of the *mexicano*'s boot.

"Look at me, Charity," Ian demanded.

Spittle seeped from the corners of his mouth. She saw her former fiancé as nothing but absurd and ridiculous, a caricature of the man she'd given up everything to follow. Never had she seen him act so strangely—his behavior was positively lunatic! *Gads, what did I ever see in him, above his handsome veneer and Papa's disapproval?*

Granted, he could be dashing and attractive in a sandy-haired, gay-blade sort of way; and, granted, he could be charming at times, but her most foolish mistake in judgment in all the years of her life had been falling for this cock of the walk now behaving as cuckoo as the wooden bird in Mutti's hall clock.

Charity stole a glance at Hawk, who was eyeing Grande with a coolness of composure. If one were to disregard that business of kidnapping and ransom, there was nothing insane about her feelings for the Indian.

"Look at me, dear one!" Ian planted his hands on his knees and leaned toward her, his wine-scented breath no treat. "You are mine, Charity McLoughlin. And I will train your nasty tongue to serve rather than taunt."

It was all she could do not to laugh.

Chapter Thirteen

For the next quarter hour or so, as Ian and Grande uncorked another bottle of wine and availed themselves of its contents, Charity wondered how in the world she and Hawk were going to get free. Or if they would.

Once again her wrists were strapped, this time with a rope that ate into her flesh. These bindings hurt more than Hawk's manacles ever had, for her rope bonds had been tied by someone Charity was ever more inclined to consider a madman.

She might well die a virgin, for she'd never take Ian's hand in matrimony. But she yearned for Hawk to take her hand and lead her away. Or was it *astray?*

"I would like another drink, señor." Grande, his fingers slack on the six-gun butt strapped around his ample hips, swayed close to the campfire. "I am thirsty."

"Me, too." Ian chugged from the bottle before handing it over to his companion. "I drink to my bride!"

In your dreams. Not for the first time that night,

Charity stole a glance at Hawk. He leaned toward her, his voice low. "What's he scared of?"

"Growing old in Laredo," she snickered.

"Besides that. You were his fiancée—you should know what frightens him."

"Ghosts."

"Good. What about the fat one?"

Charity watched the Mexican pass the wine bottle back to Ian. She recalled a night in the desert village of Shafter, just before Rangers had ambushed Adriano and the others. "Actually, I do know what Señor Grande is afraid of." She whispered something to Hawk.

As he nodded in satisfaction, Charity's line of sight settled on the two men gathered at the fire. Ian, his voice shrill, was ridiculously puffed up with bravado.

"The Indian will hang from the courthouse eaves in Laredo." Ian again passed the bottle to Grande. "And Gil McLoughlin will praise me for saving his daughter from the red bastard."

"Sí." Tilting back his unwieldy head, Grande quaffed the bottle's remainder and belched. "He will hang."

"Gimme back that"—Ian hiccuped—"wine."

Charity mimicked one of Hawk's habits; she rolled her eyes. *What would your father say, Ian, if he saw you now, uncouth and crazed?* She knew what her own papa would say: "I told you so." What did it matter, what either father thought? Both Campbell Blyer and Gil McLoughlin were far removed from the situation.

She whispered to Hawk, "I'm so sorry. This is all

my fault. I am an abomination. If I hadn't—"

"Forget it."

She took one more look at Ian and Grande. Neither man was paying any attention to the prisoners, both caught up in their bacchanalian revelry. "We may never get away from them," she bemoaned.

"Wrong. You wait and see."

Shortly thereafter, both Ian and his sidekick were weaving drunkenly, their behavior causing Charity to wonder whether they were under the influence of something other than alcohol. "Those must've been awfully potent bottles of wine."

"Thanks to Sam Washburn. He laced them with one of his concoctions. Learned how from the Kickapoo people over in Mexico," he explained.

From the offhanded tone of his voice, Charity surmised that Hawk was not of the Kickapoo tribe.

"Sam said I should use the wine on you," he was saying, "in case you continued to be contrary."

"Thank God you didn't."

Her chest tightening anew, her shoulders tensing, she glanced at the fallen horses. "It's my fault the team is dead. It's my fault you've been shot. Everything is my fault."

"Charity, don't." Hawk spoke tenderly. "You think little enough of yourself already. And now's not the time for fretting over the horses or my shoulder."

What he said was true—she didn't hold herself in high esteem. But since she had sided with Hawk when Ian Blyer appeared, Charity's faith in herself had strengthened. But what of her faith in Hawk? "I wish you didn't hold me for ransom," she said.

"It hurts to know that both you and Ian want nothing more than my papa's money."

It seemed as if an eternity went by before a sound passed Hawk's lips. "Maybe I didn't want to admit it, even to myself, but I had more than just ransom money in mind when I kidnapped you in Laredo . . . The truth is, from the moment I saw you in that cafe, I—"

"What café?"

"Where you were eating breakfast with another woman. It was a week before I took you away." He exhaled. "My heart didn't tell my head, but I knew then that I would have to have you for my own. Ransom or no ransom."

Her head reeled; her heart soared. He was not the greedy foe who had stolen her from Laredo! This was the grandest moment of her life—Hawk wanted Charity for *Charity!*

He undercut her bliss. "Don't get the wrong impression. I haven't given up on the ransom. And even if I had, you're still going home to mend fences."

"That's not for you to decide." Her solemn words were spoken with firmness. "I've been called feckless and willful and unworthy to carry the McLoughlin name. And if the day comes to pass that I want a reconciliation, it will be my decision and on my own terms. But I can't foresee that ever happening."

"Don't you think the Old One might be worried about you?"

"Stay out of my business, Hawk."

"Fair enough." His hawkish gaze turned to their

captors. "Charity, I have a plan. Scaring the hell out of those two. They're ripe for it." He explained his strategy, ending with, "Got it?"

"I do."

"Good. Think you can crawl away from this wagon?"

"Absolutely."

"Good girl." He paused. "Charity . . . before we start this, there's something I want to tell you. You'll have to stay with me when we get away. Trust me. I mean you no harm. But you're still my captive. If you don't want to face your father, I promise not to make you."

"Thank you." She smiled at him. "Hawk . . . I want *you* to know something. I wasn't planning another escape. I need you. You've got to help me get aboard a ship bound for Europe. Maybe you—"

It was on the tip of her tongue to ask him to join her, but his recent admission didn't carry with it a commitment for the future. Plus, she was still uncertain of her own feelings.

"I'll make certain that someday you're compensated for your time," she said.

"Where are you going to get passage money?"

"I haven't figured that out yet." He spoke not a word, and she pleaded, "Say yes, Hawk. Say we make a partnership."

"That I cannot promise."

"Wouldn't you agree we're partners of a sort already?" She took quick notice of the bizarre duo dancing around the campfire, then gave Hawk her full attention. "We're in this together."

"Enough talk. We've got work to do."

Charity nodded, bid him good luck, and got moving. Rolling onto her stomach, her hands laced behind her, she slithered from the wagon wheel. Hawk did the same—she hoped he wouldn't do any further damage to his wounded shoulder. As she ate south Texas dust, she made the wagon's opposite side. Hawk was there already. As planned, they positioned themselves back to back. His fingers worked at her rope bonds and within seconds, freed her. She almost whooped with joy.

She flipped over and took care of Hawk's tethers. Both jumped to their feet, then made for diverse sides of the campfire, Hawk grabbing articles from the buckboard before he crouched out of sight. Never had she heard an authentic Indian war cry—her experience being limited to girlhood games of cowboys and Indians with her siblings and cousins—but improvisation was the order of the night.

Her fingers held tightly together, she patted them rhythmically against her lips. Her cry of "waa, waa, waa, waa . . . waa, waa, waa, waa," rose into the air. She stopped abruptly when she saw she had gotten the two men's attention, then ducked for cover. She heard a rattle of something that sounded like bones clapping together, then a drawn out hiss.

"Mae-no-mae-cay," echoed across the prairie.

Another rattle filled the night air.

Disoriented, Ian and the fat man looked at each other.

"Indians, Grande?"

"No. Culebras!" As if a blue norther had ripped

into him, Grande shivered, his gigantic body quaking like a bowl of jelly.

"Snakes?" Ian took an unsteady step over the licking flames and recoiled. "Ow!" He swerved backward, unsteady. "Izz beautiful." He stared transfixed at the orange and blue fire. "Izz the call of maidens in the night. They all favor my Sharity. Come to me, Sharity."

"Loco in la cabeza. No muchachas. Culebras!"

Hawk tossed a whip, which landed very close to the campfire. Eyes on the twisted rope not ten paces from his feet, Grande trembled anew. His shaking hand reached for his six-gun, but he dropped it to the ground. Open-mouthed, Ian stared at the coiled object for a moment, then tried to focus on his accomplice. Apparently reality, as they saw it at the moment, dawned. The Anglo and the Mexican stepped back.

"Culebra!"

"Ye God." Ian's eyes bulged. "A python!"

Just then, Hawk, a light-colored blanket over his head, surged from the brush, his arms spreading wide and his fingers gyrating like a specter's. "Whooooo!"

"A ghost!"

"La fantasma!"

Their eyes as wide as saucers, their hair standing on end, Ian Blyer and his Mexican retainer took off on foot for parts unknown.

"What fortune," Charity declared gleefully.

"I think the big one peed his britches!"

As they had been doing for the past ten minutes, Hawk and Charity leaned against the buckboard and laughed at the frenzied flight of Ian and Grande. "Ian—did you see how wide his eyes got?" Charity said, her voice shaking with mirth.

"Nothing like seeing a ghost." Hawk, using his uninjured arm, grabbed her to him. "Angel, you were wonderful." He gave her a loud smacking kiss. "You're a fine partner."

Partner? Hope swelled within her as she leaned into his embrace.

Hawk just might go for the Europe idea. All sorts of possibilities were awakened inside her.

But first things first.

She studied his injured shoulder. "Did Sam send medicine that we can doctor you with?"

"Quit worrying. I'll be just fine."

"If you insist. But if that wound starts to look nasty, don't say I didn't warn you."

"All right." He raised a hand in surrender. "I'll get the salve."

While Hawk slathered the thick unguent on his flesh wound, Charity stared in the direction Ian and Grande had taken. "Do you think they'll be back?"

"They might."

"How will we keep away from them?"

"Change course. Stick to the road. With travelers around, Blyer and his lackey won't be as eager to cause trouble."

"Aren't you afraid someone might see us? Might think to rescue me?"

"Somehow that doesn't strike me as a problem. You had your chance to be free of me." Hawk screwed the lid closed, wiped his fingers on a rag, then cupped her jaw with his hand. "Tell me something. You could've gotten away. Why didn't you?"

She stepped aside, turning to hug her arms. How could she answer him? Once she had been open and forthright about her dreams, but where had her relationship with Ian led?

The midnight dampness sent a shiver through her. A merry life abroad had its appeal, yet she yearned to be held in Hawk's embrace and learn the secrets of loving as well.

Be that as it may, she couldn't bring herself to tell him—a silly, cowardly reaction, she knew. But how could she confess that she had changed, beginning with his anger over the horses? Or that she knew exactly what she wanted, once she saw him and Ian together and could compare the two? How could she admit that his confession of liking her for herself was what she had waited a lifetime to hear?

She needed a man like Hawk.

A muscle ticked in his jaw as he watched her. "Charity, must I remind you . . . ? You're still my captive."

Was she? Oh, he had her under his control, but she felt a change in their relationship, as if they were bound together by a different sort of tie.

She was with him, but she was there of her own free will.

"Why didn't you run?" he asked.

"We're both in a bind," she reasoned. "You've fallen to kidnapping, and I've fallen out of grace with my family as well as the law. We need each other." Not giving him an opportunity to comment, she rushed on. "You could go with me to Europe . . . Why, you'd be the toast of Gay Paree, an attraction amidst the swank salons of the grand republic."

"Being an oddity doesn't interest me."

The insulted pride in his voice and eyes took her aback. "Gads, you're touchy. I meant no offense. As handsome as you are, all the ladies would be swooning at your feet." On second thought, maybe that wasn't such a bright idea; Charity found herself jealous at the thought of his being admired by other women. "I've been thinking—"

"Always a frightening concept," Hawk cut in wryly.

"Now, now, don't be testy. Listen up. You probably don't know it, but I'm a master horsewoman." She waxed exuberant. "I can ride and rope and do all kinds of bareback tricks. So—"

"Bareback tricks?" he said, his eyebrows arching. "Don't tempt me to ask for an explanation."

"All right. I'll just show you sometime." Confidence building inside of her, she continued. "About my idea—let's form a Wild West show. Perhaps you could learn to shoot straight. Hmm. Forget learning to shoot. You could do knife tricks, though you might want to work on your aim. It's quite off."

His laughter filled the air as he patted the knife he had collected from the ground a few minutes earlier. "If you're talking about divesting Blyer of nothing more than his hat, all I set out to do was scare him. Killing doesn't interest me. I come from a peaceful people."

"Hawk, Comanches scalped my aunt years ago."

She searched his expression. "You aren't a Comanche, are you?"

"No."

"What are you?"

"A man."

She needed no reminders of that! Her eyes filled with the sight of Hawk under the moonlight, she shortened the distance between them and placed her palm high on his solid chest. "And I am very much appreciative."

"Careful. The virgin is beginning to sound like a wanton."

"And that distresses you?"

"Yes."

"I—I thought you wanted lovemaking." Her voice faltered as she gazed into his dark eyes. "Was I wrong?"

"By totem! There are things you don't understand. And now is not the time for explanations."

He hadn't said he didn't want her; and from the sound of his voice, she knew it was simply a matter of time before his mighty arms held her. A satisfying feeling, to say the least.

Hawk faced the pair of horses Ian and Grande had abandoned in their dispatch. "From the looks of that gelding, I'd say it's lost a shoe."

"Yes, I think so, too. And Syllabub—she's Ian's mare—can't pull the buckboard. She's too noble a chestnut for that kind of work. Looks like we'll have to abandon the wagon."

"Which means we'll have to ride double."

Charity entertained a mental image of them, bodies locked tight atop a horse. She blinked. Quite a brazen scene. So what? She wanted to be brazen for Hawk.

"All right. We ride double." Charity leaned down, grabbed the hem from the back of her dress and brought it forward to tuck into her waistband. "I'm ready."

Hawk's eyebrows arched. "Not too uncomfortable with that show of legs?"

"No."

"You never cease to amaze me."

Amazement worked both ways. She hadn't figured Hawk for priggish. *Well, I did demand respect.* It seemed as if years rather than days had passed since she'd made that demand.

"Where are we headed?" she asked.

"Uvalde."

"Why there?"

Hawk wheeled around to march toward Syllabub. "Because I said so, that's why."

Charity stared at his retreating form. He repacked his knapsack, gathering the items most necessary for their journey, then hooked them as well as her small valise over the saddlehorn.

Why Uvalde? she wondered. Did he have an accomplice waiting there? What did it matter, an accomplice? She considered herself no longer his captive. This time on the prairie was her opportunity to change Hawk's mind about what the future would hold. So why worry about a sleepy burg lying west of San Antonio and southwest of Fredericksburg?

Chapter Fourteen

High noon.

In the far northern distance, Hawk saw the promise of hills, the beginning of the Balcones Escarpment that heralded the edge of Hill Country. Between there and here lay Uvalde.

On the mare Blyer had abandoned, Hawk rode forward with Charity behind him, his grip and her valise secured at their sides. With only a trio of hours sleep since deserting the buckboard last night, they were riding double toward the powwow with Maisie McLoughlin.

To keep his mind off the upcoming meeting, as well as the feel of his virgin angel so near yet so far away, Hawk damned saddles. A white man's folly, they were uncomfortable things. And this one's horn ate into his groin, what with Charity's weight pushing forward with each clomp of hoof, yet no doubt about it he liked the feel of her legs cupping his backside.

He glanced to the side and downward. And got an eyeful of one of those exposed legs. Did she know what she was doing to him—what she had been doing to him!—showing her calves like that? He had run his tongue along many well-turned ankles, but Charity's beat all.

Come on, Uvalde.

Quickly.

Squinting at the Columbia blue sky, Hawk exhaled and rested the side of his hand on the pommel. He ached to get their relationship on an honest basis, yet he had lied time and again. She didn't like liars. Hawk knew her father; McLoughlin neither abided nor forgave speakers of false tongues. And Charity was his daughter.

Tell her, you lily-livered coward. Just get off this mount, sit Charity down, and tell her the truth. Unacceptable. He hadn't brought her this far to jeopardize his assignment on a lonely stretch of Texas. He had given his word to take Charity to the Old One, and he felt that was the best thing for his angelic hellcat. Case closed.

But there was a case quite *unclosed.*

It was never far from his thoughts, Charity's crime. Somehow they must convince the authorities of the truth, that she hadn't known Gonzáles's true intentions. First, he must get her promise that she'd let him represent her. If she allows me to defend her, Hawk corrected after his conscience reminded him about all his lies, bald and of omission.

Once she and the Old One had smoked their peace pipe, then this man and this woman could work on their own peace.

"It sure is hot today, isn't it, Hawk?"

"In more ways than one," he mumbled, her tight hold getting to him in a thousand ways.

"When will we reach town?"

"Not soon enough," he replied in another mumble. "Probably by tomorrow night. Got to ford the Nueces first."

"Hawk . . . have you given any consideration to the Wild West show? I really think we could take Europe by storm. Don't worry about a thing—I'll do the promoting and riding. Of course, you can do whatever you do best . . ."

Right. Argue torts in front of an assemblage of thrill-seeking Europeans set on watching a performance of daring and oddity. On second thought, Charity's idea wasn't much different from a courtroom.

She leaned her cheek against his back, and he was of a mind to throw good sense to the wind and let his sable-haired hellcat show him a few bareback tricks right here and now. *Wah'Kon-Tah. I am only a man!*

Attempting to shake off his lustful thoughts he asked, "Aren't you forgetting something? The case of the State of Texas versus Charity McLoughlin."

"Don't worry about a thing. I've got that all figured out. Now back to our plans. I want you to promise me—"

"I am *not* interested in any Wild West show."

"What *are* you interested in?"

"Uvalde."

"What's so unique about that place?"

"Every place is unique."

The afternoon of the twenty-sixth found Charity

more impatient than usual. She and Hawk were nearing Uvalde, yet after all his growls and innuendos and blatant bids for lovemaking prior to her handcuffing the now-dead team, he hadn't even lifted a finger in an effort to take her virginity.

And, drat him, he was certainly keeping his own counsel about his plans.

She might drat the man, but each minute, each hour, each of their two days together atop one horse, Charity thought him all the more intriguing and attractive. And he smelled nice, too. Yesterday and that morning, he had allowed them to take baths in the river.

And his knapsack did hold a change of clothes. More than one. Today he had dressed as a cowboy, sans hat and shirt. He'd said he wanted the "feel of the sun on my shoulders."

As Syllabub plodded toward Uvalde, Charity leaned her cheek against Hawk's naked back. She felt the taut pull of his muscles. Why didn't he want her?

What do you expect? You don't know a thing about loving a man, you ninny. What would it take to excite him? She recalled the kisses they had shared. Her lips pressed against his shoulder blade.

"Don't."

"Why?"

"Because it hurts."

"This isn't your injured shoulder. Which is, by the way, looking ever so good." Deliciously good.

"Don't you understand one damned thing about a man? You touch me anywhere and I hurt."

She frowned. What did he mean? She seemed to

recall Olga having written something on the subject. Something about a man's universe being centered between his legs. "Ignore it," her sister had said. Well, Olga wasn't here right now. Charity's arms tightened on Hawk's waist. In another intrepid move, she ran the tip of her tongue along his salty flesh.

"*Wah'Kon-Tah*'s mercy! Don't."

"You certainly are sensitive."

"Yes."

"If you reach a sexual peak, will you quit hurting?"

"Jesus, Lord of the paleface." Hawk's mouth had pulled into a grim line when he twisted around to eye her. "Who schooled you in such talk?"

"You didn't answer my question."

Again he faced forward. "Charity . . . you're asking for ravishing with talk like that."

"I know."

His hand froze, the reins suspended in midair. "I thought you were saving yourself for some special man."

She had two choices, to advance or to retreat. Her fingers moved up to his chest, pressing against his flesh. "I *have* found a special man. You."

"Charity . . . you don't even know me."

"You could change that. You could be honest."

"I'm not going to be telling you anything. And I want you to cease with that wanton talk of yours too."

Momentarily crushed, Charity told herself that time would change his heart. She felt confident of this. Hawk might not be talkative, but he was a darned good listener, most of the time. And she trusted him. *Gads,* she realized, *I really do!* And there was a closeness between them that she had never before experienced.

She fidgeted on the saddle—so what if Hawk tried to evade her touch? "What's it like living in an Indian village?"

"Like hell."

He said no more.

The mare plodded onward. The Texas sun was unremitting. If hell had a name, Texas was it. Of course, the brush country was behind them, having given way to the rugged terraces of the Nueces River valley. But what about the place where Hawk had been reared? Was it Texas?

Fearing another rebuke, she stated cautiously, "I imagine it rather wild, Indian living."

He finally spoke. "Wild? Not in a long time."

"My mother said Indians love dancing."

"That's part of our culture, but dance is only a diversion in these times. Life on a reservation is government agents shouting orders and doling out rations. It's being told where to live and where not to hunt. It's hearing the Great White Fathers tell you where you can go. And where you cannot. And whom you cannot fight."

It must be quite an oppressed life, the nature of which she had never gathered from the tales of red men told her by Papa and Mutti. Charity surmised aloud, "I think you were born a hundred years too late. That was a time for red men to fight other red men, with your own set of rules. Back then, you could've ridden bareback across the plains, your war lance at the ready for any brave or buffalo having the misfortune to cross your path. I think you would've been a lot happier, Hawk. I don't think kidnapping for ransom would've ever entered your mind."

He glanced over his shoulder once more, and his fingers patted the hand holding him tightly. "Funny you should say that. Sam Washburn said almost the same thing." A moment lapsed. "You don't know me at all. Yet you know as much about me as a friend of long-standing."

So, she surmised, he'd known that reprobate for some time. That *had* to mean Hawk hailed from Texas. Perhaps he was an Apache. No. She knew enough about Apaches to know they hadn't the size and stature of Hawk.

"I'd like to know more about you, really I would." She recalled the night he'd captured her, when he had said that Indians revered children. "What's it like, life for an Indian child?" she asked.

"Difficult."

"It must have troubled you to see that. Will you use the ransom money to feed and clothe them?"

"I've done what I can for the young ones. And they will know my generosity in the future."

"Then I hope you get some money from Papa. He can certainly spare a bunch of dollars. It'll be a worthy cause." She laughed. "How much are you going to ask for me?"

"How much do you think I ought to ask?"

"Oh no you don't. Don't make me put a price on my worth."

"I think you're worth at least twenty dollars."

For that, he got a swat on the thigh. "Stop that! You wouldn't go to all this trouble for a gold piece."

He mumbled something under his breath, which she could have sworn was, "I'd go to Timbuktu and back for your golden piece."

She shivered with excitement. "How do you know about Timbuktu?" she asked.

"I've been in the white man's world long enough to know about the lands across the seas," he answered smoothly. "Tell me, Charity, do you like children?"

She wondered why he was changing the subject. "I love children. I used to dream of having a dozen papooses."

"So did I."

"Did you ever think you'd found the woman who you'd want to give you those babies?"

Hawk chuckled low in his throat. "As a youngster I spoke for a wife. But she hasn't accepted my bid. Not yet."

He might as well have slapped Charity. Why hadn't she considered that he might be in love with another woman? She consoled herself. He wasn't with his adored, and anything could happen. She'd make it happen!

She had no wish to hear him expound upon the woman of his dreams. "What about buffalo hunting and scalping settlers? Did you ever do those?" she asked teasingly.

"Charity, I've never scalped anyone in my life."

"I'm disappointed." She decided to give him a dose of what he'd just given her. "I thought you were as brave and courageous as Fierce Hawk of the Osage."

"F-Fierce Hawk?"

"Yes. He hails from Indian Territory. Fierce Hawk was the brave of my girlhood dreams." *But no more.* "You know what? Before my sisters and I were even born, he asked our mother for one of us in marriage. Isn't that romantic?"

"Touching," he replied hoarsely. "I, uh, I never imagined you had such ideas."

"I most certainly did."

She told him about the Osage boy who she'd heard had grown up to be a respected lawyer and lobbyist in the capital. Hawk didn't comment on her tale, holding himself still, quiet.

She figured she knew what was troubling him. "You're jealous of Fierce Hawk."

"Why . . . why would I be jealous?"

"Remember the café? Remember those nights when you wanted to have your way with me? You *are* interested in me as a woman, though you've been doing your best to make me think otherwise. So why wouldn't you be jealous of another man?"

His shoulders tense, Hawk dropped his head backward ever so slightly. His hair brushed at her mouth. She heard his ragged intake of breath as he demanded, "Tell me more about this Fierce Hawk."

"I always thought him terribly noble and clever." She brushed her nose against his black hair. "And wildly handsome. My mother said in a letter that he *is* wildly handsome—naturally I pressed her for a confirmation as soon as she arrived home last April. Mutti thinks the world of him, that he's smart and awfully diligent. He's the sort, like you, who could and would outwit Ian and Grande."

"Imagine," he said in wonder. "As a girl, my whimsical hellcat was daydreaming over a red devil."

"I'm not a girl any longer. And they were more than daydreams."

"You mean you fantasized about bedding this warrior?"

"I have."

"What did he do to you in your dreams, this Fierce Hawk?"

"All the things you've done to me. And more."

Again, Charity felt as well as heard Hawk's sharp intake of breath. He said, "Like what? Did he kiss you and love you till you were bruised and aching, truly ravaged? I'll bet he never ripped your clothes off in haste to have you. I'll bet he never tossed your legs apart and thrust his shaft into you before you knew what was happening."

"Well, no. I figured him a gentle and considerate lover. Are you gentle and considerate?"

"I'm capable of being."

"I yearn for such. Like the night you caressed between my legs—you didn't know I knew what you were doing, did you? I want you to touch me that way again. Will tonight be the night?"

"No!"

A jackrabbit darted across Syllabub's path, and the mare reared her head and pitched her riders to the side. Charity momentarily lost her grip on Hawk's waist; when she regained her balance, her grip had fallen a couple of inches. His man-thing pushed at the placket of his britches, and her breath caught in her throat at the swollen feel of him. She jerked her hand upward. *Why did you do that?* Being brash of voice somehow hadn't extended to her actions.

Her face went hot.

She yanked herself as far back on the saddle as possible, away from his stock-still body.

You silly ninny of a virgin. He probably would've liked for you to play with him. Gads, where did she get that idea? Weren't women supposed to do nothing more than lie back and let the men do all the work? That was what Olga, last winter in Spain, had confided. Charity had a lot to learn about men. Men? The only man she wanted to please was Hawk.

Right then he leaned forward in the saddle. Obviously his attention was captured elsewhere, and she damned the intrusion.

"Trouble," Hawk said. "Someone's in trouble ahead."

Chapter Fifteen

Charity craned her neck around Hawk, catching sight of a splendid carriage stopped along the roadway. Its front wheel had come loose, and the vehicle tilted toward a ditch. A statuesque lady, plumed and dressed in low-cut finery, stood with her arms crossed while she impatiently tapped a toe. Pacing up and down, a portly man gestured from the carriage toward Uvalde and back again.

By now Charity and Hawk were within earshot. "How dare that yeoman abandon us! If I ever lay eyes on Smithers again, he'll swing from a yardarm!"

The lady motioned in the riders' direction. "Look, Norman. Someone approaches."

"By Neptune, I hope they stop." Norman cupped his hand at the side of his mouth. "Ahoy, there, mate—mates! Would you be of a mind to lend a hand?"

Hawk slid from the saddle, helping Charity to her feet. The couple hurried to them.

"What a sight for sore eyes." The man extended a hand. "I am Norman Narramore of Galveston and this is my wife, Eleanor. And who might you be?"

"I'm Charity McLoughlin," Charity piped up. "And this is Hawk."

The lady offered a greeting to Charity before turning to her companion. "How nice to meet you, Mr. McLoughlin."

"I'm not Mr. McLoughlin."

"He's just plain Hawk," Charity explained. "He's an Indian, you see, and his people don't name . . ."

Her words trailed off when she saw that the couple wasn't listening to her explanation. The middle-aged gentleman was staring open-mouthed, eyeing Hawk as if in a whole new light. Eleanor Narramore—she must have been in her late forties—uttered, "My word, Mr. Hawk, you could have fooled me. You don't look at all savage. Are you a half-breed by chance?"

Hawk swung toward the carriage. "We'd better get that wheel fixed," he said irritably.

"Let's do find some shade, dearie." Eleanor Narramore dabbed her forehead with a lace handkerchief. "Let the men take care of the dirty work."

The two women retired to a prickly pear-dotted mesquite grove.

With Norman Narramore barking orders, Hawk set about repairing the carriage wheel. *Wah'Kon-Tah,* he was peeved that the couple—or at least the wife—had instantly pinned him as white. He had taken to basking in Charity's assessment of him as Indian. He had played the part of savage to the hilt.

Charity.

What was he going to do about Charity? She wanted him, probably not as much as he wanted her, but . . . how long could he hold her off? "You won't at the rate you were talking."

"What did you say, mate?"

"Nothing," he replied to Narramore, then got back to his thoughts. Her confessions about Fierce Hawk had nearly knocked him off the back of that mare. All along he had known Charity would recognize his full name, but he'd never thought she'd been carrying a torch for Fierce Hawk.

I am Fierce Hawk. my angel.

Therein lay the problem.

One of the problems.

One of many problems.

What was he going to do now? He must *not* wait for the Old One's appearance in Uvalde. Once they reached town, Charity must know everything. Tonight would indeed be the night.

For truth.

Aggravated with himself and with the world in general, he turned to the blustering carriage owner. "By totem, don't just stand there, man. If you've got a jack in this contraption, get it."

From a distance of fifty or more feet, Charity heard Hawk shout for a jack. He was certainly being testy. Probably because of their interrupted love-talk. If not for the carriage mishap, they would be . . . *Don't be a ninny.* Hawk might have warmed up a bit, but she realized he would have gone no further than bold talk—which dismayed her.

If only she knew the art of seduction . . .

"Sure you won't have some lemonade?" asked the titian-haired Eleanor—she had told Charity to call her by her first name. She gestured to a wicker hamper. "It's quite tasty."

"Maybe I will have a glass."

After Eleanor had handed one over, Charity murmured an "mmm" as the tart-sweet beverage slid down her throat. "I haven't had anything this cool and savory since leaving home."

A perfect brow arched, as Eleanor's assessing gaze swept over Charity's travel-worn gingham. The woman carefully posed a question. "Where are you and your husband headed?"

"He's not my husband." Charity saw no reason for subterfuge. And, she felt comfortable being in the company of a female; she hadn't realized just how much she'd missed Maria Sara. "We make for the port of Galveston."

"Aren't you off route? You seem to be headed for Uvalde."

"A mere detour along the way."

Eleanor set her glass atop the closed hamper. "You're a lovely young woman, and Hawk is a most handsome young man. Much more handsome than any Indian I have ever seen. But I find it peculiar, your alliance with one of his kind."

"Not so peculiar," Charity assured her. "Hawk is as good as anyone in this whole wide world. As good, if not better."

"I meant no offense."

Charity studied Eleanor's candid face. She supposed there'd be no harm in being truthful with the woman. "Actually, he holds me for ransom," she confided.

Shocked, Eleanor widened her eyes, her voice falling to a whisper. "Norman and I will help. But we must be clandestine in our efforts, else the Indian might . . . Redskins are capable of all sorts of depredations. Never fear, poor girl, we'll get you to your loved ones."

"There is no need for that. I've chosen to go along with him. If I never see my family again, it would be too soon."

What did she really feel in her heart? To prove that she wasn't a worthless McLoughlin, she had to make something of herself. First things first. She must do something about that smuggling business. Once she was safely in Europe, she intended to make enough money to hire a brilliant lawyer who would clear her name. The source of these funds? The Wild West show, of course. Papa wouldn't be too impressed with her accomplishment. But Mutti would love the idea. *Darn it, don't be thinking about them!*

She glanced at Eleanor, who asked, "Are you sure Hawk is what you want?"

"Yes. We're going to be partners." And a whole lot more, once she learned the secrets of lovemaking.

"You're a peculiar young woman."

Not getting an argument from Charity, Eleanor turned wary eyes toward Hawk, who was hammering at the wagon wheel. Ping, ping, ping. The sounds of his labors matched the beat of Charity's heart as she took her own good look at him, seeing well-defined muscles working beneath glistening bronze skin.

What was taking so long with that blasted wheel?

Why do you ask. Ninny? He's stalling so that he won't have to listen to your silly prattle and have to suffer your inexperienced pawings.

Oh well, she reasoned, maybe he was just holding back out of respect.

Again she took a gander at Hawk. But this time she saw more than just his physical appeal. In her life she hadn't had a lot of friends, not close ones. And she had never had a man friend. What was he to her, besides the object of her feminine desires? She and Hawk had worked together toward a common goal—getting free of Ian and Grande. They had talked; rather, he'd let Charity do most of the talking, but he had begun to loosen up. What was he to her? A friend.

From the distance she heard the faint sounds of Mr. Narramore giving orders to Hawk, who barked his replies. His back turned to the carriage owner, Hawk continued to hammer the wheel back into place.

A gloved finger went to Eleanor's upper lip. "Your Hawk doesn't appear to be a man easily molded."

"He is quite stubborn. But I'm working on it."

"You must be quite in love."

Love? Hardly. Yet what about her fluttering heart and the weakness in her knees? That wasn't love, was it? There was no denying, at least to herself, that Charity ached for his lovemaking. Apparently he, on the other hand, wasn't aching for her.

Charity chewed one side of her lower lip, then hoisted a brow at the lovely Eleanor. "How does a woman seduce a man?"

The redhead nearly swallowed her tongue. "My, you are brash."

"Yes. And I'm in a hurry. I want to seduce Hawk. Tonight." Charity finger-combed a pesky strand of long hair from her cheek. Once they reached town, her first stop would be a general store and its toiletry and dress sections. "I want to be his woman."

"Tell me, do you still have your virtue?" When Charity nodded in the affirmative, Eleanor said sadly, "Oh, my dear, do think twice before you give away such a precious prize."

"You sound much like my mother. Always, she drilled it into my head, as well as my sisters', that we must keep ourselves pure for marriage."

"A wise woman, your mother."

"Is it wise, turning one's back on one's child?" Charity asked bitterly.

"A mother's love never dies. A woman can forget a man, she may shun all she has held dear, but she never forgets her child."

"I'd like to think that true."

"I speak the truth, believe me. I am a mother. I have two sons. Beau and Jeff. No matter what they do to worry Norman and me, we never stop loving them."

"Your sons are lucky boys."

"Men. Beau is twenty and eight. Jeff is two years his junior. But enough about them." Eleanor smoothed the skirt of her silk dress. "A moment ago you spoke of home. Where is it?"

"The back of that mare for now. Where do *you* live? Pardon me; your husband said Galveston." Turning her regard to the sleek coach and its even sleeker repairman, she smiled and softened her tone."Where are you traveling to?"

"Kerrville. Norman has purchased a ranch there."

Charity assessed the portly gentleman who appeared the sort never to have touched a rope, much less a branding iron. "New to ranching?"

"We are. Norman has spent his life as owner of a steamship line, and isn't too keen on the idea, but I prevailed upon his good nature. Frankly, I'm tired of salty air and hurricanes," Eleanor explained with a moue of distaste. "It's the open range for us from here on out."

"Good luck with it." Charity hesitated. "You say your husband owns a steamship company?"

"Yes. The Narramore Line. We sail passengers back and forth to France."

Charity knew the firm provided luxurious accommodations; she had sailed on their liners thrice. "And he still owns it?" When Eleanor nodded, Charity asked, "Do you think he would hire me and Hawk in exchange for passage to France?"

"No, no, no, no, no. We're indebted to you. We stood under the broiling sun for hours"—to emphasize this last point, Eleanor mopped her brow—"and at least four parties traveled by without even acknowledging our dilemma."

"People can be callous."

"Can't they, though? But you and your Indian

brave didn't leave us coughing in a dusty wake. Thus, Norman and I will be honored to compensate you for your kindness. How would two tickets from Galveston to Le Havre suit you? Complimentary, of course."

How did heaven suit her? Charity clapped her hands. If only Maria Sara knew how everything was turning out! Turning out? There was still the matter of provoking Hawk into her arms.

Stopping to study her benefactress, Charity squared her shoulders. "Eleanor . . . will you or will you not impart to me the secrets of seduction?"

Chapter Sixteen

For days Hawk had been anxious to reach Uvalde, but now that he and Charity had arrived, he wasn't so sure. It remained his task to explain things to her. What he had to say demanded the right time, the right moment. Tonight. There was still several hours of sunlight remaining.

The Narramore carriage pulled into the Wayfarer Hotel's porte cochere, and Hawk, pulling up the rear, reined in the mare before handing Charity to the street. Somehow unable to meet her eyes, he took a second look at the town that he had first passed through earlier in the month. With its peaceful, gracious airs and its mammoth oaks whose wide branches bowed heavily to the ground, Uvalde was atypical of this part of the state.

"Well, we're here," Charity announced. "What next?"

Hawk rested his palm on her shoulder. "I've got a few things to take care of. Meet me at the hotel?"

"Of course," she agreed.

Hawk gauged her expression. From the look on

her captivating oval face, from the unfulfilled passion in her blue, blue eyes, he knew he need not fear she would try to escape from him. If for no other reason than to appease her curiosity. Curiosity, hell. Her eyes had made a grand sweep over him, leaving little doubt in Hawk's mind—she wanted to continue with what they had started atop that mare. As it had earlier that afternoon, Charity's boldness and brazen passion worked against his steadfastness.

That and . . . *She's been fantasizing about me for years.* Damn, that made Hawk feel good. He felt a stirring in his groin, the second time that day. He felt even taller than his six-four. Probably, though, he should have put a stop to her confessions about Fierce Hawk. But her talk had so thrilled him, he had been unwilling, even unable . . .

Wah'Kon-Tah, he was in a fix. Wanting her. Her wanting him. Lies and disguises. A powwow with Maisie McLoughlin. He had a feeling bad medicine was on the verge of raining down.

Charity tilted her head to the side. "Tell me, Hawk, what sort of business are you about?"

"Getting that mare taken care of, for one. I'll take her to the livery stable, then send a telegram to Laredo. Let Blyer know where he can collect his mount. After that, I'm going straight to the sheriff's office. Best let it be known Syllabub was abandoned. I won't tempt a horse-thievery charge."

"Good idea."

She set off in the hotel's direction, and Hawk went about his errands, renewing his acquaintance with the lawman who had traded him manacles for a set of dominoes.

Next he made a stop at the local bathhouse. He wanted to be presentable when he confessed everything. He garbed himself in a checked shirt, leather vest, and denim trousers, then stopped at the general store to buy a pair of boots and an oyster-colored Stetson. He then made his way to the Wayfarer.

He saw her through the hotel's picture window. His exquisite angel. Charity, who'd fantasized about him for years.

Waiting in the deserted lobby, she wore a new dress low in cut, blue in color. The shade brought out the turquoise hue of her big, black-lashed eyes. And her long sable hair was combed atop her head with fetching curls brushing her shoulders. His fingers tingled to loosen that mass and let it fall to her waist.

Hawk found it difficult to breathe, so in thrall was he with her beauty, yet he forced his feet forward . . . toward his evening of reckoning.

She rushed to meet him. "My, you look nice. But I must admit, I've grown rather fond of seeing you in your breechclout." Her nose twitched. "You smell nice too. That's herbal toilet water, isn't it?"

"I, uh"—he swallowed the peppermint that Sheriff Tom Ellis had offered him—"I'd better see about renting some rooms."

"Not to worry. I've taken care of everything." Lifting her fingers, she dangled a sole key. "They had but two rooms vacant and the Narramores have taken the other."

His eyes took in the lobby. "Place looks pretty empty to me." Even the desk clerk was nowhere to be seen. "I'm sure an extra dollar or two would cause an extra room to turn up."

"No, no. I've already tried that. No luck." She made a poor liar.

"Then I'll sleep outside."

"You will not."

From the determined lift of her chin to the adamant glint of her eyes, Charity McLoughlin was a woman of purpose. *Looks like you're in trouble, Hawk.*

He glanced through the window to the street outside. "Sun's going down." Damn, what was he going to do? His stomach growled. What he had to say might be made more palatable by a couple of full stomachs, his and hers. "Possibly Mr. and Mrs. Narramore would like to join us for dinner."

"Oh, no. They're taking it in their room. Actually, I've ordered supper up as well."

"It's going to waste."

"Now, Hawk. Maiz taught me it's a sin to waste."

He grabbed Charity's hand and led her out to the street, none too gently. Of course, she griped and complained, but Hawk remained determined; he got her to the nearest café—an establishment with little to recommend itself—sat her down, then smiled tightly. "What would you like for dinner?"

Pouting, she sniffed. "Nothing."

"Don't be like that. We need to talk, and a hotel room is no place for it."

The waiter approached. "*Willkommen.*"

Bald and pot-bellied, he displayed a set of large

teeth that showed signs of decay plus the leavings of food. Using a grayed towel, he wiped a couple of dead flies from the table into his hand. Though David Fierce Hawk's upbringing didn't lend itself to fastidiousness, he found the café positively unappetizing.

The waiter said something that was unintelligible to Hawk; Charity answered as unintelligibly; apparently in her mother's native tongue.

"What did you say to him?" Hawk asked as the man disappeared behind a swinging door,

"I said we aren't interested in eating here."

"You got that right."

They left. But instead of returning to the hotel, they walked past the town square and continued on a westerly course through the streets of Uvalde.

"Why, that looks like a park," Charity said, pointing to an area that in no way resembled the lush beauty of Washington's public grounds, in Hawk's estimation.

It did, however, sport an area cleared for ball games, though no players were in sight. A mother launched her chortling child on a rope swing. Large and scruffy and barking to high heaven, a black dog chased a white cat. A young boy, pushing a hoop by a stick, ran amid the oleanders and ancient oaks. From the trees a chorus of birds got in their last squawks before sundown.

"Let's have a seat, shall we?" Hawk motioned to a bench. "There looks good."

Charity sat down in the middle. Hawk squeezed one hip against an armrest. He fidgeted. *Wah'Kon-Tah! Why am I not brave enough to speak?*

A vendor pushing a cart plodded down the path in Hawk and Charity's direction. *"Raspas. Muy delicioso. Raspas!"*

"Mmm." Charity waved a hand and called to the man in Spanish. "I'll have one." She jumped to stand, then turned to ask, "Would you care for an iced treat, Hawk?"

"No, thanks."

The vendor, a diminutive Mexican with a thin mustache that curled at the edges, made a show of packing the concoction of shaved ice and purple syrup into a makeshift cup of brown sack paper. Charity, clapping her hands, squealed in excitement with each of his movements. Hawk smiled at her childlike enthusiasm.

Singing a Spanish song of love, the vendor pushed the cart down the path. Between bites of the *raspa,* Charity joined him in song; she danced as she ate. Did she realize how lovely she was? Hawk doubted it. She had no idea of the power she had over him.

He noticed that the park was beginning to clear out, that the sun was turning to ribbons of orange and blue against the western horizon. Twilight fell.

Hawk concentrated on Charity. A woman wrapped in the giddiness of a girl, with the wildness of the untamed and probably untamable thrown in for good measure—that was Charity McLoughlin. As a boy he'd had no use for giggling girls. How strange, life. At the age of seven, he had chosen a wife. And the boy hadn't wanted one who giggled. Twenty years later, the man yearned for Charity's girlishness and high jinks.

She wouldn't be so merry, once he explained himself. For the first time, Hawk wondered at the wisdom of his plans as well as Maisie McLoughlin's. It might not be a good idea, forcing Charity to face her family. She didn't need the McLoughlins. *You have me.* Together, they could face anything the world threw at them.

And that was how he intended to approach the truth: with an alternative.

"Charity . . . why don't you sit down?"

"Mmm, soon as I'm finished with this." Dancing before him in the muted light, she leaned forward to give an ample view of two charming attributes. "Would you like a lick, my darling?"

Yes. "No."

"It really is tasty." She smiled.

He loved her smile. He loved her nice teeth. He loved the way she looked . . . and felt. And what about her crazy, undisciplined ways? Realization hit him. Hit Hawk hard. He loved this crazy woman.

The luckiest day of his life had been the afternoon in '69, when Lisette had visited his village. No, that was the second luckiest. The most fortunate day of Hawk's life was when he had said yes to Maisie McLoughlin's strident appeal to rescue her great-granddaughter.

Charity's tongue flicked over the ice. Her free arm moved upward, as if reaching for the sky. "It's a wonderful evening, isn't it, Hawk?"

If not for the truth that must be told.

"Did you want to talk about something?"

"Later," a craven voice replied. His voice.

Finished with the shaved ice, she crumpled the

paper cone in her hand, then reached to place it on the park bench. He got a whiff of rose water.

Don't do this to me, Charity. I ought to be telling you— "Let's see if we can't find a decent cup of coffee somewhere," he said.

"Rather warm, isn't it?" She patted her bosom. "That *raspa* did nothing to cool me down. How about you? Are you hot?"

What a question. Again he fidgeted on the bench.

She stepped toward him. "Look at you, all dressed in leather. You must be burning up." Her fingers worked his vest away from his shoulders. "Take this old thing off."

"Don't."

"Hush." She knelt between his legs. One hand flattened on his shirt, her fingers inching between the buttons. "You have such a nice chest. So hard, so manly."

"Please don't."

By now, the buttons were unfastened to his waist, and she pressed forward. Her parted lips settled against his breastbone; her forefinger fiddled with his neckchain. He felt the tip of her tongue on his heated flesh. As if infused with a pint or more blood, his rod stiffened.

A quick glance across the park assured Hawk of their privacy. Yet wouldn't it be better, he wondered, if someone were to interrupt them? To hell with *better.* He needed to do the interrupting.

He grabbed her up and to him, pressing them both against the back of the bench. "Have mercy, Charity. Don't do this."

"Me? Those are your fingers on my breast. And you're me holding me so close . . . Not that I'm complaining, you understand. Besides, what difference does it make, who is the aggressor? We're partners."

"We shouldn't do this."

"Balderdash." She squirmed onto his lap, and her fingers maneuvered to the hard evidence of his arousal. Stroking and cupping him, she whispered, her voice husky with emotion, "I've heard men enjoy being played with. I find it exceedingly enjoyable. Do you like it, Hawk?"

"Yes." The word hissed past his constricted throat. "Yes."

And then he was kissing her. Or was it, she was kissing him? What did it matter? Before he knew it, he had her on the ground, darkness covered them. Somehow her clothes were gone. Somehow he had gotten out of his. The grass soft beneath them, Charity soft beneath him. And fiery hot as an oven beneath his fingers. All his longings erupted into a frenzy of want and need, passion and desire. He adored her—his glorious mixture of innocence and minx.

"My hellcat angel," he murmured raggedly and swept his fingers to her jawline.

"My darling savage."

He touched her bottom lip with the side of his thumb. "I have wanted this for so long."

He knew what they were doing was wrong. There was nothing settled between them. It shouldn't be this way. Charity was a white woman of means, a woman to be revered. The woman he loved. She deserved her first mating to be in a soft bed, with legal bindings.

But no matter what his head said, his body was done with listening.

Chapter Seventeen

It thrilled her, the imminent success of her seduction, knowing that Hawk would continue with their lovemaking. The clement breezes of the dark gray evening whispered over her flesh, the soft grasses cushioned and cradled her, and the insistent touch of her man sent a fire of passion raging within her.

Naked beside the hard, hot strength of him, she heard him ask, "Would you trade me now . . . for Fierce Hawk?"

"You're all I want." She inhaled deeply as his fingers caressed her arm, her breast. "Only you, my darling."

"Remember that, angel mine. Remember that."

"Remind me." As Eleanor had schooled, Charity moved her fingers in a bold circle around one manly nipple. "Am I all you want? Just me for me?"

"I've waited a lifetime for you and you alone."

Her heart seemed too large for her chest, so swollen was it for him. He guided her to her back, his lips seeking the peak of her breast. With strong, sure strokes he suckled her; her fingers held him there. Her nerves came alive at his touch. It felt good, and right, the two of them together.

Her fingers delved into his hair, which had been cinched at his nape, freeing the raven-black strands from their binding. Likewise, his hands worked the pins from her head.

His raspy voice tickled her ear. "Don't ever put your hair up again. I like it wild and free—like you are, my hellcat angel. Wild and untamed and perfect."

"Who is the most wild here? Surely not I."

He was caressing her body with sure and experienced fingers, with sure and experienced lips. For a split second she recalled wanting to lose her virginity to a husband as inexperienced as she was, but what a foolish notion that had been. No man but Hawk could thrill her this way. She marveled at his skill as a lover. Thanks to Eleanor's advice, she didn't need much coaching herself, at least in arousing him.

Charity's fingers smoothed over the taut lines of her adored savage, resting on the turgid, hooded tip of him. "You like this, don't you, Hawk?"

"You know I do," he replied hoarsely.

She sighed at the thrill of discovery, at the wonder of him. How differently they were made, yet Nature had matched them ideally. Her fingers moved downward, encircled him. "I've never felt anything so hard, yet so satiny," she admitted in an awed whisper, wishing for light so that her eyes might feast upon him.

"Your innocence refreshes and pleases. And now I shall please you."

She murmured low trills of satisfaction at the feel of him . . . at the feel of what he was doing to her. No inch of her flesh did he leave untouched. He explored the shape of her breasts, her waist, her hips, her legs. She yearned for more. And then his inquiry moved between her thighs . . .

"Open for me, sweet hellcat. Ah, yes."

Never had she imagined that lovemaking would be so splendid, not even in her girlish fantasies, not even in her womanly thoughts of Hawk. Her head spun, her senses whirled at the gentle, sure movement of his forefinger at her kindled nub. Hotly, intensely, from the dip of her throat to the lobe of her ear, he blazed a trail of kisses. She quivered at the sensation.

"Kiss me," he whispered in her ear.

Her lips parted for him, and his seized hers. He tasted of peppermint, sweet and hot. Instinctively, she met the movements of his ardent tongue. They played with each other—darting, challenging, retreating only to taunt each other again. The ache that had begun low in her body spread throughout her limbs, begged for something—*something!*

"I hurt," she murmured when he rose up to cup her face with his hands and look into her eyes. "I need . . . Oh, Hawk, I don't know what I need."

"Me. You need me. As I need you."

In the dark of night, she knew he looked at her searchingly.

"Take me, Hawk."

The hard, long length of him settled at the mouth of her most private place. The silver ornament around his neck, heated by his flesh, fell to the cleft between her breasts, seeming to brand her as his. His fingers curled around her shoulders. Once more his lips met hers. And then—his thumbs and fingernails dug into her shoulders, causing a flash of instant agony, as he thrust hard . . . branding her for real, as no bauble could.

So intense was the pressure of his grip that she barely noticed the searing pain of his entry, yet she cried out.

He didn't move. Lodged high inside of her, he released his grip on her shoulders. "I knew it would hurt you. I figured it would be better if I took your attention away from the tearing."

"I—I'm fine. Very fine." To be filled so fully, oh, my, it was a miraculous feeling. Yes, her virginal body protested the invasion, but now she knew what it was like to be a woman. Hawk's woman. "Give me more."

He did. He thrust; he pulled back; he thrust again. And again and again. She wanted to meet his rhythm, but was that what she was supposed to do? Eleanor hadn't said anything about it, their chat having been cut short when Hawk had gotten the carriage wheel fitted firmly in place. *Should I do as my body suggests?* After all, there had been some talk of going on instincts.

As if he read her mind, Hawk reared up to look down insistently at her face. "Give me more, my Charity. Meet my lovemaking. Move with me."

Oh, yes.

Their tongues tangled anew as they moved together in life's most beautiful cadence. Wild. They were wild with the need for each other, and her blood continued to throb hotly through her veins, as if Hawk were her very life source. Her toes inched over and between the back of his thighs to curl and anchor at the top of his calves. "I can't seem to get enough of you," she moaned, gasping for breath.

"You've got all I can give," he said. "And honey, I don't think you could find anything much bigger." He bit her lip playfully.

"That's not what I mean. I am filled to my limit, yet I seem to be on a precipice, on the verge of tumbling over."

He chuckled, or was it a growl? "That's exactly what is happening."

One long, sure stroke accompanied his words. She bucked beneath him, and he growled his approval. Whirling, whirling, whirling . . . she lost the ability to make sense of anything except for Hawk. Hawk, her darling Hawk. And then it was as if something burst within her. Something wonderful and luscious and infinitely satisfying. She tumbled into it.

"I love you," she cried.

At that same moment she heard Hawk groan harshly and felt him pulsate within her. He said something in his language that she knew must be an expression of release and gratification.

With a shudder he gently lowered his body atop her. She nestled her head into the crook of his uninjured shoulder; he rested his cheek low at her ear. His lips settled against her throat. It seemed as difficult for him to breathe as it was for Charity.

"Thanks be to *Wah'Kon-Tah,* you're wonderful."

He rolled over slowly, guiding them to their sides, sliding out of her. "So wonderful."

"So are you."

Tenderness in his tone, he asked, "Are you all right?"

"Why, yes. Why wouldn't I be? Good gravy, I've never felt better in my life!"

She intended to write Olga and divulge her own information. Olga ought to know just how much she was missing by her adherence to Victorian mores!

"Charity, I want to give you something." When she assured him that he'd already given her the best possible thing, he shook his head. "I mean this." He pulled the silver neckchain over his head and wrapped her fingers around it. "Wear my totem, Charity."

"I will be honored to," she replied, her heart bursting with happiness.

He slipped the silver, turquoise-adorned chain around her neck, the heat of his flesh transferring to hers. "It matches your eyes, you know. Turquoise is a special stone to some Indians. Your eyes are special to me."

Her fingers flattened over the chain as well as its warmth. "May I tell you something? My mother used to tell a story of a dear Osage lady. Red Dawn. When my parents were guests in her village, Red Dawn loaned Mutti a turquoise necklace. She had traded an Apache for it."

"I traded an Apache for this one."

"Why do you sound troubled?"

"Didn't mean to." He rolled to his knees at her

side and reached for his shirt. There was a note of regret in his voice when he said, "Let's get dressed." Bending over her, he added, "We'd better get you cleaned up first."

Without another word he gently rubbed the folded shirt between her legs. His touch was soothing. Marvelous. And it left her aching for more of his attentions. A glance at his again-stiffened shaft—how lovely it was, limned by the moon and the stars in the heavens and the stars in her eyes—assured her that he was likewise inclined.

"Charity . . ." He swallowed, then tossed the blood-stained shirt aside. "Charity, did you mean it? When you said you love me."

"It may have been spoken in passion," she replied honestly, scanning his dear and savage features. "But it was spoken from my soul."

"Will you promise me something? No matter what happens, remember I meant you no harm."

She looked at him questioningly.

"We'd better get back to the hotel," he said. "We need to talk."

Earlier, he'd said a hotel room was no place for a chat. But everything had changed between them. She had realized the depth of her feelings for Hawk, and they had been together in the most intimate of ways. A hotel-room conversation with her beloved would suit her just fine.

"Is this the time you're going to tell me everything about yourself?" she asked.

"Yes."

* * *

Maisie McLoughlin had been waiting in the lobby of the Wayfarer Hotel for over an hour. It was a high-priced inn, considering the amenities—Maisie liked value for her dollar. The rooms were spartan at best.

"Highway robbery, if ye ask me," she groused to her driver, "the asking price of these rooms."

Heinrich Weingard flushed. "Please, *meine gnädige Frau.* the clerk . . ."

She didn't care if that money-grubbing, air-sniffing room peddlar heard her. The man—probably English, being that laziness was all over him like a second skin—had kept his own counsel about Charity until a whole quarter had crossed to his greedy palm. Once the coin was tucked in his dungarees, he had become quite talkative.

Charity was indeed registered. And town gossip had reported that a lovely young woman, a stranger had been seen at a local eating establishment with a strapping young man who fit the description of Fierce Hawk of the Osage. Maisie had marched right over to the café where they had been spotted, only to find it closed.

Where were the lass and the lad?

Maisie marched to a horsehair sofa in a corner to the left of the door and sat down. A spring pinched her behind. "The stuffing is worn out," she complained to Heinrich. "Go fetch my folding chair."

The Fredericksburger nodded and quit the lobby.

"Ye got any cigars?" she asked the desk clerk, who was picking his nose and reading a book.

"Nope."

"Well, then, get off your arse and go fetch me a

couple."

Naturally, it took another exchange of specie. But she finally got rid of the man. She didn't want anyone around when Charity showed up.

A nicely dressed couple descended the staircase. The woman, a plump redhead—as buxom as Maisie had been in her heyday—held onto a gentleman's arm. He looked pleased as punch. Maisie concluded they must have been up in their room doing what Fierce Hawk *had better not* be doing with Charity.

"Evening," the man said to Maisie as they strolled by.

The lady nodded in greeting, then strolled on toward the door, saying to her man, "Norman, my dear, what do you suppose happened to our young friends?"

"Don't be daft, Eleanor." He opened one of the double doors, then led her outside.

In the now deserted lobby, Maisie drummed her fingers on her knee, hoping Fierce Hawk had gotten her great-granddaughter into line. And that big Osage buck better not have broken her maidenhead. He just better not have.

"Ye old fool. They've been together betwixt Laredo and here, and he's a hot-blooded Injun." Her eyes squarely on the lobby window, Maisie sucked her teeth. Anything could have happened. "Well, if he's done her wrong, I'll be making sure Fierce Hawk does right by the lass."

Then Charity would be settled. Afterward, the lawyer would see to that smuggling business. And in time . . . "Great-great-grandbairns. Do ye think ye'll live t' see the day?"

At that moment a young couple stepped in front of the window. Charity! And the Indian.

When they entered the double doors, Maisie got a good look at them. They didn't see her—she knew they didn't. Charity and the red man had eyes only for each other.

He wore a Stetson, britches, boots, and a leather vest. No shirt. His bare chest glistened with sweat. Charity's hair was a mess, grass particles sticking to it. Her dress looked as if an iron had never run across it. An Indian gewgaw hung from her neck. And she had the satisfied look of a woman thoroughly debauched.

With a sigh of resignation, Maisie decided she'd have to make Fierce Hawk do right by the lass.

Bones aching, she stretched to stand. "Thought ye two would never be getting here. I'm early, lad, I know, but ye're looking fit, the both of ye."

Two dark heads snapped around to stare open-mouthed at the old woman. Charity's eyes rounded with horror. Fierce Hawk grabbed her upper arm, pulling her to him.

"It's going to be all right," he murmured. "I will make it all right."

Charity looked from him to Maisie McLoughlin and back again. "You know each other."

Lord, she dinna know . . . Well, she did now. And there was no going back. "Thank ye for getting her here in one piece, Fierce Hawk."

Her body stilling in shock, Charity recoiled.

For the second time in Maisie McLoughlin's life—the first being when she'd made an awful blunder with Gilliegorm and Lisette that had almost cost them their marriage, near the beginning of it—she feared she had done the wrong thing. But it was too late now to do anything about it.

"*You* are Fierce Hawk?" Charity's voice was barely above a whisper. "Fierce Hawk of the Osage?"

"I can explain."

"You lied to me. Lied!"

Tears glistened in Charity's eyes. Maisie had never seen her cry, save for when she'd been a bairn. *Lord, what have I done?*

Shoulders hunched in betrayal, Charity took a stumbling step backward to point a finger at her great-grandmother. "You put him up to this."

"Charity, honey, let's talk." Fierce Hawk reached for her hand.

"Talk? You are way too late for that." Five feet eight inches of furious woman whirled on him. "I will never, *ever* forgive you!"

Chapter Eighteen

Double crossed.

Lied to.

Heartbroken.

As daylight approached, Charity was all these things. In the darkened hotel room she had rented when life seemed rosy, she lay desolate on the bed. Alone. And that was how she wanted it.

Her body still sore from the night's grassy interlude, she cursed her betrayer. The name Fierce Hawk fit him well. No bird of prey was more adroit at picking clean the bones of its victim.

Tears flowed freely in her heart, yet not a drop had fallen from her eyes. She demanded they fall, but they didn't. She supposed that for too long—all her life—they had been stoppered. Yet nothing in her past hurt as much as she hurt right now.

Why hadn't she made the connection between him and the Indian of her childhood dreams? Hadn't he, on the night that he grabbed her from that street in Laredo, said something on the order of, "You'd never convince a jury . . ."? That was a lawyer's verbiage. There had been other incidences.

And, my God! Had she really gone on and on about the Fierce Hawk of her fantasies?

Her head tossed from side to side on the pillow. How foolish she must have seemed in his eyes, an obtuse female ripe for his deceiving. He had said he wanted her for herself, a lie that had slipped past his forked tongue with ease.

"And, God, why didn't I keep my mouth shut? Why did I tell him I love him?"

Every time she had allowed herself to be vulnerable, the situation had exploded in her face. Never again would she tell anyone that she loved them, no matter how much she felt she could trust them.

Never.

Ever.

Not as long as she lived.

Suddenly, it seemed as if she could neither swallow nor breathe. She burrowed her face into the pillow and wished that she were a million miles away from herself.

A knock sounded on the door to the hotel room. Not the first one of the night. There had been a dozen or more since she had locked herself away there. And she responded the same to this one. "Go away."

"It's me. Eleanor Narramore. May I speak with you?"

Eleanor. The kindest person she knew, save for Maria Sara. She needed someone to talk to. Charity opened the door. And the dear woman opened her arms. Obviously, Eleanor knew something of her troubles.

As kindly as any storybook mother, Eleanor

smoothed Charity's wild hair and patted her back. "I've brought a decanter of brandy. Can I interest you in a snifterful?"

"You can interest me in the whole damned bottle."

"Let me light a lamp. It's ever so dark in here."

Within moments, the golden glow of a hurricane lamp flooded the room. Charity's eyes protested the invasion. She spied her friend pulling the hotel room's lone chair to her bedside.

"Would you like to talk?"

"Yes." Charity covered her mouth with a palm before forcing her fingers to her lap. Eleanor handed her a snifter of spirits, which Charity quaffed rather than sipped. The brandy burned a path to her stomach. At least it gave some semblance of life to her broken heart. "I have been wronged. I fell in love with an agent of the McLoughlin family."

"Hawk seems an honorable man. And he is quite distraught. You should see him. He is beside himself with concern for you."

"Ever the noble savage, isn't he?"

"Mrs. McLoughlin is concerned, too."

"Eleanor, if you've come up here to play the devil's advocate, you can take your leave right now."

"I am not the devil's advocate. My concern is for you, young lady. And my heart goes out to your pain. It is a terrible thing, being lied to."

"How much do you know?"

"Everything. Your granny and your Indian are in the lobby waiting for you to come down. She was eager to talk."

"And I wonder where I get my big mouth?" A dry chuckle passed her lips. "Oh, Eleanor, I never imagined it would turn out this way." She reached for the brandy, refilled her snifter, and swallowed its contents in one burning gulp. "I thought Hawk was my soul mate! I imagined we'd take Europe by storm, and . . ." Her words trailed off. She felt as if her entire body were an empty cavern. "I—I thought he was on my side."

"I understand." Eleanor sighed. "Feeling the way you do, I hope you didn't go through with your seduction plans."

"I did."

"Lord have mercy."

Squeezing her eyes closed at the memory, Charity added, "I did as you said. I touched him in many places. And I went on instincts. Oh, Eleanor, it was so beautiful! Yet now it is tarnished and tattered."

"And he never uttered so much as a whisper about himself?"

"Not enough for a simpleton like me to put together." Beating her fists against the top of her thighs, she raged against Hawk. Damn him! Damn the traitor! "Eleanor, I've got to get away. I must get out of Uvalde at first light. Perhaps before. I don't *ever* want to see Hawk's—excuse me, Fierce Hawk's face again."

"Are you certain this is what you want?"

"Absolutely."

"Then, of course, Norman and I will help." Eleanor tapped a forefinger against a lower tooth thoughtfully. Looking up, she said, "We must get out of the hotel, and you must avoid the lobby. Do you think you can climb down a rope?"

"Yes."

"What am I thinking? We don't have a rope. I know! Let's use the bed linens."

Already Charity was gathering the sheets together and knotting them. The makeshift ladder finished, she tossed it out the window to the ground, then climbed out onto the catwalk girding the second floor. Daybreak lit the sky. Using all her strength, she lowered herself over the ledge and began to slide slowly down. But just as she reached the apex of an oleander shrub, insistent fingers closed around her hips.

"Dearest, I've been waiting for you."

Oh, God, not Ian!

Didn't she have enough problems? And after their last confrontation, what could his intentions possibly be?

Yet she allowed him to guide her to the boardwalk before taking a long look at her former fiancé. Once again he appeared the gallant dandy. He breathed out a breath of fresh and unsullied air as he spoke her name. His hair was combed and shining with pomade, and he wore a cravat and other fine attire—a Prince Albert coat and a derby of fine beaver skin.

I wonder what Hawk looks like in cravat and spats? She cursed her thoughts.

Moving back several paces, Charity addressed her former fiancé. "Ian, I want you to leave me alone," she said firmly.

"I cannot do that, dear one. I love you."

"Even if what you say is true, you must know

that I don't return your feelings. After the other night, you would *have* to know that."

"Oh, I don't hold that nasty business against you. You were under a strong negative influence, as was I."

Yes, the influence of her savage betrayer.

"Will you forgive me?"

She sized him up skeptically. "You're certainly agreeable, considering you ran like a scared rabbit when Hawk and I spooked you."

"No greater love hath a man than I for you."

"Than for what you think I'm worth, don't you mean?"

"I admit the money is important. We cannot live by bread alone." Morning light flickered in his eyes. Ian put a hand over his heart as if to punctuate his sincerity. "But if I were forced to choose between you and gold, you would most assuredly win."

"That wasn't what you said when I arrived in Laredo. And you were off your rocker for the want of Papa's money not so long ago."

"When you arrived in Laredo, my father had been bullying me about finding a job. I have told you this before. And how would you feel if your adored one were caught with an affections-stealing savage? Isn't that call for insanity?"

She related to his feelings of betrayal.

With a flourish, Ian offered her his elbow. "I've rented a carriage, and have provisioned it well. Will you accept my guard? We will go anywhere or do anything that pleases you."

How she had longed for Hawk to say those words. But his utterings had issued from a deceiver's tongue. Her eyes lifted to Ian Blyer. She knew that his affections, too, were false.

"Charity?" Eleanor called downward. "Are you all right?"

Charity looked up at the window, where Eleanor was bent over the sill. Charity had two choices. Europe or Ian. But the continent had lost its appeal, for her dreams had been tied to the wretch waiting in the lobby to laugh in her face. No, there would be no Paris or Madrid or Wild West shows for Charity McLoughlin. Those things had been the silly dreams of a girl.

And what makes you think you could have made a success of it anyway?

If there was anything she wanted, it was to hurt David Fierce Hawk.

But how could such a ninny as she hurt him? She glanced up and down the street, catching sight of Señor Grande and a half dozen other people in the distance. Wagging tongues would enjoy relating the story, should she leave with Ian. It would damage the Osage, discovering that she had gone from his arms to another's.

This thought swayed her as Ian's cajoling never could.

I'll escape Ian as soon as we're past the city limits.

Vengeful she might be toward her true lover, but . . .

"Ian, have you collected Syllabub?"

"Yes. Grande will ride her."

"I must have your assurance on something. Promise me you won't press charges against the Indian for horse theft."

Ian nodded. "I've told Sheriff Ellis that I left Syllabub stranded and that you saved her for me."

"Thank you."

"Charity?" Eleanor's voice was more insistent. "I ask you, are you all right?"

Placing her palm atop Ian Blyer's proffered forearm, she stared straight ahead and shouted upward, "I am quite fine. My fiancé has rescued me."

Eleanor Narramore hadn't finished telling Hawk that Charity had left on the arm of another man before he was out the hotel's front door and flying after her. *Wah'Kon-Tah,* it hurt, her turning to Blyer at the first opportunity.

He caught her and her foppish companion just before she put her foot on the step of a carriage.

"If you take one more step, I'll shoot those horses and blow Blyer's head off," Hawk warned as he came abreast of the duo.

"Number one, you're unarmed. Secondly, you can't shoot." Charity hoisted herself into the carriage's interior.

Indignant, Blyer huffed, "Be gone, red menace."

Hawk reared back and plowed his fist into the man's pompous face. Blyer's body went airborne, careening against the coach's open door and landing in a thud on the ground. Blood seeped from his thin nostrils. His lights were out.

Señor Grande lumbered toward them. Hawk decked him too.

In one giant step Hawk hauled himself to the car-

riage's portal, reached in, and grabbed Charity. "Get away!" she yelled. The toe of her shoe caught him in the chin; he reeled but didn't waver, neither from his intent nor from his feelings for her.

"You're going with me."

"I am not."

Somehow, he got her wiggling, fighting form out of Blyer's carriage. Depositing her facedown on the ground, Hawk towered above his seething Charity. She blew a strand of hair out of her eyes and, propping herself up on her elbows, imparted a look that could fry eggs on a winter's morn.

From the corner of his eye, he spied the tall, thin personage of Maisie McLoughlin, her bonnet askew, rushing to them. "Charity," she called out, "I must speak with ye."

"Stay back, ma'am. This is between me and her." He bent to haul Charity up and to his chest. "Are you ready to talk?"

Charity wasn't in any mood for conversation, but Hawk didn't let that stand in his way. Past a crowd of curious onlookers, he herded her through the hotel lobby, up the stairs, and into the room she had escaped from. He pushed her inside before turning to lock the door and pitch the key out the window.

She eyed her improvised ladder of linens.

"Don't even think about it," he warned hurrying to untie the knot of sheets from its bedpost mooring. When he had finished, he dusted his hands and advanced on her. "You're going to tell me why—*why*—you would've even considered taking up with

Blyer again."

Her bosom heaving, she lifted a palm to ward him off and backed away. "Because I want to. And because I want *nothing* to do with you."

"Don't say that. It'll make you as big a liar as I've been."

"You'd like to think so."

Hawk reached out to her fingers, only to have her pull back from him. Had she given no thought to what they might have begun already? It was on the tip of his tongue to ask how she would view all this, were she to discover that his seed grew within her. Instead, he asked, "Would it help if I say I'm sorry?"

"No."

"Would it help if I say I wanted to be truthful?"

"No."

"Would it make a difference to you if I tell you that I lo—"

"Nothing would make a difference. Nothing!" She turned to the window and hugged her arms. "How you allowed me to blabber on and on. Letting me suggest the blacksmith trade to you. Letting me believe you can't read and write. And—oh, Lord!—all my jabber about the Wild West show." She shivered. "Imagine, David Fierce Hawk in a Wild West show."

"Angel, I loved listening to your dreams and schemes."

She wasn't appeased. "You betrayed me. You led me to believe you were someone you are not. And you *promised* I wouldn't have to face my father, yet all the while you were leading me into a family trap."

He took a step toward her; his eyes locked on her huddled form. His fingers reached for a strand of her hair. He whispered, "You don't know how much I wish things could have been different between us. But that is the past, and nothing can change it. We have the future, though."

She whirled around, her eyes ablaze. "We have no future. I'll never forgive you."

"Because I kept my identity secret? Or because I brought you to Maisie? Charity, if I'd told you my name or anything about myself, you would've guessed at the truth—I couldn't risk it. It's best that you reconcile with your family. I've thought so all along. But we could—"

She interrupted him. "As I told you the other day, how I live my life isn't your concern."

"I beg to differ."

"Don't make yourself into something you're not."

Is that what he was doing? Had she lied in the park when she'd told him that she loved him?

"I am curious about something," she said. Rigid and unforgiving were the eyes that had gazed at him in love and passion only the previous night. "Should I address you as Mr. Hawk or Mr. Fierce Hawk? Or will just plain 'Fierce' do?"

"Hawk. I'll always be your Hawk."

"No. You will never be anything but a bad memory." Again, she put distance between them and presented her back. "I would appreciate it if you would take your leave."

They were getting nowhere. Hawk felt as if his chest had taken a bullet.

He heard a fist pound the outer door. "You in there," called a voice from the corridor. "We're not having any hanky-panky in the Wayfarer!"

"Leave 'em be, ye jackanapes! If it takes buying this hotel lock, stock, and barrel, I'll be making ye listen t' me."

"Perhaps, madam, we *could* talk."

The disturbance in the corridor was quickly quelled. Hawk heard no other sound but his and Charity's breathing. He closed the distance between himself and his beloved, his fingers curling around her shoulders. "Forgive me. I need to hold you in my arms and make you understand how much you mean to me."

Her eyes were like chips of frozen turquoise when she rounded on him once more. "How much did my great-grandmother pay you to kidnap me?"

"Not a dime."

"What a shame. You had to put up with me for nothing. How sad."

"Stop it, Charity. Money has never meant anything to me. I have all I'll ever need. I did it because the Old One asked. And because I wanted to see you for myself. I, too, have had fantasies over the years. Of you."

Charity stared at him for a moment, a maelstrom of emotions crossing her face before she turned to plant her palm on the rail of the bed. "Well, the deed is done and your curiosity is satisfied. Go on back to Washington, or wherever it was you were summoned from, and leave me be."

"Can't. I mean to put us to rights."

"Over my dead body."

"Your very alive body is what I'm after. I am your lover. Your first lover. And I shall be your last."

"You *were* my lover. Past tense. Furthermore, you will never, ever touch me again."

"You mean, like this?" His fingers moved to her breast. And her quivering response—pure woman—belied the malice of her expression. "You can't forget me," he said. "I won't allow it."

She swatted his fingers. "I won't allow myself to remember."

He grabbed her into his arms. "You'll allow it. For the same reason we made love last night. Because you love me."

Her teeth clenched, she beat her fist against his chest. "Lust was all I felt for you. Believe me, it has passed." She snapped his totem from her neck. "Take this back."

He closed his fist around the neckchain. A nerve ticked beneath one eye. "You will take it back someday. Someday you'll wear my totem with pride."

"Never! And just why would I want any reminders of your pawing me?"

His body stiffened, his anger rising. "I beg to differ on who was pawing whom. I seem to recall that you were the one with your hands all over me. I believe I was the one pleading with you to stop."

She made a fist and socked him in the eye.

Chapter Nineteen

After she had struck him, Hawk had made a silent retreat out the window, and deftly negotiating his way along the catwalk, had set off for parts unknown. Charity sat and stewed. How was she going to get out of the locked room? Maisie answered her thoughts by putting a key in the lock and making a cautious entrance.

"Are ye gonna be angry with yer poor old granny forever?"

"Yes." Charity refused to meet the old woman's eyes. "You've really done it this time, and I hope you're satisfied. Oh, Maiz, why did you interfere? Why didn't you leave me alone?"

Maisie stood firm, her silver head leveled. "If I have t' be answering that, then I havena done a good job of raising ye."

Always, Olga and Margaret and young Angus had gotten their parents' attention, so the job of dealing with Charity had fallen to the family matriarch. And she was old, so old. Maisie seemed to have aged ten years since the previous May. Charity regretted her part in the change she saw in her great-grandmother.

How she had suffered under the impression that the old woman was through with her! And now she had been proven wrong. This realization worked against the raw fury that had festered in her since the previous night, but she was not ready to give any thought to forgiveness.

Maisie took a step toward her. "Canna ye ken? I love ye, and I want yer happiness."

"You picked a fine way to show it, sending *him* after me."

"He's a good lad, that one. A fine, upstanding man. Educated, ye know. And he's got money from a grandmaither—"

"All you think about is money."

"If ye'd ever been without it, ye'd know the importance."

"I've been without it. The most important thing, as I see it, is love. And I don't have that."

"Ye're wrong. And if ye coulda seen the lad agonizing over ye last night, ye'd know his feelings are true."

Charity pulled a face. "You're such a romantic, Maiz, that you can't tell love from a guilty conscience."

Her patience wearing thin, Maisie wagged a finger. "Listen here, I've got seventy years on ye, ye whelp. Don't be advising me on life and love. I've lost a country and a man and all the bairns of me body. I've seen war and more war. And I've been seeing a lotta love exchanged in this nasty ole world of ours. Like with your maither and faither.

If ye ever knew the hell Lisette and Gilliegorm had known, ye wouldna be turning a nose up at a fine lad like Fierce Hawk."

"Oh, please."

"Give the lad a chance, and ye won't be sorry. Splash some water on yer face and fix yer hair 'fore I take a broom to yer britches. We're going home. The three of us."

"I have no home."

"I'll not be listening t' that sorta blather. I am going home, and ye're going with me, and that's that."

"Think again."

For the stretch of a minute, they glared at each other. Maisie gave in first.

"Mind if I sit down?" Not above using her advanced age as a tool of persuasion, she rubbed her hip, then teetered toward a chair. "These old bones are aching. Ye know the trouble I've had since that horse threw me last Hogmanay."

Not being able to help herself in the face of the old woman's discomfort, Charity rushed to her great-grandmother and lent a hand in helping her to the chair.

"Thank ye, darlin'. Granny does need help from time t' time." Maisie patted her hand. "Had a god-awful time getting here. Thought that carriage was gonna break ever' bone in me body. Havena got enough meat on me arse anymore. Don't get old, lass. 'Tis a terrible thing."

"You do look thin."

Her chin trembling, Maisie sighed and the motion accentuated her slight frame. "Havena been able to eat, with ye being gone from home and not knowing ye were okay. Figured ye were in Laredo, but for all I knew, ye coulda been lying dead in a ditch."

Charity stared at the floor. "I didn't wish to trouble you. And I thought you were finished with me, after what you said that afternoon I left ho— I left the Four Aces."

"I was trying to pound sense int' yer head."

"Well, I didn't see it that way."

Bright old eyes found their mark. "Guess I had better be getting back home. Going with me, lass?"

Charity shook her head.

Maisie rubbed her hip again. "Fetch me a glass of that brandy. I could use it, what with the jarring trip ahead of me. Sure hope I doona get laid up somewhere . . . sickly and without a loved one t' care for me. Or t' see t' a proper burial, should it be coming t' that."

Charity wouldn't be able to live with herself if something happened to Maisie while she was away from home chasing after her great-granddaughter. *You're being gullible again.* Charity straightened her spine. "You won't be alone. You said yourself that Indian is going with you."

"He willna. Unless you go too."

What a noble savage! "You will do fine. You may be ninety, but you'll be fine at a hundred and ninety."

"Least that sweet Maria Sara has some respect

for old age. She—"

"What do you mean, Maria Sara?"

"Dinna tell ye? She and her lad are waiting at home."

Maria Sara and Jaime. At the Four Aces. All in one moment Charity was thrilled, aghast, and dismayed. "No telling what sort of poison Papa has filled her with about me."

"Yer faither isna home. Neither is yer maither."

"When are they expected?"

"They are not. I doona need to be telling ye that Senate is in session and your faither never neglects his seat."

It had always been difficult for Charity to tell when her great-grandmother was fibbing. Maisie was a master of half-truths and false impressions, yet . . . She was old, she was kin, and it was a long carriage ride between here and the Four Aces. "I'll see you to the gate of the ranch. And that's the extent of it."

A smile as wide as Texas burst across Maisie's face. "Thank ye, darlin'."

"Before you go thanking me, let's get something straight. We travel alone. That—that Indian won't be going with us."

Where she would go from the entrance to the Four Aces, she wasn't certain, but it wouldn't be in any direction other than that dictated by Charity McLoughlin.

What a day. In his office, Sheriff Tom Ellis

tugged his ten-gallon hat low on his creased forehead and leaned back in his squeaking chair to lace fingers over his growling stomach. Tired and hungry, he parked booted feet on a scraped-up old desk the good citizens of Uvalde County had provided him.

He was looking forward to a nice pot of beef stew his wife, Barbara, was fixing up. It felt right fine being a family man. Come sundown, he would go home, sit down at the table, and have his girls crowd around him. Amanda would tell him about the boys at school; Abigail would jabber about going off to college. Afterward, he'd challenge the ladies to a game of dominoes.

Tom sure did like those ivory dominoes he'd beat ole Hawk out of.

The front door burst open, interrupting his musings of domestic bliss. "Sheriff, I must have a word with you."

Well, hell. "So, Blyer, you done woke up from your nap."

"It was not a *nap.* I was unconscious after a brutal pummeling."

"Ain't got time to nitpick over word choices." *Dinner's getting cold.* "Whatcha want, Blyer?"

"Look at me when I am addressing you. I am the son of Senator Campbell Blyer, I'll have you know."

"Yep, I know." Just like his father, this one liked to throw his weight around. Tom lowered his feet and looked past swirls of dust motes to eye the dandy. "Looks like ole doc Ruman took care of ya real good, Blyer. In my born days I ain't never seen so many bandages wrapped round one feller's noggin."

Blyer put a hand to his face. "Yes, I was seriously assaulted. As was my employee, Mr. Rufino Saldino of Nuevo Laredo, Mexico. I am here on behalf of both of us to press charges against one David Fierce Hawk. Address unknown."

Tom clicked his tongue, then reached for one of the peppermints he always kept handy. Rolling the candy from one side of his mouth to the other, he thought about the day's events. After that ruckus over at the Wayfarer, ole Gabe Weatherwax, the night clerk, had come rushing in, jabbering about two fellows being beat to a bloody pulp. Near as Tom could figure, one punch each had been enough.

After seeing Blyer and his big Mexican *amigo* toted off to Doc Ruman's, Tom had had to listen to this tongue-wagger and that tongue-wagger bending his ear about Senator McLoughlin's girl and her man-troubles with Senator Blyer's son and some good-looking Indian that turned out to be a Washington lawyer.

Tom could have told those ladies a thing or two about ole Hawk. Fine fellow, that one. Doggone good dominoes player, too.

But poor ole Hawk, looks like he'd gone and got his hands full of trouble. The McLoughlin girl and her old granny had skedaddled sometime before noon, that rich couple that had been staying over at the Wayfarer saw the ladies off.

Every busybody in Uvalde had come out for their farewell. Couple hours after that, Hawk, decked out in Indian duds and riding a fine dun stallion bought from the livery stable, had left. Probably to ride after his lady.

Giggling and simpering, the unmarried ladies of the town had hotfooted it over to Helmut's Café to jabber over the good-looking buck. The older ladies had showed up, too. Even that dried-up old schoolmarm Miss Carmack had participated. A few of them had clucked over the Blyer dandy, too. The café hadn't seen that much business since it opened its doors last year.

All of this while outlaws had been going about the monkey business of breaking the law—like stealing a pig from poor old lady Moore. And right before lunch, Rufus Haysmith got caught exposing himself in front of the little Metzger girl. Then a couple of young fellows got into it over a poker game at Estelle Hamilton's saloon; even as they spoke, one of the boys was lying dead over at the funeral home. His pregnant widow was crying over him right now.

But did the tongue-waggers give a darn about any of that? *Naw.* Common folks liked knowing rich folks was just as common as they was. Tom Ellis had enough to worry about, what with folks like poor Mabel Moore and the little Metzger girl and that widow woman crying her eyes out.

He crunched down on his peppermint while giving Ian Blyer a hard look. "Round here, the law don't mess between men when they fight over a lady."

"Charity McLoughlin is no lady."

"Now, son, watch what ya say. I know ya was engaged to the lady, and calling her anything less ain't dignified. Your pa wouldn't like it, your being less than mannerly. Ole Campbell Blyer cottons to keeping up a good front."

The peacock sniffed. "Sheriff, I left Laredo with every intention of being a gentleman to the young woman. I'd learned that she had fled from justice on the arms of a ruffian, yet, to save her reputation, and to bring her to the authorities, I and, my man Rufino Saldino, overtook their party."

"Rufino Saldino? Ain't he that scalawag what's been in and outta trouble for years with the Customs House in Laredo?"

"Charges have never been filed against Mr. Saldino."

Tom shrugged. "Get on with your story."

"As I was saying, Mr. Saldino and I overtook Miss McLoughlin and her party south of here. I tried my best to convince her to throw herself on the court's mercy, but she refused."

This story held about as much water as Barbara's cooking sieve, to Tom's way of thinking.

The peacock continued. "She and her Lothario stole my horse, and—"

"Hold on there, Blyer. The man Hawk done come by here yesterday, 'splaining hisself over the chestnut, and he was on the up and up." No use pointing out his relationship to ole Hawk. " 'Sides, ya told me last night the lady rescued your mare."

"I was less than honest—a gentlemanly gesture on my part. I thought to save face for the woman." Blyer dusted the arm of his coat. "May I sit down?"

Again Tom shrugged. "Makes me no never mind."

Blyer lowered himself into a straight chair, then crossed his legs. Tom Ellis had never had any use for a man that crossed his legs like that. Seemed kinda sissy to him.

"I have much to say, sheriff."

Doggone it, Tom was hungry and tired, and how long was this plucked peacock going to keep him from Barbara and the girls? A man sure had to put up with a lot of bull hockey to put food on the table. "If ya got more to say, Blyer, get on with it."

"Are you familiar with the Shafter silver-smuggling ring?"

"Yep. That lawyer feller Ellersby, outta San Antonya, come in here a couple days back and was jawing about it."

"I can assist in solving the case."

"Seems to me ole Al Ellersby said 'twas settled. Gonzáles and his boys got theirs from the Rangers."

"Not all of the miscreants were killed."

The Sheriff watched as ole Prissy Britches, a smooth smile moving across his pasty face, settled a forearm on his desk. Tom chuckled. This ole desk had long been needing a good dusting.

"Miss Charity McLoughlin was involved in the crime. Deeply involved. She was the money carrier. She, sir, is a fugitive from justice."

"Them's serious allegations, son. 'Specially against the daughter of Senator McLoughlin. He's a mighty powerful man in Washington. I shore would hate to be in your shoes if—where'd ya get those silly lace-up things, by the way?"

Blyer looked on the verge of blowing up, which made Tom decide he ought to watch his step with this one. Rich folks never had been much for a sense of humor.

"All men are created equal in these United States, sheriff. And no matter how high or mighty the culprit, we must all face the letter of the law when we break it."

"Ya know what, son. I think ya sound like a woman scorned. 'Sides that, ya ain't got no proof of Miss McLoughlin being tied in with that Gonzáles feller."

"On the contrary. As we speak, the Mexican government is handing over a dossier on the woman. It will be in my father's hands by tonight. Already the silver mine owner, Jerome Hunt, is in Senator Blyer's office in Austin. If you don't believe me, feel free to send a telegraph asking for confirmation."

"What're ya suggesting I do?"

"The McLoughlin woman departed Uvalde this afternoon, I've been told. Form a posse—after you've sent wanted-poster information across the telegraph lines—then ride after her."

If Blyer had been any other man, Tom Ellis would have picked him up by his ear, tossed him out the door, and advised him to work on his courtliness. But, doggone it, Campbell Blyer wasn't a man to cross—the son rode the father's coattails.

'Course, the lady was riding some pretty powerful coattails, too.

But all Tom wanted to do just now was get ole Prissy Britches here out of his office. "Don't worry 'bout nothing, son. Ole Tom'll take care of ever'thing. You just go on about your business. Ride that fancy carriage on outta here. Or maybe ya might wanna take the train on into Austin, so's ya can meet up with your pa and that mining feller real quick-like."

"I can trust you to send the telegrams and form a posse?"

"Shucks, yes," Tom assured him. "I'm on my way to the telegraph office right now."

Dad-burn-it, that stew was going to be ruined before Tom Ellis could wrap his mouth round a spoonful of it.

Chapter Twenty

Charity attempted to block out her great-grandmother's voice so she could concentrate on nothing. She rather warmed to the void, though the carriage ride repeatedly brought her back to her senses. How could it not? They were traveling through passes in the rocky, rough section of Texas known as hill country. Even on level ground, horseback riding had always beaten this bumpy, bone-jarring mode of transportation for comfort.

Riding close to Hawk had been thoroughly enjoyable. *Don't think about that knave!*

She cooled her sweltering face with one of the fans Maisie kept handy in the carriage. "Why can't we open the curtains? We're not getting a bit of breeze."

"We've been traveling since day before yesterday, and all ye've done is complain about yer comfort. But when ye had a chance to stretch yer legs and get a better attitude aboot yerself, what did ye do? Ye dinna even get outta the carriage in that bonny town, Leakey." Maisie flattened her wrinkled lips and shook her head. "Ye're an abomination of a whelp, Charity McLoughlin."

Hawk, too, had called her an abomination. All the while he had been lying to her, deceiving her, he had called her all sorts of names. Hellcat. Spoiled. Angel. His own.

Swallowing proved difficult.

Maisie raised a silvered brow before screwing her mouth into yet another demonstration of disapproval. " 'Tis no wonder Fierce Hawk hasna ridden after us. Probably, all ye did was gripe and complain to the lad. Till he was fed up to the gills. Men doona like that, I can tell ye."

"Thank you, Maiz. I needed that. And I really appreciate your making me feel worse than I already do."

" 'Tis time ye started thinking, period. Ye're in a heap of trouble, lass, what with that smuggling malarkey. But did ye appreciate me going to the bother of getting ye an attorney? No. Did ye accept the lad's apologies? No. Did ye say 'aye' to his marriage bid? No."

"Marriage bid?" *Pray, I didn't hear right*. "There was no 'marriage bid.' "

"He dinna say nothing about marrying ye?" Surprise burst on Maisie's face, surprise supplanted by aggravation. "Why, that jackanapes. Why, I *demanded* the lad do right by ye, and he—"

"You did *what?*"

"I told Fierce Hawk he had t' marry ye, now that ye are ruined."

Charity could have died right then and there of

mortification. She burrowed her face into the seat's leather squabs, squeezing her eyes closed. "How could you?" she asked, her voice pained. "You've taken away whatever pride I had left. Don't you understand me at all? I don't want a husband my great-grandmother has to coerce to the altar."

"It dinna take much coercing."

Oh? Then why hadn't he mentioned it at the Wayfarer? "Even if he were to show up and get down on his knees to beg, I wouldn't marry that red devil," she said, hoping and praying she meant it.

"Ye will once yer faither finds out aboot yer spreading yer legs for Fierce Hawk. Gilliegorm will load that shotgun of his, and—"

"I thought you said Papa wasn't at the Four Aces."

"I lied."

Charity might have forgiven her great-grandmother for interfering in her life, eventually. At some point, she might have overlooked a lot of things, since she did love Maisie, but the old woman's last admission was too much to take.

Charity picked up the brocade clutch devoid of money once more, thanks to the purchases she had made in Uvalde. Purchases meant to impress a sly Indian who had taken her virginity as well as her pride. Her mouth set in a rigid line, she stared at Maisie. A sanctimonious expression met her resolve. Charity said, "Once we reach Kerrville, you can go on by yourself. It's not that far from there to Fredericksburg, and Heinrich will make sure nothing happens to you."

"Ye mean to desert me?"

"Parting ways isn't desertion."

"Well, doona be waiting for any Kerrville. Here is as good a place as any. Doona let the door hit ye as ye're leaving."

Unable to believe her ears, Charity gaped at Maisie. Until last May they had been thick as thieves; a more staunch champion Charity could never have hoped to find. That was last May. This was now.

Perhaps she had misunderstood the old woman. "You want me to leave? Right in the middle of God knows what?"

"Aye."

Not believing that Maisie could be capable of such hard-heartedness, Charity said raggedly, "Maiz, you know it frightens—" She stopped herself from groveling, though her fear of the wilds urged her to grovel, plead, beg—do anything to keep from being put out alone. But her pride had already taken too severe a beating.

"And ye'll be taking nothing but yerself when ye go."

"Fine," Charity said, opening the carriage door and ordering the driver to stop at once.

The carriage jerked to a halt, unsettling the occupants.

Charity pushed the door outward, jumped to the ground, and landed on her feet with a thud. Hill country beauty met her regard; Heinrich's concern drifted to her ears. "Fraülein Charity, what are you doing?"

"Leave the lass alone. She is thinking she has all the answers. Let her find out that isna so. Drive on."

"But, *meine gnädige Frau,* we cannot leave her here."

"I said drive on!"

It just about killed Maisie, driving off and leaving her precious lass on the roadside. Time and again, the temptation to tell Heinrich to turn back got to her, but she forced her lips together and sat on her hands, lest they reach for the carriage door. Charity needed to learn a lesson.

"She's got t' be learning how lucky she is," Maisie said aloud. Yet once more the urge to call Heinrich came over her. "Don't do it. Fierce Hawk will be finding her. Or I'm not Maisie McLoughlin."

It took a couple of days after receiving Sheriff Tom Ellis's telegram for Gil McLoughlin to reach the capital in Austin, the roads being sorry at best. He wore out a Four Aces's stallion as well as a hired one, and the trip about broke Gil's tailbone.

But he was not a man to take slander lying down. The Blyers were doing their best to sully the McLoughlin name, had even involved Jerome

Hunt of Shafter and the Mexican and United States governments in their scheme. Trouble was, Gil feared it might not all be slander. Charity, he was sure, had been up to her usual tricks.

By an exchange of a dozen telegrams, Tom Ellis had tried to soften the situation, had said he couldn't imagine Miss Charity being mixed up with that Mexican bunch. Her father knew better.

She's my child–mine and Lisette's–goddammit. So why can't she accept our love. and toe the line? All Gil had ever asked of her was to behave herself. It seemed beyond her abilities, if not beyond her ken. But dammit, he loved that girl.

"I'm getting too old for these kinds of shenanigans," he griped to himself, glancing south down Congress Avenue. "Damn that girl."

Wiping sweat from his brow, he stomped into the new granite capitol building housing both branches of the state legislature.

"Why, Senator, how nice to see you," a page called, nearly stumbling to bow when Gil's legs ate up the space between the front door and Campbell Blyer's first-floor office.

Gil didn't reply; he was a man with a mission. With the heel of his hand, he thrust open the door marked CAMPLELL BLYER. The heavy door rattled on its hinges. Two men turned. One had a bandage wrapping his head; the other one, older, wore spectacles.

Ian Blyer tugged at the hem of his waistcoat. "What are you doing here?"

"McLoughlin," muttered his father.

Gil was across the room in two fiercely determined strides. He drew back his fist and plowed it into Ian Blyer's astonished, already battered face. The coxcomb went flying backward into a file cabinet. "That's for my girl, you son of a bitch."

"See here, McLoughlin, you can't burst in here and—"

"Shut up." Gil spun around, his fist raised anew. "You're next."

For two days Hawk had been following the McLoughlin carriage. At a respectable distance, of course. This afternoon, as he and the stallion he'd dubbed Firestorm weaved through a pass in the conical hills, Hawk caught sight of something out of place amongst the limestone mounds, the cedars, the live oaks. A person. A living being with long, dark hair.

Could it be?

He kicked Firestorm's flanks.

What the hell? he wondered. What was some woman doing out in the middle of nowhere? Unless of course that woman was Charity McLoughlin. Who was capable of just about anything. He got closer and closer to the lone form.

He inhaled sharply. It was indeed Charity. Now what? When last they had faced each other, she had sent him off with her fist. He didn't suppose Charity would open loving arms to him now.

Loving arms? Did he even want her to? He couldn't stop thinking about her jeers. But he had made a promise to the Old One. Legal aid. Maisie McLoughlin had tried to extract from him a promise that he would marry her great-granddaughter as well, but after that last time in the Wayfarer Hotel, Hawk hadn't been eager to commit.

Right then Charity turned her head, and when she caught sight of him, she propelled herself forward in a run.

He was tempted to let her flee.

She had wounded his pride with her scathing remarks. Yet seeing her gave him pause. She'd been angry, and she'd had every right to be.

He kept Firestorm on a forward path. There were a few facets of Charity McLoughlin that he needed to accept.

Again, Hawk dug his heels into the stallion's flanks. His fingers yanked at Firestorm's mane as horse and rider cut in front of her. The stallion pranced beneath him. Hawk took a full look into cold, cold eyes.

She was backing away from him.

"Where is the Old One?"

"Kerrville is my best guess." As she said those words, Charity continued to backtrack. "Do keep to your path. I'm sure you'll find her at the Narramore ranch. I imagine she'll be staying the night with them."

"She's not what I want. You are what I want."

By now Charity had set a wide arc as her course, and her hair streamed in the wind. Pulling up the hem of her blue dress—the same one she'd worn the night they had made love—she became fleet of foot.

David Fierce Hawk, late of Indian Territory and the District of Columbia, might not have been handy with a six-shooter, but he was a master horseman. Within moments he caught up with the fleeing woman and leaned down to grab her into his arms; turning her facedown, he settled her across Firestorm's back.

"Let me go, damn you!"

One elbow drove into Hawk's upper thigh. Her knees attacked the stallion's shoulder. Thankfully, Hawk had bought a mount of strong back, else poor Firestorm would have collapsed under the weight of her indignation. Hawk affixed his grip to Charity's waist and gave Firestorm a couple of meaningful kicks before setting off toward the nearest foothill.

"Damn you, put me down!"

"No. I'm not done with you."

Raising herself up by a thrust of elbows into the mount's side, she turned a seething face to Hawk. "Well, *I* am finished with *you!*"

He remained unaffected. At least on the outside. Each move that Firestorm made toward the foothills, Hawk became more and more mindful of the feel of his uncharitable Charity. His shaft grew harder and harder as his palm skimmed along her spine, curved around her waist, then migrated across her delectable behind. His fingers inched up the material of her skirts.

"You're not wearing pantaloons."

"Right. I've decided I like my *freedom.*"

"I approve," he said while his palm caressed, stroked, and unsettled her. It took him a couple of seconds to realize she wasn't fighting his touch. "You said I would never have you again," he said, slowing the horse's pace, "but I shall prove you wrong."

Questing, his fingers moved up and between her legs. It was all he could do to hang on to Firestorm's mane as Hawk thrust his middle finger into the place his shaft had deflowered in Uvalde. *Wah'Kon-Tah,* she was wet. And she moaned.

Firestorm reared back his majestic head, imparting a look that asked what-is-this-about? *Truth. This is about the truth.* Hawk was determined that she would declare herself anew. Before this day was over, Charity would admit her love and desire and hunger for David Fierce Hawk. Or he would die trying to make her.

"Show me a bareback trick, Charity."

"No."

"Yes."

"Why?"

"Because you want it as much as I."

"I hate you, Fierce Hawk of the Osage."

"You think so. I shall prove you wrong. But for now, forget all that has happened to tear us apart. Rise up and show me your skills."

His hands reached under her arms, bringing her to face him, her legs straddling the mount. Her mouth cleaved open. Hawk's lips swooped to hers. Jesus, Lord of the paleface, he thrilled at her response.

"Say it, Charity. Admit you lied about our time in the park."

"I will not."

"Say it." The fingers of one hand captured the tip of her cloth-covered breast. "Now!"

"I—I lied."

"Tell the truth. You went to Blyer just to punish me."

"I—I did."

Satisfaction—ah, it was wonderful. All of a sudden, they were ravenous, craving nothing but each other. Hawk ripped open her bodice, his fingers conquering the heavy mound of one breast. She leaned in to his touch. It became more insistent; he increased the pressure on her nipple. "Don't. Stop. Don't stop," she whimpered. He did not.

"Play with me, sweet Charity.."

She did. He bade her to touch him; her fingers swept aside his breechclout. Overly ready for her eager fingers, he felt the release of his first drop of seed as her fingers slid back his foreskin. Hawk couldn't breathe, much less think.

Suddenly her fingers pulled back from him, and she wailed, "I can't forget your deceit! And now—! What are you doing to me?"

He tucked the hem of her skirt into what was left of the dress's bodice and guided her upward, her hair cascading around him. Her womanly place sank and tightened around his shaft. At last he replied, "I am ravishing you."

Chapter Twenty-one

Thoroughly sated yet still hard of heart, Charity eyed her exacting lover. In the aftermath of their bareback coupling, they stood on the ground. Hawk, having ravished her body, now attempted the same with her heart. His voice a seductive growl, his eyes insistent, he demanded, "Admit you love me."

Her inner thighs warm and sticky from their lovemaking, she backed away. The heel of her slipper caught on a rock and prevented her escape. Thankfully Hawk didn't close the distance between them; he stood, arms at his side, his bare chest heaving.

"You've proved yourself a master of my passions," she finally replied. "I grant you that."

"Your passion is tied to your love."

Was it? Her love had been tied to trust and friendship—and lies, as it turned out. "Hawk, just leave me be. Please."

"What if my papoose grows within you?"

She had given thought to this possibility many times since leaving Uvalde. Each time she reacted the same way. Uncertainty battled with delight. Her future was clouded . . . She was alone in the world . . . But she would love any child of her body. *His child. too.* What they had shared before she discovered his perfidy was wonderful, perfect. But this wasn't a perfect world.

"The babe would want for nothing," she replied, vowing that she would make life easy for the little one, even if it took bowing and scraping to Papa. "And mind your own business."

"Any child of ours is my business. I'd do right by you both. If that doesn't sway you, think of this. If you do carry my seed, and if the courts deal with you favorably and both you and the babe are allowed to live, Gil McLoughlin would make it his business to see that his grandchild is born with a proper name."

She blanched at his grim declaration. Backing into Firestorm, she grabbed the horse's saddle to steady herself. "I won't be pushed into anything," she asserted wanly.

"Would it take my pushing you to let me become your attorney?"

Incredulous, she stared at him. Her lawyer? After all that had happened between them, he thought to insinuate himself into her life by acting as her counsel—as the defender she would have to trust with her life? And possibly their child's?

She laughed dryly. "That's an insane idea."

"I don't think so."

"Even if I did agree, which I won't, wouldn't it

pose a conflict of interests? An attorney shouldn't be bedding his client."

"I haven't had you in a bed." His eyes, now smoky with desire, penetrated her. "Not yet."

In spite of everything, a wicked and wanton part of her yearned to be abed with Hawk, a soft mattress at her back, sun-kissed linens musky with their mating surrounding them. And, Lord have mercy, she ached for another journey to that wondrous place where there was no beginning nor end, where a moment's breathlessness erased all thoughts of right or wrong or in between.

"Will you let me represent you in court?" Hawk asked.

She studied the ground; beneath her slippers were patches of grass parched by the relentless heat of late summer. Autumn would soon make its brief appearance in these surrounds. Without a friend in court, where would the dying season find Charity McLoughlin? She had few avenues. Broke, desperate, deceived, betrayed, possibly with child, she had to face facts. *I am a criminal.*

If a seed grew within her, she must protect it.

Yet . . .

Her eyes leveled on Hawk's high cheekbones and bronze visage. "I will not allow anyone whom I do not trust to serve as my advocate," she said.

"Without me, you will hang, Charity McLoughlin. You will swing from the rafters of some courthouse in Texas. Probably the one in Laredo. In full view of Senator Blyer and his son. Do you know what happens when a person dies by the noose? Their face turns purple from lack of air. The neck snaps. And their bowels loosen. Will you have that for yourself, Charity McLoughlin?"

Cringing, she turned from Hawk. Her eyes surveyed the hilly wilderness, devoid of humans save for herself and the Osage lawyer—a couple torn asunder by lies but united by damnable passions. Where did they go from here? And she wasn't thinking about the craggy hills of Texas.

"How would you plan to represent me?" she asked.

"By a plea of innocent. We would tell the truth and beg the jury's mercy."

"Others have never been disposed to believe me."

"Trust your fate to my hands. I will free you."

Once more she turned to him, searching his eyes, seeing in them unshakable confidence. Yes, Hawk had infinite self-assurance, while she had none. "You aren't a criminal lawyer. You are a lobbyist, a man of government."

"You have no idea what I am capable of."

She laughed nervously. "On the contrary. I know very well. Lies. Deceit. Cunning. Wiles. Molestation."

"All the qualities of a good attorney, angel mine. All the qualities." He took a step forward. "I'll serve you well."

A slick tongue had he, yet she would fight her weakening resolve. "What about your work in

Washington? Surely that needs to be addressed."

"Washington is over and done with. I mean to become a Texas lawyer."

"You can't be serious. Why?"

"Like you, I have broken with my people."

For once, she was speechless. After a moment she realized she was staring at him open-mouthed. "How can that be?" she finally asked. "Mutti said you are your people's most stalwart advocate, that you worked night and day, not only for the Osage nation but for other Indians as well."

"I did. But they have no more use for me. And I am through with them. They have settled for what the Great White Fathers have doled out. And I would never have settled for anything less than fair play."

Sadness laced his eyes as he squinted into the sun. "When you said I was born too late, you were right. The eighteenth century would have been the time for me." He laughed ruefully. "Or better I should have been born an Apache. They are neither peaceful nor subdued. Unlike my people."

"But you aren't an Apache and this is the nineteenth century. What do you plan to do with the rest of your life?"

"After defending you, I'll open an office in Austin. As your father advised."

"Papa gave you advice?"

"You find that hard to believe?"

"Well, I . . ." She shuffled her feet. "P-papa

does have his prejudices. Of course," she rushed on, "you are mostly white; I'm sure he thinks of you as such."

"He doesn't." Curt were Hawk's words. "Senator McLoughlin knows I am, and will always be, proud of my Indian blood."

"As well you should be," she commented. "And please don't take offense at my words. I know my father as a very obstinate man."

"He is that."

Thinking aloud, she said, "From what I've heard, you are—or were—a man of high ambition and dedication. I'm sure that appealed to him."

Charity recollected all her jabbering about Wild West shows. She had been asking a brilliant attorney to form a motley crew of entertainers. How ridiculous.

Blood rushing to her cheeks, she swallowed the lump in her throat. Unable to meet his gaze, she pointed out, "Good lawyers expect compensation. I would never allow any McLoughlin to have a hand in it. And I have no money to pay you."

"I think something can be worked out." His lips twitched into a lascivious grin. "Services for services."

She scowled at his brazen offer. If there was anything to be thankful for, it was that there had been no further talk between them of honorable intentions, marriage-wise. She would die before accepting any shotgun wedding!

"If—if!—I agree to retain you as my defender, we must get something straight. You will be paid in cash alone."

"Really? Did you happen upon a pot of gold between Uvalde and here?" His teasing tone grated on her nerves, especially when he added, "Or did you fall in again with someone like Adriano Gonzáles?"

She wouldn't dignify his questions with an answer. "You will be paid in time. For now, though, understand that I will not allow what happened in that park in Uvalde and atop that stallion to happen again."

"You didn't enjoy the sweetness of our flesh . . . together as one?"

The leavings of him still painting her womb and thighs, she longed to answer the call of her desires. If she did, she would be powerless against any whisper he issued, any touch that he elected to give. *Don't let him!* For too long she had been a pawn in the tournaments of others. No more. "I will have you for my attorney. If you agree to keep your distance."

"Charity . . . in Uvalde, you said you loved me."

"I lied," she lied.

Hawk took a backward step to fold his arms over his chest. "Then you are a bigger liar than myself. You've tarnished your halo."

"Is this how you mean to start our client-attorney relationship, by questioning my word and degrading my character?"

"A lawyer needn't think his client is honest in order to give good representation."

His remark cut to her marrow. "We are not discussing my part in the Shafter debacle, are we?"

"You're absolutely right." His eyes now as hard as brown bullets looked her up and down. "Okay, we'll do it your way. We keep our distance, at least where the needs of our bodies are concerned." He scanned the wilderness around them before he uttered another syllable. "Charity, I promised not to make you face your father. I won't. We have alternatives. We can head back to Laredo. You must turn yourself in before word gets out that you were involved in the Gonzáles gang."

"Ian may have informed on me already."

"If that's the case . . . well, we'll cross that bridge when we get to it." Hawk rubbed his brow. "We're nearly to Kerrville. Better we should go on to there before turning back. We need proper clothes and you need a horse of your own."

They reached Kerrville before dusk. Charity waited on the far side of the Guadalupe River while Hawk visited Schreiner's store as well as the livery stable. Twilight was beginning to fall when he returned with the goods.

"We've got trouble," he announced without preamble. "There are wanted posters nailed all over the place. Your name is on them."

She shuddered and trembled, feeling as if the earth had opened to toss her into the pit of perdition.

"Charity, we've got to get your family involved. You need their help as never before."

The Four Aces Ranch.

Charity and Hawk reached the McLoughlin property three days after they had crossed the Guadalupe. She'd vowed never to approach the place again, but that vow she would have to break—for herself and for her child. If there was one. She couldn't take any chances.

Nevertheless, it took all her strength of will to ride, head held high, up the carriageway leading to the mansion on the hill. The two-story limestone structure was encircled by roses, spreading oak trees, and close-clipped grass; it was to the untrained eyes, she supposed, a beckoning scene. But home had never seemed so forbidding. Papa was here.

She slowed the mare Hawk had purchased for her in Kerrville and glanced at him. Gone was his Indian garb, left behind on the banks of the Guadalupe. Proud of his heritage he might be, but he meant to downplay it here for her benefit. No jury would be impressed by a breechclout and bare chest. And Papa remained to be faced.

"We mustn't tarry," Hawk said, walking Firestorm close to Charity's mount.

Her courage failed. Her eyes closed. "I—I can't do it. I can't go on."

"Yes, you can. You can and you will. You've got to make peace. Your very life depends on it."

Would Papa back her, though?

Her gaze settling on Hawk, she saw that he

was assessing the house as if he had never seen it before. Pulled out of her melancholy, she said, "You seem to be looking at the place in a whole new light."

His brown eyes welded to the blue of hers. One palm flattened on his thigh, the other clutching Firestorm's reins, he winked at Charity. "You're very perceptive. In a way, I haven't seen it before. When I was visiting, it was merely a mansion on a hill, a place that showcased great wealth. Now I see it as the home where you were reared.

"I see a small girl, growing up amidst horses and privilege. Alone in a large family. Misunderstood and mistreated. Perhaps not intentionally. But what does it matter, the intent? It hurt you, living in this palace."

Charity found herself taken aback at his insight. And at that moment she felt a certain oneness. She wanted to make peace with Hawk. That didn't mean going hog wild for the love of him, or revealing to him that she still carried a torch. They needed to settle a few differences, it was true. But it seemed important that she understand the man she had once taken to friend.

"Will you tell me about your childhood?" she asked impulsively.

A hint of a smile played over Hawk's chiseled lips. "I'm pleased to hear you're still interested in me."

"Don't make too much of it. I'm curious, that's all."

"So you say," he murmured. "I'm flattered by

your curiosity. But you do have more pressing business at the moment."

Her regard turned to the house on the hill. "Yes. Papa." She put her heel to the mare's flank. "I'd better talk to him by myself."

"Agreed."

Chapter Twenty-two

Lisette McLoughlin had never been so happy nor so troubled in her life. How wonderful it was, having Charity home, right here in the solarium. And how awful it was, the noose hanging over that dark head. *Gott in Himmel.* What was to be done about the girl?

For twenty years she'd been frustrated over her defiant triplet's actions. Charity had caused a world of problems throughout that time. Why couldn't the girl realize that she was doing nothing but destroying herself with willfulness and impetuous behavior?

In spite of everything, though, Lisette loved her daughter. Always had, always would. And her conscience gave a reminder: she, too, had been guilty of willful acts. If Lisette had always done as expected, she wouldn't be married to Gil.

"I don't want to be here."

Lisette listened to her daughter's words. Charity stood with her chin up, her shoulders squared, ardently defiant.

"It must be difficult, coming home after our

row of last May," Lisette said. "But you are here, and we must face . . . what we must face. How can I help you?"

"Hadn't you better get Papa's approval before you ask that question?"

"Your father is a levelheaded man, Charity, and I have long depended on his wise counsel. But I make my own decisions."

"Levelheaded? You never see his faults, do you? He's a hothead if there ever was one."

"Did you come home simply to criticize him?"

"No." Charity glanced out the window before studying the floor. "I'm here because I . . ." Her words trailed off. Why was she here?

"I am glad you're home. Every night I have lost sleep, worrying about you."

"You could have written to me. You could have sent a telegram to Laredo, at least on my birthday. You could have done a lot of things."

"You could have, too."

Turning on the ball of her shoe, Charity faced the window. She said not a word. Lisette reminded herself of the futility of trying to reason with her daughter, for her words had always fallen on deaf ears.

She decided to hone in on the positive. "I am happy you're home," she repeated.

"Are you? Are you really?"

"I am."

"I . . . it's good to see you, Mutti." Charity closed her eyes. "I've missed you. I didn't realize how much until I saw you."

Her heart aching with pain and love, Lisette extended her arms, then pulled them back when Charity made no motion to reciprocate.

Chuckling hoarsely, Charity said, "A while back I remembered something. I remembered that Christmas I broke your mother's crystal bowl. It was one of many times that I disappointed you. I'm sorry for each of them."

"The bowl was merely a possession." Fate had given them one more chance for closeness. Lisette had to put aside her doubts and misgivings—or there might not be another opportunity. "I'm sorry that I wasn't more understanding of you."

"I did give you a heck of a time, didn't I?" Charity flashed her mother a scamp's grin. "I meant to, you know. I did everything I could to get your attention."

Lisette rolled her eyes. "You certainly were a handful. I tried to be patient with you. I wanted you to know that you were special to me. Are special. You have a very special place in my heart, Charity."

"But you prefer Olga and Margaret and Angus."

"That is not true. I love each of you equally. Each of my children has a private spot in my heart." Again she opened her arms to her daughter. "Don't stay away from me."

Charity faltered; she stared at the floor, shuffled her feet. She refused to take the first step of the ten that distanced her from her mother.

Lisette approached her. "Come here, *Liebchen*."

Charity's dark head elevated. Blue eyes—shaped

so much like her father's blue-gray ones—went from defiant to hopeful, and she sailed into her mother's arms.

"I have missed you," Lisette whispered, cradling her willful triplet in her embrace. It felt indescribably splendid, touching her daughter and knowing that Charity had returned. Here, the family could protect her, both from herself and from her crime. Lisette patted the waves of near-black hair. *"Ich liebe Dich."*

"Oh, Mutti . . ." Charity seemed to be fighting an internal battle. Moments later, a victor was declared. "I love you, too."

It was a poignant reunion for Lisette; her child who was no longer a child in years but so much so in spirit returned her love. Maybe there was hope for them.

When at last they drew apart, Lisette suggested they sit awhile, and led her daughter to the solarium's wing chairs.

"I was told Maria Sara and her son are hereabouts. Are they?" Charity inquired.

"Ja. They are in town this afternoon. With your cousin Karl. He should have them back by late evening."

"Karl would be wonderful for her."

Lisette didn't wish to discuss either her nephew or Maisie's paid companion, either singularly or as a couple. Especially since there was something about Maria Sara Montaña that troubled her. What it was, she wasn't exactly sure.

Eager to tell Charity all the news of the household, yet unsure how it would be received, she pushed Maria Sara and Karl from her thoughts. Her fingers as jittery as her nerves, she touched the diamond pendant suspended from her neck; Gil had given her the jeweled heart back in Kansas, back in the darkest days of their married life. Since then she had touched it a thousand times, as if the heart were a talisman.

Lisette McLoughlin had always been a woman of steel nerves, yet at this moment, how she needed her husband.

Try to keep your words light. "We have a surprise for you. Margaret is expected home in a couple of weeks."

"Margaret? All the way from university?" Suspicion marked Charity's features. "She was sent for, wasn't she?"

"Ja."

"I see." But it didn't appear as if Charity saw anything at all. "What about Angus? Where is my brother?"

"Your father sent him away."

"Sent him away? Has he done something wrong?"

"No. Gil thought it would be best if Angus wasn't around for a while. Until the, uh, the scandal dies down."

"Oh."

Lisette noticed that no question had been posed about Gil's whereabouts. *Well, are you surprised, considering the hurts each wreaked on the other?*

"Enough about other people." Anxious for her

daughter to broach the subject of the smuggling charge, Lisette said, "I want to know what has been happening with you."

In short, terse sentences, Charity told so much yet so very little. Her flight to Laredo; the unveiling of Ian Blyer's true character; the desperation that had driven her into being an unwitting accomplice to smuggling. "I am not guilty, Mutti. I promise you, I'm not."

"I never thought you were."

"You never questioned . . . ?"

"Never."

Charity's expression softened. "Thank you."

Lisette picked at a piece of lint that adhered to the chair arm. *"Liebchen,* you haven't mentioned David Fierce Hawk."

Charity's mouth tightened into an expression her mother knew well: aggravation. "I guess Maisie blabbed everything."

"No," Lisette replied honestly, "I didn't know there was an everything. I only knew that he was sent to Laredo to fetch you."

"What did Maiz tell you?" Charity asked too quickly.

Intuitively, Lisette knew there was much, much more to the story than she had thus far been able to gather. "That you were unhappy about being fetched."

"That's the truth," Charity muttered. "About Hawk, he is with me. Well, not exactly. He's gone into town to talk with the sheriff." She squirmed on the chair. "You see, he's going to be my attorney."

"You didn't ask him in? You didn't want your attorney at your side this afternoon?"

A blush spread across Charity's cheeks as she averted her eyes. "We . . . *I* thought it better if he stayed away for a while."

Lisette studied her daughter carefully. *Mein Gott,* the girl must have lain with the Osage lawyer. Lisette almost laughed. And cried. When she had met Fierce Hawk, in '69, she'd had a suspicion that the McLoughlins had not seen the last of him. Her instincts had been correct.

But why like this?

Lisette wouldn't press her daughter on the matter, not now. There would be time for that later, if Charity wasn't candid on her own.

But, oh, poor Charity. History repeated itself, for the daughter was apparently as vulnerable to jeopardies of the heart as her mother had been, so many years ago. Well, unlike Lisette's first brush with a man, Fierce Hawk was like Gil, admirable and honorable. Perhaps Charity hadn't, and wouldn't, experience the hell of courtship gone awry.

But what about Ian Blyer? *Doesn't she know heartbreak already?*

That awful cock of the walk's greediness had been apparent to everyone, save for Charity. While she had the ability to make quick and canny judgments about most people, Charity was blind to the faults of those she yearned to please. In her too trusting heart she couldn't—or wouldn't—see truths. But once her illusions were shattered . . .

Take heed, Lisette. She didn't marry Ian Blyer. What *had* she done with Campbell Blyer's son, though? Lisette figured it was best not to give that too much consideration.

She thought about her husband. Gil would be furious if he found out his daughter had coupled with either man. In Gil's eyes, both were unsuitable mates for a McLoughlin daughter. Then again, few potential spouses met up to Gil's tough standards for his children.

The problem wasn't confined to Charity's lack of will in staying pure. Gil, Lisette knew, had many bones to pick with the girl.

"Where is Maiz?" Charity asked, obviously wanting to change the subject.

"As soon as I saw you riding up, I told her to stay in her room."

"And she agreed?"

"Ja."

"Doesn't sound much like Maiz. But then, she's as angry with me as I am with her."

"I'm surprised about this business between you two. You never quarreled in the past."

"She never interfered in my life before."

"Well, she is old. And she wants your happiness. You know she stops at nothing to get her way."

They both chuckled.

Charity abandoned the chair and walked to the window, turning solemn. "You know that Hawk has broken with his people."

"He said as much when he arrived here in August. And it is the talk of Washington. But I trust he'll do fine in whatever life he chooses. I . . . I'm sure you feel the same way."

"All I care about is how well he defends me." Charity moved toward the door. "I think I'll take a short nap. I find I'm quite weary."

Charity was in the east wing of the house, headed toward her childhood bedroom, before she turned and started back to the solarium.

Such motherly understanding had given Charity a world of peace. And Mutti hadn't even demanded her to explain many things that were, Charity supposed, glaringly apparent. If their new understanding was to be successful in the long run, she would have to meet her mother halfway.

She didn't regret admitting her love. It had always been there, though she had tried to deny it. Time after time after time. And she had more to say.

Her mother still sat in the velvet-upholstered wing chair. Lisette McLoughlin had grown plumper over the past five months, her daughter assessed. Sweets were her solace. And tiny lines now radiated from the corners of her blue eyes. A streak of white lightened the already fair hair that grew above one side of her forehead. Mutti was still beautiful.

"I thought you were going to nap, *Liebchen*."

"Mutti . . . Hawk is more than my lawyer. I

have . . . He is my lover. I gave him my virginity."

Lisette exhaled in relief. "I'm glad you didn't give it to Ian Blyer."

Astounded, Charity gaped at her mother. "All my life you've lectured me about keeping myself pure for marriage. You aren't going to lecture now?"

"No." Lisette rose from the chair. Once she faced Charity, she took her hand. "I think David Fierce Hawk is a wonderful man."

"Good gravy."

"Do you have any idea why I cautioned you against giving too much of yourself?"

"Propriety?"

"Has nothing to do with my worries for you, my child. Experience taught me to advise caution. You see, I, too, had my own Ian Blyer. But I gave him what I should have saved for your father. And he almost ruined my life."

"Oh, Mutti darling, I never imagined . . ." Charity marveled over the courage it must have taken her mother to admit such a thing. She slipped her arms around her mother's shoulders. "I'm so sorry you were hurt."

"Hurt has its way of healing. I found your father, and for him, I am eternally grateful. Be glad you've found David Fierce Hawk. He, too, is a good man."

"Maybe. Probably. But he has hurt me." She couldn't forget how Hawk had deceived her, how he had thrown her in the lion's den."Hawk hurt me with his lies. He plotted against me. And he fooled me into thinking he was someone he is not."

"Sometimes, my child, lies must be told."

"Is that supposed to make them hurt less?"

"I don't know, *Liebchen*. I don't have all the answers."

"Mutti, you're shattering all my illusions," she chided gently. "I'm going to think you want to be more of a friend than a mother."

"I'd like to be both."

"I'd like that, too."

Mother and daughter embraced once more. Afterward, Charity excused herself to take the nap she had started for earlier. As she took a step to leave, Lisette captured her hand. "I can't help but wonder why you haven't asked about your father."

A feeling of dread and apprehension flooded through her. "You're right, Mutti. I didn't."

"I think you should know . . . He is—"

"Has something happened to him?"

"I'm afraid so."

Suddenly Charity felt faint."Wh-what? What happened?"

Lisette laced her fingers. She swallowed. She cleared her throat. Nervously, she fingered the diamond pendant that hung around her neck. At last she replied, "Your father is in jail."

Chapter Twenty-three

Crickets chirped over the slight breeze rattling the leaves; pastured cattle lowed on the hill. Ribbons of lantern light beckoned from the stable's tack room. As he walked into the long brick building, Hawk heard the comforting sound of horses neighing and snorting. Since he had not had the greatest of days, an after-supper ride on Firestorm might do him good.

What would be better? If Charity were to get up from the dinner table and follow him out here. He ached for a frank, unheated discussion with her. Earlier that day, when she'd asked about his childhood, he figured his way had been paved.

In the formal dining area he had decided she needed someone to talk with. Conversation had not been easy at the table. Tension between Charity and the Old One had loomed like thunderclouds and lightning on the horizon.

It wasn't Charity who joined him in the tack room.

"Left supper kinda abruptly, dinna ye?"

Aggravated that Charity's kinswoman had followed him out in place of his beloved, he frowned at Maisie McLoughlin. "I was looking for a bit of and peace and quiet."

"The meal *was* kinda spirited."

"Why wouldn't the family be upset? It's not often a United States senator finds himself in an Austin jail for defending his daughter's honor."

"What is Fierce Hawk gonna do about her honor? Now that ye've had yer way with her." A sly grin stole across Maisie's wrinkled lips. "Are ye forgetting yer promise to wed her?"

"Mind your own business."

"She *is* my business, ye scalawag."

"In the matter of whom Charity accepts as a husband, it's no one's concern but hers. And her intended."

"Could be. Keep something in mind, though. Her reputation. It suffered for running off with Ian Blyer. People like t' be talking about such as that, but talk has a way of dying down, in time. Some things are forever. No decent man will be having her, now that ye've lanced her maidenhead."

Hawk shuffled, uncomfortable. "Ma'am, Charity soon meets the sheriff to turn herself in for a hanging offense. And all you can think about is marrying her off?"

"Will ye be having her hang with yer bairn in her belly?"

Shoulders stiffening, Hawk queried, "What do you mean by that? She's not with child."

"How do ye know for sure?"

He didn't. But he refused to discuss the matter further, unless it was with Charity herself. "She's not going to hang. I won't let her."

"Are ye going to be marrying her before or after the trial?"

The meddling old tomahawk would give no mercy, would she? "If she'll have me, I'll marry her. But I'll do the asking at the proper time, do you understand?"

Maisie nodded. "Just don't be taking too long aboot it. I willna be having a big stomach poking at the waist of the wedding gown."

The Old One turned and marched out of the tack room, out of the stable that was suddenly to quiet for his liking. Hawk strode toward the door, meaning to find and confront Charity in the great house, but he stopped short with a sigh and, lifting an arm above his head, rested his forehead against the door facing. Did Charity carry their child? Would she know already?

Wah'Kon-Tah, don't desert us.

While the idea appealed to him, a child between them, Hawk knew that such was the last thing Charity needed right now.

"I've got to talk with her," he muttered under his breath.

He hurried back to the house. A snippet of conversation over the dinner table had informed him that Charity's room was upstairs in the east wing. The children's wing, Lisette had called it. No one but Charity would be sleeping in that side of the house.

But was she abed yet? Hawk breathed in relief when he looked up at the second floor and saw a light shining from one window. Hiding his boots behind a rosebush, he shinnied up the vines that grew on the wall behind it, then levered over the windowsill.

Curled up in a chair, wearing a wrapper and bed slippers, Charity started when he said, "It's me."

Wilting back in the cushions, she shivered and grasped the single braid that lay over one shoulder. "You scared me. Crazy as it seems, I thought it might be Sheriff Untermann here to arrest me."

"I told you at supper—I talked with him this afternoon." Deciding it would be best not to discuss all that had happened in Fredericksburg, Hawk crossed the Oriental rug, stopping at her feet. "He's agreed to let you come in of your own free will, once your father is back."

"I guess I'm just jumpy." A look of disappointment emptied the spirit from her eyes. "I noticed at dinner . . . You cut your hair."

"Needed to be done. For professional purposes." Goading her, he asked, "Like it?"

"Not particularly. You don't look very Indian anymore."

"Then I have counted coup," he teased. "I look white."

"You always did. I just wanted to see the savage in you."

"You saw me the way I wanted to be seen."

His gaze caught on a show of ankle. Her eyes

traveled up to him. The look they exchanged was one reserved for lovers who had experienced total rapture and wanted it again. He swallowed, feeling his blood simmering with desire. He had lived twenty-seven years without making love to Charity, but now that he knew the infinite satisfaction of her, he felt as if he couldn't live another moment without being inside that wet, hot place of hers.

She broke the visual contact. "You'd better leave, Hawk."

"In time."

"No. *Now.*"

"Can we call a truce?" he asked. "Because, believe me, I won't want any more arguing between us."

She sighed. "I'm not up to it, either."

It was then that Hawk noticed a decanter of spirits on the table beside her chair. A near-empty snifter, plus a clean one, sat next to the crystal bottle. "You don't have to drink. I said I'll get you out of this mess. And I will."

"I know." Tentative trust shone in her eyes, yet it was overshadowed by worry. And a fist pressed against her belly. "It's just that . . . well, everything is so complicated."

Tell me about it. Hawk went for a Queen Anne chair, scooted it close to Charity, and sat down. He leaned forward and took her hand. Thankfully she didn't pull it back. "Angel, there's something I need to ask you."

"Does it have something to do with the sheriff?" At his shake of head, she asked, "Does it have anything to do with the change of venue you were going to ask for? From Laredo to here?"

"No. I, uh." He cleared his throat. "We, uh." Again, he cleared his throat. His fingers tightened on hers. "Have you had any indications that you might be carrying our child?"

"No." Her nails pressed into the heel of his palm. "Thank God, no."

Hawk should have been pleased. But her expression of relief got to him. Did she despise him to the extent that bearing his child was abhorrent? *Get serious. She's being exceedingly wise.*

"Don't look so worried," she said. "I got my monthly this afternoon."

"Oh."

Hawk straightened. Instinctively, perhaps shamefully, he sniffed the air. It had a slight tinge to it, of woman and of taboo. In his village, the women exiled themselves to separate lodges during their unclean time. There were few things more forbidden than laying with such a woman. Yet . . . Hawk found himself oddly enticed by the thought of making love with Charity right now.

Jesus. Lord of the paleface.

Attempting to master his wits, he spoke on more pressing matters. "How about pouring me a shot of that brandy?"

She nodded, then did as bade. He took a sip of the good stuff. French, he decided. Cognac. At least ten years old. The McLoughlins did have excellent taste in spirits. As an Osage, Hawk had never been much of a drinker; his people shunned firewater for the most part. In Washington, though, he had imbibed to a certain degree, and had found that his taste buds were finely tuned.

Leaning the chair on its two back legs, warmed by the liquor that swirled through his veins, he looked at Charity. *Wah'Kon-Tah,* she was beautiful. His eyes seized upon the thrust of her breasts, high and proud, that pushed at the silk wrapper. No babe would go hungry at her font. His babymaker, curled into trousers grown suddenly tight, protested the confines.

Charity was looking him up and down. "Are you wanting to make love to me, Hawk?"

"Yes."

She placed her slipper-shod feet on the rug; her fingers laced on her lap. "I thought we agreed . . . And you promised to . . ."

"Right."

"Anyway, my stomach is in knots from the pain."

Her bald admission felled his lascivious thoughts. No woman had ever spoken so frankly to Hawk, yet he was pleased that she felt so comfortable with him, even if their past few days together had been less than ideal.

He couldn't help but ask, "Does it hurt badly?"

"I feel as if a fist is yanking and twisting in my stomach. It's clawing the blood out of me."

"What a pity." Concerned, he placed his palm on her knee. "Is there anything I can do to help?"

"I think so. Let's have another drink. Liquor seems to help my malady."

He was only too happy to oblige. They both took sips of the cognac, though it was plain to see that she didn't relish hers with the intensity that he did his. She screwed up her mouth and set the snifter aside. He took another swallow, savoring the rich taste. "I think we should get married," he blurted, then mentally kicked himself. With no child between them, what was the purpose?

"Married?" Her eyes rounded. "Whatever for?"

Because we want to. "It's the right thing to do."

Wariness painted her oval features. "Has Maiz been talking to you?"

"She has."

Those features fell. "I'm not interested in marriage."

"Were you ever? Say, before the Old One showed up in Uvalde."

"No."

"What *were* you interested in?" he asked, disheartened.

"Europe. And our being together in that mad idea of mine, the Wild West show." Charity surged from the overstuffed chair. The hem of her wrapper swaying, her back to Hawk, she glided over to the tester bed. One hand wrapping around a post, she glanced upward. "What are *you* interested in?"

"Your freedom." *And the Wild West show. provided you—What about Austin?* "Once you're free of the charges against you, we can decide whether we are right for each other."

She whirled around. The motion exposed the rise of one dusky-tipped breast. "We aren't right for each other. Never were, never will be."

"You're wrong."

"Am I?"

"Yes." He abandoned the straight chair to stride over to her. "You were promised to me, you know."

"I wasn't. My mother said she didn't promise anything. You asked. But she didn't promise."

"Is it that you don't want to tie yourself to an Indian, Charity?"

"You should know better than that, Fierce Hawk of the Osage. Especially after Uvalde."

"What if what happened in Uvalde hadn't happened?"

She frowned. "I thought we were going to keep our relationship strictly business, yet you've invaded my bedroom and you're asking leading questions."

"Can't help myself."

A dry laugh passed her throat. "I guess I can't keep my own word, either."

"Then answer me. What about your feelings for me?"

"I told you I'd fantasized about you, almost all my life. I waited years for you to rescue me from myself."

"I still could."

"Get me free, then we'll talk about it."

She was dismissing him, wasn't she? He had to make certain. "Tell me something. Would you be willing to live on a reservation?"

"You said you aren't going back to the territory."

"I won't. I was speaking speculatively." To his way of thinking she needed to understand who he was and where he'd come from. "Would you be willing to dirty your hands with the chores of an Indian woman? Would you, a white woman who knows the splendors of this place, be willing to live in a mud lodge?"

"I can't cook. I don't clean. And I certainly don't like sleeping on the ground."

"You wouldn't have to do any of that. But I would expect children. Lots of them."

She paled. "We . . . we're talking about the future, when the present isn't settled."

"Keep talking like that," he said, forcing lightness into his tone, "and I'll think you don't have faith in my abilities as a defense attorney."

"You ask too much." Forced coolness chilled her statements. "I keep seeing that hotel lobby in Uvalde. And how you and Maiz were in collusion. Now you're talking about a passel of children. You certainly have high regard for your powers of persuasion."

"I do. Now—answer me. Do you or do you not want children?"

"If God grants me the time on this earth, I want many children. But not yours."

Hawk would change her mind. Of this he had no doubt. But he figured a change of subject was in order. "This afternoon you wanted to know about my childhood." He raised a brow. "Still interested?"

She squeezed her arms under her breasts, then sighed. "Yes."

Good. Scooting around her, Hawk took a couple of steps to the side of her bed. He unbuttoned and shrugged out of his shirt, then eased onto the bedcovers. One hand going to brace his neck, he looked at her. She stood at his side, her long braid brought forward over one shoulder and falling to her waist.

"Get in bed, and I'll tell you everything."

"I told you. No lovemaking."

"I just want to hold you closely," he replied in earnest.

He inched across the bedclothes, arcing his arm to pat a place beside him. "Come to me," he murmured, luring her with his voice, his eyes, his being. "Come to me, my curious hell-kitten."

He knew she stifled a laugh.

She eased onto the fresh, clean sheets. Hugging the opposite side of the bed, she asked, "Were you a happy child?"

"Yes. I had everything I wanted, near-about. The only trouble was my parents' displeasure that I wanted to be more Indian than they expected."

"How could that be?"

"My mother Laurann would've been pleased if I'd acted the good white boy. My father wanted whatever my mother wanted. He's a henpecked sort of fellow."

"Then you were as misunderstood as I."

"There's a chance of that."

Charity turned her face to him. "My mother always said, as a boy, you were a warrior in training for battle."

"We've discussed this before. I was born a hundred years too late. There are no more wars for the peaceful Osage people."

"I wish you could've been whatever you wanted."

Hawk scooted over to drape an arm across her waist. "Had I been born in the 1700s, we would have missed each other." He rather enjoyed it, pushing her to her limits. "Would you have wanted that, Charity, never knowing me?"

She moistened her lips. "No."

He grinned. "You do know me. And I don't ever intend to let you forget me." He caressed her hip. "I *am* the Fierce Hawk of your fantasies."

"Oh, Hawk, don't you see anything? It's not Fierce Hawk I want. It's *you.*"

Turning still as a statue, Hawk gazed into her eyes. "Fierce Hawk and I are one and the same. Can you accept the truth?"

"Must we talk so much?" Her fingers moved to cup his jaw; one calf moved to the bend of his knee. "Can't you simply take me back to the road . . . where we—where I—was naive to what you and Maiz concocted? Can't you simply make love to me, without making me *think?* As you did in the park. I want to be in the storybook that is me and you . . . a captor and his captive, eager for nothing but each other."

For days he had prayed for her to say these words. Yet . . . Inwardly he bemoaned the ironies of life and tribal proscription. As if they had minds of their own, though, his fingers trailed to the top of her thighs, finding the extra padding. *Don't do it. Back off.*

He pressed his shoulder blades to the mattress and slammed his eyes closed. Fingers, soft and feminine, slid up his throat, over his jaw, and stroked a closed eyelid. His brazen angel—oh, how she tempted him.

He swept her palm to his lips, pressing a kiss to the warm center, and he laughed in the face of taboo. He pulled Charity into his arms; she went eagerly. Raising up, he slanted his lips over hers. His hands searched for treasures found and conquered in Uvalde and atop Firestorm. Once more, he and she were driven by passion, wanting and needing and demanding. There was little foreplay needed.

"Take me," she demanded. "Now."

She ripped at his buttons, and britches went flying. He swept aside any barrier to his entry and took her with one hard stroke. *Wah'Kon-Tah,* he prayed, you are wrong. It's good in here! Good, wonderful medicine for what ailed him.

"Hawk," she murmured, her fingers digging into his back as he plunged into her, time and again. "Fierce Hawk. David Fierce Hawk." Her hands moved to his ears. "David," she whispered lyrically. "Such a beautiful name." Her lips parted; her tongue darted to his lower lip. "You do wild things to me . . . David."

Never had he allowed anyone to call him by the name his mother had given him. It simply wasn't

Indian. But on Charity's lips it seemed right.

He smiled. "Call me anything you like." *As long as you call me.*

At that moment he felt her tremor. Her head moved from side to side, and Hawk quickened his movements. The pressure in his groin increased, demanding relief. She tightened around him, and he lost control, spilling himself into her.

"I don't hurt anymore," she admitted as he held her in the afterglow of their lovemaking.

It wasn't so awful to make love at a time like this, he realized. Even yesterday—even an hour ago!—the mere contemplation of making love like this would have made his skin crawl. Had he changed so much? He wondered if he wasn't as Indian as he yearned to be.

Chapter Twenty-four

In the shadows before dawn, Charity lay in Hawk's arms. Unable to rest after their night of wild lovemaking, she stared at the dimly lighted room, the room where she had grown up; it had held her childish hopes and dreams, her disappointments and tears.

Twenty years old, and I'm still in hot water.

Rather than dwell on that, she concentrated on Hawk. He looked so peaceful sleeping beside her. Peaceful and happy. But she knew he wasn't a happy man. And she yearned to know more about what had made Hawk Hawk.

The tips of her fingers caressed his temple, then swept down his strong jawline. He groaned in his sleep, then opened one eye. "Is it morning?"

"Almost dawn."

He opened the other eye. " 'Morning." His arms went around her, pulling her to him. Seemingly contented, he dozed off again.

She would have none of that.

Blowing a stream of air across his closed eyes,

his nose, she tickled his chin. "Wake up, sleepy-head."

He chuckled, batting his eyes at the intrusion. "Vixen, didn't you get enough last night?"

"No."

"How are you feeling?"

"Wonderful."

"Besides that," he said with concern in his tone. "How's your tummy?"

"You cured what ailed me."

He raised himself above her, one hand sliding beneath the crook of her arm, and she delighted in the unkempt look of him. She took in the clipped hair, the straight brows above his heated and dark gaze, the high-boned cheeks, and his sensuous lips. He smelled warm and manly and all Hawk. Once more her passions built. Maybe later she would chide herself over being aggressive in coercing him to lovemaking, but not now.

Nevertheless, she did congratulate herself on keeping mum about *love*.

"Cured what ailed you, you say?" he said. "I guess that makes me a shaman."

"What is a shaman?"

"A medicine man."

"You do have all the right medicine."

Feathering a kiss on the tip of her nose, he said, "How about I try . . . making sure you feel good all day long."

Suddenly the sun broke through the windows, reminding Charity of what the day would bring. But what was wrong with a tad more lingering?

"Hawk, I want you to make good on your promise. I want you to tell me all about yourself."

He pulled away to lie back on the pillow. "What do you want to know?"

"Tell me about your family.".

"My mother is white, but you know that. My father—Iron Eagle—is a half-breed. He's chief of the Osage nation. And I have a sister, Amy. She's married to a brave from our village. They have two daughters and another papoose on the way."

"Why didn't you go back to them, once you left Washington?"

"A difference of opinion on the settlement of whites in the territory."

"I take it you weren't for it?"

He nodded. "Whites have grabbed enough land. What was given in treaty to Indians ought to stay that way."

She observed the conflict of emotions that flickered across his face. *How awful it must be, being an Indian.* Before, she hadn't given much consideration to Hawk's troubles. He had once called her an angel of broken wing. His own proud wings had been clipped by these modern times.

Her fingers touching his face, she said, "I'm sorry. I wish it weren't too late to turn back the tide."

He brought himself up to a seated position, then swung his naked legs over the bedside. "Time to get dressed. This'll be a busy day."

Though she hated it that he cut short their conversation, she couldn't argue against his reason for making an exit. Charity was struck with guilt. They shouldn't have made love. Hadn't she forced him into a promise of business only? Hadn't she wanted to keep her distance? *You have no strength of character, Charity McLoughlin.*

As Hawk pulled on his britches and began to button them, he said, "You should get dressed, too. Your father will be home this morning. And we've got that business with the sheriff to attend to."

"Do you think I'll be jailed?" she asked, pushing an arm through the sleeve of her wrapper.

"I'd say you won't, being you're a McLoughlin."

"That didn't keep Papa out of the Austin jail."

Suddenly she laughed, picturing her law-abiding father being thrown in with the criminal element. Laugh she might, but she was pleased and proud that he had punched out Ian and Campbell Blyer—in the name of Charity McLoughlin.

Before yesterday, she would have never thought him capable of such a move. Did Papa care more for her than she had imagined?

"Charity . . . do you want me with you when you speak with him?"

"No. He is something—someone—I must face on my own."

Minutes after Hawk exited her bedroom, Charity was tending to her female-needs and plucking at the soiled sheets that held the scent of man and woman. Giving the sheets a final tug, Charity wadded them into a ball, then rushed to the large bathroom that had been built the previous year from an adjoining sitting room, and was supplied by an elaborate system of cisterns and aqueducts designed by Margaret and a cadre of her confederates, all well-schooled in Roman architecture, among other disciplines.

"Me, myself, I think I've done good just figuring out how to *use* all these contraptions."

Her actions in the bath were meant to keep her mind off the upcoming confrontation with her formidable father. Charity filled the porcelain tub with cold water, grabbed a bar of soap, and bending at the waist, she scrubbed at the sheets. At last, the tainted water swirled down the drain; she leaned back to rub the perspiration from her brow.

A pain low in her back, spreading around to her tummy, announced what she already knew. This was her time of the month. Always, Charity had been plagued with menstrual cramps; sometimes they had sent her to bed for the duration. Strange, she hadn't hurt when Hawk had made love to her, and the pain wasn't vicious today.

"Oh, Hawk—what am I going to do about you?" she wailed under her breath. And then she recalled their night together. "David. I like that name."

"Charity?"

She jumped upon hearing the feminine voice, then straightened. Maria Sara Montaña stood in the doorway. So lovely and perfectly coiffed was her petite friend. So lovely—and so welcome!

Standing, Charity brushed her hair over her shoulders—it had come loose from the braid, thanks to Hawk's questing fingers. She opened her arms. "Oh, Maria Sara, it's so nice to see you."

Her friend crossed the bathroom floor tiles to accept her hug. Stepping back, she said, "I have been worried sick about you. I was so afraid that things would not turn out as Oma had hoped." Maria Sara smiled. "But it appears that my worries were for nothing. You and the Indian lawyer . . . Well, you have taken him as your attorney."

"Don't you mean, as my lover? Obviously, you've seen the wet sheets, and have formed an opinion."

Maria Sara lifted a shoulder. "I could not help but notice the two snifters on your table. Especially after just passing him in the hall."

"Who else saw him?"

"No one."

"Good. You won't say anything, will you?"

"Of course not."

Charity beamed. In the name of friendship she launched into a brief account of what had befallen her since the night Hawk had snatched her from a street in Laredo.

"I heard there was a disagreement in Uvalde," Maria Sara said. "Between your Indian friend and Ian."

"Ian is difficult to get rid of."

"Some might not want to be rid of him."

Baffled, Charity scrutinized Maria Sara and the curious expression on her face. "Is this a riddle?"

Charity asked. "Are you trying to tell me something?"

Waving her hand dismissively, Maria Sara shook her head. "No, no."

"But why did you say *some* might want Ian?"

"He is a handsome man. Many young women are drawn to him."

"Well, I am not. Looks are only skin deep, you know." Charity rolled her eyes. "Good gracious, I sounded just like Maisie, with that skin-deep business."

The *mexicana* shuffled her feet and braided her fingers together. "Charity, *amiga*. I have been talking with Oma. She wants to—"

Aggravated, Charity cut in. "Please don't let her manipulate you into the middle of our fuss."

"I cannot help but be concerned. You are both very important to me, and it hurts me that you are at odds." Maria Sara took a step in her direction. "Would you please speak with her?"

"I'll think about it," Charity hedged. Hoping to get off the topic, she said, "Enough about me. What about you? I understand you've been seeing my cousin Karl Keller."

"Not . . . not really."

"Why not? Can't I infer something from your trip into town together, Jaime in tow?"

"Karl insisted."

"Karl insisted?" Incredulous, Charity shook her head. "Bashful Karl *insisted.*"

"He's not as shy as one might imagine."

"Still water runs deep, eh?"

"You might say that."

Sitting on the tub's rim, Charity leaned forward. "He's a fine man, my cousin."

"I—I know. That is what scares me." Maria Sara stared at the floor tiles. "He is much too good and decent for me."

"Bah! You are wonderful."

"Are you forgetting my employment in the brothel? Are you forgetting that I bore a child out of wedlock?"

"You *sang* in a brothel—you never sold your body. And Karl is no flower of purity, believe me."

"He's not?" A spark ignited in Maria Sara's eyes.

"Of course not."

Immediately Charity regretted her loose way with words. Tales of Karl had spread like wildfire through the family after that awful stepmother of his had seduced him, then made a point to let her husband catch them in the act. If Maria Sara were to find out . . .

"What I mean is," Charity corrected, "he's not a youth. And all men his age have some experience."

Maria Sara shook her head. "I don't think so. I think Karl is a virgin."

Right. And Martin Luther founded the Mormon Church. Charity drew a bowlful of cold water, went for a wash cloth, and began to bathe her face. "How is your son?" she inquired.

"The Four Aces suits him."

"I'm glad. And I'm glad you're out of Laredo." Noting the other woman's lack of an enthusiastic reply, Charity set the cloth back in the sink. Was something wrong? Of course not! Maria Sara would be candid if something were bothering her. Friends didn't keep secrets from each other.

"Maria Sara, you don't know how much it means to me, your giving me money when I was trying to escape from Ian."

"It was nothing."

"Nothing? It was a sacrifice. And I will repay you. Someday."

"Repayment is the last thing I want. And I'm doing fine, now that Oma has hired me."

"And where does the morning find my meddlesome great-grandmother?" Charity asked.

"Oma is in your father's study."

Then Papa was home. Charity felt as if the whole contents of the sink had surged up to douse her face with icy reality. She began to shake. "I . . . I'd better hurry getting dressed."

"Would you like for me to help you?"

"No. But please send in one of the servants."

Maria Sara nodded.

"I'm glad you're home, my friend," Charity said gratefully.

"Me too, *amiga,*" Maria Sara replied as she turned and exited the bathroom, leaving Charity to her thoughts.

Within a minute or so, Graciella was hovering over Charity. "Which dress would you choose, señorita?"

"The gray muslin." It ought to be austere enough.

Corseted, bustled, brushed, and made fit, she trudged toward her father's study. The walk reminded her of what it must feel like, taking the last steps to the gallows. What would Papa do, once they were face to face?

Chapter Twenty-five

Thankfully, Maisie was no longer in her Gil McLoughlin's study.

The large room was just as Charity remembered it. A hardwood floor; massive, dark furniture upholstered in deep wine leather; walnut paneling. Between the pair of casement windows, looking out over the many acres of the Four Aces, hung a painting of longhorn cattle. Their fierce faces, decked with expansive horns, were painted in the foreground of massive dust clouds that billowed up to the cerulean sky.

Behind the huge desk a rack of horns dominated one wall. They spread a good eight or nine feet, commemorating a bull that her papa had admired and loved—Tecumseh Billy, who had led the way to Kansas on each of Gil McLoughlin's cattle drives and had paved the way to McLoughlin riches.

Cattle drives were now a thing of the past. Barbed wire laced the Chisholm Trail. Railroads ferried cattle to northern markets. After a peaceful retirement, Tecumseh Billy had died of old age, with a campfire and singing cowboys surrounding him. He rested in a proper grave not far from the main house. An era had died with him.

"You're back."

Charity jumped at her father's voice. No welcome imbued his tone. Barely looking at her, he cut across the room to settle into the chair behind his desk. Papa was just as she remembered him. Ungiving. Scowling. Disapproving.

"You're back, too." She refused to cower. "How was jail?"

"About like seeing my wayward daughter. Like hell."

"How very kind of you."

"Sit down, Charity. Do you want a cup of coffee?"

Her father reached for a coffeepot and poured a mud-thick cup of the brew. He waited for her to reach for it. She did—why be any more ornery than necessary? But she didn't sit down. She wanted to have the advantage of looking down at him.

He gave her a hard once-over. "Pleased with yourself?" he asked.

"Must you make this so difficult?"

"You've made it difficult, Charity McLoughlin. Sit down, dammit, and I mean *now.*"

She sat, though with some difficulty, thanks to her bustle. "Thank you, Papa, for defending my honor with Ian and his father."

"You have shamed us all, Charity."

Her shaking hand reached for the coffee cup.

She scalded her tongue on its thick contents. "I suppose I have."

"Suppose? No supposing about it, girl. You have."

Though she had spent her life trying to get her papa's attention, she could have done without it now. "I—I'll be leaving now."

"You, by God, won't."

The force of his words assaulted her. "Must you shout?"

"What am I—what is everyone—to think, daughter? You ran off to meet one man, returned with another, and you've got a bounty on your head."

"I didn't mean to carry money for Adriano Gonzáles.

"You didn't *mean to?* What in bloody hell does that mean?"

"I didn't know what I was doing, until it was too late."

"That seems to be the story of your life." Gil McLoughlin leaned forward to plant an elbow on his desk. "Just what have you been up to with that Indian?"

"Hawk is my attorney, and—"

"Not anymore he's not. I brought a team of lawyers from Austin to clear the family name. I fired Hawk, not ten minutes ago. And if he knows what's good for him, he's headed off my property."

"You fired him?" Pushed past her limits, Charity rose from the chair. "How dare you do that?"

"Same way I've done everything in my life. Quickly. Forcefully. Unhesitatingly."

"You can't fire him. *I* hired him. You have no say over me."

"That so?" Papa parked his elbows on the chair arms and steepled his fingers in front of his sun-dried, fifty-year-old face. "I seem to recall you haven't reached your majority. Seems to me I still have legal control over you."

"And you love having that control, don't you?" She glared at him. "But I won't be controlled. I *will* find Hawk and stop him from leaving. No. I'll make certain he takes me with him."

She whirled around, making for the door, but her father's words stopped her. "For another roll in the hay?"

"What?" Again, she faced her father. "What makes you think? Mutti—she told you didn't she?"

"She told me nothing. I was going on a hunch. And on the boots that Manuel found beneath your window." Gil McLoughlin closed his eyes, and his mouth pulled into a grimace. "Damn."

"Don't concern yourself, Papa. What is between me and Hawk is between me and Hawk—and no one else." She grabbed the doorknob, giving it a twist. But the door opened too quickly—Charity stepped back as David Fierce Hawk marched forward to the study. "I—I thought you had left," she murmured.

"Never." Hawk's fingers brushed her jawline. "I'd never desert you, my darling."

She was glad her father had heard his declaration, and she was even more glad, seeing him. "I knew you wouldn't desert me," she bluffed, *"my darling."*

"Tell me, Hawk," said her father. "Am I going to need to oil my shotgun over this affair?"

Oh, no. Not Papa, too! "Leave it where it is," she said. "I have no intention of marrying. Ever."

"Charity," Hawk whispered. "Let me handle this."

For once, she was relieved to hand over control.

She followed Hawk into the depths of the study. He helped her into a chair at the side of her father's desk. Without being asked by Gil McLoughlin, Hawk sat down in the chair she had quit. "In case you've wondered what I've been up to since you ordered me off your property, McLoughlin, I've been firing those Austin lawyers you brought home. They're past your gates as we speak."

"Why, you son of a bitch," Papa shouted, rising up from his chair and nearly toppling it behind him. His eyes hard, he ground out, "You looking for my bullet between those Injun eyes of yours?"

Charity shivered; she knew her father was capable of making good on the threat.

Hawk lifted his palms. "Hey, the lady hired me. What can I say? I wouldn't be much of a defender if I didn't look out for her best interests. And if you don't approve . . . *too bad."*

The room went silent as Papa eyed Hawk. Charity's heart thumped. Papa never let anyone thwart him. What would he do next?

Amazingly, the meanest bull in the Lone Star State sat down in his chair and sighed. "You truly think you can free my girl from the charges against her?"

"I'm certain of it."

Papa stared at Hawk, then at Charity. She could tell that indecision was roiling within him. She held her breath.

"I won't fight you," he said at last, to his daughter's surprise and ámazement.

"Good," said Hawk. "But we need your help. Charity needs her family at her side."

"I would *never* desert my daughter."

Never had she been so proud of her papa! She fought the urge to surge to her feet, fly around his desk, and throw her arms around him.

Her papa rubbed his chin with his thumb and forefinger. "I'll hand this to you, Hawk. You've got balls."

Oh, dear. It wasn't over yet.

"Watch what you say." Hawk shifted uncomfortably. "There' s a lady present."

"Don't tell me how to talk in front of my own daughter!" he barked. Yet Charity saw a grudging respect for Hawk in her papa's countenance.

"Since the lady in question happens to be the woman I love, I will remind you to watch your tongue."

Hawk loved her? Charity shook her head to clear it. Had she heard right? She stared at Hawk. From the forthright look on his face, she knew she had. He loved her!

Right then, all her problems seemed insignificant.

A couple of hours after the showdown in Gil McLoughlin's study, Hawk, driving the McLoughlin buggy with Charity on the seat beside him, caught sight of Fredericksburg.

Charity was in a delightfully good mood, considering their destination. She hadn't mentioned what might happen at the sheriff's office, and neither had he. Like a pup welcoming the sun on a warm day, Hawk basked in her high spirits. He said nothing of his avowal of love, but he noticed she didn't bring it up either. Well, a buggy ride culminating in her surrender to the authorities probably wasn't a good place for talk like that.

Reaching the eastern edge of town, Hawk stopped the buggy to allow a funeral procession to pass by. Situated to their right was a hotel, a widow's walk dominating its facade. Just as the last of the cortege rolled down the street, a boy, appearing to be aged four or five, darted out of the hotel. He held a toy boat in his sturdy grip.

Charity lifted her hand, waving to him. "Chester! Chester Nimitz! How are you?"

The light-haired youngster—handsome and hardy, the type, any father would be proud of—ran forward to stop below Charity. "Hello, Miss Charity. Where have you been? Why don't you teach Sunday school anymore?"

Charity a Sunday school teacher? Hawk had a

hard time picturing that. Nonetheless, he realized there was no end to the many facets of his archangel.

"I've been away, Chester," she said to the youngster. "It's good to see you. Is that a new boat?"

"Yes, ma'am." He held up the miniature frigate, displaying it proudly. "Isn't it nice?" He tapped the bow against his solid chest. "I'm going to go down to the sea in a tall ship someday. Did you know that?"

"Oh, yes, Chester William Nimitz, I know. You've told me many times. I'll bet someday you make these United States proud."

At that moment a uniformed woman with an obviously grim disposition charged from the hotel. Catching sight of Charity, she imparted a look of vast disapproval. "What are you doing out of jail?"

"Can I go riding with Miss Charity, Miss Agatha?"

"No! Get inside." She cuffed his ear. "It's time you washed up for the meal, young man."

"Yes, ma'am." Waving the frigate at Charity, the boy was pulled by one hand into the hotel.

"His nursemaid never did care much for me," Charity said as Hawk made a right turn onto a broad avenue, headed west. "Apparently her opinion of me has been strengthened by the wanted posters."

"Don't concern yourself with her." Not liking the dip Charity's mood had taken, Hawk decided to change the subject. "Tell me about this town."

"Need I say it's sleepy?" Charity took a handkerchief from her reticule and blew her nose before continuing. "This is the Hauptstrasse. That means 'main street' in German."

"Go on."

"Fredericksburg was settled in the mid-1840s by immigrants from the northern regions of the German states, the duchy of Nassau-Hesse for the most part. The Kellers didn't arrive till the 1850s."

"I know your blood is a veritable ketchup of heritages, like mine, but you don't seem very German to me."

"I must take after Papa's side of the family, the wild and woolly Scots."

Hawk laughed. "You aren't woolly, but I won't argue the wild. I like wild."

Just as she turned to smile at him, a trio of matrons pointed and covered their mouths with their hands. Hawk was glad Charity didn't see them, and to make sure she wouldn't, he motioned to the opposite side of the street. "What are those funny little houses?"

The dwellings were stone, compact, and looked too small to rear families in.

"Sunday houses. Farming families live in them on weekends. They drive in Saturday mornings for market, then stay on for church. They usually eat their Sunday meal here in their little homes away from home."

Now that he thought about it, he did smell sauerkraut and boiled sausage. The citizenry of Fredericksburg must be gearing up for a meal that would be graced by their prayers, he thought. All was God, home, and apple pie. Or in this case—God, home, and pickled cabbage.

He said, "Good, honest citizens. Respectful of the law. And of propriety."

"You forgot—they also fight for their country. Fredericksburgers have fought for America since the Great Scott went to Mexico."

"Did they fight Indians, too?" Hawk asked, knowing what her answer would be.

"Yes."

By now they had driven through the main part of the business section and were nearing the sheriff's office, which was located close to the courthouse and the all-purpose Vereinskirche building. More people stopped to gawk at Charity and to gossip behind their hands. From an attorney's standpoint, Hawk didn't like the looks of the place.

He had considered asking for a change of venue from Laredo to here. Not a good idea, he decided. These people would never understand her.

Yesterday he'd ridden into town to make some purchases designed to outfit himself like a proper attorney, and he had spoken with the sheriff as well as the district judge recently arrived from Laredo. By taking the train as far as San Antonio, Judge Pierce had beaten Hawk and Charity to Fredericksburg.

Yesterday Hawk had been pleased that the ambivalent Pierce was in town; it would make the job of petitioning for a change of venue less cumbersome. His opinion had changed, thanks to the hostility on display today.

That, and his visiting a local beer garden the previous day. He'd done some talking with a few of the English-speaking locals about the McLoughlins in general. He'd found out that while they revered the family, they were inclined to look unfavorably on the angel of broken wing known as Charity McLoughlin.

While each had commented on how she had been a spirited and mischievous girl who loved children to a fault, only one or two had mentioned that the other McLoughlin girls had overshadowed her. "The girl has been nothing but trouble to her father and mother for the past few years, and a child should honor her father and mother," was the general consensus. At the time Hawk had hoped it was their beers talking.

Bringing the horse and buggy to a halt in front of the sheriff's office, Hawk once again went over in his mind what he would say inside.

"I'm scared," Charity said brokenly.

That made two of them. Hawk had made a lot of promises. Thus, not taking any chances on a particular deity, he prayed to God as well as to *Wah'Kon-Tah* that he could stand and deliver. "Everything will be all right, angel mine."

A rotund man, wearing suspenders and a ten-gallon hat, ambled out of the building. Sheriff Josef Untermann. "It is about time you two got here," he said in a thick accent. "I was beginning to think I would have to come after you, Fraülein

McLoughlin."

Hawk expected Charity to quail at the sheriff's harsh words and condescending airs, but she didn't. With enormous courage she stood up tall in the buggy. "I have never given you any call to say such a thing, Josef Untermann. And I am here. Let's get this over with."

Her head high, and refusing the help Hawk offered, she descended the conveyance. Unruffled, she marched into the sheriff's office. Already Judge Noble Jones was there.

Jones, a portly man in his sixties, reigned from a wing chair out of place in the spartan, dusty office. The chair had probably been brought in special for the occasion, no doubt meant to intimidate. He wore an expensively tailored suit sporting a gold watch chain, a starched shirt, silk cravat, and polished boots. A monocle fitted against his left eye and magnified the censure in his gaze.

What had happened to his *laissez-faire* attitude of the previous day? Hawk wondered.

"Sit down. Both of you." Judge Jones gestured to a couple of straight chairs while Sheriff Untermann settled behind his desk.

"Young lady, I am aggrieved that it's come to this," said the judge. "Your family deserves better than the scandal you have brought upon them."

Uh oh. Townspeople must have been talking with him. Hawk cast a furtive eye at Charity, telegraphing a message, *Let me do the talking.*

"You don't know my family," Charity blurted

out anyway. "So don't concern yourself with their feelings."

An agitated flush crept up Jones's throat. "Campbell Blyer warned me that you're a piece of work, young lady. I should have listened to him."

"While you do," said Charity, "I'll be considering the source."

That's right. Antagonize the man before they even got started. Hawk could have wrung her neck, especially when she made a face at His Honor!

Jones looked as if he were red enough to pop a vein in his neck.

The sheriff announced, "You're going to jail, Fraülein."

"Please. Just listen." Hawk instructed his client, then turned his attention to the judge who might well sit for her fate. "Sir, we have two requests. First of all, we don't see how it would serve the People of Texas if Miss McLoughlin is incarcerated before the trial."

"I will not have a criminal walking free in my streets," the sheriff declared.

"Judge Jones, Sheriff Untermann, Miss McLoughlin is not a criminal. She was an innocent victim in a plot devised by the late Adriano Gonzáles of Nuevo Laredo." Hawk stood to face the two men. "I beg you both to have mercy on this lady of upstanding character and refined sensibilities. And on all the McLoughlins." He smiled at Charity, who chewed at her bottom lip. "Leave her free until her case comes to trial. And let that trial be in . . . San Antonio."

"San Antonio?" was the chorus of three.

Jones said, "Why there? What is wrong with Laredo?"

"Miss McLoughlin would not be able to get a fair trial in the hometown of her accusers, the Blyers. As for San Antonio, it is a city harboring no prejudices against the young lady."

With any luck Hawk could get the Bexar County district attorney to drop the charges due to insufficient evidence, though he wouldn't bet on it.

"What do you think, Judge?" Untermann asked.

"I'll take the matter under advisement."

It was the best Hawk could ask for. For the time being. He murmured, "Thank you, your honor," and leaned to shake the man's hand. "When might we expect to hear from you?"

"Soon."

Chapter Twenty-six

As Hawk nodded his head in thanks, Charity glared at Judge Jones. She appreciated Hawk's decorum in her defense, but she was not going to sit like a bump on a log while some pompous judge gave wishy-washy answers about her fate.

She started with Sheriff Untermann. Seemingly nonchalant, she leaned to the side to gaze out a filmy window. "Oh, my. Is that Hildegard Stahlberg I see going into Kreitz's Store? Why, I haven't seen Hildegard in the longest time." Charity turned her innocent wide eyes on the sheriff. "How has she been doing? And do tell me how your good wife is getting along, while you're at it."

Josef Untermann squirmed. "We aren't here to discuss Fraülein Stahlberg."

"Right." But Charity knew she had him on the run. Batting her lashes at Judge Jones, she smiled again. Laying the fingers of one hand across the back of her opposite one, she studied her nails and said, "Noble Jones. That name does ring a bell with me. Aren't you an elder in the First Presbyterian Church of Laredo?"

Jones puffed out his chest. "Yes, ma'am, I am."

"I know a woman who used to work in an establishment called Pappagallo's in Nuevo Laredo. Are you familiar with that broth—er, that *establishment,* Judge?"

"I don't know what you're getting at, Miss McLoughlin."

"Charity, don't," warned Hawk.

She ignored him, saying to the judge, "As I remember, the woman said there was a silent partner in the operation who hailed from these parts. Aren't you—"

The judge coughed nervously.

She turned to Hawk. "Ask them again. Ask them again about your petitions."

He looked as if on the verge of strangling her, but he said, "With the court's approval I move that Miss Charity McLoughlin remain free until a jury has been seated in the district court of San Antonio."

"Granted."

Freedom. Oh, it was lovely. Even if temporary in duration. Charity rejoiced at the judge's decision, especially since her freedom hadn't been tied in with anything to do with her papa or his money. A little old-fashioned blackmail had gone a long way.

"Isn't it marvelous?" she asked Hawk as they rode toward the Four Aces.

"No."

"You can't mean that."

"You embarrassed me, Charity." Hawk snapped the reins over the horse's rump. "And you left yourself wide open to charges of extortion."

"Oh, pooh. I didn't extort anything."

"Let me tell you something, lady." He glared at her. "I represent the accused in the case of the People of Texas versus Charity McLoughlin. And from now on the accused will keep her big mouth shut. Understand?"

His aggravation and anger took her aback. Unwilling to surrender, she asked rather snidely, "Does this mean you're not interested in a celebration?"

"Right."

"I never thought your ego was so fragile."

"Why don't you shut up? For once."

"Please don't be upset with me, Hawk. I felt I had to do what I did."

"Charity McLoughlin, I have never hit a woman in my life, but if you say *one more word,* I am going to slap you."

You and whose army?

They rode back to the Four Aces without so much as a sideways glance passing between them. They didn't speak at supper that night. And he didn't visit her room at bedtime. It was enough to make a girl cry.

If she were capable of crying.

"You hurt his pride," Maria Sara told her at breakfast the next morning. "He is staying away to lick his wounds."

Of course her friend was right.

Just before lunch Lisette came out to the stable, where Charity was grooming her Andalusian mare, Thunder Cloud. "Would you like to talk, my child?"

But Charity was in no mood for conversation.

At dinner that night Hawk's place went unoccupied. Once the dessert was finished, Gil McLoughlin made his excuses and went outside for a smoke. Maisie joined him for a cigar of her own. Charity went looking for Hawk.

He wasn't in his room. He wasn't at the stable, and he hadn't taken Firestorm out. One of the stableboys informed her that Hawk had gone on a walk. Since the acreage of the Four Aces was immense, Charity decided not to set off on an odyssey across the ranch. Vast acreage? It really had nothing to do with her hesitation. She couldn't bring herself to take off into the dark of night.

When she trudged back into the house, Maisie pulled her aside and gave her a tongue-lashing for "not letting the lad do the job ye gave him." This was not what Charity wanted to hear, especially from her meddling great-grandmother.

"I know my own faults, thank you very much."

The next morning Johnny the stableboy told her that Hawk had collected Firestorm and without so much as a word had ridden out. Charity walked from the stable into the harsh light of day. Right into her Papa. "If you're looking for Hawk, he's gone to San Antonio. He's meeting with people at the courthouse."

"Oh."

"In case you're wondering why he didn't tell you, I'll wager he didn't want to chance your demanding to go along."

Why argue her papa's reasoning? Charity had come to the same conclusion.

"He told you what happened with Sheriff Untermann and the Laredo judge?" she asked.

"I don't need some redskin to tell me what goes on in my own hometown, goddammit."

She took a long look at her father. The sun seemed to halo behind him. His Stetson shadowed his arrogance. Yet for the first time in her life, he didn't intimidate her. Once, Mutti had said that Gil McLoughlin was more bark than bite, and Charity decided that that was so.

"Why don't you like Hawk?" she asked. "Just because he's an Indian?"

"Hell's bells, missy, he's hardly an Indian! He's three-quarters white! What I don't like is that he's stolen my baby!"

Charity blinked at him in surprise. *Had a stranger thing ever happened?* Tart as she pleased, Charity parked a fist on her hip, and teased, "Why, Papa, I didn't know you had a baby. Is it a boy or a girl? Does it belong to my mother?"

"Get outta here, Charity McLoughlin, before I

dust your britches."

Charity's heart skipped a beat. Her papa was laughing. And it was a sweet, sweet sound.

Over the next week Charity tried not to think too much about Hawk. Or about his absence. Naturally her resolve was overridden from time to time; each time she conjured up his image she prayed Hawk would return quickly so that she could try to make amends.

He stayed away.

A cool front moved in, lowering the taxing Texas heat and ushering in the first blessed hints of autumn. Workers bailed hay and moved the Four Aces herd to the best pastureland; hogs were butchered and hung in the smokehouse; Manuel the head gardener and his helpers picked the last crop of tomatoes. Still, Hawk didn't return.

Charity conjured up all sorts of scenarios about what he was doing.

On the fourth morning of his absence, Charity brought to mind advice Maisie had given her over and over. "An idle mind is the devil's workshop," she told herself.

She kept herself busy with needlepoint, with long rides on Thunder Cloud. She honed her trick-riding skills on a favorite cutting horse. And she spent time with little Jaime.

What a precious child. While in Laredo she'd never really gotten to know Maria Sara's son. Furthermore, she hadn't had much opportunity to observe him with his mother. But since both mother and child had been at the Four Acres, Charity came to a conclusion that troubled her. Maria Sara had something against Jaime.

This worried Charity.

It was wrong, she figured, the way Maria Sara chided the boy over the most minor infraction of behavior—he was only a toddler, for goodness' sake! Too often the mother left the boy to the care of others. He simply wasn't accepted for himself. Charity couldn't help but identify with young Jaime.

Yet she warned herself not to make judgments. Perhaps she was making too much of Maria Sara's seeming neglect. Hawk's absence left her cross, to say the least.

But she was never cross with Jaime.

On a bright Saturday morning—a cool and pleasant one—Charity went to the room he shared with his mother. The boy jumped up and down, shrieking with glee when he saw "Shartee."

He toddled across the floor and threw himself into her arms. She cuddled him to her, drinking in the child's sweet scent. *I want a baby.* Good gravy.

"I'm here to collect your son," she said to Maria Sara, who was brushing her beautiful blond hair into curls atop her head. "Manuel says the pumpkins are lovely this year, and I'll bet Jaime would love to see them. After that, we'll take a nice walk through the hills and search for arrowheads."

Arrowheads. Indians. Hawk! *Gads. Don't start thinking about him again.*

"Jaime will like that," said Maria Sara.

"Would you care to tag along?"

Maria Sara shook her head. "I promised to go with Oma. We're calling at the Keller ranch."

"Maiz has taken quite an interest in my cousin." Charity lifted a brow. "But I'd think you and Karl should be past the matchmaker stage by now."

Maria Sara smiled. "We are." Her friend's tone grew serious. "But there is much to iron out between us."

Charity tickled Jaime's chin, setting the child to giggling. "You two will be fine. Then you'll have more time for the boy."

"What do you mean?"

The two friends had never had words, and Charity warned herself against borrowing trouble. "I only meant that I will be happy to see you settled and content." Setting Jaime to his feet, she took his hand in hers. "Have fun today, my friend."

"Charity . . . perhaps you and Jaime would care to accompany us?"

Being in her great-grandmother's presence wasn't high on Charity's list—she still hadn't forgiven Maisie for abandoning her in the wilderness, not to mention that other business—but Maria Sara *would* be with her son, a rare occurrence. What could hurt in saying yes?

Ten minutes later, the four of them climbed

aboard Maisie's carriage, setting off for Karl Keller's ranch. Charity decided she would not let the Old One get to her.

Old One.

Good heavens. I'm even starting to think like Hawk.

Chapter Twenty-seven

Still in her dressing gown, Lisette McLoughlin looked from the bedroom window and watched Maisie's carriage depart down the hill. "Where do you think they're going?" she asked her husband as he walked into the room.

"To Karl's." Gil paused. "I'm thinking that fancy Mexican gal is going to throw a shoe, once she finds out your nephew broke up his own father's marriage."

Frowning, Lisette recalled the terrible happenings, once her brother Adolf had discovered his second wife had taken his surviving son to her bed. It had almost killed the already lame Adolf.

Finally, Lisette replied to her husband, "I don't care much for Maria Sara Montaña. Don't ask me why. Mother's intuition when it comes to her children's friends? I hope she isn't taking advantage of Charity's friendship."

"I hope not, too."

"Anyway, the situation between Karl and Maria Sara isn't our problem. We have enough to worry about. With that smuggling business." Lisette continued to watch the carriage. "On the positive side, it's good to see Charity and Maisie in spitting distance of each other."

Gil chuckled and rattled a drawer knob. "My guess is that's exactly what they'll be doing. Spitting at each other. Those two are more alike than either would ever admit to."

"Ja. Willfulness did carry down through the generations to Charity." Lisette added a chuckle of her own as she watched the carriage become smaller and smaller in the distance. "We misnamed our girls, I'm thinking. I named our sensible and studious triplet after Oma, when I should have demanded 'Margaret' for the most stubborn of them."

"Maybe I should have named Charity after you. You've been known to be pretty willful yourself, pretty wife."

Lisette turned to her husband. Fresh from a bath, he stood nude as he searched through his bureau for undergarments. Even after all their years of marriage, the sight of his naked, battle-scarred body still thrilled her.

"We are alone, *Liebster."*

His blue-gray gaze flew to the blue of hers. The union suit dropped from his grip. She moistened her lips as a slow smile played across his mouth and his blue-gray eyes canvassed her form.

"It has been weeks since we made the best use of a Saturday morning, my husband . . ."

"My sentiments exactly."

Reaching behind him, never averting his gaze, he

clasped a bottle of bay rum, then splashed a goodly portion on each side of his face.

"You don't need that to excite me," she said.

"I know."

Gil's feet ate up the space between them. He kissed her passionately, his hands going to all the places he'd had so many years to relish. And it was past noon before they spoke about anything . . . except for what would pleasure each other.

As he helped her into her corset, she said, "Gil, why do you think Fierce Hawk has been gone so long?"

Her husband's hands stilled on the laces. "What makes you think of that son of a bitch?"

"I wish you wouldn't call him names. He is Charity's choice as, uh, as attorney."

"They're lovers. But you knew that, didn't you?"

Lisette nodded. "Our daughter told me. Did she tell you?"

"No. But I guessed it, and she denied nothing."

"I think they're in love."

"Charity never did have the sense God gave a gnat."

Whirling around, Lisette shook a finger at her husband. He bent to nip it. But she forced herself not to be deterred by the eroticism in his action.

"Don't talk about our daughter that way," she said. "She is bright as can be."

"Bright, yes. But devoid of horse sense."

"She can't help being the way she is. And, Gil, I'm happy to have her home."

Tucking the tail of his shirt into Levis, he

stomped across the bedroom to retrieve his boots.

"Aren't you pleased to have her back?" Lisette asked.

It was a half minute before he answered, "I am. Now that I've had some time to digest it. I just wish we could rejoice in her homecoming. But we can't. Not with her crime muddying everything up."

"Her 'crime' has nothing to do with your attitude, does it? You're angry because she brought a lover with her."

"You got that right."

"Would it make you feel better if they married?"

"Lisette McLoughlin, have you lost your marbles? There is no way I'd welcome him into the family."

"If you don't, we may end up losing a daughter over it. Because I think they are meant for each other. And I think they'll be together forever."

His brow drawing inward, Gil studied Lisette. "Do you really think so?"

"Ja." She went over to smooth silver-streaked black hair from his forehead. "I think they will be as happy as we have been." *If they are given the chance for happiness.*

"How could anyone else be as happy as we've been?" His hand closed over hers. "How could any man love a woman as much as I love you?"

"What a seductive tongue you have, husband." Lisette winked at him. "But we shouldn't get off the subject of the younger set. Tell me something. If Charity were to say that she and Hawk are going to be married, what would you say?"

" 'How much is it all going to cost?' "

Thrilled that he had backed down, she swatted his firm buttocks. "Don't play the penny-pinching Scotsman with me. I know better."

He moved her hand around to the front of him, and she said, "Whatever am I going to do with you?"

"I have an idea . . ."

"Don't look at me that way, Gil McLoughlin. We've just done what you're proposing to do. And you are *not* as young as you used to be."

"Wanna bet?"

A knock on their bedroom door pulled them apart. Gil accepted a folded piece of paper from the servant Graciella. After thanking the girl, he read the note, then said, "Our Margaret will be home tomorrow."

"How wonderful!"

The Keller ranch—situated in view of Fredericksburg's most famous landmark, Cross Mountain—was nowhere near as sprawling or as wealthy as the Four Aces, but it showed prosperity. Barns and outbuilding sparkled with fresh paint, as did the modest main house. Polished and shining, a buggy and a buckboard were parked alongside the residence. In the distance horses, oxen, and cattle grew healthy and hale on the grasses painstakingly planted and tended by Karl Keller's mexican hired hands.

A lot of this prosperity, Charity knew, had come from her parents' generosity in the early years of their marriage. The Kellers hadn't been rich by any stretch of the imagination, so Papa and Mutti had helped Uncle Adolf and his first wife out. Then Aunt Monika died. After the three younger Keller boys succumbed to the cholera pandemic of 1883, the McLoughlins had given even more assistance.

The Keller ranch thrived. Uncle Adolf met and married a painted lady from New Orleans, Antoinette Harpe. And oh, how Uncle Adolf adored her! But she wasn't satisfied with her limping, older husband. She turned her violet eyes to her stepson. In the aftershock Uncle Adolf had left for a self-imposed exile in San Antonio.

Antoinette had left, too, and Charity didn't give a darn about her destination.

"Charity, are you all right?" Maria Sara asked, pulling her away from dark thoughts.

"Of course."

She turned to the *Mexicana*. They stood on the front porch, Maisie and Jaime dozing in the wooden swing suspended from the ceiling. Karl had gone inside to collect a tray of refreshments.

"I think I will join those two in a short nap." Maria Sara, yawning and patting her mouth, glided to a divan that hugged the porch wall. "I stayed up too late last night."

"Only you?" Charity winked. "Or should you be adding Karl?"

Maria Sara curled up on the sofa. "*We* stayed up too late last night. Chatting."

Humming a particular tune from *Lohengrin,* Charity cocked her head. She started to say, "I'm going to see what my cousin has to say about all this," but saw that the blonde had fallen asleep. Charity entered the house and made her way to the kitchen. Burly and broad-shouldered, the blond giant was squeezing lemons into a glass pitcher.

"You look right at home in the kitchen," Charity teased and pulled out a chair to sit in it. Resting her elbows on the table and dropping her chin onto the backs of her braided fingers, she eyed the starched shirt and slicked-back hair. *I'll bet he's wearing clean longjohns, too.*

"Since I know you like to spend Saturday mornings in town, playing checkers with those old goats who hang around the poolroom, and since I know you *hate* anything that smacks of domestic skills, I'd say you're going to a few pains to impress Maria Sara."

"Nosy." Laughing, he lifted the lemon, squeezed, and shot juice onto Charity's nose.

As she batted at it, she gave a fleeting thought to the last time she had seen lemonade. How were Norman and Eleanor Narramore? When they had said their goodbyes, just before noon on the day Charity and Maisie had departed from Uvalde, the Narramores had wished her all the best, and Eleanor had said, "If you need help, please don't hesitate to let us know. We'll be at the Dollar Five Ranch in Kerrville."

Charity decided that as soon as she reached

home, she would write to them, let them know she remained free, and give the trial's location. *Maybe I'd better wait until I know the date.*

"Has the cat gotten your tongue, Cousin?" Karl leaned toward her.

"Did you say something?"

"I did. I was thanking you. For your responsibility in bringing Maria Sara to Fredericksburg."

"Think nothing of it." Charity picked up a slice of discarded lemon, sprinkled salt on it, then sucked the last of the tart juice. Her mouth pursed, her eyes squinted, she said, "Like her a lot, do you?"

"*Ja*. I do."

"What do you think of Jaime?"

"Ah, he is a fine child." Karl poured a cup of sugar atop the lemon juice. "Any man would be proud to claim him." On a frown, he added, "I cannot understand why his father has not seen after the boy."

"That makes two of us."

Adding water to the mixture, Karl asked, "Do you know the man?"

"No. Maria Sara never talks about him."

"I think she sees the boy's father each time she looks at Jaime."

"Do you? I think Jaime looks just like his mother, what with his fair hair and blue eyes."

"Maybe his father is fair."

"I never thought about that. And I suppose it's none of my business."

"Mine, either."

Huh. She glanced around the kitchen, then said, "This place could use a woman's touch. Maria Sara is quite a homemaker. She's clean as a pin, and you've seen how she sews for Maiz. You ought to taste her enchiladas. Mmm, mmm. Are they delicious."

"I have tasted her cooking. It is delicious." He shook the spoon at Charity. "You needn't make a list of her virtues. I don't need a push in wooing Maria Sara."

Charity salted another discarded lemon, blurting, "Maria Sara thinks you're a virgin."

Karl turned beet red. "You are as meddlesome as Oma."

Was she? Oh, dear. But . . . "You shouldn't let Maria Sara hear about Antoinette from anyone but you."

Turning his back to get glasses from the cupboard, he replied, "I know."

"She'll understand. I know she will."

"Will she?" Karl's voice was low, agonized. "There are things . . . I am afraid she will not understand about me."

"Karl, you're a grown man. She doesn't expect you to be some sort of paragon."

"She is a lady. She'll be shocked if she learns—" A glass dropped from his fingers, crashing to the drain board.

"Learns what?" Charity asked as she gathered the glass shards and placed them in the waste can.

"There are things you don't understand about me."

"I might if you were straightforward."

Ducking his head and jamming his fingers through his hair, he replied, "You are an innocent girl. I cannot speak of . . ."

"I'm not innocent. I've taken a lover. So, go on. Tell me."

"You? *You've* taken a lover?"

"Well, don't look so astonished. As Maiz always say, there's someone for everyone. Even me."

"I didn't mean that you cannot attract a man, Cousin. What I meant to say was, I thought you would stay pure for marriage."

"I didn't. Now—tell me what you're afraid of."

He sank to a chair and covered his face with a hand. Charity barely heard him say, "I am depraved."

Rocked from her moorings, Charity gripped the table edge. "Oh, dear."

"I enjoy copulation over-much," Karl explained. "With Antoinette I learned this. And I am afraid I will shock Maria Sara."

Inside, Charity seethed against that Antoinette. What was wrong with Karl that he had been attracted to such a viper? "I guess that makes two of us, depraved. Must run in the family, or something." Charity stood and put her arms around her cousin. "Karl, try to forget Antoinette. Go on with your life. Maria Sara needs you."

"That is my hope."

"I think that I should collect my great-grandmother and Jaime, and we should head back to the Four Aces. If you have any idea of making something permanent with Maria Sara, you two ought to have a good, honest talk."

Karl nodded. "You are right, Cousin."

Chapter Twenty-eight

Madre de Dios, what was on this man's mind?

For hours—it was now approaching sundown—Karl had sat beside Maria Sara on the creaking porch swing; he had said absolutely nothing to her, had simply gazed across his land, as if he were in a trance. Occasionally a blush colored his thick neck, as if his own thoughts embarrassed him.

He's found out about Pappagallo's. He yearns to tell me he is not interested in seeing me again. And he's too shy and sensitive to blurt it out.

His shyness gave her pause. While Maria Sara was desperate for the security that a good marriage would assure her, it worried her that Karl might not have enough passion to quench her carnal thirsts.

Perhaps she should give the gentle giant an avenue of escape. "Karl . . . I should be going home."

"Not just yet. Please." Yearning eyes turned to her. "Would you like another glass of lemonade?"

She glanced at the empty pitcher. "No, thank you. If I drink any more, I shall swim home."

"I . . . I want your home"—he swallowed—"to be with me."

"Oh, Karlito, *mi querido* . . ."

She almost laughed at her words, thinking what people in Vera Cruz would say if they heard her call such a big man "Karlito."

He grasped her small hand in his big one. "I have money in the bank. Property. Cattle. And I am lonely. I want you to be my wife."

What more could she ask for—besides a voracious lover? "You don't know me."

"Yes, I do. I know you are as lonely as I am. I know your smile makes the sun shine in my heart. I know you would like to have a home of your own." He brought her fingers to his lips. Once more the flush crawled up his neck. "I know that I have a grand passion for you."

Grand passion? Indeed his eyes held the promise of it. She took a covert look at his masculine bulge; it showed promise.

"You are a lady. And I am a man of vulgar needs. I hope I haven't shocked you."

"You have not." The sun began to shine in her heart as well, but Maria Sara cautioned herself against getting her hopes up. "There's something I must tell you. This awful page from my past—"

"If it's about the boy, I have guessed that you weren't married to his father. It matters not to me."

She angled toward him. "Karlito, are you certain?"

He nodded. "I want to raise Jaime as my own."

But what about the brothel? "Your words please me. My heart pounds as I think of the life we could have together."

She left the swing and moved to one of the porch's wooden support posts. She couldn't face Karl, though she heard him stand and approach her.

"Stay back," she pleaded. "There are things that you must know."

A chicken ran across the yard, cackling as it headed for its roost.

"What are these things?" Karl asked.

"When I met the man who gave me Jaime, I was a respectable girl in Vera Cruz. My family has a sugar plantation there, understand, and the Montañas are held in high esteem, thanks to my father and his wealthy adoptive parents.

"It was unthinkable for a young lady of my station even to be seen without a *duenna,* yet I fell victim to the advances of an adventurous young man from Laredo. He promised his love and all his wealth, though his fortune paled in comparison to that of my family. He said we would marry. But my father refused to grant permission."

"Go on."

But she couldn't. Anger raged through her. She hated Ian Blyer! He'd offered Charity everything; he had made a fool of himself over her, more than once; he had even followed her to Uvalde. He had never followed Maria Sara Montaña as far as *el baño!* But she would avenge her honor. Someway. Somehow.

At last she spoke. "The *sinvergüenza* seduced me under a poinciana tree. I thought he was in love with me. But that was not his motive. He meant to impregnate me, then demand my hand as well as a portion of the Montaña wealth. My father was unimpressed."

"He sounds as evil as the blackguard who pulled the wool over Charity's eyes."

Maria Sara went still. "He *is* Ian Blyer."

"Gott in Himmel. I will snap Herr Blyer's neck between my hands!"

"No, no. You mustn't." *Vengeance must be mine.*

"But your honor is at stake. And Charity's."

"Karl, promise me you'll say nothing to her." Maria Sara had no wish to hurt Charity. By hurting Ianito, both women would triumph. "It would wound her, knowing the truth. It need never come out."

"You are right. And there is no reason for you to feel shame, Maria Sara." He folded the small woman into his bearlike embrace. "I understand."

"But I haven't finished my story." Once more she pulled away from him, then hugged her arms as if a blue norther had suddenly swooped down. "I followed Ianito to Laredo. I pleaded with him to help me and our child. He refused. I had no money—my parents had disowned me. I made a pact with the devil. If *el diablo* would see me through the birth and give me a healthy child, I would do anything to keep a roof over our heads and food on the table."

"What did your predicament force you into?" Karl asked slowly.

"I accepted employment in a brothel."

Karl slammed his eyes closed.

"But I never sold my body," she lied.

"Explain how you worked in a whorehouse and didn't sell your body."

"I sang. To entertain, I sang."

Doubt marked Karl's square face. "I have never heard you sing."

"I will never sing again. It reminds me too much of that time. That place. Pappagallo's."

Karl gasped. "Pappagallo's?"

"Yes. It is in the boys-town section of Nuevo Laredo. A wretched place filled with girls as desperate as I was. For a year and a half, I was the singer there. Until last month."

"That was *you?*"

They stared at each other, both disbelieving. Both incredulous. Maria Sara blanched. Then she remembered where she'd seen him before!

His lip quivered. "That was *you* at Pappagallo's."

He tried to liken the whore from across the border with the regal lady before him. How ironic. That she—That he—Suddenly Karl threw back his head and roared with laughter. Once more he looked at Maria Sara, seeing her in a whole new light. Why she was as wicked as Antoinette!

"I remember you. All painted up, wearing that

see-through nightgown, sprawled against that battered old piano."

"I trust you enjoyed what you saw."

Karl gave another bellow of laughter. "What a *Dummkopf* I have been, not recognizing you. Of course, you aren't wearing all that paint, and you're buttoned to the chin. A year ago, I saw you. I offered the host—he was known as Señor Grande, I recall—fifty dollars for your favors. He demanded a hundred. And I only had fifty in my pocket."

"No one ever came up with the money Grande asked for me."

The memory of that night in Nuevo Laredo made him catch his breath. Feeling his lids half shutter his eyes, he relaxed against the porch wall. "Want to know the truth? I was demented for the want of you that night. I thought about going outside to knock some poor soul in the head to get another fifty dollars. But I could not bring myself to do it. So I settled for one of the fifty-cent girls. I don't even recall her face, much less her name. When I had sex with her, I imagined she was you. All painted up and wearing that see-through gown."

Karl bent toward her, lifting her chin with the crook of his finger. "If you'll have me, I still want you for my wife."

"Are you insane?" she asked, disbelieving.

"That night in Mexico is all the more reason to want you."

"You cannot be serious. You . . . you are a decent, upstanding man, a pillar of society."

"My private life has nothing to do with that." His hot lips covered her cold ones, his imagination running to what she could do between his legs. "At Pappagallo's, after I finished with the whore, the host gave me the opportunity, for two dollars, to watch you with him and another man. You were chained to the better looking of the two to a contraption."

Maria Sara's eyes rounded.

Karl clasped her head, squeezing. "So don't lie to me about not selling your body, not if you want to be my wife."

A corrupt laugh dispelling her gloom, Maria Sara arched against him. "I want to be your wife. And your whore. Like I was to El Aguila and that bastard Grande. If . . ."

"If?"

"If you can prove to me that this"—she unbuttoned his fly and grabbed him—"will keep me pleasured."

Randy as a rutting boar at her lasciviousness, he ran his hand along Maria Sara's hip. "Then we will be married." He pulled her onto his lap. "Provided you'll paint your face and wear nightgowns that I can see through."

"I would be willing to do that."

He fumbled with the buttons of her dress, then delved into her, biting an already erect nipple. Maria Sara's mouth parted while a gasp of approval slipped past her lips. "But tonight . . . tonight we won't be needing any clothes at all."

"You are right, *querido* Karlito." She covered his hand, pressing him to her. "We don't need them tonight."

Getting to his feet, he carried her into the house.

Ian Blyer stomped into the modest house that his father had rented in Austin. He pushed past the open-mouthed housekeeper. Charging into his father's study, he demanded, "Father, why did you advise Jerome Hunt to drop the charges against Charity McLoughlin?"

Campbell Blyer, seated at his desk, took off his spectacles and rubbed his eyes. "Because matters have gone far enough, and I am embarrassed at your behavior."

Ian balled his fists. There had been a time when he would have backed down when faced with his father's displeasure. But too much was at stake, for Ian Blyer had not given up on exacting his punishment against the chit who had humiliated him. Charity McLoughlin had two choices. Become his wife. Or swing from a rope. In either case she would regret crossing him.

And Campbell Blyer *would* help his son, or Ian would make him suffer too. "Do you think it matters to me that you're embarrassed?"

"It would be sensible if you'd give up this vendetta you have against the McLoughlin girl. I offered Jerome title to my property in Laredo, in exchange for his agreement to drop the charges."

"Next you'll be hectoring me about finding a job." Ian took a furious look at his father, and for the first time saw him for what he was. A shriveled old weasel. "You aren't on my side."

"Ian, you're making a fool of yourself, prancing around the capital, demanding retribution."

"The McLoughlins got to you, didn't they?"

"As I understand it, Senator McLoughlin has hired attorneys. The best in the business."

"Thank God Jerome Hunt didn't listen to you."

"Be careful what you thank the Lord for, Ian. The truth may win out." Campbell Blyer rose and approached his son. His eyes were moist. "Do you really want it known that your own father was a part of Gonzáles's organization?"

"You buffoon. You mindless buffoon."

"Will you have me exposed to my voters as an outlaw?" Campbell pleaded. "I realize you find this all hard to believe, your father tying in with miscreants, but I was desperate. Your losses at the gaming tables were expensive."

Ian cut over to where his father hid the whiskey. Pouring an overly healthy shot, he quaffed it. "I've known you were involved from the beginning. Who do you think ordered Adriano Gonzáles to hire you in the first place?"

"Oh, my God." Traumatized, Campbell grasped the back of a chair for support. "Not you. Not my only son. Not my hopes for the future."

"If you harbor hopes for the future, at least where your own hide is concerned, you will do exactly as I say. Or your constituents will see your feet waving beneath a scaffold." Ian took a look at the embroidered slippers shodding his own feet. "And perhaps your handsome son's, too."

Shaking his head, his eyes closing in dismay, Campbell Blyer replied, "What do you want me to do?"

Chapter Twenty-nine

A general air of celebration—advanced by Gil McLoughlin, Lisette, and Maisie—ruled in the Four Aces dining room that night. On the journey between the Keller ranch and home, Maisie and Charity had patched up their differences, thanks to an out and out apology on the matriarch's part.

And Margaret would be home tomorrow.

No one made mention that Maria Sara hadn't returned from visiting her suitor. Nor did anyone say anything about Hawk's prolonged absence, though both subjects kept surfacing in Charity's mind.

Had a proposal of marriage been extended by her cousin to her friend?

And what kept Hawk in San Antonio?

"Wouldn't you care for a glass of champagne to go along with your sponge cake?" Lisette asked.

The footman Diego stepped forward, presenting her with a chilled bottle of French champagne. Charity glanced at the untouched dessert in front of her before shaking her head in reply.

Her father asked, "What's the matter with you?"

"A bit of a headache," she replied truthfully.

"Too much showering her old granny with forgiveness, if ye ask me." A satisfied smirk settled on the old woman's face. Maisie leaned to pat her great-granddaughter's hand. "Thank ye, darlin', for doing it. I love ye, ye know."

"I love you, too," Charity whispered, suddenly wondering why she had held back her feelings for so long. This was her family, after all. Her *family!* "I love all of you."

Papa put down his fork. "Does that include me?"

"Why, of course. I love you most dearly, Papa."

Her mother and great-grandmother murmured in joy.

Quietly, her father addressed her. "I love you, too, Charity, my daughter."

"Oh, Papa."

She looked into his eyes. Tenderness and honesty and fatherly concern were there. She knew her papa would stand beside her through thick and thin. Everyone had rallied around her, as she had once been certain they would not.

Charity McLoughlin had waited her entire lifetime for this moment.

A lump in her throat, her eyes glistening, she whispered, "I am sorry for the pain I've caused you and Mutti. And the rest of the family. You have my word that I'll do my best to settle my past wrongs. I yearn to make you proud of me. And I shall always—always!—work to earn your trust in the future."

"Diego! Pour more champagne." Papa beamed. "I've been waiting a long time to hear my baby say these things!"

Her head cleared as Charity reveled in her father's approval. Had it been such a long time since she had expressed her feelings? Good gracious! She couldn't remember the last time she had said anything of a loving nature to her papa.

You expected love, when you never gave it!

Rising from the table, she walked to where her father sat at the head of it. With no hesitation she hugged his wide shoulders. "Oh, Papa," she whispered as his familiar scent filled her nostrils, "I always think of you like this, smelling of bay rum and the sun. I'd forgotten how good it feels to hug you."

"Then give your papa a kiss." His forefinger tapped his lips. "Right here. Don't miss your mark—or I'll dust your bottom!"

To a round of laughter from her mother and great-grandmother, Charity hit the bull's-eye.

"Sit right here beside me," said Gil as he motioned for a chair to be pulled up. "And let's make like the McLoughlins."

"Wonderful idea, Papa."

Never had Charity felt so close to her kin. Never.

The family fell to reminiscing about days gone by, with recollections of friends far and wide, old family lore, and silly tales of Gil's boyhood in Inverness and Maisie's unsuccessful attempts to keep him from searching for the monster in the Loch Ness.

When the last dish was cleared away, Lisette asked, "Is anyone interested in a game of bridge?"

Papa groaned. Bridge-playing wasn't one of his favorite pastimes. Since they couldn't play a threesome, Lisette made another suggestion that met with almost unanimous approval. "Let's turn in early, so we'll all be rested up and ready for Margaret's arrival."

The McLoughlins gradually removed themselves from the dining room, but Charity wasn't ready for bed. She was too exhilarated over the events of the evening, her *real* reunion with Papa and Mutti and Maisie.

And Margaret would be home tomorrow!

Charity changed into a simple blouse and trousers, and walked to the stable. Thunder Cloud would enjoy a good grooming, and Charity would welcome the opportunity to get her mind off her thoughts. Opening the stall door, she gave the gray mare a loving stroke on its forelock.

Charity had chosen the horse while in Spain, visiting Olga and Leonardo—the Court and Countess of Granda—at their holiday cottage in the coastal village of Marbella. Oh, what a delight the adventure had been, riding the gray beauty—Thunder Cloud's mane and Charity's hair whipping in the salty wind—and dodging the quicksand that hid in the shores of the Mediterranean!

Spain.

Europe.

The Wild West show.

Hawk. *Hawk!*

Darn.

Could nothing keep Charity's mind off him?

She took up a currycomb and gently attacked the snorting Thunder Cloud's coat. "Where is he? Doesn't he know I am frantic to see him?"

Lifting her majestic head, Thunder Cloud looked at her mistress and stamped its front foot.

"Don't be so haughty, missy." Charity gave a love-pat to the mare's rump. "If you had a man like Hawk, you'd miss him, too."

It was then that the subject of her declarations stepped out of the shadows.

Charity dropped the currycomb.

To hide her embarrassment at being caught talking to a horse, as well as her joy at Hawk's return, Charity flipped her head nonchalantly. After all, the rat had been listening to her, for heaven's sake, and he had been gone *way* too long.

Don't even look at him, she ordered herself.

But immediately, her eyes were filled with Hawk.

A Stetson pulled low on his bronzed brow, he held a cigarette in his mouth. When he doffed the hat and tossed it atop a nearby hook, her casual stance abandoned her. Lantern light played over his closely cropped Indian-black hair, shooting highlights of blue through it, and her fingers itched to smooth those satin strands. For beginners.

Squinting past a curl of smoke, he asked in a low voice, "Do much talking with horses?"

"Do much lurking in stables?" she queried, and

opened the gate to the corridor, stepping out of it to face him fully.

"Just rode in." He ground the glowing end of the cigarette beneath his foot. "Took a catnap. You woke me, yammering to that mare of yours."

Moving as nimbly as any feline, he stepped closer. A stalk of straw clung to the shoulder of his chambray shirt, which Charity brushed away. She got a whiff of man and horse and leather, and it was a combination wholly appealing. So near to him, she noticed a certain weariness to his dark eyes, a certain tenseness to his mouth, and she lifted her fingers to massage away his cares away.

"I apologize for disturbing you." Her palm cupping the smooth blade of his jaw, she gloried in the warmth of his skin. Or was it the heat of her own? "It's good to see you, Hawk," she whispered.

She fully expected his lips to lower to hers, but those expectations were not met. He simply patted the back of her hand before taking two steps in retreat. What was wrong? *Your memory's grown short, ninny.*

"Hawk . . . I know you're put out about that business in Sheriff Untermann's office. I want you to know, I realize I overstepped my bounds. It was your place to speak with Judge Jones, and you were handling the situation just fine."

Planting his elbow on the gate leading to Thunder Cloud's stall, he crossed one booted ankle over the other in an attempt to appear collected. "Charity, I don't deny you caught me off-guard, but I've had a couple of weeks to think about it, and I know you're no scurrying church mouse."

She straightened, pleased. But he hadn't finished. *"However.* I will *not* stand for your interference where this case is concerned.Got it? You *will* do whatever I tell you."

She squeaked like a scurrying church mouse, then twitched her nose and made as if she had a couple of long front teeth. "Yes, sir."

Throwing back his head, Hawk laughed. "Now, honey, don't work too hard on it. I like you just the way you are. In matters that *don't* pertain to the courts, anyway."

Oh, this was a grand evening!

Boldly, seductively, Charity took a gander at his riding attire, drawing mental pictures of what lay beneath. "My bed is so big and empty. It's been lonesome, having you away."

"I've been lonesome, too."

"Then let's do something about it."

"Bad idea."

She stared up at the frown further emphasizing the weariness in his face. "Why not?" Before giving him a chance to answer, she came to a conclusion. "Something went wrong in San Antonio, didn't it?"

"No problems from that end. Your court date is set for December 15."

"I must write the Narramores and tell them," she said, thinking aloud. She cocked her head. "There was no mention of putting me in jail there, in the meantime?"

"There was. Judge Peterson demanded bail."

"Bail? Oh, goodness. Whatever did you do?"

"Stood good for it."

Good gravy. Not only did she owe him for professional services, she would have to come up with bond money as well. "How much was it?"

"Ten thousand."

"Dollars?"

"They weren't interested in beads and feathers."

"Good Lord. Where am I ever going to get that sort of money? Wherever did *you* get it?"

He shrugged. "By use of my letter of credit from Robber Baron's Bank, Baltimore."

"There's no Robber Baron's Bank in Baltimore."

"That's what I call the reputable establishment of Planters & Merchants."

She had heard of that financial institution; it catered to the wealthiest of the wealthy. She recalled Maisie saying something about Hawk inheriting money from a Maryland relative, and he'd mentioned something about having security of purse, but she'd had no idea that he was *that* well-off."You got the money from Papa."

"You're accusing me of lying?"

"Hawk, darn it, let's don't get in a sparring match. Please explain yourself."

With no more passion than if he were speaking about the weather, he replied, "My mother's grandfather owned a railroad on the eastern seaboard and a half-dozen coal mines in West Virginia. I fell heir to them after Laurann's mother died."

"Dear me."

"I'm surprised your parents never told you."

"Hawk, it's in exceptionally bad taste to gossip about the wealth of others." Maisie, of course, would have no compunction about such a thing, but Maisie was a special case. "Goodness, I'm amazed. My Indian warrior turns out not only to be an attorney but also a railroad tycoon and a mining magnate."

"Wrong. I sold out. Railroads have been one of the white man's tools to overpower the great tribes of this country. As for coal mines, they exploit the poor working man. I wanted no part of either."

"Your thinking seems quite liberal."

"I have my opinions as to right and wrong. And I fight for right as I see it. Such as the cause of Charity McLoughlin." He brushed a loose strand of her hair over her shoulder. "If you don't mind, I think we should go with propriety on this issue. I'd rather we didn't discuss my bank accounts."

That was fine with Charity. She was greatly concerned with how she would ever come up with *ten thousand dollars* to repay him. And an even greater concern . . . Why was he being so standoffish?

"Hawk, we have been apart for two whole weeks. Don't I even get a kiss hello?"

Chapter Thirty

Eyes liquid with desire and anticipation met his gaze. But Hawk had his misgivings, big misgivings, not to mention the three little words that he had yet to hear from Charity. She hadn't so much as whispered them since that night in Uvalde.

And taking his physical needs into consideration, he knew that if he kissed her, there would be no stopping there. She continued to close the distance between them. He swallowed hard, hoping to marshal his wits, and gazed at the whole of his beloved angel.

Her waist-length hair, wavy as the waters of the Atlantic, thick and dark as richest sable, billowed past her shoulders. She wore britches and a shirt, yet the manly attire did nothing to diminish her femininity. Her breasts, large and proud, strained at the soft cotton's buttons. The flare of her hips . . . ah, but they were enticing.

No one, not even from a distance, would mistake her for a man. Or even a boy. She was all woman. Rounded, feminine, tall. Jesus, Lord of the paleface, Hawk wanted her kisses.

How would he be able to turn her lips swollen and cherry-red with desire from the insistence of his lips? His groin throbbed. His heart ached for her touch, for her surrender. For his Charity, his ivory angel. The past weeks had been all too lonely.

"What about a kiss?" she asked, her voice sultry.

"Not tonight."

"Why not?" Disbelief and uncertainty flashed in her blue gaze. "You said you aren't still mad at me. You said nothing went wrong in San Antonio. And you can be certain I'm not interested in your wealth."

In answer to her question, Hawk said, "None of that is what's troubling me."

"Don't you . . . Don't you want me?"

"I want you more than I want the air that I breathe or the sun at dawn or the stars at night. I love you, Charity McLoughlin. And that's why I'm going to keep my hands off you."

"I don't understand."

"We're alone in this stable. And a kiss would lead to lovemaking."

"I should hope so!"

"And what will we do if you get in the family way?" Squinting at the ceiling, he raked his fingers across his scalp. "Sam Washburn met me in San Antonio. I asked if you could've gotten with child while you were unclean, and he said it was doubtful. Women aren't fertile then."

"You talked with that *toad* about our intimacies? And what do you mean, calling me unclean? Of all the nerve. Is nothing sacred between us? I've never been unclean in all my life—save for when I was out there in the wilderness thanks to you! I ought to take a crop to you."

"Cut the indignant act," he demanded. "You and I have business to discuss."

For a moment he thought she might actually go for the riding crop, so furious was she, so clenched were her fists. At last, in a self-consciously controlled voice, she responded, "By all means, let's get to it."

He strode to a bench that ran along the stable's interior, motioned for her to follow and to sit, and he settled on the hard seat. *The last time the two of us occupied a bench . . .* Refusing to reflect on Uvalde, refusing to meet the eyes that rained blue-hot fire, he reached into his pocket for a smoke.

"It's dangerous, smoking in here," she said. "There's enough fire between us to set this place ablaze. Or is there?"

"Charity, don't. Not now." Hawk poked the cigarette back into his breast pocket. "Let's go over your case one more time." On the horseback ride to the Four Aces, they had discussed it, over and again, but Hawk had to be certain he hadn't missed anything. "You thought you were bringing Cuban cigars into Texas from Mexico. A crate of them. And you're certain that no one was still alive, besides Rufino Saldino, also known as Señor Grande, knew you were in the dark about the money?"

"He was the only one I had contact with, until I reached Shafter. And Ian knew, of course, after he caught me burying the cash."

"Did you tell anyone else that Grande had offered you employment?"

"Only Maria Sara. She's the one who introduced me to him. He ran Pappagallo's for Adriano, you see."

"Did you wonder why he didn't bring the 'cigars' across the border himself? Or why he didn't get one of his girls to do it?"

"Hawk, I was hungry. And my rent was due. He offered me work. I wasn't going to look a gift horse in the mouth."

"Understandable." He doubted her reasoning would hold up in a court of law. Hawk planted his palm on one thigh.

"We'll subpoena Maria Sara to testify on your behalf."

"But what about Ian? You know he's ruthless. And the Blyer name means a heck of a lot in south Texas."

Actually, Hawk would have liked to have finished what Gil McLoughlin had started in Texas's capitol building. "I'll drill him about his motives for wanting to see you hang. Paint him as a man thwarted in romance, out for blood in the aftermath of rejection. And Sheriff Tom Ellis has agreed to testify about Blyer's confusing statements in Uvalde."

Hawk went on. "Besides, the McLoughlin name carries more weight than Blyer's. We must play it to the hilt. Don't fight me on this, Charity."

"I won't. You see, I've made peace with my family."

Hawk studied her face. She smiled. A lovely, serene smile. "I'm waiting to hear the details," he said.

"There aren't a lot of them. Tonight, well, tonight Papa and I buried the hatchet. I think we'll be okay from here on out."

Hawk took her hand in his. "I am pleased, sweetheart. We need all the help we can get." *It will make the hell you face in San Antonio easier.*

"What next?" she asked.

"I've hired some investigators to go to Shafter and Laredo. I'll be joining them in Laredo later this month."

"I don't want you to go."

"Charity, we have no choice in the matter. I've got to be prepared for the trial. Well prepared."

"I suppose I understand."

"Don't be petulant. I won't be gone long. And I want you to meet me in San Antonio by the first of December." She asked him why he wanted her there so early. "I want people there to see you. You've got to show the good citizenry of San Antonio that you are a McLoughlin beyond reproach."

"If you insist. My uncle Adolf lives there. I guess I could stay with him."

"Not acceptable. I've checked Adolf Keller out, and he's a drunk unworthy of your association. You'll reside at the Menger Hotel. I've already made arrangements. We need to find you a proper chaperone, though. What do you think about calling on the Old One?"

"Forget it. I love her. We're on speaking terms. And she'd be eager to help. But I don't want her interfering in my life."

Neither did Hawk, now that he thought about it. "What about your mother?"

"I'd rather have Maria Sara."

"Since we're calling her as a witness, it's best she not be thought of as your close companion."

"There's Margaret. My sister might be willing to look out for me."

"Charity, she's away at school."

"She'll be here tomorrow. And if I know Margaret, she'll be eager to help me."

Margaret McLoughlin was fit to be tied.

After being pulled from her advanced studies on European history—right in the middle of semester—her sister wanted her to prolong her stay and spend no telling how long in San Antonio, playing nursemaid.

"I won't do it." Though she had been known to falter under her sister's pressure, Margaret was adamant. This time. "I came home only because our father demanded it. I've got to think about my studies. I must return to school. As soon as possible."

Charity's face fell.

They were standing in Margaret's bedroom.

Charity huddled against the four-poster, as if she were some discarded waif waiting for a crumb to drop from a passerby. Margaret kept unpacking her steamer trunk for what she anticipated as a short visit.

"Maggie," said Charity, "I need your help."

Maggie. Her sister called her by that diminutive only in times of greatest desperation, and it was all Margaret could do to keep her resolve. "I wish you wouldn't do this to me. You know I have a hard time saying no to you. But please realize, I may lose a whole semester of school if I accompany you."

"You have the rest of your life for school."

"You'd say that, since you never cared for it. You don't understand that my studies keep me going."

"And learning about the past will make your future bright?"

"Correct." Margaret poured a cup of tea from a pot that a servant had left a few minutes earlier. "I don't understand why you need *me*. I've been told you have a dear friend living here. Maria Sara, isn't it? By the way, where is she?"

"I haven't seen her since yesterday. She and Cousin Karl have . . . It seems they have made a match. At least that's what her note said. She's staying with him."

"Rather in bad taste, wouldn't you say, staying with a man who is not one's husband?"

"Don't ask me to pass judgment on others."

Margaret watched dots of pink form on her sister's cheekbones. *Hmm.* Charity must be living in a glass house; that would explain why she wouldn't throw stones. Fierce Hawk of the Osage must have done more than agree to be her attorney. Margaret was on pins and needles to ask about him. She would. Shortly.

"Why don't you ask Maria Sara to act as your companion in San Antonio?"

"Hawk intends to call her as a witness. And he doesn't think we should present ourselves as great friends, lest the prosecutor get ideas that she would lie for me."

"That makes sense." Margaret eased into an overstuffed chair and eyed Charity over the rim of the teacup. "Too bad your Hawk was in town when I arrived. I can't wait to get a look at him." She took a sip and watched pride light her sister's eyes. "Imagine, the young brave from the Territory showed up at last. I never dreamed it would actually happen."

"He is a dream come true."

"Tell me, Triplet, are wedding bells in the offing?"

"No."

"I'm sorry to hear that. I've always thought a special man would be your ticket to happiness. And I know you. From the sound of your voice, from the look in your eyes, I know your Hawk is that special man."

"Oh, Margaret, you've always been so bright."

That was what everyone said. Sometimes Margaret McLoughlin wished she were anything *but* bright. At times life would be more pleasant, would that she could bask in the bliss of ignorance.

If she hadn't been so smart, she wouldn't have discovered that Professor Frederick von Nimzhausen was out to steal the meat of her dissertation and sell it to Academic Press in New York. If she was a silly twit, she would still be reveling in his glib praise. *If I don't put a stop to his treachery, a bank draft will be resting in his breastplate.*

"Hawk says he loves me," Charity was saying. "But I can't—I refuse to tell him the same. I did once, but I'm scared. As much as I trust him—as much as I want to trust him, anyway—he conspired against me. And I can't forget it."

"If you can't forget, then simply forgive."

"Forgive?"

"That's what I said," Margaret replied, sounding very like their father. "If you love the man and he loves you, forgive the past. You won't be sorry for it. Just forgive him and be done with it."

"Why didn't I think of that?" Charity's face brightened. "Oh, Margaret, you've always been so smart! What in the world would I ever do without you?"

Margaret wondered the same. "You might want to go and find your Hawk. And get on with the forgiving."

Straightening her back as well as her hair, Charity replied, "Yes. You're absolutely right." She stood. "But, sister, first things first. Will you go with me to San Antonio?"

Although she had spent most of her life being aggravated with Crazy Charity, there was a bond between them that couldn't be denied. No one, except for that simpleton Olga, could infuriate Margaret as Charity could. Yet she couldn't turn her back on her. Her arguments had been for naught. Margaret accepted that they had been futile from the beginning.

Enjoy your money and your stolen acclaim. Frederick.

"You win. I'll go with you to San Antonio."

Charity charged from the bed, threw her arms around her, and laughed with glee. "I knew you would, I knew you would. I knew I could count on you, my precious sister!"

Chapter Thirty-one

She burned to get on with the forgiving.

Right after Margaret had agreed to accompany her to San Antonio, Charity went searching for Hawk. Surely he'd returned from town by now! He wasn't in the house. Firestorm's stall in the stable? Empty. Frustrated, Charity set up camp in the solarium to await Hawk's return. Midnight came and went. When the new day dawned, he had still not returned.

Once she had finished her breakfast, Charity wandered restlessly out into the rose garden in the rear of the house. The gardener Manuel, a sombrero shading his weathered and amiable features, pruned branches from the fading bushes. Charity asked him to turn over his clippers and then shooed him away.

Chopping at this dead limb and at that dead limb, and dodging the leaves that fell from the ornamental plum tree that shaded the area in summertime, she tried to likewise snip off her thoughts of Hawk. Impossible. Charity had never been so confident of the future, what with the family having fallen in behind her, but the foundations of her confidence were crumbling under her feet.

Suppose Hawk had changed his mind about defending her? Suppose he just didn't want her anymore? Suppose he never returned?

Oh, for heaven's sake. What was the matter with her? Hawk was not the kind of man to run out on a commitment. *Says who? Didn't he run out on his Osage people?*

He would not run out on her. He had twice declared his love. His reason for keeping his distance from her probably rested on his concerns over starting a child. Charity acknowledged that his was sensible reasoning. Yet, strangely, crazily, she took a fancy to the idea of having his baby grow in her womb.

"You've lost your mind," she mumbled under her breath.

If only the trial was behind her.

From the corner of her eye, she spied Graciella leading young Jaime into the rose garden. "The boy, he wants to play outside, señorita."

Setting the clippers aside, Charity opened her arms to the child. "Hello, munchkin. Do you have a kiss for Tía Charity?"

Nodding vigorously, he planted a wet one on her lips. "*Donde* Mamacita?"

Charity's eyes shot to Graciella, who lifted her palms in uncertainty. Keeping her voice light, she told Jaime, "Your mama has much to do today."

Manuel rounded the house. "Señorita, I peek the pumpkins thees morning. Meebe the boy, he would like to help Manuel?"

Squealing with joy, Jaime scampered to the elderly gardener, and the two of them headed for the pumpkin patch. Charity was of a mind to go along on the expedition, but changed her mind. She intended to find out what was keeping a mother from her son.

Graciella, fingering one of the braids that lay over her shoulders, stepped forward. "Señorita Charity, it is not my place to say anything. But I cannot help myself. Señorita Maria Sara . . . she should not stay away so long from her baby."

Although these were Charity's sentiments exactly, she wouldn't speak against her friend. She was even more set on seeking Maria Sara out, though, since she didn't want gossip to spread in her absence.

"Maria Sara has business in town," Charity lied to the servant girl. "It's taken longer than expected, that's all."

"Sí, señorita."

Graciella walked into the house. Charity brushed her hands and sleeves with determination. What had been keeping her friend?

Just then, her hat at a jaunty angle, Maisie McLoughlin marched toward her. The oldest of the living McLoughlins stood tall and lean; ten feet separated the two women. "Have ye run the lad off?"

There was no doubting who she meant.

"Hawk will be back. Soon." Charity, using her fingers, snipped at a dead rose leaf.

"Ye ought t' be getting the lad's ring on yer finger."

Charity tossed another dead leaf to the ground. "Doggone it, Maiz. Would you give it up? I'm fighting for my life right now. I don't need to be thinking about a husband and keeping him happy!"

Or about growing Hawk's child.

Maisie, remarkably spry for all her complaints of late, marched ahead to halt her button shoes just short of her great-granddaughter. "I need to tell ye something."

Dread flooded through Charity. "What?"

"I sent the lad on purpose to Laredo. And it dinna have nothing t' do with anything but matchmaking. I like that lad. I think he would make ye a fine husband." A timid look so uncharacteristic of Maisie McLoughlin crossed her aged features. "Do ye know why I think the lad is right for ye, my darlin'?"

Charity chuckled, relieved. "I have no idea," she replied "I almost hate to find out."

"That Fierce Hawk may be able t' suffer yer tongue, but he's got more t' him than that. He reminds me of my own sweetheart. My Sandy. Alexander McLoughlin may not of lived t' an old age, but he was a giant of a man."

Since she had known her great-grandmother as a widow only, Charity had never been able to picture Maisie as a wife. *She was young once, and in love.* "It must have been difficult, losing your man."

"Not a day goes by that I doona think of him."

Tears welled in the old woman's eyes, much to Charity's surprise. Maisie never cried! *Neither do I. Are we, as Karl charged, much alike?* Not such a terrible thing. Maisie had character that had not diminished over the space of ninety years. And wouldn't if she lived to be as old as Methuselah.

Charity wiped away the tears now streaming down the ancient face. Pulling the shivering Maisie closer into her embrace, Charity whispered, "I wish I could have known him."

"Ye will someday. When we all meet in heaven." A tentative smile lit her face. "I'll be seeing him soon. I am old. So old. Surely God willna be needing me here in his earthly domain too much longer."

"Don't talk like that. I can't stand the thought of losing you," Charity said in all honesty.

"No one lives forever, darlin'. And my work is near-on finished here. Once I see you married and settled, then I can go t' me grave in peace."

"I've no plans for marriage."

"Ye should, lass. Ye and Fierce Hawk . . . Will ye make yer old granny happy? Will ye marry the lad afore something happens t' me, and I'm put in me grave a troubled woman?"

Here we go again. If and when Hawk broached the subject of marriage once more, Charity would have to be certain Maisie had nothing to do with it. "Don't put me on the spot. Please don't."

"Is there something wrong with the lad?" Uncertainty replaced cunning in Maisie's expression. "He isna some sort of pervert, is he?"

Suddenly Charity knew exactly how to deal with her meddlesome great-grandmother. She plucked a drifting plum leaf from the air. Feigning nervousness, she crumbled the leaf, then turned to walk to a garden chair. Seated, she chewed her lip in exaggeration. She heaved her shoulders and chest up and down, as if to get control of herself.

Maisie advanced to her chair. "There *is* something wrong with the lad."

"Well, I didn't want to say anything." It was all Charity could do not to grin. "It is personal, you know. And highly inflammatory against his character . . ."

"Get on with it."

"Well . . . he has the nastiest habits when we're alone. He picks his nose and breaks wind."

Maisie sighed in relief. "The lad isna perverted! Most men do that, oncest they are sure of a woman."

Uh, oh. "Papa never does such things!"

"I dinna say every man."

Drat. Charity covered her eyes with her hands. "There's more . . ."

"Tarnation!" Her hand sweeping to her face, Maisie knocked her hat aslant. "What else child?"

Not being schooled in perversions, Charity was unsure how to proceed. Yet she recalled something Maria Sara had said one night in Laredo, when they had drowned their troubles in tequila. Maria

Sara had mentioned a whore in Nuevo Laredo who enjoyed having two men at once. While Charity liked teasing Maisie, she wouldn't smite Hawk's character by placing him in such a compromising scenario.

"Maiz, it's too awful to tell. Please don't make me."

"I willna be left hanging by tether hooks. Speak up, lass."

Was there anything—*anything!*—that Olga had mentioned? Wringing her hands, Charity searched her mind. Futilely. Then suddenly she thought of something. One time, while she had been on a roundup with the cowboys, she had overheard them teasing each other. "You see, Maiz, it's like this. Hawk's male equipment is awfully tiny."

Parking her knuckles on her lack of hips, Maisie leaned forward. "Ye must think I am blind in one eye and canna see outta the other."

"Excuse me?"

"I ought t' take a strap t' yer ankles, Charity McLoughlin, for lying." A gnarled finger poked at Charity's nose as Maisie made herself clear. "All a woman has t' do is look at the crotch of his britches t' tell ye're lying."

"What were you doing gawking at his private parts?"

"I may be ninety, but I ain't dead!"

Charity threw back her head and laughed. Trying to regain control over the situation, she pulled herself together and pointed out, "Watch what you say and do, Maiz. Or Sandy will turn over in his grave."

Not to be outdone, Maisie replied, "My Sandy will be needing the exercise."

There was no prevailing over Maisie McLoughlin. Thus, Charity gave up. At least she allowed her great-grandmother to think so. Once Maisie had bounced into the house, Charity took the opposite direction.

She saddled Thunder Cloud and made for the Keller ranch. She had to know what was keeping Maria Sara from her son.

"Karl and I are going to be married."

"I'm delighted, Maria Sara."

Giving a prayer of thanks to the Lady of Guadalupe that she had washed away the face paint and put on respectable clothing before Charity's arrival, Maria Sara opened the front door even wider and gestured for her friend to enter.

She closed the door as Charity swept into the room and scanned it.

Her own eyes searched for any signs of the past day's—and night's—sexual activities, and Maria Sara found none. How humiliating it would be if Charity discovered that she and Karl were ravenous for each other.

Karl's carnal appetites met and exceeded her own, and what a lovely thought it was, that they would have the rest of their lives to slake them. It wasn't love she felt, but she knew she would never get enough of his purple-headed prize. All the men in her past—the extremely ugly or disfigured men who had been willing to pay a fortune for her favors—had been dissatisfying lovers, unworthy to be considered in the same breath as Karlito. Ianito had fire, but his soul was the devil's.

A voice in the back of her mind assailed her. What about El Aguila?

But Rafael Delgado had never offered her the respectability and security of marriage. El Aguila—a man of danger and mystery and inborn talents as a lover—didn't have to offer anything beyond himself; women swooned at his feet. It had taken a whole bottle of tequila to interest him in so much as one night of sex with Maria Sara. It had taken another to cajole him into a threesome.

Moist between the legs from her thoughts of Karlito and El Aguila, she couldn't help but wonder—not for the first time today—what Charity's Indian looked like naked. She found Hawk wildly attractive, for in his fierce mystery he resembled El Aguila of Chihuahua.

She wondered what it would be like to have both the Indian and Karlito at once. Such would hurt Charity, she knew. *You could be careful and not rouse her suspicions.*

Yet the thought of Karl bedding another woman roused Maria Sara to jealous fury. She would kill any *puta* who even thought about touching Karlito's oversized testicles.

Evil thoughts have you. It was as if Sister Estrella of the convent school were shaking a finger at her in castigation. *I cannot help myself. Ianito turned me into a whore,* she replied to her vision from the past. For the hundredth time Maria Sara Montaña made a silent vow: Ian Blyer would pay for everything he had done to her.

She calmed herself and eyed Charity, who was staring at her with big, beautiful questioning eyes.

"I'm sorry, but your cousin isn't here at the moment," she explained. "Karl's foreman called him away."

"Actually, I'm here to see you."

"I am pleased, *amiga.* I would like to ask you to stand up for me in the wedding."

"I will be honored to do it."

In the center of the room, Charity stopped and turned to face her friend. There was a peculiar mien to that familiar face, Maria Sara noticed. *I wonder what is troubling her.*

"The wedding will be a week from this Saturday. Here at Karl's home. Already we have spoken with the peace justice." Maria Sara smiled. Taunting the nun of her visions, she wondered once more what Fierce Hawk looked like unclothed and if he would be interested in a ménage à trois. "I am so very, very hopeful for the future."

The peculiar look vanished from Charity's face, and was replaced by one of pure delight. She bent at the waist to hug Maria Sara. "Best wishes to you both."

"Thank you."

Charity stepped back. "What plans do you have for Jaime?"

Maria Sara shrugged. "I am sure Graciella will be happy to look after him until the honeymoon is over."

Charity's smile instantly disappeared. "Maria Sara, Graciella Garcia is not your servant. She has her hands full taking care of the McLoughlin family. You would do well to put your son's welfare—"

Irked, Maria Sara clenched her teeth. "You owe me, Charity McLoughlin. I helped you when you were trying to leave Laredo."

Charity refused to quail. "You're right. I do owe you—money. But this isn't a matter of money. This is a matter of a mother's responsibility for her child. Jaime asks for you. What are we to tell him?"

"Tell him that I will come for him when it pleases me."

"Don't you miss him? Maria Sara, what do you have against your precious baby?"

Actually, she hadn't given much thought to Jaime, save for the time Karlito brought up the subject. Her *alemán* lover and future husband had suggested they fetch the boy, but Maria Sara had reminded him of the sacrifice in privacy they would have to make.

But Maria Sara knew she must make certain that nothing happened that might jeopardize the security of her upcoming marriage.

"I do miss *mi hijo*." The lie passed her lips with the ease of flowing honey. "But you must understand, Charity. I am in love and I want to be with my Karlito every moment of the day. Cooking and cleaning for him. And getting to know him. Please do not think that anything improper has taken place between us, though. I am staying in his guest room, of course. Your shy cousin is a gentleman."

"Right."

"You have your Fierce Hawk. Surely you can understand."

"Yes, I understand what it is, wanting to be with the man one loves."

Maria Sara searched her friend's features. Was all not well with the lovers? Perhaps the threesome would be easier to arrange than Maria Sara had thought. Tonight, she would ask Karl what he thought of the idea. Even if he was not interested, he would delight in talking about it.

Get Charity out of the house so that you can be ready for Karlito. To placate her friend, she said, "Be assured, *amiga.* I will collect Jaime as soon as the honeymoon is over."

"Good enough." A tentative smile brightened Charity's expression. "Do you need help planning the wedding?"

"No. Everything is under control."

Of this Maria Sara was confident.

Chapter Thirty-two

There was a threat of rain in the air that Friday afternoon.

Twelve days had gone by since Hawk had left to make what he thought would be a quick trip to the telegraph office in Fredericksburg. He returned to the Four Aces dusty and tired, his heart dull with pain. He needed to find Charity. Never had he needed her so much.

He found her in the south pasture, riding bareback on a black cutting horse. He started to call out to her, but changed his mind. Settling himself down on the ground, he rested his back against an oak trunk. It felt good just to look at her. He had been so occupied with his grief the past few days . . .

Her hair was pulled back into a ponytail that swung from side to side; she wore denim britches and a cotton shirt. Her feet were shod in boots. Leaning over the horse's neck, she lifted her feet behind her, pointing them toward the graying sky.

Then, fluidly, she dropped the reins to grab the mount's neck, twirled her body, and swung her legs beneath his underbelly. All the while the horse raced onward. Hawk heard her exclaim in glee. As easily as if she were stepping onto a curb, she contorted to the horse's back again. Like an acrobat, she planted her palms on wide shoulders and levered to stand on her head.

Stand on her head! While riding into the wind, as if a war party were on her tail!

"You do know the bareback tricks," Hawk whispered, his lips curving into a grin when she angled down to seat the mount once more. "You ought to have your Wild West show."

He brought himself to his feet, and strode into the clearing. She saw him and her face lit up. Waving, she pulled the black steed to a halt and dismounted. Her neck was beaded with perspiration, wet tendrils of hair curling against her forehead.

"Long time no see," she called, walking toward him.

"Too long."

His eyes caught on the wet material clinging to her shirt. She wore no camisole. Her proud breasts were clearly outlined. The sight of them, the sight of her, elevated Hawk's need for her.

'harity gulped, tearing her eyes from Hawk. "Plowrong needs cooling off. So do I. I'm going to walk him down to the stock tank. Go with us, Hawk?"

"Be glad to."

A couple of minutes later, and without conversation between them, they arrived at the manmade pond. She led the horse to the water's edge; he drank. Throwing back his long-maned head, he blew water from his nostrils into the air.

"He's pleased with himself," Charity commented.

"As well he should be. The two of you put on quite a show."

"Did you enjoy watching us?"

"I enjoyed watching you."

A soft rain began to fall.

Hawk drank in the freshness of the air. He wanted to bask in raindrops . . . and to bask in Charity's presence.

Her eyes held questions. She would know what had kept him away for so long.

"I'm going to take a dip," she said. "Want to join me?"

"I do."

She tied Plowrong to a tree, then stripped off her clothes. Hawk grew hard, watching her. Absently, he plucked at his own clothes. Her rear end swaying, she darted knee-deep into the water. Hawk remained ashore, his attention captured by the sweet dimples of her behind.

"The water is wonderful." Raindrops wetting her long, long hair, she bent and splashed water on her face, then faced him. "I am not unclean."

"I will never think of you as unclean again."

She smiled at his answer. But Hawk stood still. If he made love to her now, they might both regret it later. If a child were conceived.

Life mocked him with its cruelties. Once upon a time his life had seemed simple. The Indian boy would grow up to take a McLoughlin girl as his wife, they would make papooses, and he would teach those little ones the ways of his people. Reality had taken a different course. He loved a woman in jeopardy of her life, a woman who lusted after him, but didn't love him.

And Hawk had begun to doubt himself, thanks to the past few days. He wasn't an Indian. He wasn't a white man. He was nothing more than a quarter-breed lost in both worlds.

The rain shower stopped, but rain continued to fall in his heart.

He needed Charity. All these days of being without her found him weak of will. He couldn't stay on the bank forever. One way or another, he had to plunge into life.

Not being able to contain himself any longer, Hawk charged into the water, into its bracing chill. He dove for her. Capturing her knees, he brought her down. She went willingly, and her arms wound around his waist. The naked feel of her, warm within these cool waters, drove him wild. His elbow bracing them both, he held her closely and gazed into her eyes of turquoise. He spat water to the side, then said, "Put your legs around me."

She wrapped her arms around his neck. Her legs fitted to his waist. He felt the tangling of their pubic hairs when he rocked his pelvis forward. The water's buoyancy made it seem as if they were flying on a magic carpet. Turning her to where his back lay against the mossy floor of the pond, he thrust upward, entering her.

It was as if he had found the heavens.

A small laugh bubbled from her throat as she flipped her hair over one shoulder.

He gazed up at her. "Why did you laugh?"

"I was thinking of a lie I told Maiz."

Shaking his head, Hawk wondered if he would ever understand this woman. He pushed deeper into her.

"Hawk, there's something I want to tell you. I—"

"No talking. Not this time."

His lips slanted up to hers, his tongue sliding into her sweet mouth. Her womanly place tightened around him, and he let go with his desires. Surging and surging, he gave and took. It might have been minutes, it might have been hours, the span of their lovemaking. Hawk knew not. All he knew was that she was what he needed, what he had always needed.

His nerves afire with the tingling that assaulted his lower spine and all his lower reaches, he bent his neck to capture an erect wet nipple between his lips. Tugging on it, he heard her moan of delight. And he felt the tremor that shook her. Knowing his own climax was imminent, he pulled out, his seed washing away in the swirling waters.

"Why . . . why did you do that?" Charity asked.

He tightened his arms around her. "So we'll have nothing to regret. Later."

"Are you ready to tell me where you've been?"

Charity asked as Hawk combed his fingers through her hair.

He didn't reply.

Orange ribbons of dusk slashed across the western horizon. The lovers lay on the bank, their arms and legs twined; Charity's head nestled against Hawk's shoulder. Darn it, why wasn't he answering her? If he kept his own counsel, how could she tell him that she not only loved him but also had forgiven him that nasty business with Maisie? "I'm waiting for an answer."

Lifting himself up on an elbow, Hawk studied her cutting horse. "What were you doing riding a stallion? They aren't good mounts for women."

"Plowrong doesn't seem to mind. And he's the best mount in the stable for trick-riding."

"What happened to Thunder Cloud?"

"She's not for tricks. Plowrong fits the bill," Charity replied impatiently. "Hawk, I won't let you—"

"Why is he called Plowrong?"

"He's not the sort for a plow. Margaret and I came up with the name a couple of years back, sort of as a play on words. A plowright makes plows. The opposite of right is wrong. Get it?"

"Not entirely." Hawk chuckled. "How is your sister?"

"She's fine. And she's agreed to accompany me to San Antonio."

"Good. Anything else of importance been going on that I should know about?"

"There's a wedding tomorrow. My cousin and Maria Sara. Will you attend?"

"Am I on the guest list?"

"Of course."

"Then I'll be there." He shivered. "It's chilly. And night is falling. Let's get dressed."

Charity would have rather lain in his arms till morning light, but now that their lovemaking was over, she realized the air did hold a chill. They dressed. She sat back on the ground, signaling him that their discussion wasn't over.

Hawk eased down. They sat face to face, their knees touching. "I'm glad it stopped raining," he said. "Else we'd be drenched."

Enough chatter is enough chatter!

"Hawk, I won't have you dodging the subject of where you've been."

Hawk sighed. He swept his hand across his face before replying. "I went to the Territory."

Aggravated that he'd been gone so long without so much as a note to tell her he was all right, Charity commented, "Awfully quick trip, if you ask me."

"I took the train as far as Dallas. Caught it again on the return."

It was on the tip of her tongue to point out that trains did have their uses, but she changed her tune. "Didn't you tell me you weren't going back to your reservation?"

Pain etched Hawk's face. "Charity, I went into Fredericksburg and sent a telegram to the agent's office on the reservation. I got a swift reply. Earlier that morning . . ."

"What? What happened?"

"My father died."

Dear God in heaven. How awful Hawk must feel! The very thought of losing her own father sent chills down her spine. She instantly regretted the tone she had taken with him. She touched his face tenderly. "I am so, so sorry for your loss."

"Thank you." He kissed the center of her palm. "I had to go back to the territory and comfort my mother and sister. I apologize that I didn't send word to you."

"Under the circumstances, I understand." Charity reached to hug his chilled body. "Is there anything I can say or do to help you?"

"Try to understand me. That's what I need."

"I want that most dearly."

Night fell as Hawk spoke about how much he wished that he could have made peace with Iron Eagle before it was too late. "Thankfully, my mother and I have mended fences."

Later, he admitted how much it had hurt him, the Osage people calling him away from Washington on the heels of the land rush. "They're letting the Great White Fathers run over them," he said.

It troubled Charity, his turning away from his people. She had done the same with her family. She realized just how lucky she was that a reconciliation had been thrust upon her.

"There's something I want to tell you." She

placed her hand atop his knee. "Thank you for making me face my father and the rest of my family. You made me face myself."

He covered her hand with his own. "I was confident you'd feel this way, eventually."

She tried to picture the Osage reservation and Hawk's reunion with his tribe. "You mentioned your family but said nothing about how others of your people received you."

"Several resent that I have left them."

"They want you back?"

"Some of them."

"And you have no regrets?" she asked.

"I have many regrets," he agonized. "For years I worked for the common good. It's impossible to forget all that I strived for."

Caught between two cultures, he was a man tortured—Charity saw that clearly. He might think that he could thrive in the white man's world, but she knew otherwise.

"Don't you see, Hawk? You're as guilty as I was. You deny yourself if you deny your heritage. If you don't go back to your people, you'll be forever running from yourself."

The black of the cloudy night prevented her from gauging his expression, but she knew he was frowning; she could feel it.

"Hawk, the Osage need you. As an attorney, as an advocate. Don't quit on them." He spoke not a word. She pushed on. "Austin doesn't need you. Your people do. Go back to the Indian Territory and fight for what is right."

"Can't do it. Won't do it. Your trial begins in a month."

"Once it's over, there's nothing to stop you."

"Nothing?"

"Nothing."

Hawk jackknifed to his feet and loomed above her. "Plowrong looks as if he could use a nice big bucket of oats. Let's get him back to the stable."

"He's not starving. I am. To continue this discussion."

She said these words, yet she wondered if she shouldn't have. Perhaps it would be better not to push him, what with all he had recently gone through. People shouldn't make decisions while grieving that they would be bound to live with later.

Chapter Thirty-three

"He's not starving. I am. To continue this discussion."

In the dark of the clouded night, with the after-rain freshness of the air filling his nostrils, Hawk stared down at Charity as she said these words. He wanted to leave. He wanted to stay. He wanted her love.

Yet she had said there was nothing to keep him here.

He walked to the pond and cast his gaze upon the argent waters. "Charity, have you ever stopped to think that we might have a future together, you and me?"

"Yes. How could I not?" Standing, she narrowed the distance between them. Her palms settled on his chest, and it was all he could do not to cover her hands with his own. Suddenly clouds moved away from the half moon and lit up her features. "I . . . I love you."

Her words vanquished his grief over his father,

vanquished his uncertainty about where the road of life would take him. He wrapped his arms around her, burying his face into her sweet-smelling hair. The strength of their love flowed between them. Hawk moved his lips to her parted ones. Their kiss was tender, loving. "Thank you for telling me," he murmured against her ear. "And I'm thankful you didn't say it in the heat of passion. Like you did before."

"I do reserve the right to say it . . . anytime." She tightened her arms around his neck, her breasts thrusting against him. "That's only fair."

"Right. That's fair enough." He laughed. "You never do let me have the last word, do you?"

"Another right I reserve." On her tiptoes, she rubbed her nose against his. "And I reserve the right to keep after you. Hawk, my darling, please think about what I said. About returning to your people."

"If I go it will be because honor dictates it."

He dropped his arms from Charity and, turning from her, walked along the bank. She didn't protest.

He thought about what she had said. He didn't like the idea of going home. He didn't belong there, though he felt a responsibility to the tribe. While on the reservation, he'd been uncomfortable with the old ways, had been eager to return to Charity and her world. *You've changed. Hawk. You weren't born in the wrong century. You want the white man's ways for your own.*

Yet the new chief as well as the council of elders had begged . . . What did he owe them? He felt honor-bound to return.

If he did, Hawk wanted Charity at his side. And how could this be? His recent visit to the reservation had convinced him that she wasn't meant for an Indian woman's life.

While his mother had adapted, despite the circumstance of her maternal family's wealth, Hawk feared Charity would never be able to adjust to the dismal, harsh surroundings. Nor was she the type to accept the social strictures of a town like Austin. She was wild and impetuous, perfect for the excitement of the thing she dreamed of, a Wild West show.

But what if they had made a child from their mating in the pond? Sam Washburn had cautioned that pulling out was no guarantee there'd be no babe. Jesus, Lord of the paleface, even if she wasn't with child . . . The Old One was wise. By his taking Charity's virginity, he owed her the respectability of marriage.

Give her the benefit of the doubt. She might be happy on the reservation.

He swung around and found her within a few feet of him. Hugging her arms, she watched him closely. He breathed in deeply. "Charity, would you go with me to the Territory?"

The night grew quiet, the slight breeze ruffling the leaves the only sound. Then a coyote howled in the distance; the plaintive cry echoed in Hawk's ears. His heartbeat thundered through his chest as he waited, waited, waited for Charity to reply.

He took two steps. He saw uncertainty in her eyes. Eventually, he was the one to speak. "You'll be free of the smuggling charges. Soon. And you've got to consider the future. You stained your reputation, running after Blyer. But I took your virginity. If you ever intend to marry anyone, it had better be me. Or you'll have a helluva lot of explaining to do on your wedding night."

"Did you speak with Maiz before you came out here?"

"What does she have to do with it?"

"Possibly nothing. Possibly everything. Tell me, and tell me honestly. How much of this is my great-grandmother's doing?"

He wouldn't lie. "The Old One never backs down."

Charity retreated, stopping a half-dozen feet away. "So, like your sense of honor to the Osage, your sense of responsibility binds you to me."

Irritated, he replied stiffly, "I think that is uncalled for. Yes, the Old One is waging a campaign. And, yes, it is a factor in my asking for your hand, but I recall we have exchanged vows of love, so a simple yes or no will be sufficient."

"No!"

Anger and disappointment knifed through Hawk. *Wah'KonTah!* He had tried to be honorable and she'd tossed his honor back in his face. Never would he ask again. "Goodnight, then," he said, and left her to her thoughts.

* * *

Why did you tell him you love him?

Charity rushed into the house. While her heart went out to Hawk over the loss of his father, and while she sympathized with the dilemma he faced about the Osage, she couldn't help but be furious with him now. Why did everything have to go wrong on the heels of her admissions of love?

Why couldn't Hawk have lied and said honor had nothing to do with it?

Margaret must have heard her footfalls in the hallway, for she was entering the bedroom even before Charity had thrown herself across her bed.

"I know your Hawk is back," said Margaret. "Apparently parting was not such sweet sorrow. Or at least the reunion wasn't."

Charity buried her head in the pillow, and mumbled into it, "Go away."

She heard a familiar tinkling, and opened one eye to see her sister pouring cognac into a snifter. "Put that stuff away. It reminds me of Hawk." And of the night he had made love to her in this very room. "Go away."

Sitting on the edge of the bed, Margaret tapped her shoulder. "Drink. I won't take no for an answer."

Turning over, Charity punched up the pillows behind her head. "Give it here." She took a sip. "Ugh. I've never liked cognac. I don't know why Mutti insists that it be left in everyone's bedroom."

"To soothe tensions at the end of the day. Have another sip, Triplet."

Doing as she was told, Charity realized there

was method to her mother's madness. She did feel somewhat better. She glanced at Margaret. "I'm at my wit's end."

"You and Hawk had a difference of opinion?"

"He asked me to marry him. I said no." Charity took another sip. "He didn't ask in the name of love. He wanted to make an honest woman out of me!"

Margaret tossed back her head and laughed. "Your Hawk is to be pitied. He hasn't learned that no one *makes* my willful sister do anything."

She tossed a pillow. "Margaret McLoughlin, don't you dare laugh at me!"

Her expression schooled, Margaret gave an apology. "What is wrong with making you an honest woman?" she asked.

"Because Maiz put him up to it. Because he's worried that people will think me a tart. Can you imagine him worrying about my *purity* when the whole world knows I'm going on trial for my life! I want him to ask for my hand in the name of love. I want him to love me so much that he can think of nothing else except dragging me by the hair of my head to the altar!"

"Well, Triplet, it could be some sort of cultural thing. I've heard the noble savage puts great stock in the approval of his elders—I really must study more about the native society. Dang, there's never enough time to learn everything."

"Maggie!"

"All right, all right. Anyway, I don't see anything wrong with his wanting to impart to you respectability." Margaret squinted in deliberation. "If you ask me, which you have, I think you're too much the romantic and Hawk's too much the practical sort when it comes to love."

"Possibly."

"No, definitely. Your romance has progressed too fast. You should ease back from it. Don't be so eager to yield to his charms. Then you'll find out who he is more interested in pleasing. Maisie or himself. Or *you.*"

Charity decided to give this advice some thought.

Saturday night arrived.

On horseback, and far from prying eyes, Ian Blyer watched as wedding guests flocked to the ranch of Karl Keller. Tonight that betraying *puta* Maria Sara would finally get a ring on her finger. Ian didn't like the idea at all, though jealousy played no part in his disfavor.

"Damn the bitch," he ranted under his breath. "I should have known she would take refuge with the McLoughlins."

But Ian had never imagined that she would have been able to insinuate herself so deeply into the McLoughlin family that one of their own would take her to wife. Undoubtedly she'd be eager to ingratiate herself with her new kinfolk, and would hop on the witness stand to contradict everything Ian Blyer had to say.

The whore could ruin his plans. Ruin them!

His fingers clamped the reins tightly. "I must get rid of her."

He had until the trial's beginning to come up with a clever strategy for murder.

Chapter Thirty-four

Saturday night, with a gathering of family and friends in attendance for the torchlit outdoor nuptials, Maria Sara Montaña became Mrs. Karl Keller. From the back of the crowd, Hawk watched the ceremony with an ache in his heart, especially as he gazed at the blue-frocked maid of honor.

Did the vows get to her, as they had him? No! Not once did she look his way, before or during the ceremony. And she'd avoided him all day, even on the trip to the Keller ranch in her father's gilded coach.

Once the couple had kissed, sealing their exchange of vows, the guests rushed forward to congratulate the newlyweds. Hawk—in no frame of mind for a celebration, especially one of marriage—lagged back to watch Charity give hugs to the bride and groom, then glide over to the Old One, who wore a flowered hat and a dress decorated with a string of pearls; her bustle gave a suggestion of curves to the ancient bones.

Hawk moved closer and heard Charity compliment the Old One's attire. While he didn't care for seeing Charity's hair piled atop her head and hidden by a wide-brimmed hat, she had never looked more lovely to him, what with her light-blue, cameo-enhanced silk dress that nipped at her waist, emphasizing all that Mother Nature had bestowed upon her.

He wondered if Charity would become thin in her old age. What made him think he would ever know how she'd look in her dotage? He accepted a shot of whiskey from the Four Aces's top hand, the old-timer Ed Roland.

He watched Charity turn to a group of locals; Hawk noticed they were curt and eager to snub his outlaw angel. Momentarily her shoulders slumped, then she hoisted her chin and acted as if nothing had happened. But Hawk knew she was hurting. Despite his anger, he felt the urge to rush her from censure, rush her into the cocoon of his protection.

Don't do it, he warned himself. She needed to get used to rebuke; it would toughen her hide for San Antonio.

He watched a cadre of women as they uncovered dish after dish of food. A quartet of cowboy musicians filled the air with music, mostly of the German and hoedown variety. From a fire-pit that belched the delicious scent of barbecued beef, a couple of men unearthed a cow's head that had been wrapped in wet burlap and buried earlier that day around a nest of coals.

"Eeeee-hah!" a male guest, brandishing a carving knife, shouted to announce the barbecue. Quite a number of people thrust plates at the carver. Hawk wasn't hungry in the least.

He grieved for his father. He grieved for his inability to choose between the white man's world and the Osage. He grieved for an uncertain future where he and Charity were concerned.

The musicians struck up a polka, and the newlyweds strolled through the crowd of well-wishers. Taking a long draft of mediocre bourbon, Hawk watched the bride. There was something about Maria Sara that needled him. He couldn't put his finger on it, but if he had to make a guess, he would say it had something to do with the slyness that flashed in her eyes from time to time.

He would be glad to get to Laredo, where he could search for other witnesses to testify on Charity's behalf.

Charity.

Once more his eyes found her. Flanked by her parents and Margaret, she stood by the cake table and sipped a cup of punch. Her sister, who wore a brown frock and had her hair yanked into an unbecoming bun at the nape of her neck, chatted with her. Although a stranger might not be able to tell them apart, had they been clothed in matching clothes, Hawk would never mistake the two.

Margaret was all business.

Charity was all fire.

" 'Tis a pithy one, our Margaret." Maisie had found Hawk. "A lass of purpose and determination. In anything she sets out t' do."

"I've met women like her," Hawk replied. He'd *known* a few of them, too. He took another drink. Once a man cracked through that type, they were tornadoes in bed. Provided the man did as he was told, he thought with a chuckle.

"Aye, Margaret is dedicated t' the path of success, wherever it leads."

Hawk took another swig of bourbon; the Old One continued.

" 'Twasn't so long ago that ye might have gone t' Laredo t' abduct Margaret, had she been the triplet there."

Where would the path have taken them? he wondered. Right to the Osage reservation. In no time Margaret would be orchestrating the activities of the tribe, finding new ways to grind corn. No doubt she'd turn the place on end, demanding a seat in the council of elders.

"Are ye thinking aboot what woulda happened, had ye met Margaret first?"

"Excuse me," Hawk said in exasperation.

He did an about-face, finished off the glass, then accepted a refill, this one from a flask offered by a boisterous cowboy whose white shirt contrasted with the black of his string tie and suspenders. Hawk chose not to make conversation. He continued to study the two sisters.

Margaret had character all right, but she was no match for Charity in looks. His hellcat angel was the only choice for him, even though his spirit lay shattered at the bottom of the chasm separating their hearts. If only he could touch her. If only . . .

Feeling the effects of the liquor, he went to her, weaving a bit. Torchlight reflected in the blue of her eyes when she nodded at him. Nodded! Nothing else. While her sister and their parents tried to make pleasant conversation, Hawk had to restrain himself from picking Charity up and carrying her away to a place where no chasm existed.

Forget it. You took a big chance at the pond. Don't ask for bad medicine.

The quartet struck up a waltz; Gil led Lisette onto the makeshift dance floor, and Margaret said to Hawk, "I noticed you haven't danced tonight."

Though he wanted to grab Charity into his arms, he'd never mastered the waltz and wouldn't make a fool of himself by trying. He took another swallow. "I don't dance."

"I'll teach you." Margaret smiled. "If you're interested."

"Some other time."

He scowled at Charity, who did not offer lessons. She pirouetted to her father's foreman and tapped his shoulder. "Ed Roland, I believe this is your dance, sir."

Hawk wheeled around, almost stumbling as he charged away.

"Not the romantic sort, are you?" he heard Margaret say as he blended into the crowd.

The Old One found him again. This time she

touched on her favorite subject: "ye doing right by the lass."

"I've asked for her hand. She said no. Now quit on it."

Starting to make an about-face, Maisie said, "I will be seeing what Charity has t' say about that."

He caught her skinny arm. "Don't. For God's sake, don't."

"Ye call in the name of the Almighty? Are ye a Godfearing man, Fierce Hawk of the Osage?"

"Yes. I believe in God as well as *Wah'Kon-Tah*. A man needs all the help he can get in this life."

"Well, ye could be worse."

Again she set a course, and again Hawk stopped her. "Leave Charity alone about marrying me. We'll work out our problems on our own."

"I have yer word on that?" At his nod of agreement, the Old One said, "I'll be trusting ye t' do so."

Instead of marching toward Charity and her dancing partner, she filed over to her grandson and his wife, who had stopped waltzing to speak with the bride and groom.

Hawk had it to the gills with celebrating. Unfortunately, he had ridden over with the McLoughlins; he was trapped. The best he could do was find a somewhat deserted area, and wait out the party.

Hawk maneuvered himself to a dark corner near the ranch house. From there he watched a cowboy slap the bridegroom on the back. Karl Keller turned to listen to what the man had to say. The bride glanced at her new husband, then at Hawk. Picking up a bottle of champagne from one of the cloth-covered tables, and with a glass in her other hand, she started toward him.

Now probably wasn't the time to discuss her testimony, but what else was there to do? So Hawk didn't shy away when she came abreast of him.

Looking up at him with sultry eyes, she held the bottle aloft. "Your glass needs refilling." Her lashes fell demurely. "May I do the honors?"

Hawk shrugged. Champagne tinkled into his glass. Maria Sara, her line of sight traveling upward once more to settle on Hawk's face, sipped from her own glass. There was something entirely improper about all this, Hawk suspected.

"Are you willing to travel to San Antonio and testify on Charity's behalf?" he asked quickly.

"But of course. She is my dearest friend and we are now cousins by law. I would do anything to help her."

"I hope you mean that."

"Why wouldn't I?"

He drank the sparkling wine. "You tell me."

"I am concerned about one aspect of the proceedings." Maria Sara's hand tightened on the neck of the bottle. "It will not do for my employment at Pappagallo's to come to light. Do I have your assurance that when I testify to introducing Rufino Saldino to my friend, you will not mention my connection to that house of ill-repute?"

"You have my assurance." Hawk would have promised anything at this point. "Is there anything else you can think of to help the case?"

"Señor Hawk, must we discuss such dismal doings? This is my wedding, you know."

Hawk took a backward step; she took a forward one. He took another step, and again she stepped closer. He detected a bitch in heat.

She smiled under the moonlight. "I have been wanting to talk with you."

"About what?"

"You do not look like an Indian. I have seen many in my country. They have diluted Spanish blood. You do not resemble them at all."

"Am I supposed to be complimented?"

"Actually, you and I share a common bond." She refilled his glass anew, and it was obvious that her hand hadn't brushed his by accident. "It is rumored that native blood flows through my veins. Such has to do with an ancestress from the village of Coatlpoala in Mexico."

"How interesting," Hawk commented dryly.

"Coatpoalans—the pagan ones—have been known to be maneaters."

Interest somewhat piqued, Hawk eyed the woman anew. No doubt she was a man-eater. Without regret, she would chew up a man's flesh and spit out the bones. *I wish Charity and I weren't depending on her.*

"Charity looks as if she's lonesome," he said and started to take his leave. He weaved. Definitely, he'd had too much to drink.

Karl Keller called to his wife, and she waved to Hawk before saying, "We must talk again."

Not until absolutely necessary, he wanted to call after Maria Sara Keller.

Chapter Thirty-five

As the bride returned to her husband's side, Hawk thought about Charity. Despite his frustration with her, he couldn't help but wonder what it would hurt to take a stab at making amends.

But he saw that she was dancing with her father, and she looked happy—not at all like she was missing him. Well, if he couldn't assuage what ailed them, he could at least relieve himself. He had had too much alcohol. He retreated to the privacy of a dark wooded area a few hundred feet from the wedding festivities. Legs braced, he unbuttoned his fly. Finished with his nature call, he made to put his appendage back in his trousers.

"You are as I imagined."

He started at the sound of Maria Sara's voice. Suddenly a small hand clamped around his rod. It was a sobering experience.

"Ah, *hermoso, muy magnifico,*" she whispered, her champagne-scented breath hot against his skin. "How big does it get, Señor Hawk?"

Sickened, yet somehow not surprised at her advance, he lied, "Not any bigger."

"Ah, but you are wrong. I feel it growing."

"Maria Sara"—forced patience—"we've all been drinking. Don't do something you'll regret in the morning."

"There will be no regrets."

Under his breath Hawk muttered a base oath. He tried to yank away from her clutch, yet winced in pain from his effort. "Get away," he demanded. "Stop!"

Insistent, she did not let go. Her fingers fondled him, and his emotionless sex continued to grow from the external stimulus. Hawk had the urge to push her away—to swell for anyone save for Charity was both unthinkable and repulsive. But if he pushed, he knew the man-eater would tear him from the root.

"My, my, look how much bigger you have gotten." She licked her lips while her fingers clung to him. "I should like the feel of you pounding me into the grass."

"Get away," he ordered, agonized. He gritted teeth. "Now!"

"Do you not wish to give me a wedding present?" She squeezed him where it hurt the most.

"I—I b-bought you a silver b-bowl."

"We will use it to wash with. After. Do you not find me beautiful, Señor Hawk?"

"Not particularly." He pried at her fingers to no avail. "Will you have Charity knowing her friend is untrue?"

An evil laugh, which made Hawk's skin crawl,

filled the air. "I am not worried," she said. "What Charity does not know will not hurt her. She is busy with her parents. And are you not man enough for the both of us?"

Hawk had had one romp of the sort favored by Romans of the empire days. Never again. "What exactly are you after, Maria Sara? A quick roll in the grass before you consummate your marriage?"

"I am interested in three together. I am quite skilled at it. You will enjoy my arts, as did Grande and El Aguila."

"Suppose your husband were to find out about this?" Hawk asked in desperation.

"Ah, but he is here already."

She released her hold, and Hawk stuffed himself back into the safety of his britches. Quickly. At that moment Karl Keller stepped from behind a tree.

"My wife wants you to join us in a celebration of our marriage."

Maria Sara looped her arm around her bridegroom's crooked elbow. "Won't you stay behind when the guests leave, Señor Hawk?"

Hawk gaped at the newlyweds. They were mad, deranged! "Not interested."

Keller scrunched his shoulders, obviously angry. "You do not think my Maria Sara is comely?"

"The two of you make me sick."

Keller tightened his fist, and no doubt he meant to plow it into Hawk's face, but a male shout from the distance stopped him. "Line up, boys! We're fixing to have a dollar dance. Where's the bride? We'd better be finding the new Mrs. Keller!"

"You're being summoned," said Hawk.

"Ah. I am." Crooking her fingers, each in turn, she motioned to Keller. "Come, *mi novio*. We do not need him. Señor Hawk is much too conventional for our tastes."

Hawk shook his head in disgust. Get to Laredo, promptly, he told himself. *Promptly.* And find someone close to the smuggling who could testify on Charity's behalf. But whom?

Latching onto any clue, he recalled the names Maria Sara had dropped in her talk of a threesome. Grande. Was she referring to Señor Grande, also known as Rufino Saldino? What about El Aguila? "The Eagle," Hawk translated under his breath. Who was the Eagle?

Hawk packed the next morning. Before taking his leave, he cornered Charity in the library. "Watch your back with Maria Sara. She is not your friend."

"What makes you say that?"

Hawk hesitated before answering. "She made more than a pass at me last night."

"Oh, Hawk, you were drunk. And upset over your father. Not to mention being upset with me." Charity waved a hand in dismissal. "It was her wedding reception, for goodness' sake! I'm sure you're making a mountain out of a mole hill."

He thought to ask if she'd like to take a look at

the bruises on his private parts, but decided against it. Besides, if she truly loved him, she would have at least had the courtesy to be jealous.

"You're right. I'm making too much of it." He grabbed his hat. "I'll see you in San Antonio, Charity."

"You're leaving without kissing me goodbye?"

"Yes." Halting short of the doorway, he asked over his shoulder, "Ever hear of someone called the Eagle?"

"No."

Mid-afternoon of December first—a chilly day—Charity and Margaret checked into a suite of rooms at San Antonio's most elegant hotel, the Menger.

From their balcony, Charity caught sight of the historic Alamo grounds, where Colonel Travis and the Mexican general Santa Anna had faced off in the fight for Texas independence, in 1836. The San Antonio River, really no more than a wide creek with a grassy bank, meandered to the south. A cobbled and busy street separated the river from the hotel.

But Charity didn't ponder the surroundings too long. She kept thinking about Hawk. And his warning that Maria Sara wasn't her friend. She shivered despite the cashmere cape that draped her shoulders.

There was truth to his words.

Ever since the wedding, Maria Sara had been

anything but friendly, and hadn't bothered to collect young Jaime after the honeymoon. Two days previous, Gil McLoughlin and Charity had taken the youngster to his mother. In a curt manner Maria Sara had shoved the weeping boy into the house and had slammed the door in Gil and Charity's faces.

That evening, in an effort to make peace with her friend, Charity had returned to Karl and Maria Sara's home. Blocking the entrance, Karl's bride wore a flimsy night frock that she clutched at her throat. "Charity, we are not receiving guests."

Embarrassed, Charity had replied, "My apologies for interrupting you. I'll visit another time."

"Wait until I call on you."

Jaime, now crying from the interior, tried to scramble around his mother. "Shartee! Want Shartee! Mean Mamacita—"

"Munchkin . . ." Charity bent and widened her arms.

Maria Sara hustled him back into the house. "Go to Karlito. *Rapido!*"

Charity stood her ground. "Why are you so cruel to your baby?"

"He is an awful child! As is the father, as is the child. I don't expect you to understand, but I do demand you to stop meddling!"

Once more the door got slammed in Charity's face with such force that the sound echoed in her head.

Such hostility toward Jaime as well as herself

tore her heart, then and now.

The bitter gust of wind that slapped at her face was nothing compared to the fears that plagued her. *Please don't let little Jaime suffer.*

What had happened to the woman who had been her friend in Laredo? More importantly, how was Karl being treated? Well, her cousin was a grown man more than capable of standing up for his own rights. Furthermore, he loved children and would be protective of his stepson.

Feeling a bit assuaged, she wondered if Maria Sara would make good on her promise to testify.

And had Hawk discovered the mysterious Eagle's identity?

Hawk.

I miss you. I love you.

Hawk . . . Obviously he cared not for her standoffish tactics. Which, she decided, had been Margaret's worst piece of advice in all their twenty years. If he were to want marriage for love's sake, she must not give him call for grievance.

What could she do to undo the damage already done? It seemed as if years rather than weeks had passed since he left. Thankfully, he was expected soon in San Antonio.

"Charity? Charity! You'll catch your death out on that balcony, and we don't need any more invalids in the family. Come inside and put your things away."

Heeding her sister, Charity entered Margaret's sleeping room."I wonder how Maiz is doing," she said.

Margaret shook out a dress, ran a coat hanger beneath its shoulders, and turned to hang the garment in an armoire of French design. "Let's pray she's doing better."

Charity unfastened her cape and folded it across a chair back. "If my prayers can heal her broken leg, then she'll be on her feet in no time."

Striding across the room, Margaret jerked open the velvet draperies that hung at the tall windows. Light spilled into the room that was decorated in dark, flocked wallpaper, and it reflected the impatience in her big blue eyes. "Maisie took a needless risk, if you ask me, getting on a horse after she hurt herself last New Year's. She ought to realize that she is old as the Seven Wonders."

Indignant, Charity propped the backs of her hands on her hips. She had the urge to say that Maisie McLoughlin was the eighth wonder of the world, but held her tongue. "That's not very nice."

"It wasn't *nice,* her being selfish enough to jeopardize her health to prove how invincible she is. Her accident is keeping our parents from being here with you. When you need them the most."

Charity stared at her sister. Margaret had always been testy, but since her return from university, she had been positively difficult.

"I'm surprised Father was able to make it in to town to reinstate your trust fund, what with Maisie acting as if—"

"Sister, what's the matter with you?"

"Nothing!"

Drawing near her, Charity put her hand on her

triplet's arm. "It's me, isn't it? You're angry because you had to leave school in mid-semester. I'm sorry, Sis. Really I am. But I want you to know how much I appreciate your sacrifice."

Irritably, Margaret shook off her touch and stomped over to her steamer trunk to pluck at the contents. "For Pete's sake, must you turn everything to yourself? Believe it or not, you are not the only person in the world with troubles."

When they were children, such remarks would have gotten Margaret a sock in the eye. But Charity as a woman read much into her sister's tone. "You've had trouble with a man."

Holding a pair of pantaloons, Margaret's hand froze in midair. In slow motion, she set them aside. "Yes."

Charity went to her now hunched-over sister, and put her arms around the shaking shoulders. Tears spilled, wetting thick black lashes. Poor Maggie.

"Sis, go back to him. As soon as you can catch a train out of here. Make everything right." *As I intend to do with Hawk, once he gets here.* "Please."

Reddened eyes and nose turned up to her. "No. If I never see Frederick again, it would be too soon."

Frederick? Margaret, gorgeous Margaret, brilliant Margaret was pining for someone named *Frederick?* Well, on second thought, the name did conjure up images of tweeds and pipes and fireside chats. No doubt he was exactly Margaret's cup of tea.

"Um, Sis, what did Frederick do to you?"

"Everything!"

"Oh, dear." Drawing all sorts of conclusions, Charity said, "It's awful what we women do in the name of love." She dug for something, anything. She recalled how she'd felt in Uvalde, and drew her mouth into a frown. "They know our vulnerabilities and play on them, until we are mush in their hands. And we give our purity as if it were no more than a colored ribbon."

Good gravy. Charity had sounded positively Victorian. Well, it was for Margaret's good.

"Are you out of your mind? Frederick is a man of refinement and culture. He did *not* molest me." Hot indignation squared Margaret's shoulders. "He stole my research papers on the Spanish Inquisition and its causes and effects on the voyages of Christopher Columbus, for Pete's sake!"

It was all Charity could do not to laugh. She might have known that any grand passion of Margaret's would be somehow connected to her work.

Margaret wiped her nose with a handkerchief. "Excuse me for being a watering pot. I got upset over *that.*" She pointed to a telegram. "Frederick is going to dedicate his book to me."

"Isn't a book dedication a special thing?"

"Not in this instance!"

Margaret made no sense at all. For once.

A knock on the outer door demanded Charity's attention. "I'll see who it is," she murmured.

A uniformed bellman—blond, hazel-eyed, youthful, freckle-faced—stood in the corridor. "'Afternoon, ma'am." Barely disguising his approval, he took a gander at Charity. "There's a gentleman in the lobby, and he bids the Misses Charity and Margaret McLoughlin come down. A Mister Hawk."

Her first honest smile in weeks burst upon Charity's face. "Tell him I—*we*—will be right there."

"Yes, ma'am." With a crisp salute he tapped his heels together. "If I can be of assistance during your stay at the Menger, all you have to do is ring." Striding jauntily down the hallway, he called over his shoulder, "I'm Ted."

Charity rushed to the mirror, pinched her cheeks, and patted her hair. "Hurry, Margaret. We mustn't keep him waiting."

"I'm not going. You two should greet each other—"

"But Hawk said I shouldn't rouse suspicions by being seen without a chaperone."

"For Pete's sake, you'll be in a public lobby."

Margaret had returned to being logical.

Chapter Thirty-six

Charity stopped at the foot of the Menger's staircase and grasped the bannister, lest she swoon at the sight of David Fierce Hawk. Although there were others in the hotel lobby, she had eyes for no one but him. Spats fastened over his shoes, he stood tall in the middle of the spacious marble room, conversing with a gray-haired man.

Hawk looked like the consummate attorney, clothed in a striped cravat, a white silk shirt, and a charcoal-colored woolen suit of impeccable cut. In a room full of Texas's richest and most powerful men, Hawk's self-confidence overshadowed all but his tall, dark, and commanding good looks.

I have missed you, my darling.

He reached for a silver-tipped cane.

Good heavens.

Had something happened to make him lame, like Maisie? When he tucked the cane under his arm and moved sideways with all agility, Charity gave a gasp of relief. It was only a prop, another of the trappings of gentility. When she had been chained in Sam Washburn's hovel, and again in

Uvalde, she had wondered what Hawk would look like in cravat and spats. Now she knew.

What she had imagined nowhere near lived up to the real thing.

She swept toward him. As she approached, she caught his scent. He wore the same brand of toilet water he'd worn the night they had first made love. In Uvalde. No more did she resent memories of that place. No more.

Remembering to address him formally, she murmured, "Mister Hawk."

Fluidly, he turned and bowed. "Miss McLoughlin, how very nice to see you." His formal mien belied the look of stark desire that flashed in his dark eyes, which pleased her to no end. "Miss Charity McLoughlin, may I present the honorable Osgood Peterson, judge of the district court."

"Miss McLoughlin." Peterson bowed as well.

"His honor will be overseeing your trial," Hawk explained. "By the way, I was under the impression that you had a chaperone here in San Antonio. Where is your good sister?"

Charity couldn't very well tell them that Margaret was crying her eyes out over some stuffed shirt's book dedication. "Margaret is indisposed. A headache, you see."

"How unfortunate," said the judge. Small gray eyes decked by silver spectacles drilled into Charity. "A lady should never be seen in public without a chaperone. And in light of your purpose in visiting our fair city, I would think you'd be especially sensitive to decorum . . ."

Indignation flared within her. "Would you have me drag a sick woman from her bed, your honor? Just for some silly show of propriety? And what should I be afraid of, perchance? That you two natty gentlemen might drag me into the courtyard and ravish me on the spot?"

Hawk rolled his eyes as Osgood Peterson reeled, his manicured fingers flying to his heart and covering most of his cravat and all of his old-fashioned stickpin. Charity knew she'd done it again, even before the judge choked out, "Miss McLoughlin, have you no shame?"

"Bellman," Hawk shouted. "Please be good enough to summon Miss Margaret McLoughlin!"

The amiable Ted shot up the staircase.

And Charity realized it was imperative that she make amends. "Sir, your honor. I was reared on a cattle ranch, and we aren't as proper as you San Antonians." No use pointing out that she was one of a kind on the Four Aces. "I fear that my reckless behavior brought me to the dilemma of the accusation against me in the first place. I—"

"Hers is no admission of guilt," Hawk cut in. "Miss McLoughlin, I believe, is trying to point out that she is capable of erring in judgment. She became a pawn in the devious Adriano Gonzáles's scheme—"

"Please save your opening remarks for the jury, Mr. Hawk."

His eyes closing in momentary supplication, Hawk gave a nod, and Charity continued. "Anyway, as I was going to say, I hope you will excuse my bluntness and lack of polish. I will be more careful in the future."

Hawk shot her a look that said, "Don't make promises you can't keep."

From Judge Peterson's expression she might as well have been addressing the potted palm that grew near the lobby's grand piano, so she took another tack and smiled her most winning smile. "Are you by any chance related to Miss Henrietta Peterson of this fair city? I knew the beauty at—"

Charity started to mention the boarding school where she'd had the misfortune to be paired with the incredibly homely, overly pampered and adored, vicious-tongued Henrietta, but she her cut short her reminiscence. Boarding schools taught proper behavior. Or tried to.

Peterson scrutinized her anew. "Henrietta and I are most certainly related. She is my daughter."

Charity feigned shock. "Your daughter? How is that possible? Why, you couldn't be old enough . . ."

Hawk gestured to her to *cease and desist*.

The judge fairly preened under Charity's praise. She embellished shamelessly, mentioning the "lovely" Mrs. Peterson, who played the harp as if "angels were singing."

"My dear, could I interest you and Mr. Hawk in a cup of tea? The Menger serves an excellent cuppa."

He extended his elbow and Charity placed her hand on the proffered arm. "I'd be delighted. And you, Mr. Hawk? Are you interested?"

Hawk's countenance conveyed interest in strangling her. "Of course. Ah. Here is your sister now."

Dressed as dowdily as a schoolmarm, yet looking lovely despite it, Margaret swept forward, and the quartet retired to the swank holds of the Menger dining room.

"You amaze me."

Alone at last, seated at a table for two in an obscure café in west San Antonio, Charity peered at Hawk and at the open collar of his silk shirt. Gone was his cravat and suit coat. "Somehow I get the impression you damn me with faint praise."

Hawk leaned his chair on its back legs. "Think again. All I've got to say is, you amaze me. You had Peterson wrapped around your little finger."

"Are you angry with me?" she asked, worried. After all, there was that business in Fredericksburg.

The waiter, garbed in a loose white outfit, lit lanterns as she spoke; he then went to the kitchen. A mariachi band tuned their guitars. One other couple sat eating; they occupied the far corner. Letting out a lone howl to announce nighttime, a skinny tan dog guarded the entrance.

Charity waited for Hawk's reply.

At last he righted the chair and leaned forward to chuck her chin with his forefinger. "Who could be angry with success?"

It was on the tip of her tongue to allude to the "who" as being David Fierce Hawk, in Sheriff Untermann's office. *Why do you keep asking for trouble?* "The afternoon was successful. Aren't you pleased that I figured out a way to get shut of Margaret, as well as the judge? If you ask me, I think we're lucky, their finding a common interest in the Catholic kings of Spain. Whoever the Catholic kings are . . . were. It got her an invitation to the Peterson home for a meeting of minds, didn't it?"

"It was clever of you, turning the day's conversation to history. A subject you guessed Peterson was interested in."

"And knew my sister is a scholar of," Charity added for Hawk. "I couldn't help but notice that the judge wore a stickpin fashioned in a replica of the Alamo. Margaret has one. A beau gave it to her during the fiftieth anniversary celebration of Texas independence, in '86. Anyway, I figured the judge had an interest in bygone days."

"Astute observation, Miss McLoughlin." Hawk, shaking his head in wonder, crossed his arms over his chest. "You might make a society hostess yet, since you can so ably assess the strengths and weaknesses of others, and you know how to use them in pairing up like minds."

Yet his complimentary remark seemed to trouble him.

She wanted nothing to trouble him. She wanted to be held in his arms before midnight, and she would do all she could to make that possible.

Unfortunately, the mariachis strolled over to circle their table. The lead singer asked if they were interested in a tune.

Charity had no wish to share Hawk's attention with musicians, but Hawk nevertheless handed over a silver coin.

It seemed as if they sang and strummed forever! But the warbling crescendo finally came, and Charity passed a dollar to the lead singer while whispering, "Go next door. Or some place out of here."

Since they were used to playing for pennies, the men were eager to depart.

Hawk rubbed his chin, then said, "I found out something while I was on the border. It doesn't have anything to do with your case, but I thought you might want to know as a point of interest. You were dead wrong about Judge Noble Jones being a silent partner in that Nuevo Laredo whorehouse. There is an Anglo with power across the Rio Grande, but it isn't Jones."

"Who is it?"

"Don't know. Not yet. I've got some investigators working on it, though." Hawk took a sip from his cup.

"Well, I don't want to think about my legal troubles tonight. Please, no more."

With a constrained smile Hawk agreed. "We've got to talk, though. No later than tomorrow, say a carriage ride at noon. Agreed?"

"Agreed." Her eyes on Hawk, Charity sipped from a cup of creamy Mexican hot chocolate. "I hope *our* evening will be successful . . . on a personal level," she said. "Interested?"

"I'd have to be dead not to be interested. But I told you I wouldn't tempt getting you pregnant."

"You didn't seem to be worried about it that evening in the pond."

"Wrong. I took precaution." His bronzed face paled. "Did it not work?"

"It worked. And it could work again . . ."

"Don't tempt me. I am not without my weaknesses. Such as when you cajoled me into bringing you here. But as for continued intimacies between us, there won't be another time."

Ever? She couldn't stand the thought of *never.* Or of even being away from him another day . . . "You said you'd get me free. Surely the trial won't last long. I don't see why we must deny ourselves."

"I do." He paused. "I'm going back to the territory, once you're free."

While she had urged him to do so, a heavy weight settled in her bosom. Soon he would be leaving her. Forever! But maybe not. Why not make a stab at seeing if there wasn't a bit of the romantic in Hawk? In the past he'd liked her unconventional way.

"Not so long ago you asked me to go with you." Was she insane, asking for trouble? What about Maisie? Would he agree for an elder's sake? Or for nobility's? *Charity, don't be a naysayer.* "Is there a chance you might again extend the invitation?"

"None that I can think of."

The weight in her heart increased.

"Why . . . why not?"

"You'd be miserable on the reservation."

Was Hawk becoming too much a white man for his own good, worrying about how she'd react to life in the territory? A savage would kidnap her away . . . and never look back or worry about a darned thing.

"How do you know I'd hate reservation life? Maybe I would love it. I'd love it anywhere you are." Lacing her fingers in her lap, she studied them rather than look Hawk in the face and chance seeing his refusal. "Especially if I was your wife."

She heard him groan. He pulled her arms from her lap and twined her fingers with his, atop the table. "I never thought I'd hear you say you want to be my wife."

She felt the warmth of his fingers, yet . . . Was she imagining that he drew away in spirit?

"Well?" She swallowed, borrowing nerve from somewhere. "What about it? Or are you waiting for a more formal proposal?" She got to her feet, walked around the table, and dropped to one knee. "David Fierce Hawk, will you marry me?"

A myriad of emotions flashed in his eyes. "I . . . Don't do this."

"It is already done," she replied, her fears rising anew.

Hawk shook his head. "I'm sorry, angel, but I don't think making marriage plans is a good idea. Our worlds are too different."

Pride cried out for her to stand and run. But how could she, when her heart was sending broken shards through every vein in her body? She wouldn't reach the exit before falling apart.

Buck up! Don't let him get the better of you!

Forcing a bright smile, she got to her feet. "Okay. Our worlds are different. You're right. Absolutely right." She coerced her lashes to bat, then laughed. She prayed her tone was light. "But don't ever say, David Fierce Hawk, that I never asked for your hand."

"I'm glad you see the jest in all this."

Ignoring the sarcasm in Hawk's words, Charity tossed a hand upward. "Just call me the court jester."

Chapter Thirty-seven

"She asked *you* to marry *her?* And you said no? Never in my fifty years have I heard anything like it." A bulbous nose took on a redder hue. "Have you got rocks in your head, boy?"

Sam Washburn looked incredulously, expectantly at Hawk. On this, December the second, the two men sat on the balcony of Hawk's second-floor suite of rooms located at the opposite end of the Menger from the McLoughlin quarters. The norther that had turned the air brisk over the past few days had been blown away by warm southern breezes. Making use of the balmy morning, Hawk and Sam shared a pot of coffee, a plate of sourdough biscuits, and Hawk's confidences.

"Hawk, I thought you was plumb daft for the girl."

"Drink your coffee."

They had been speaking candidly, so why was Hawk now reticent about the subject of Charity? Before he could settle his mind on this score, Sam spoke again. "Did it hurt your pride, her sending that money to you a while ago?"

"It made a statement."

A big statement. Not an hour earlier, not long after the banks opened, Ted had delivered a package containing fifteen thousand dollars. The message the young man relayed was, "The court jester says this is in payment for bond as well as services rendered. Wonder why she called herself the court jester?"

Hawk hadn't wanted her money. In fact he'd forgotten about any monies due. And he didn't want to talk about it.

"How's your room, Sam?"

"Why, I'm dancing in high cotton. Never seen nothing so fancy since the last time I was in New Orleans, in '80. My friend, thank you for helping me get past that sniveling desk clerk."

Sam had had some trouble getting registered, since the Menger management had been less than enthusiastic about booking "riffraff," until Hawk had intervened.

Sam dunked a biscuit in his coffee. "I always told you—playing up your white blood does have its privileges."

"Blood had nothing to do with it. Money talks around here."

"Money and a smile that could charm the step-ins off the most dried-up old maid in town, you mean."

Hawk doubted the male desk clerk had been impressed by his smile; not as impressed as he'd been with a few influential names Hawk had tossed around—McLoughlin being the primary one.

"Tell me," Sam implored, "why you said no to your gal."

Hawk, dressed in trousers and a casual shirt, leaned back in the Morris chair, crossed his arms, and tucked his hands under his armpits. "I asked her once to go to the Territory. She said no."

"The answer seems plain enough to me," said the physician. "Don't go to the Territory. And, like she told you, forget that Austin idea, too. Find out what would please your lady, then set your sights her way."

"Once upon a time . . . she had a hankering for a Wild West show, for staging it in Europe."

"How do you feel about it?" Sam chewed a biscuit, the effort raising his two-inches-long beard up and down. Several crumbs clung to the coarse salt-and-pepper hairs.

"The idea has its charms."

"Remember ole Lick Salt outta the Cherokee nation? Back in '81, he and his buddy Man-Who-Hears-Voices tied in with Healy and Bigelow in their medicine show. I understand Lick Salt is looking for a new set-up."

"Interesting." Faces flashed through Hawk's mind. A dozen braves who would be perfect for a Wild West extravaganza. "Wonder how our friend Calm Waters of Fort Smith would feel about touring the continent?"

"That ole satyr?" Sam's belly rolled as he laughed. "Why, he'd never quit running after the ladies long enough to swing a tomahawk for an audience."

Hawk grinned and took a big sip of coffee. "While I was at the Four Aces, I met several cowboys looking for a change."

"An operation like yours and your lady's, why, it'd be needing a sawbones, wouldn't it?"

"You, perhaps, Dr. Washburn?"

Sam blew a stream of air across the back of his curled knuckles, then dashed them across a lapel of the suit coat that had faded from black to shades of shiny dark green. "No one never had no complaints about my doctoring . . ."

"I'll keep that in mind."

"Sounds like your show'll work." Hitching a thumb to the French doors leading into the hotel, Sam added, "Get outta here, boy. Meet up with your lady Charity, and tell her, 'Let's round up our entertainers, sugar pie.' "

"It's not that easy, Sam. The Osage need me. The new chief asked me to go back to Washington. He wants to make certain our interests are watched over."

Sam shook his gray head and scratched his whiskered chin. "I thought you said you didn't wanna take Charity to the reservation. Now you're talking about Washington."

"I'd be dividing my time between both places."

"If the little woman dudn't want the Indian life, leave her in Washington." Sam clicked his tongue. "My friend, since you ain't answering me, I take it you don't cotton to that idea."

"I don't. What's a marriage of separate lives?"

"Well, all I can say is, you need to talk with

your lady about all this. Get ever'thing smack dab on top of the table, like a whole deck of cards." Sam winked. "Seems to me you ain't giving her the credit she's due, seeing how she's a gal daring enough to ask for a feller's hand. I warrant Charity McLoughlin turns out to be a whole bagful of surprises."

Hawk lit a cigarette, took a couple of puffs, and ground out the tip. Sam was right; "bag of surprises" fit Charity like a second skin. As he lifted a piece of tobacco off his bottom lip, Hawk's face split into a grin.

"She is one fine woman," he admitted. "And I've done what many have done. I haven't given her enough credit."

With a knowing look, Sam asked, "Remember that time I said you was a warrior without a war? Seems to me the little lady's given you the battles you been needing, boy."

"You're absolutely right. She is perfect for me." Laughing now, he cuffed the wise Dr. Washburn's shoulder. But he turned solemn, thinking about how his interests weren't the only ones to consider. "Whatever the case, I'm not doing any talking about the future. Not until her trial is over."

"You sure seem confident you can keep her head outta a noose."

"Of that, I've never had any doubt."

But could he? Hawk quit the chair. Time after time during his last visit to the border, he'd run into blank walls. Charity's defense, beyond her own word, hinged on Maria Sara's testimony.

Plus whatever Sheriff Tom Ellis could say to smite Ian Blyer's character.

And the prosecutor, who had filled the courthouse's rafters with his guffaws when Hawk had asked for the charges to be dropped, was lining up witnesses. Texas Rangers and *federales,* and the silver mine owner; all could attest to the crime, but they couldn't necessarily testify to Charity's part in it.

The one person who could send her to the gallows had a believable story. Ian Blyer had found her in possession of the cigar boxes filled with loot. It had been Blyer she had confessed to. He had taken the money from her and had turned it over to the authorities.

Hawk stomped into the suite, calling over his shoulder, "I'm meeting the McLoughlin sisters at noon for a carriage ride. Time to get dressed."

Impasse.

That was the only word that Charity could think of to describe her love affair with Hawk. As the open-air carriage lurched, setting off from Alamo Plaza, she gazed at him. Dressed impeccably, he sat across from her and her sister; he wasn't looking her in the eye. He chatted with Margaret.

So be it.

Charity turned her scrutiny to the busy streets the carriage took on its journey southward. She listened to the clip-clop of horse hooves. She noticed Christmas decorations that wound around lampposts and were prominently displayed in shop windows. But she couldn't keep her mind off Hawk.

He had no intention of exchanging I-do's with her, or even continuing their love affair, for that matter. So why had she bothered making herself as pretty as possible? What was the use of being laced into a corset that constricted her breathing? Her new shoes pinched her toes. Her new baby-blue silk foulard dress, trimmed with ribbon of midnight blue, might as well have been sewn from a flour sack, for all he seemed to care.

If there was anything in her appearance that she could pat herself on the back for, it was that she had pinned her hair atop her head and had half hidden it under a large Gainsborough hat. While dressing, she had chosen the hairstyle and its accompaniment to impress any prospective juror who might see her driving along the maze of San Antonio's streets. But she knew for a fact that Hawk liked her hair brushed free and wild.

Serves you right, drat you, Hawk.

They had reached a less crowded part of the city. From the distance she glimpsed the outline of the Pioneer flour mill as well as the lovely section of new Victorian homes in the King William District; they were owned by well-heeled citizens, primarily of German extraction.

"I think we should call on Uncle Adolf," she said, interrupting a spirited discussion on the demise of the Roman Empire.

"Bad idea. Your folks may have set him up in

swank surroundings, but he does not have the best reputation in town. His drinking is legendary," Hawk replied and Charity wished a bug would fly into his flapping mouth. He added apologetically, "I hope you'll forgive me for passing judgments, Miss Margaret."

"Think nothing of it, sir. He is to be avoid—" She leaned to the left as they approached the Keller home. "Look! That's Antoinette coming out of Uncle's house. And . . . And that's Uncle Adolf right behind her. Triplet, when did they get back together?"

"Speed up, driver," Hawk ordered.

"I didn't know they were reconciled," Charity replied to her sister. "Poor Uncle."

"Duck. For heaven's sake, duck, Triplet. Or they'll see us."

The sisters huddled low in the carriage as it raced by Adolf Keller and his former wife. After they turned the corner, the conveyance nearly tipping on two wheels, Hawk said, "You're foiled. They saw you."

Charity and Margaret, both red-faced, adjusted their *chapeaux*. "Undoubtedly Uncle will be paying us a call," said the more conservatively dressed of the two. "As soon as he finds out where we're staying."

"Don't you imagine he knows already, Miss Margaret? There was an article about your sister in the *Express* this morning."

Still peeved at Hawk, Charity said, "Are we going to sit here and chat about trivialities? I seem to recall you had a purpose in mind. Discussing my case."

"You are certainly testy today," Margaret observed.

Hawk brushed his cravat. "Let's do get down to business. Charity, I can't get something out of my mind. That Eagle fellow. I have reason to believe he exists, and it's a longshot, but I have a suspicion he might serve our case. Is there anything you can remember that might help us?"

The Eagle. El Aguila. An eagle was featured on the Mexican flag, Charity recalled, putting aside her aggravation to concentrate on priorities. " 'Eagle' is a popular word and name in Mexico. It has to do with nationalistic pride. The former president Santa Anna was called after such a puissant bird."

Heavens, I hope I didn't use "puissant" wrong, or Margaret will correct me. What if she did? Charity realized that her sister would mean it in the spirit of help. Margaret always wanted to help her.

Margaret said nothing, and Charity continued. "At least a dozen men in every Mexican village call themselves the Eagle. Halcón," she added, eyeing Hawk, "doesn't enjoy the Eagle's popularity, but a handful of Mexican men are known as the Hawk, too."

"That's very observant of you," Margaret said. "I had no idea you mulled the nature of Latin mankind."

"Your sister is quite perceptive." In salute,

Hawk touched a forefinger to the brim of his hat. "Her cleverness has always amazed and pleased me."

"Indeed." Margaret, who had never cottoned to anyone appearing more clever than she, tightened her full mouth.

Hawk's compliment spreading through every vein in her body, Charity straightened; she smiled at him. He winked. "Go on."

"There is an area in northern Mexico that teems with rattlesnakes. Once, I heard Señor Grande make mention of the place—he does have an unnatural fear of snakes, you'll recall, Hawk. Anyway, Grande knows a man who captures those rattlers. For some God-knows-why reason. I believe his name is Rafael Delgado. Or maybe it's Reuben Delgado, I can't recall for certain."

"Is there a point to all this?" Margaret asked.

"Yes, Sister, there is." *Maybe.* "I'm wondering if the rattlesnakes might lead us to the eagle. The Mexican flag features an eagle with a serpent between its beak. Maybe Rafael—yes, his name *is* Rafael—likes to think of himself as an eagle with a serpent in its mouth!"

"For heaven's sake."

"I'm convinced it's a fair guess," Charity said, pleased with herself. "Hawk, Rafael Delgado lives in the state of Chihuahua. In the foothills below the mountain, near the town of the same name."

"Chihuahua. I'd never get an investigator in to such a rural area and back by the start of your trial. And there are no guarantees that Delgado is our man." Hawk bowed his head in concentration. He recalled Maria Sara's admission. Glancing at Charity at last, he said, "The Eagle knows Grande. I have it on good authority that they are, um, acquainted."

"Rafael Delgado is more than acquainted with Grande. One evening in Laredo Maria Sara told me she'd heard at Pappagallo's that the two men coupled the same woman at the same time. I think she said Senor Delgado was drunk, and—"

Hawk's eyes lit up. "Charity, angel mine, we've found our eagle!"

He lunged across the carriage, shoved his hands around her waist, and gave her a loud, smacking kiss. His hat as well as her Gainsborough went flying to the street. He was being totally improper.

And Charity loved it.

Maybe there was hope for them yet, she thought, and brushed her fingers through his now-tousled hair.

Chapter Thirty-eight

When the trio returned to the Menger, the bellboy dashed Charity's hopes for a speedy powwow with Hawk on the nature of their personal relationship.

Ted sauntered over to Margaret. " 'Afternoon. There is a Mister Ian Blyer asking after you, Miss Charity."

No one bothered to correct young Ted's mistake in identity. Charity's gaze flew to Hawk. He started to take her hand—she knew he wanted to from the look in his eyes—but he stopped for the sake of appearances

Charity shivered. All along she'd known Ian Blyer would arrive in San Antonio. Yet after Laredo, after she and Hawk had scared Ian and Señor Grande away, after Uvalde, she had held on to the hope that he'd had enough—an unrealistic hope, considering the Blyers had been the strongest proponents of her apprehension and arrest for smuggling.

Margaret asked, "Where is Mister Blyer? Is Senator Blyer with him?"

"In his room, Miss Charity. He's alone." Ted clipped a salute and started to turn. "Almost forgot. Your father's in your suite."

Hawk tipped the bellman, then led Charity and her sister upstairs.

"Papa, how is Maiz?"

"She's on the mend. Complaining about everything." A grin spread across McLoughlin's face. "And demanding to come to San Antonio."

"Thank God she's all right."

A smile as wide as the Lone Star State stretched across Charity's expressive face, and for the first time Hawk noticed a strong family resemblance between father and daughter. He didn't dwell on it.

Hawk had heard the concern in Charity's voice, had seen the distress in her eyes, and witnessed the relief that flooded through her now; he loved her all the more for her anxieties being centered on the Old One's welfare rather than on the malignant turn of events instigated by Ian Blyer's arrival.

My crazy, sweet, beloved pussycat. The young woman who had once professed to be through with her family, yet obviously loved them extravagantly. *You did right, Hawk, bringing her back to the fold.*

This was no time for self-congratulations. Hawk said to the sisters as well as their father, "We've got to send someone to Mexico. We must find the Eagle."

"The Eagle?" McLoughlin questioned. "Who is he?"

Hawk took his place beside Charity. "We're not certain he'll be able to help our case. But I suspect he might shed light on the investigation."

Margaret started to enlighten Gil McLoughlin about their speculations, but Charity interrupted her. When she had finished her tale, their father shook his head. The back of one hand bracing an elbow and the whitened knuckles of another propping up his chin, McLoughlin paced the sitting room. "You're sure we're not chasing down a dark alley?"

"I'm sure of nothing," Hawk replied and squeezed Charity's shoulder. *You'd best speak with Maria Sara, see what else she's got to say.* "We must search all alleys."

"Who do you suggest we send?" McLoughlin queried.

"Sam Washburn." Hawk gave a thumbnail sketch of his trusted friend. "If anyone can get back in time for the trial, it's Sam."

"I'm going with him."

"Papa, you can't go charging off to Chihuahua," Charity said.

"Young lady, I am not as old as I look!"

"But what if something happens to you?" Margaret asked. "We can't take that chance."

"You girls are as bad as your mama, clucking over me like a hen with her young." Despite his words, McLoughlin beamed with fatherly pride. "I didn't build an empire by being a coddled chick!

I'm going to Mexico. And that's that."

Hawk chuckled warmly when Charity, love and respect dancing in her eyes, embraced her papa. "Thank you. And take care of yourself."

Within an hour both Gil McLoughlin and Sam Washburn were aboard an El Paso-bound train, the first leg of their trip to Chihuahua. And Hawk had sent a telegram to Fredericksburg, requesting Maria Sara's presence. Posthaste.

The evening her papa and Sam Washburn departed, Charity sat alone in her suite. Margaret was attending a harp recital at Judge Osgood Peterson's home. Hawk—her dear, darling Hawk, who had stolen a few moments to tell her he loved her and that everything would work out for them!—kept a distance for propriety's sake.

Charity worried about her father. Take care of him, she prayed. And she was concerned about Sam Washburn, too. She appreciated the lengths he was going to to help her. Maybe Hawk's toady physician-friend wasn't so bad after all.

She was fortunate, so fortunate to have so many people in her camp. Except for that smuggling business, she had everything on her side. *I've been lucky since the night Hawk kidnapped me.*

A series of knocks on her door announced a visitor. Hawk, she prayed. She was wrong. Her luck had run out.

Ian Blyer flashed his teeth.

She backed away in surprise when he brushed

past her, prancing into the sitting room. Reeling around, he bowed to kiss the back of her hand, but she jerked it away.

"Charity, how well you are looking," he said, tenacious as a bulldog, slimy as an eel. "I have missed you, dearest."

"Get out of my suite."

"Is that any way to speak to your husband?"

"I beg your pardon?"

He lifted a brow; his voice and visage reeking of histrionic indignation. "You don't recall our marriage, dearest? Such a lovely August evening it was in Nuevo Laredo, reciting our vows and promising love everlasting."

"What trick are you up to now?"

"Your freedom." Ian sashayed over to the liquor cabinet and poured himself a tumblerful of Scotch whisky. Sweeping a hand across his blond temple and taking a hearty swig, he smiled his oily smile. "I have the perfect plan to free you."

Charity took sidesteps toward the bell chain. "Do tell," she said and would have rather had an explanation from the henchman himself.

"A husband need not testify against his wife in a court of law. I am willing to recant my deposition . . . provided you are willing to make a few concessions."

"Aren't you forgetting something? We aren't married."

"Aren't we?" He flashed the sort of smile that would have charmed her last spring. "I have at my disposal not only our marriage license but also a witness to the nuptial rites."

"Have you got that witness in your pocket, perchance?" she gibed.

"Figuratively, yes. Rufino Saldino is at my beck and call."

Oh, yes, she thought with a shudder. Señor Grande again. "You should be careful of picking allies," she said with disgust. "He rode with Adriano Gonzáles."

"He did? Rufino? No." Eyes that had enlarged in astonishment now bent in skepticism. "You must be making jest. And can you prove such a claim against my man?"

Rather than give Ian the enjoyment of a negative reply, she asked, "And what about the esteemed state senator from Laredo? I understand he isn't registered here. Is he still in your hip pocket?"

Ian's mouth twisted. "Father does whatever I tell him."

"Doesn't sound much like Campbell Blyer. Then again, he'd like to unseat my papa and take his place in Washington. So I imagine he rather enjoys rubbing McLoughlin noses in the dirt."

"Excellent assessment." Ian advanced one step. "Enough about him. I am waiting for your answer."

She took another sidestep. "Ian, your offer is ever so kind," she said snidely, "but if you recant anything, won't that brand you a liar in the eyes of the law?"

"Surely Judge Peterson will understand, man to

man. I'll explain it away as a honeymoon squabble that tore us apart." He studied the amber liquid in the bottom of the clear tumbler before settling his avaricious gaze on Charity. "Anyway, I do not give a fig how I am seen. As long as I have you."

"You mean my papa's money."

"I do have a tendency to link the two."

"You honestly think my father would accept you into the family? After you've slandered our name?"

"Why depend on His Nibs? Sources tell me your trust fund has been reinstated. I look forward to its benefit."

Thankfully, she didn't need to depend on this piece of backwater scum for her freedom. Hawk would free her! "Rest assured, I want no part of your scheme."

Ian laughed sinisterly. "I shall grant you time to reconsider."

"I've had all the time I need. Now get out!"

Setting the glass aside after sloshing its paltry contents, he stepped toward her. "I made a grievous mistake, playing the gentleman with you. Foolish of me, not fathoming you were ripe for a man. Now . . . I will not leave until I've tasted what you have served the red bastard."

Frightened, she twisted to the right and lunged for the bell chain. Something heavy struck her, knocking her from her feet and the wind from her lungs as she fell to the floor. The heavy object—Ian!—landed atop her.

He covered her mouth with his hand to silence

her scream. "Don't make me get ugly with you."

Ugly? When had he not been ugly in his dealings?

"You have your choice, Charity. You can allow me to announce our marriage. Or you can face a jury. Either way, I will know your supple body." His hand receded. "Which do you choose?"

"The jury."

"Foolish, foolish Charity. You never did possess good sense, did you?"

"She's got a man in her room," Maria Sara said to her husband when they approached Charity's hotel door. "Her Indian lover, no doubt. Should we return later, *querido?*"

"No." Karl stepped up to the entryway. "She must know that we are here to support her."

They were. Back home Maria Sara Keller had been put off by Charity's conduct over Jaime, and it still irked her. But to spite Ian and to pave the way for his fall from grace, Charity must be freed of the charges against her.

Karl pounded on the door. "Cousin, it is I and my wife."

The door burst open. Disheveled, Charity held the knob. "Help me! Ian means to harm me!"

Slicking back his hair, Ian Blyer stepped forward.

"You!" Maria Sara hunched in anger.

"We meet again," said Ian. "And is this your husband?"

Drawing back his fist, Karl Keller plowed it into Ian Blyer's face; the smaller man crumpled onto the floor. "You are through hurting the women I cherish."

After a thorough trouncing that drew the hotel management's presence, as well as that of the several guests, Ian begged for Karl to stop the beating.

His chest heaving, Karl eyed the assembled crowd. "He has learned his lesson."

Charity wasn't so sure. While the night manager cautioned the two men on appropriate behavior in the Menger Hotel, she shook her head in dismay. She feared that nothing would stop Ian. Nothing short of her total capitulation.

She felt Maria Sara's hand at her elbow and heard her friend address the onlookers. "Disburse. Everyone. Everything is under control."

Karl echoed her words, and the crowd receded. Even the management departed after Maria Sara assured the night clerk that there would be no more trouble. Ian, meanwhile, was wiping his bloodied nose with what had been a pristine handkerchief.

"*Amiga,* we should go into your room."

Charity nodded through her daze. In the interior, she heard Karl insist, "You are not coming in here, Herr Blyer!"

"On the contrary. I have something to say that you will want to hear."

Figuring it had to do with his preposterous

scheme, Charity collected herself. "You've said your piece. And you have my answer."

"This has nothing to do with you, dearest. This has to do with Maria Sara."

Warily, she saw him step toward Karl's bride. As usual he was arranging his hair just so. "How is my son?"

"Silencio!" Maria Sara hissed.

"What is going on?" Charity asked slowly.

A diabolic smile spreading on his swollen face, Ian ignored Maria Sara and smirked at Charity. "You didn't know Maria Sara Montana—pardon me, *Mrs. Keller,* is the mother of my son?"

Shocked, Charity pressed the pads of four fingers against her suddenly throbbing forehead. Jaime was Ian's child? Why had Maria Sara kept it a secret? What else had Maria Sara kept a secret?

The tiny *mexicana* clung to her towering husband. "Be gone with you, Herr Blyer, before I finish what I started in the hallway."

Brushing his vest-coat, Ian replied, "I will be leaving. But before I go . . . Charity, dearest, didn't you know that the new Mrs. Keller has been my spy since last May?"

Charity's eyes begged Maria Sara for a denial. But the beautifully coiffed blond head turned away from her. Betrayed, Charity wilted onto a chair. Why—oh, why!—hadn't she seen through her?

I should have. I should have suspected her from the beginning. I should have been wary of her offer of friendship when it came so soon after I found Ian out.

His despicable deed done to perfection, Ian took himself from her presence. Charity wished Maria Sara would do the same. She did not. Her taffeta skirts swaying like a bell, she rushed forward to drop down beside Charity's chair.

"You must hear me out, *amiga.*"

"Not interested." By now both Kellers hovered closely, trying to placate her, but Charity bought none of it. She wanted facts, not lip service. Her gaze fastened to her cousin, she asked, "How much did you know about all this, Karl Keller?"

He blushed. "I am ashamed to admit how much."

Traitors both! "What did you seek to accomplish, Maria Sara, by aligning yourself with Ian?"

On a drop of her chin, she replied, "He blackmailed me into being his pawn. But I have done nothing to help him in a long, long time! You must believe me."

"You ask too much."

Ground out in a guttural pitch so unlike the speaker's usual quiet and melodious tone, a Spanish epithet was spat past clenched teeth. "Ianito. He is the one who is responsible for all our pain. He is the one who should pay for his sins!"

Karl calmed his wife. "Cousin, she means well. Please have pity."

"I need time to think about all this."

"I understand." Karl exhaled. "I have rented a small house close to La Villita. We will be here when you need us."

Hateful though she knew it sounded, Charity asked, "Is *Ian's son* with you?"

"He is *my* son now."

"Are you treating the munchkin well, Karl?" Eyeing first her traitorous cousin, then his devious wife, Charity felt a catch in her chest. "Are you both treating him well? Because if you are not, I will do everything in my power to see that he's taken away from you."

Chapter Thirty-nine

"Querido, Charity wasn't pleased that we left Jaime at the Four Aces."

Karl frowned at his wife as they quit Charity's suite and began to descend the staircase. "She has many things to be unhappy about. And after Herr Blyer accused you of being his spy, I wonder why you worry about your son now. I would think—"

"I am not worried about Jaime." Not missing a step, much less a beat, Maria tittered and waved fluttering fingers. "Your Aunt Lisette is taking good care of him."

"You never worry about Jaime. You are a cruel mother, Maria Sara."

"When we have children, it will be different, *querido."*

Karl gulped down the bad feeling that rose in his gullet. Though he adored his bride, although each day and each night his adoration grew, and while he would do anything to keep her happy, it troubled him, her attitude toward the child of her flesh. No matter the father, she should love her baby.

And with her dearth of affection for Jaime, just how capable was she of loving a husband? Or of being a friend to Charity? Something about Maria Sara didn't ring true.

Before Karl could further ponder the situation, a male voice boomed up the stairway. "Didn't expect you this soon. Only sent the telegram this afternoon." Hawk climbed toward them. "Did you literally fly from Fredericksburg?"

"We left home yesterday," Maria Sara replied. "We know nothing of a telegram."

It bothered Karl, seeing the attorney again. While he enjoyed sharing fantasies with his bride, he hadn't been all that interested in going through with Maria Sara's idea of a threesome. He supposed his traditional upbringing had prevailed.

"I supposed . . . *we* supposed Charity would need us," Maria Sara said.

"My cousin needs *you,*" Karl amended, putting everything in the proper perspective. "She is in her suite. There has been some trouble tonight."

Wordlessly and with fear widening his eyes, Hawk took the stairs two at a time.

"Too bad he was not interested in the threesome," Maria Sara commented in a provocative tone that her husband had come to know well. "He is very energetic."

Shut up about threesomes. At the bottom of the staircase, Karl extended his hand to help her along. Just then he heard a voice from over his shoulder. A familiar female voice calling his name. The familiar scent of lily of the valley drifted to him. A voice and a smell from his past.

He couldn't help but smile.

It was wrong, his reaction.

Maria Sara was his cherished. She carried his name. His thoughts and fantasies and sex-making were for her. Yet . . . The toothsome blonde who peered at him so knowingly had been his first love. It had been she who had led him into the world of base desires. Did a man ever forget his first delve into the salacious?

"Mon chére, what are you doing in San Antonio? It has been months since I have seen you. And who is this woman?"

"I am his wife." Maria Sara then insisted hotly, "And just who are *you?"*

"His *amour."*

His lover! Karl's *lover!* Maria Sara Keller could not stand the thought of her husband with this obvious whore. Maria Sara wanted to claw the *puta's* eyes out! Right here in the Menger Hotel lobby.

And the worst part of it was, Karl was looking at the blonde as if she were a sight for sore eyes!

"I am Antoinette," the woman explained dulcetly. "Antoinette Keller. Have you not heard of me?"

Why did she carry the Keller name? "My husband does not speak of the whores who kept him occupied before he fell in love with me."

Ignoring Maria Sara, the French *puta* slithered

to Karlito. "You have married, *mon chére?* How very regrettable. It was always my vision that you would return to me."

"Liebling, uh, I mean, Antoinette, my wife and I must be going."

Maria Sara stared at her husband. "What does it mean, this term *Liebling?"*

Antoinette smiled. "It is a German term of endearment." Her lush mouth parted, and she moistened her lips with a little pink tongue. "Has Karl not called you such?"

Before Maria Sara could pounce on her antagonist, Karl grabbed her arm and fairly dragged her out to the porte cochere. As did the chance encounter, the bracing night air of December slapped Maria Sara in the face.

"What does that *dama* mean to you?" she demanded, angrily. "Why is she a Keller? And do not try to claim her as some long-lost cousin. Only an idiot would be fooled into thinking you are related. Why did she say she is your beloved? How long has it been since you fornicated with that whore?"

"Watch your language, *meine Frau.* Someone will hear you."

He was right. In light of the upcoming trial, it would not do to draw attention. And a half dozen bystanders were staring at them. "Who was that woman?" Maria Sara whispered.

"My father's wife."

"What does she mean to you?"

"She was the first woman I lay with."

If a stiletto had been in Maria Sara's reticule—despite their need to keep up appearances!—she'd have rent her husband's heart. "You still love her."

"*Nein*. She was a passing fancy."

"You are lying, Karl Keller."

Her husband hailed a livery coach.

Despite the beating he had taken, Ian Blyer felt euphoric. He straightened himself up. A quick bath. A styptic pencil to the small cut on his jaw stopped his bleeding; the swelling wasn't as bad as he feared. A fresh change of clothes did wonders. By nine-thirty he'd made himself presentable again.

Splashing a lavish amount of cologne on his stinging cheeks, he gave himself a mental pat on the back. All right, Karl Keller might have prevailed in fisticuffs, but Ian had made his point. He had undermined Maria Sara with Charity.

While Charity had scoffed at his idea to free her, he felt confident her mind would change . . . once the tide started turning in the courtroom.

Whistling, he left the Menger and rode Syllabub to Beethoven Hall. Already his father and a group of citizens, roughly a score of them, were there. He made a proper showing as a politician's proud son, smiling and waving and speaking to the assemblage. Then his father took the podium.

"Friends, I am here with you tonight to announce my candidacy for the United States Senate." Stunned silence met his revelation, and

Campbell Blyer pushed his spectacles up the bridge of his nose. "Tell me, will you return a man to Washington who has brought shame on the State of Texas?"

A few spoke up to answer. "No!"

Campbell cocked his head. "One cannot help but wonder—with the daughter certain to be convicted of a felony, how effective can the father be? Now, I ask again. Will you return Gil McLoughlin to Washington?"

This time there was a resounding "No!"

"Good. Will you send me to Washington?"

"Yes!"

The crowd surged forward to speak with the candidate. He let it be known that he would return to Laredo by next light, "to study on how I can best serve our common interests."

It was an hour before the Blyers were able to leave the assembly hall. Each second had increased Ian's fury at his turncoat father. Both sat their horses, then rode toward the Menger, riding through a secluded and darkened section of town. It was bitter cold, as the fickle Texas climate could turn without a moment's notice.

Campbell complained about the norther. "I don't want to travel in this sort of cold."

"Funny you should mention that." Ian reined in. "What did you mean, you're returning forthwith to Laredo? You *will* stay with me until this business with Charity has been settled."

Campbell shook his head and braced his wrist on the pommel. "I will not. You must go it alone."

They argued for minutes, perhaps a quarter hour, but Campbell wouldn't budge from his stance. "I'm not waiting for dawn. I am leaving now," Ian's father decided. He kneed his mount, striking off in a westward direction.

Ian dug his heels into Syllabub's flanks. Catching up to his father, he grabbed for the rider's reins; Campbell tried to elbow him out of the way. Ian drew back his fist, driving it into his sire's jaw. Campbell slipped in the saddle, and the stallion bucked. With an exclamation of alarm the rider fell to the ground.

His mount whirled, his front hooves rising again. And they came down hard. On Campbell's head. Ian jumped to the ground and rushed to help his father. But it was too late. Blood and gore seeped over his shoes. His father was dead.

Ian cried out. Judas though he had been, Campbell Blyer was his father. But then a greater concern assaulted him.

"The authorities will hold me responsible for this," he said to the mournful wind. "I'll be arrested for murder!"

That wouldn't do. He hadn't finished his business with Charity.

Suddenly pleased that his father had announced he would be leaving for Laredo, Ian decided that Senator Blyer's disappearance would rouse no suspicions. "Anything could happen on the way to *Laredo.*" He made plans for evidence elimination. After quite an effort, he got the dead man atop the now calm stallion. Finding a bucket of slop water outside a doorway, Ian returned to wash down the red stains on the street.

"What can I do with the body? What about the horse?"

Well, he didn't have Señor Grande hidden in town for nothing. He found Rufino Saldino at his rented hut; Grande was playing cards with a couple of Latin companions.

"Don't discard that joker," Ian instructed barely above a whisper. "You have rubbish to discard."

By midnight, Ian was making his way back to the Menger.

The bells of the German cathedral struck midnight. Margaret had not returned from the harp recital, and for this Charity was thankful. She had wanted nothing to interrupt her moments with Hawk.

Making love was not a part of their evening. Decorum forgotten, they sat on the lyre-shaped sofa in the sitting room, holding hands. Hawk's words of comfort, as they had since his arrival hours ago, flowed through Charity like a healing tonic.

She said nothing of Ian's ridiculous plan. It didn't even bear repeating, so absurd was it. Instead, she made sense out of the evening's insanity in relation to Maria Sara and Ian. "They are both crazed as bedbugs."

Tenderly, Hawk squeezed her arm. "Angel, I could've told you that."

"Oh, Hawk, I still find it hard to stomach that she duped me! She was the best friend I ever had, outside of my family and you. What is wrong with me, that I can't tell friend from foe?"

"Don't go overboard. It's not as bad as you think. Disturbed as she is, she says she wants nothing but good for you, and we have to trust that she means well."

"At this point we have no other option, do we?"

Hawk nodded. "Unless there is a breakthrough in your case, we depend on her."

Charity stood and paced the rug. "I don't feel comforted." Her eyes turned to him. "A while back you said she accosted you at her wedding. I believe you spoke the truth."

"If that's an apology, I accept it."

"It is." Charity rushed to Hawk. "I was wrong. Very wrong. But, Hawk, my darling, I just couldn't believe that she would . . ."

"Believe it."

Charity took his big hand in hers. "What did she do?" When he told her she didn't want to know, she pressed, "Hawk, you know vague answers don't work with me."

Hawk threw his head back and exhaled. "*Wah'Kon-Tah!* What she did isn't an issue. Unless someone—perhaps the Eagle, perhaps not—can serve your case, you're dependent upon her good graces. There's no one else to vouch for your innocence."

"Because Señor Grande is on Ian's side."

"Exactly."

"Hawk, you promised to free me."

"And I did so with all good intentions. But . . ." Everything about him speaking to his uncertainty, Hawk muttered, "I am worried."

Ever since Hawk had demanded to be her lawyer, Charity had assumed he could free her. Her love didn't lessen even confronted with a show of vulnerability in the man she thought invincible. Yet . . . *What will happen if he can't pull an ace from his sleeve!*

"I may hang," she whispered in dread.

"Never!"

The boom of his loving and protective voice flowed through her, allaying her fears. She fell into the protection of Hawk's arms, trusting him with all her heart.

"I'm going to speak with Maria Sara. She's the one who mentioned the Eagle," Hawk explained. "First thing tomorrow, I'm going to see what she has to say about him."

Chapter Forty

"Toni . . . *Cawwwww, shoooo, cawwwww.* Toni . . . *Cawwwww, shoooo, cawwwww.* 'Toinette."

The rafters shook with Karl's snores; he sounded like a chorus of braying burros, as far as his wife was concerned. In their rented house near La Villita, Maria Sara punched her husband's shoulder in anger, to no avail.

Outside the wind howled, and shutters slapped against the windows. But neither the bluster from outdoors nor her husband's nocturnal bellows held a candle to Maria Sara's fury.

Karl had stormed out earlier that night, after their argument had continued at home. Upon his return—with a spent *pene,* to be sure—he had reeked of rotgut whiskey and cheap perfume. The same scent worn by that French whore, Antoinette. He had denied being with the woman. His wife didn't believe the *bastardo.*

"Cawwwww, shoooo, cawwwww . . ."

Maria Sara covered her ears with a pillow, then cast it aside. She would not rest until her foes were vanquished. Who first? Ianito or Antoinette?

"I will kill Ianito," she vowed, her words drowned out by Karl's snoring.

He had undermined Maria Sara; Charity's trust in her had been destroyed. There could be no friendship between them. Again he had shown that she was no more than Latin trash in Anglo eyes. Not once in Charity's suite had Ian Blyer taken more than a passing glance at her. And he had used the child of his loins as a pawn.

The mother had no use for the child, either, for obvious reasons, but she thirsted for the blood of vengeance.

Then she would scare Antoinette Keller away from Karlito.

Tossing back the covers, Maria Sara jumped out of bed. With all haste she dressed and slipped a knife in her skirt pocket. Her hand on the doorknob, she hesitated. Sister Estrella's voice echoed through her mind, like the shutters that flapped against the windows in the December wind.

It could all go wrong. And you owe a debt to the only person who has ever been loyal to you. You must guarantee Charity is set free.

She turned hurriedly from the door and swept to the kitchen area, where paper and pen were within reach. She sat down at the table, dipping the stylus into ink. The quick but decisive note penned, she tapped it into an envelope, then sealed it and left it on the table, where Karl could see it, should fate deem that she not return.

Tears obscured her vision as she reached for her

cloak and hurried out into the bracing night air. The wind blew the doorknob from her clutch; the door banged against the kitchen wall, sending a fierce gust of wind into the house. With determination she shut the door tightly.

In her haste, she had not looked back to see that the letter still rested in its place on the table.

Dead. Maria Sara was dead. Shot dead. On the morning of the thirteenth of December, two schoolboys found her body floating in the San Antonio River, several miles from the city. A garland of Christmas cedars wrapped her neck. It had been twelve days since Karl reported her missing.

Charity felt certain Ian's hands were tainted with Maria Sara's blood. He had been unusually quiet of late. Which spoke for itself. She prayed he would make some false move and implicate himself in the murder.

Maria Sara's funeral was held the afternoon of the fourteenth. There weren't many mourners. The widower, Charity, Hawk, Margaret. And Eleanor Narramore, who had arrived the previous night to give moral support to Charity during the trial, which was scheduled to start the next day.

Although Charity had been heartsick over Maria Sara's perfidy, she grieved at the loss. Not because Maria Sara had been the only hard-and-sure witness to her innocence. She mourned for the friend she thought she once knew.

"I'm sorry," Hawk whispered at the grave site in San Fernando Cemetery.

"Me, too."

She watched Karl take the white rose from his lapel and place it on his wife's grave, his mouth moving in a silent goodbye. *He loved her. He'll miss her.* And so would her son.

"Oh, Hawk, what will happen to Jaime?"

The widower must have overheard the question; he plodded past Margaret and Eleanor, stopping in front of Charity. "I will take care of him. He is my son by law. And by love. He is . . . was . . . Maria Sara's."

Charity's heart went out to Karl; she forgave him for keeping the truth from her. Touching his haggard cheek, she said, "My mother has offered to raise Jaime. Let her. She will do well by him."

Karl shook his head. "*Nein*. The boy is mine now."

Karl Keller trudged toward his mount, but his favorite cousin reached him before he climbed into the saddle. "Are you certain you want the responsibility of Jaime?"

"*Ja*, Charity. The boy will be loved and cared for," Karl Keller replied honestly.

His gaze turned back to the flat plain of the cemetery, where grave diggers were at work. Who had killed his wife? he agonized. But what did it matter? Maria Sara had passed on, and nothing or no one would bring her back. Never more would he hear her call his name with a Spanish inflection. Never more would she caress him with fingers hot and insistent. Never more would he know the joys and the hell of loving his Mexican lady-whore. His wife.

Tears fell, unashamedly.

Charity tried to comfort him, as did Margaret; but there was no comfort for Karl Keller. He had buried his mother. He had buried his brothers. He had lost his father over a mistake in judgment.

"It will be all right," Margaret murmured.

But these were platitudes. "Leave me alone," he said hoarsely. "I want to go back to the ranch. And to Jaime."

"What shall we do about your rented house?" Hawk asked, coming up beside them.

"There are but a few personal items there. Do whatever you please with them." Already he had filled a couple of boxes. But the chore had been too much for the widower. Maria Sara's lingering scent. Touching her filmy nightclothes. Maychance someday he could touch them without this pain in his heart. "I will take what I need only."

"Good God," Margaret groaned.

From the corner of his eye, Karl spotted Antoinette walking toward him; he turned his back. Despite Maria Sara's claims, he had not so much as breathed in the scent of Antoinette, though she had found him in a saloon on the night of his wife's disappearance—when he'd been tormented over how to make peace with Maria Sara. Antoinette had curled herself around him. As he told her then, he repeated today, "I want nothing of you."

"But, *cheri–*"

He pushed away her hand as it clasped his forearm; Karl stumbled toward the carriage. As if from far away, he heard her ask in her lilting accent, "If you do not want me, *mon chére.* should I return to your father?"

Ja.

After leaving the grave site, Charity demanded, "Hawk, I think Ian killed Maria Sara. We should tell the sheriff."

"I agree."

So did Margaret and Eleanor, but they stayed in the carriage when Charity and Hawk entered the sheriff's office. The sheriff was unimpressed with their conjectures. More than twenty witnesses placed Ian and his father at Beethoven Hall on the evening Maria Sara had disappeared. "And Mister Blyer has an airtight alibi for later that night." Sheriff Schultz spat a stream of tobacco juice into the battered spittoon to the left of his desk. "He played cards till the wee hours of dawn with some Meskin buddies."

"Might we know their names?" Hawk asked.

"Jorge Gomez, Federico Juarez, Rufino Saldino." Schultz put another wad of tobacco into his mouth, waving a hand in dismissal. "Get on outta here. I got work to do."

During their hack ride back to the Menger, Charity said to Hawk, "Señor Grande would lie for Ian."

"Twenty ordinary citizens wouldn't. And what about those other two card players? We've no reason to believe they would lie."

"If not Ian, then who killed Maria Sara?" she asked.

"Who knows?"

"Well, I still think Ian did it."

That night at dinnertime Charity, Margaret, Eleanor, and Hawk sat at a round table in the Menger dining room. No one showed much interest in the delectable meal of quail and rice, especially not Charity. Margaret and Eleanor kept up most of the conversation.

Other diners in the Menger, buffeted by gossip and lurid newspaper stories about "that McLoughlin girl," kept close watch on them. Three matrons at the nearest table made certain their conversation was overheard.

"Look at the shameless hussy, sitting there as calm as you please, as if she should even be showing her face in public."

"Which one is it? I can't tell the difference in those girls."

"There's a difference all right. One's a lady. The other's not. I certainly feel sorry for the family, having such a cross to bear as Charity McLoughlin."

Margaret and Eleanor glowered. Hawk, his face

and mouth severe, leaned over to Charity. "Let's leave."

"No," she whispered in return. "I won't give those old biddies the satisfaction."

The skinniest one said to the fattest, "Mildred, I can't wait for the hanging. Did you know invitations are already being printed?"

"My word!" Mildred chomped on a dinner roll. "Pass me that eclair you aren't eating, Gladys."

Margaret shot murderous looks at the women.

"Is that her attorney sitting there?" The third biddy, who wore a bird's-wing bonnet, nodded at Hawk. "He's mighty handsome, if you ask me."

"Not if you compare him to Senator Blyer's son," Mildred commented after devouring Gladys's dessert. "I hear she's secretly married to Mr. Blyer. He's going to testify against her because she refused to share the marriage bed."

"She refused Ian Blyer husbandly rights?" Gladys put a scrawny hand on her scrawny chest. "Mildred Beeson, how could that be? Why, Mr. Blyer is the handsomest man in Texas!"

"Then you can have him," Charity answered, making certain no one overheard but her table-mates.

Margaret and Eleanor chuckled. Hawk did not.

Thankfully the women paid their bill and departed, snubbing their noses in the process.

The red-haired Eleanor dabbed her mouth with a napkin, then placed it beside her plate. "Thank God they're gone."

"I've gotten used to such talk," Charity said.

"And I don't think we should let it bother us."

Hawk lifted his wineglass. "Certainly not."

Margaret introduced a new topic. "Mr. Hawk, I think it's terrible Karl's landlord wouldn't hand over our cousin's possessions."

"That is the least of our problems right now, though I will send someone back over there tomorrow."

"I'll talk to him." Eleanor took a sip of wine. "Women do have the upper hand when it comes to speaking with men."

"Good idea," said Margaret.

"I may be late for the opening proceedings."

"Oh, Eleanor, no." With her father gone to Mexico and Mutti taking care of Jaime and Maisie, Charity needed all the moral support she could get. "I need you here."

"She does." Hawk patted her hand, then turned to Eleanor. "Do you think you can get over there and back by nine o'clock in the morning?"

"Absolutely."

Margaret ran her thumb across the bottom of her wine glass. "Charity, I hate to say anything, being you're upset over Maria Sara, but I've got to. Your best witness is gone."

Hawk frowned at Margaret; Charity asked him, "What about Sheriff Ellis?"

"He's not a material witness. All he can attest to is Blyer's show of imbalance over Syllabub. And even that could be discounted, since Blyer had suffered a head wound."

Propping up her spirits, Charity said, "Don't be

such a naysayer. Papa and Sam will be back. And they'll have the Eagle with them. You wait and see."

"Charity, jury selection starts in the morning. We've heard nothing from Papa or Sam. We're desperate." Margaret lowered her voice. "Unless we get lucky and Ian is exposed as a no-good."

"I'm afraid she's right."

Charity gaped at Hawk's concurrence. "What exactly are you trying to say?"

"I'm trying to be practical. And realistic. We're in trouble." He rubbed his brow. "I'll ask for a delay. I'm going to Peterson's house. Tonight."

Hawk excused himself, returning in an hour to the impatient women who still waited at the table. All gossip-minded diners had exited, leaving the room deserted except for a waiter. Hawk pulled a chair close to Charity and put a sympathetic arm around her.

"No use. The judge won't grant the delay. Peterson wants it over and done with by Christmas. So it won't interfere with his holidays."

Margaret wasn't the only one to grimace at Peterson's self-indulgence, but she was the one to speak. "He's got a nerve. Questioning me until my head spun on Spanish history, making me listen to Mrs. Peterson's moronic prattle. Then he uses the excuse of Christmas to sabotage my sister. Goddamn him."

Margaret never swore, much less used Papa's verbiage.

"Oh, dear." Her face paling, Margaret lowered

her chin. "I know why Judge Peterson is vexed. Henrietta and I, well, we had words a couple of days ago. She made a cutting remark about Charity, and I, well, I told Henrietta she resembled the East African blind mole rat."

Charity laughed. She had no idea what a blind mole rat looked like, but if it looked like Henrietta Peterson, it was one ugly creature.

Turning solemn when she eyed the grave expressions of her loved ones, Charity realized how strongly her sister was pulling for her. A lot of people were pulling for her. Too many had involved themselves, had imperiled themselves. One had died. It caused her much pain, that death, for surely Maria Sara would be alive tonight, if not for her having become embroiled in this mess.

"Charity." Tenderly, gently, Hawk whispered her name. "Let's all retire for the evening. You need your rest."

Her eyes welded to his. She knew he was a man tormented; she heard it in his voice, saw it in his eyes, felt it in his touch as he buried her head against the strong wall of his chest. He yearned to free her, yet his hands were tied by circumstance. She squeezed her eyes shut. *What if he can't free me? What will it do to him?*

She knew her own fate. But her worries were for him. Once convicted, she would have mere days of torment—until her feet fell through the scaffold's trapdoor. Hawk would have all the rest of his years to suffer, knowing he hadn't been able to save her.

We may not have our tomorrows. But we do have tonight.

She said to Eleanor and Margaret, "If you don't mind, I'd like a private word with Hawk."

Chapter Forty-one

In a dusty cantina in Chihuahua City the calendar read December 14. Night had fallen hours ago. A trio of sombrero-wearing hombres sat in one corner and played monte. Beneath their table, and all about the taproom, yapping little hairless dogs with large, pointed ears jumped around like oversized fleas; no one paid them much heed.

At another table an overripe *señorita* picked her teeth with the point of a knife while her table-mates argued for revolution.

Standing at the bar, half empty glasses of tequila in front of them, Gil conversed with Sam Washburn until he felt something grabbing the ankle of his boot. A quick glance downward and Gil spied one of the "fleas," a Chihuahua pup, trying to look ferocious.

Both he and Sam chuckled amusedly at the sight, their first bit of levity in days. Their laughter increased after Sam barked back, which sent the small dog yelping in fear; it cuddled at the tooth-picker's feet, shaking and crying.

But neither man was here to enjoy the local

color. Gil asked Sam, "Think you can handle riding out tonight?"

Both men, now friends, were tired and dirty. Cactus liquor and a diet of beans and chilis hadn't settled well with either of them. Neither young, each had admitted to aches and pains brought on by their arduous travels deep into the Mexican high desert.

They had found El Aguila near the village of Santa Alicia, but not without difficulty. The man was, Gil supposed, the sort that some women would find attractive. Young, sanguine. Dark and swarthy. His physique showed none of the droop and sag of middle age. He had an air of danger.

Appearing the benevolent *hacendado,* Delgado had held court at his ranch. A bevy of comely *señoritas* had hovered around, waiting for any indication of the Eagle's slightest whim, and his whims were numerous. At Delgado's Hacienda Aguilera Real, too, the funny little dogs native to this part of Mexico, had been much in evidence.

Once Gil and Sam had finally gotten to speak to Delgado—it had taken days of kowtowing—the Eagle claimed to know nothing of Rufino Saldino, alias Señor Grande, or of Adriano Gonzáles.

Already Gil and Sam knew several things about Delgado. Paupers and potentates courted him, for he had been the greatest matador in Mexico, once upon a time. And the Delgados were one of Mexico's richest and most powerful families.

Now he walked a thin line between respectable and disreputable. When would the line snap?

"I have trouble believing you know nothing of the Shafter silver-smuggling operation," Gil had said.

Exhaling smoke from a long slim cigar, El Aguila pressed a scarred hand over his heart. "How do I know you are not a Texas Ranger?"

"You know who I am."

"Ah, *sí*. You are a lawmaker from Texas. You say."

"I am foremost a father. And my daughter needs your help. If—"

"Is she pretty, your daughter?" A leer and a flare of nostrils accompanied the question.

"She's spoken for." The thought of any daughter of his dallying with this desperado—why, Gil McLoughlin would gut the son of a bitch before he could cry for mercy. *Calm down.* "If you should remember *anything,* I'll make it worth your while." He swept his eyes across the Mexicans and their empty bandoliers. "Rebellion, Eagle, takes guns and ammunition. I can provide money for them."

"I am not a revolutionary." The cigar stuck between his teeth, he squinted past the curl of smoke. "I am a simple man of the land, happy here with my cattle and dogs and women."

"If the simple man takes on a complex memory, you let me know. My friend and I will be at the cantina in town. But not for long."

"You have my answer, *gringo.*"

Apparently Gil did have the Eagle's answer. Gil and Sam had been hanging around the cantina for two days. And there was no way to get fast word to San Antonio. Some rebels had cut the telegraph lines.

Gil tossed down the last of his tequila. "If we're gonna make train connections for San Antonio in El Paso, we'd better get riding."

In the aftermath of hearing that the judge wouldn't grant a delay, Charity cajoled Hawk into an interlude in her suite. "I just want to talk," she pleaded. Margaret, understanding, took her night-clothes and sneaked down to Eleanor's quarters.

"Would you like a drink?" Charity asked Hawk when they were alone together, with only one lamp lighting the sitting room. "*I* would."

"I'll fix them."

He pushed a path to the liquor cabinet. She followed. After pouring two snifters of cognac, he handed her one, his gaze falling to the floor. Sipping, he leaned a shoulder against the wall. There was an air of tension between them, and Charity didn't have to ask herself why.

He said, "Now that the Old One is doing better, I hope your mother will be able to attend the trial."

How could Charity tell him that she didn't want her mother in court when the final verdict was read? "Mutti won't be here. I sent a telegram, telling her to stay home. Karl and Jaime and Maisie need her more than I do. I have you and Margaret and Eleanor here, you know. Speaking of telegrams, I wonder why we haven't heard from Papa and Sam. They said they'd send word."

"The lines could be down."

Small comfort.

Charity placed her glass on a table. "I don't want a drink and I don't want to chat. I want you. I want what we had in Uvalde. And atop Firestorm. And in my room at home. And I don't want you to be careful, like you were at the stock pond." It wasn't raging passion that spiraled through her; she needed the solace and comfort of their lovemaking. "I want all of you, Hawk. All of you."

In his eyes she saw the war he fought, wanting her with the same intensity yet needing to protect her from all sorts of harms. She crossed to him and lifted her fingers to stroke his jaw. A tremor of desire quaked against her palm. Lamplight clarified the look in his dark eyes—she saw in them his own need for solace.

She arched against his solid form. "I'm no angel," she whispered, reaching on tiptoes to feather her lips across his. "I have been weeks without being held in your arms. And I can stand it no longer."

His hand settled at her waist. "We shouldn't."

She laughed low in her throat. "Good gravy, Hawk, what's the difference now?" *Don't let him know your deepest fears.* "My troubles will be over soon." *One way or another.* "Kiss me." Her fingers clamped his slim buttocks, her ankle twining behind his leg. "Or I shall have to proceed with ravishing you."

"You would, wouldn't you?"

Her passions igniting to a conflagration, she answered with a husky whisper. "I'll do anything—*anything*—to make you happy. I want to make us both happy."

"How did I ever live without you?" He pulled her tightly against him, his mouth slanting over hers. "But this is probably the stupidest thing the two of us have ever done."

"We haven't done it yet," she teased. "But I think we should tarry not another minute."

With a growl of primal need he lifted her into his arms, carried her into the sleeping chamber, and settled her on the bed. He helped with her clothes, her breasts spilling into his hands. Leaning to take one erect nipple into his mouth, he wound his fingers into the hair near her scalp. Desperation painted his actions as his loving caress stole downward to further ignite the fires of need and want.

Whispering words of love, he caressed her with deft fingers, until she begged him to give her all of himself.

He straightened; he tugged at his clothes. Soon he was standing naked—her naked savage. Her Indian, his bronzed form limned in the moonlight filtering through the windows. The glint of silver on his chest caught her eye.

"I haven't seen your neckchain in a long time." Her gaze traveled to his. "I'm sorry I made you take it back. How cruel I was, tossing your gift in your face."

He lifted the turquoise-studded chain over his head; he bent to place it around her neck, his touch stilling on her throat. "It hurt when you returned my gift. But I knew you'd someday wear my totem again. That made your anger easier to accept. Eventually."

"You never lost faith in me?"

"Angel, sometimes I wavered. But I never lost faith." She felt his smile. "Did you know the turquoise matches your eye color?"

"No." She fingered the flesh-heated stones. "Do you really think so?"

"Have faith in your beauty, my Charity. Have faith in yourself. And in me." He slid onto the sheets and pulled her to him. "Wear my totem. Know that you have my love. And that we'll have many years of love between us."

A tear welled. She closed her eyes and it spilled down her face. Never could she remember shedding a tear. "I will wear your totem till the day I die."

Morning.

Reality.

Hawk left before dawn, and Charity took breakfast in her suite on this, the fifteenth of December. She ate little, though Margaret insisted she needed her strength for observing the jury selection. She did, however, drink enough coffee to send her nerves ajitter. As if they weren't already.

When she and Hawk were making love, it had been easy enough to forget the outside world. Two in love—bodily and spiritually—could drown in the ecstacy of the moment.

One had to face facts in the light of day. She trusted Hawk with all her heart, but if they didn't get a break in her case and soon, no one—not even Hawk—could keep her from the gallows.

She wilted onto the edge of the bed, dropping her face into her hands. What would it do to Hawk, her execution?

Oh, this was no good. If he saw her like this, Hawk would be devastated. Furthermore, there was still hope. Papa and Sam could bring good news. And Ian just might be guilty of murder, and he might slip up, yet.

Margaret called into the room, "Eleanor dropped by. She's collected Karl's boxes. Said she'll meet us at the courthouse. Hawk did, too. Listen, you need to hurry. Or we'll be late."

Charity hurried. She was sure to dress in conservative attire. As she slipped on kid gloves, Margaret popped her head in the open doorway. "Triplet, uh, well, I know you don't want to see him, but—"

"Of course I want to see Hawk."

"I'm not talking about Hawk. It's—"

Charity gasped. "Ian?"

"Would you hush? There's a reporter in the corridor. He won't hear of not speaking with you."

Charity, furrowing her brow, waved a hand dismissively. The last thing she wanted was to face the fourth estate. "Tell him you're me. Tell him anything."

"He knows I'm Margaret. I can't hold him at bay forever. He says you'll want to hear what he has to say."

"Aren't reporters supposed to listen, not talk?"

"Maybe he has information that will help you, Triplet."

"All right. I'll see him."

Charity brushed the bodice of her simple brown frock, borrowed from Margaret, and lifted her chin. She marched to the door. Not inviting the reporter in, she stepped out into the hallway.

Tall and lanky, the well-dressed man who stood in the corridor was boyish looking, though Charity guessed his age at forty, owing to the gray fringe of hair that curled at his ears. He had flashing, intelligent blue eyes, not to mention dimples.

"Hi there, Miss McLoughlin. I'm Jay Rogers. San Antonio *Express.*" Quick as a blink, he pulled a tablet and pencil from his pocket. He licked the pencil tip. "What is your reaction to the news that Mrs. Antoinette Keller has been arrested for the murder of your primary witness, Mrs. Karl Keller?"

Good Lord. "I—I didn't know that had occurred."

"Earlier this morning. Antoinette Keller confessed."

Ian didn't do it? "Are you certain she confessed?"

"Yes, ma'am. Story goes the ladies got in a scuffle over Karl Keller's affections. His wife pulled a stiletto, but the French lady had a derringer on her person. Any comment?"

"I, uh, I—I'm pleased the case is solved."

Jay Rogers fell to more questions; Charity gave cursory replies. Her head throbbed. So Ian wasn't guilty—now what?

Even if her father and Sam Washburn showed up with the Eagle in tow, there were no guarantees that the man had knowledge of Adriano Gonzáles's activities.

Her final hope had died with Maria Sara.

What about Ian's "marriage" scheme? It seemed too foolish even to consider. Besides, any time she'd had any dealings with him, the results had been disastrous. Nevertheless, should she mention Ian's designs to Hawk? *Ha!* He would skin Ian alive, and then where would they be? No, it was better to say nothing about Ian's plan to free her.

But what could she do to help Hawk and herself? *I am trouble he doesn't need.* Hawk needed to return to his people and to his work in Washington. Should she somehow get her freedom, his credibility would suffer if he took a wife with a shadowy past.

Having a daughter of dubious repute had already tarnished her papa's reputation, she thought, reflecting on Campbell Blyer's malicious campaigning for her father's Senate seat. A man of the people—and certainly Hawk would be that again—needed a spotless reputation.

What choice did she have?

Whether she lived or died, Hawk deserved better than what she had to offer. Somehow, someway she must damage herself in his eyes so that he wouldn't mourn her loss. Then Hawk would be free. And he could go on with his life—with few regrets.

"Something wrong, Miss McLoughlin?" asked Rogers.

Everything. "Don't be absurd."

The reporter tucked the notebook back into his suit coat. "Nice meeting you, Miss McLoughlin. I'll see you at the courthouse." He loped off, his long legs halting at the top of the staircase. He turned to eye her. "By the way, what do you think about Senator Blyer being reported missing?"

"His whereabouts are the least of my concerns."

Chapter Forty-two

With heavy heart Hawk climbed the steps leading to Bexar County's red granite courthouse. Over the previous days he'd had faith in Blyer being arrested for Maria Sara's murder. The *Express*'s headlines dashed those hopes.

Ian Blyer hadn't killed her.

Hawk knew he must keep latching on to the belief that McLoughlin and Sam would show up, El Aguila in tow. If the Eagle proved worthless, though—Charity might be found guilty. If she went to the gallows, Hawk knew he'd spend the rest of his life—and his afterlife—tortured by what he had failed to do.

Topping the stairs to the second floor's wide hallway, he heard a familiar voice. "How doin', Hawk?" Tom Ellis, Sheriff of Uvalde County. "Ya're shore looking down at the mouth. Anything I can do to help?"

"Tell the truth. Tell the truth on the witness stand."

It was then that Hawk caught sight of a pair of

handcuffs dangling from Tom's gunbelt. Handcuffs—Laredo—Capturing Charity.

I could kidnap her again. What if the two of them just made a run for it? The authorities would ambush them before they got past the city limits. No, somehow Hawk had to free her. *Legally.*

He stomped into the courtroom. Taking his seat, he glanced at Charity, seeing the fear she tried to hide. Desperation was firmly entrenched in Hawk, too.

Marshaling his wits, he surveyed the courtroom. High ceilings. Musty. An American flag festooned the wall behind the judge's bench, and a pot-bellied stove, glowing red, sat in a corner to the right. Behind the chairs and tables for the defense and prosecution teams, a low wooden fence separated the principals from the onlookers. Today the courtroom had more than its fair share of spectators—the reporter Jay Rogers among them—all eager for the spectacle to begin.

It was then that Ian Blyer entered the courtroom. Brash as he pleased, he pranced up the aisle, halting mid-way as feminine ooh's and aah's lifted into the air.

"Emma, isn't Ian Blyer a fine-looking man?"

"Oh, yes, Abra. I hope he goes into politics, like his father."

Blyer sashayed over to shake hands with the ladies. One was not so taken with the man. "I prefer Mr. Hawk's looks, myself," she told her companions.

Hawk turned his gaze on Charity. He wondered what was going through her mind.

Blyer approached the rail and leaned to pat her shoulder. She jumped in her seat. "Dearest, don't be frightened of me." Lowering his voice to a whisper, Blyer continued. "Remember, a few well-placed words from me and you could be free. I'll be at the hotel, should you wish to talk."

It was a good thing Hawk didn't have hold of his knife, else that bastard would have found out what it was like to have his scalp lifted.

"Oyez! Oyez!" called the bailiff. "The Honorable District Court of the State of Texas for the County of Bexar, the Honorable Osgood Peterson presiding, is now in session. All rise."

Peterson, attired in his robes of office, took the bench.

Hawk yearned to take Charity's hand one last time. He caught a glimpse of the prosecutor. Lean and mean and dressed the part, Albert Ellersby shot him a superior look. Ellersby received one in return.

After the preliminaries, both attorneys went through their list of prospective jurors. Seating a jury proved frustrating to Hawk. Ellersby and Peterson disallowed all of Hawk's candidates. The rest—man after man, Ellersby's choices, seemed destined to rule against an angel of broken wing. But Judge Peterson, overruled each of Hawk's objections.

There would be no fair trial in Bexar County.

At noon Osgood Peterson banged his gavel. "We will recess until two o'clock."

Hawk led Charity, along with Margaret and Eleanor, outside. He hailed a hack. "Café Pámpana," he told the driver, then handed Margaret and Eleanor into the interior. His fingers on Charity's elbow, he whispered, "We need to talk."

Within ten minutes they had arrived at the café, the same one where he and Charity had shared Mexican hot chocolate. Where she had proposed marriage.

Margaret and Eleanor took a seat in the main eating area; it was filled with peasants. The manager showed Hawk and Charity to a private room off the kitchen. Chiles and chili powder permeated the air, and whitewashed walls were decorated in the Mexican motif—oversized painted flowers, posters depicting bullfights, tiles of Arabic influence.

Seated at a wrought-iron table, neither Hawk nor Charity was interested in food. Hawk addressed the diminutive waiter. "We'll have two bowls of *caldo*."

"Only soup, señor?"

"And coffee. Lots of black coffee."

As soon as the waiter had ducked into the kitchen, Hawk demanded, "What did Blyer mean, a few well-placed words and you could be free?"

"I—I have no idea."

"You've never been a good liar, Charity." Spying the waiter and his tray, Hawk said no more, not until they were once more alone. "Don't sit there, your hand shaking, trying to drink that coffee, and not tell me what Blyer meant."

"Did you know his father is missing?"

"Don't change the subject on me, I won't have it!"

Filling and lifting her spoon, Charity took a bite. "Delicious soup. Did you notice the tortillas they've floated in it? Much more tasty than rice or potatoes."

"Charity . . . don't dally with my patience."

She put down her spoon; coolness iced her eyes. "I paid good money for your services, so don't order me around."

Aggravated, Hawk, nonetheless, let the matter drop. He drank a cupful of coffee. He poured another from the pot the waiter had left. He nearly choked on the third, when Charity said, "Hawk, we've done some talking about our future. We agreed not to make any sort of tangible plans until I'm free, but there's something I've been needing to tell you. I am not free to make plans."

"You will be soon."

"Yes, actually I will. You see, I've decided to reconcile with Ian."

"You're lying through your teeth."

Her lip curling, she said, "You've always had the nastiest habit, David Fierce Hawk, accusing me of falsehoods—when you want to believe otherwise. If you'll get the stars out of your eyes, you'll see I'm serious."

His temper rising, Hawk slammed his fist on the table. Their dishes and cutlery rattled.

"The stars are out of my eyes."

"Good." She rose to stand and glanced at the clock. "It's half past twelve. I'd like the time between now and two to be by myself. Please make my excuses to Margaret and Eleanor."

She rushed through the café's back door.

With a furious shout Hawk swung his forearm across the table, sending plates and cups crashing to the floor. What a mess. Just like their lives.

What's the matter with you?

He'd reacted like a savage. Charity wouldn't go back to Blyer. She'd been upset by the trial's opening, that's all. She was fighting for her life, why shouldn't she have the right to make a stupid and *forgivable* scene?

He smiled.

Nothing had ever hurt her so much. Nothing. Her hands swept upward, disturbing her hair. What had been a single tear the previous night became a torrent today. Lying to Hawk tore her heart to shreds. But it was better this way. Let him think her cruel and unfeeling and fickle. She couldn't make him hate her any other way.

Her eyes nearly blinded from the cascade of tears, she pressed his totem to her bosom and hailed a hack. "The Menger."

Rushing to Ian's room, she pounded on the door. He answered her summons quickly. The mere sight of him revolted her.

"Dearest . . ." Ian, shirtless, scratched through

the tawny hair that carpeted his chest. "Shall I address you as wife?"

"Yes."

She signed her death warrant, for what was living if she couldn't be with Hawk?

Chapter Forty-three

Where was Charity?

The clock read two-fifteen. Judge Osgood Peterson sat scowling down at Hawk. His glower moved to Margaret, then Eleanor Narramore before returning to Hawk. "Where is your client, Mr. Hawk?"

"Detained, sir."

"If she's not here in ten minutes, I'm calling the sheriff. And her bond will be revoked."

Ellersby leaned back to speak with Jerome Hunt of Shafter; both men chuckled. Titters from the spectators rode across the courtroom. The gavel banged furiously. "Order in the court."

From behind, Hawk heard the heavy doors swing inward, and he exhaled in relief. Charity was here. Swiveling in his chair, he turned to eye her. But it wasn't Charity who entered the court. Pushing a wheelchair occupied by Maisie McLoughlin, Lisette walked down the aisle.

"If the court pleases," said Hawk, "I'd like a five-minute recess."

"Granted."

What had been a smile from Lisette turned to a worried frown. "Where is my daughter?" she whispered.

"What's the matter with the lass?"

Hawk tried to appease them before the gavel banged again. "Time's up. Court is in order."

Lisette took a chair by her daughter and the Narramore woman, Maisie's wheelchair dominating the passageway.

Not two seconds later, Hawk heard a boom to his rear. Turning, he saw Charity flying past her great-grandmother, who took the business end of a crook-neck cane and tried to stop her descendant. Tried to. Without a word to anyone, the defendant took her place next to Hawk.

"Where in the hell have you been?" he demanded lowly, wondering why her hair had a mussed look.

The door opened again.

Ian Blyer, a smirk on his face, strutted to the empty seat next to Jerome Hunt; naturally, Blyer's admirers hailed him. He leaned to whisper to the prosecutor. Ellersby took on a strange countenance, which didn't sit well at all with Hawk.

He leaned to do his own whispering. "Charity, what is going on?"

She refused to meet his eyes. "I should imagine the state will drop its charges."

Even before Hawk could form a question, Albert Ellersby rose to his feet, asking, "Your honor, may I approach the bench?"

Peterson nodded. Hawk went forward as well.

Leaning an elbow on the top of the bench, the prosecutor said, "Your honor, Mr. Blyer has informed me that he refuses to testify against the defendant."

"On what grounds?" Peterson asked sternly.

"He refuses to testify against his wife."

What? *What!* It was as if that statement had come from far, far away, and it nearly knocked Hawk off his feet. What was this lie? His eyes traveled to Charity; she avoided his gaze.

"This cannot be true," Hawk said to Peterson. "The defendant is *not* married to Mr. Blyer."

The judge appeared skeptical to all he surveyed. "We'd better hear what Mr. Blyer and Miss—his supposed missus—have to say about this. To my chambers. At once."

The woman who had lain in Hawk's arms last night, the woman who had said she loved him at least a dozen times before dawn, the woman who was breaking his heart came forward. Without meeting Hawk's eyes, she swept into the judge's chambers, Blyer holding her hand. Never before had Hawk had such an urge to plow his fist into Blyer's smug face, nor to grab Charity to him and shake the truth out of her.

Surely the marriage claim was some sort of a hoax.

Charity had been a virgin in Uvalde.

The judge sat at his desk, his stern visage unyielding. "Mr. Blyer, what is this? You're unwilling to testify against your lady?"

"You couldn't have said it more clearly, sir. I refuse to incriminate my wife. I am recanting my deposition."

"Odd." Osgood Peterson took a good gander at Blyer and Charity. "Odd that you would come forward with this at the last moment. It's my guess that you're not telling the truth."

"On the contrary." Blyer gestured to Charity. "Show him the marriage license, dearest."

"Y-yes, of course." Charity dug in her reticule. "We were married in Nuevo Laredo on August twenty-ninth."

"As you know, she had returned from Shafter on the twenty-eighth," Blyer put in. "At the time I knew nothing of her crime. We married. But the . . . the marriage wasn't consummated." Blyer shot a woeful expression at the judge. "This is personal. It pains me. I don't wish to offend my wife's sensibilities, your honor." He put an arm around Charity. "This will all be over soon, dearest."

Hawk's fists were clenched. Charity leaned in to Blyer.

Jutting out his clefted chin, Blyer told the judge, "My wife was experiencing a delicate time of the month on our wedding night. To my shame, I tried to force my advances, and I, well, I frightened her. She left me, sir. Left me! And my pride was bruised. I do have a reputation as a ladies' man, as you may know. I became insane. In September, I found her burying the proceeds of the smuggling operation. I struck at her by filing a report."

"Young woman, is this true?" Peterson's scowl etched wrinkles into his brow.

Hawk felt the blood drain from his face when she replied in a steady voice, "Yes."

She was a bagful of surprises, all right. He had a lot of questions. But something stopped his protests of foul play. Somewhere in the recesses of his mind, he knew that Ian Blyer could free Charity McLoughlin.

And wasn't that the most important thing here?

Yet . . . at the moment he would have gladly strung a noose around her neck—*if* he could have been assured she wouldn't die from it. He bit his tongue.

Peterson announced, "Mr. Blyer, your marriage is invalid. It wasn't consummated."

"On the contrary," the peacock declared. "We spent the lunch recess in my quarters at the Hotel Menger. The lady is now truly my wife."

No! You didn't! You didn't let him touch you! Hawk glared at her, silently demanding a denial that never surfaced. His blood surged through his ears; his gut twisted. No wonder she was late in returning to court. Little wonder her grooming was less than impeccable.

"One of the witnesses to our marriage ceremony is available." Blyer flashed his teeth. "Señor

Rufino Saldino waits to be called."

"Bring in the witness."

Hawk leaned toward Peterson. "If it pleases the court, I'd like a few minutes alone with my client."

"Granted." He motioned to the others. "We will wait in the courtroom while Mr. Hawk and Miss, uh, *Mrs.* Blyer are in conference."

Hawk closed the door behind them. She stood, her back straight, meeting his furious eyes. Her hand moved slowly up to her hair to smooth the disarrayed chignon.

"What kind of game are you playing?" he growled.

"No game. I—I'm sorry it had to come to this, Hawk. But Ian was in my life before I met you. And you never asked if he and I were married. In the beginning I saw no need to inform you."

Hawk raked his memory. He had never come right out and asked if she'd married Blyer, but she had gone to Laredo for that very purpose, hadn't she? Maisie McLoughlin had told Hawk that county clerks in *Texas* were watching for a marriage license, so he'd assumed no marriage had taken place. But if it had taken place across the border . . .

"I thought about seeking an annulment," Charity said. "Then things started to change for me and you. I saw that we weren't right for each other. You were no longer the savage I fell in love with. You became much too practical for me."

Hawk had known pain in the past, but Charity

turning against him was the most brutal blow of his life. "So be it. Let's hope it turns out well for you. Because you may not have beaten the system, *Mrs.* Blyer."

The judge, followed by Blyer and Prosecutor Ellersby, filed back into the chamber. Señor Grande was right behind them. The Mexican gave a plausible account of the marriage of Charity McLoughlin and Ian Blyer. When he had finished, Judge Peterson whipped off his spectacles and asked, "Mr. Ellersby, do you still have a case?"

"No, your honor."

"I feel as if there is something, maybe several issues, that do not hold water in this instance, but I have no choice but to dismiss the case of the People of Texas against Charity McLoughlin. Uh, Mrs. Blyer."

Damn her if she didn't curtsy and say, "Thank you, sir," then take her husband's arm.

"Just a minute, young woman." Peterson shook a finger. "We will do this by the book. You and your husband take your places in the court."

"If we must," said Blyer before planting a kiss on Charity's cheek.

Hawk could have killed them both.

He refused to look at Charity when Osgood Peterson announced the turn of events. The courtroom went wild. But Hawk kept his seat as Charity, ignoring her family beyond a "leave me alone," left with her husband.

Hawk, as well, tried to bypass the McLoughlins.

Margaret's whitened fingers clamped around the top of her great-grandmother's wheelchair. "We . . . we didn't know."

"Neither did I."

Lisette touched his sleeve. "I am so sorry."

Shaking her head in dismay, Eleanor Narramore sat wringing her hands.

Her face white as marble, the Old One shook her head back and forth. "I woulda rather had you in the family, lad. I woulda rather."

She seemed to age before his eyes. But Hawk was too heartsick to pay mind to a distraught old woman. Cold with shock, he stared with unseeing eyes out a window of the courtroom. Vaguely he heard a commotion from the entrance. The McLoughlin entourage rushed toward it. He didn't bother to turn and investigate the cause. Not until he heard Gil McLoughlin boom, "I'm here to free my daughter."

Hawk whipped around. He saw two dusty men and the crowd that parted for them. McLoughlin and Sam Washburn. They marched forward, and then Hawk heard a gasp go up from the assembly. Was it of fright? Or admiration? Even Margaret was affected by his presence.

A stranger separated himself from the crowd. Hawk didn't doubt his identity.

The Latino ambled forward, stopping at the gate. He was garbed in a wide sombrero trimmed in silver above tight britches and a bolero, both as black as the straight hair that reached his shoulders. Six-guns rode at his hips; bandoliers were strapped to his shoulders. Like heat from a furnace, mystery and danger shot from him.

"Buenos . . . tardes, amigos." The mouth peeled back to show white teeth that emphasized the scar on his jaw. "I am El Aguila."

The Eagle.

Chapter Forty-four

More than sick over what she had done—and more than devastated over what she had allowed Hawk to think she and Ian had done that very afternoon!—Charity allowed her tears to fall freely. She cared not that others in the swank restaurant saw her. She cared not what Ian Blyer thought, either.

She cried for Hawk . . . and the ashes of their starcrossed love.

"Is this any way to celebrate our good fortune and our upcoming years of connubial bliss?" Ian chided for about the tenth time and took another chug from a stemmed glass. "Drink your champagne, dearest."

"Go to hell, Ian Blyer."

Through the cloud of her tears, she spied a couple of men approach their table. Deputies, she thought dully, catching sight of silver stars pinned to their chests. Wait. Wasn't that Jay Rogers behind them?

Great. Another scandalous headline to shame my family.

Both deputies drew their revolvers, pointing them at the back of Ian's head. What was going on? Had they somehow been found out? Oh, Lord, they were going to be arrested for perjury.

The older lawman spoke. "Ian Blyer, put your hands up."

Ian's eyes rounded like saucers; instinctively, he raised his arms. In a flurry of motions, the lawmen clamped handcuffs on his wrists and yanked him to his feet.

"I beg your pardon," Ian blustered. "Do you know who you are accosting? I am *Senator* Campbell Blyer's son! I'll have your badges for this!"

They hustled him out of the restaurant. Charity sat puzzled. Why hadn't they arrested her, too?

Jay Rogers grabbed a chair and turned it around to straddle the seat. Parking an elbow on the table, he said, "Congratulations on your freedom."

"I don't want to talk to you," she said.

"Can't say I blame you, but . . . What do you think about Rafael Delgado of Chihuahua appearing in court this afternoon?"

The Eagle!

"My father—has he returned, too?" Rogers nodded, and Charity gave a large sigh of relief. "Wh-what happened with Señor Delgado?"

"Apparently he hadn't been of a mind to help, but something honorable in his nature prevailed. He followed Senator McLoughlin and Doctor Washburn to the train depot in El Paso. He—"

"Mr. Rogers, what happened in the courtroom?"

"He swore to your innocence in the Shafter silver-smuggling scandal."

"Hawk. Hawk was right all along," she whispered, mostly to herself. *My God! I hurt Hawk for nothing. Nothing!*

"The big question is, what do you think about your husband's arrest?"

"Few things could please me more."

Rogers picked up the champagne bottle, pouring himself a glass. "The paper's circulation will go through the roof tomorrow." He winked, held up his glass in a toast, and took a congratulatory sip. "You've sold a lot of newspapers for us, ma'am. Shall we drink to it?"

She wasn't interested. She yearned to race to Hawk. But curiosity was a force to be reckoned with. One quick question, and she would be on her way. "Why was Ian Blyer arrested?"

"His Mexican cohort made a big mistake, riding Senator Blyer's mount to the courthouse. The sheriff recognized the stallion immediately. Didn't take much for Rufino Saldino to confess to being an accomplice to the murder of Campbell Blyer. A few more facts came out, too. He admitting lying about your wedding.

"It turns out, Blyer was the mastermind behind the smuggling. Got his father mixed up in it, too. Blyer the younger set you up from the beginning."

She laughed in bitter irony.

"How *do* you feel about all this?" Rogers went for his notepad.

She jumped to her feet, knocking her chair to the floor in her haste. "I feel it's high time for me to find David Fierce Hawk."

She had a lot of explaining to do. A lot of begging for his forgiveness. Undoubtedly he'd never understand her reasons. But he needed to know the truth.

Charity hurried through the streets, reaching the Menger as twilight fell. Her footfalls echoed through the lobby and up the staircase as she ran toward Hawk's suite. Ted, a portmanteau under one arm, was whistling "The Eyes of Texas" while unlocking the entrance.

"Where is Mr. Hawk?" she demanded, out of breath.

"Gone. He checked out about three this afternoon. Rode out on that fine stallion of his, Firestorm."

"Where did he go?"

"Said something about the Indian Territory."

Charity sighed in frustration. She couldn't—just couldn't!—let Hawk go away without seeing him. But what could she do? A carriage would never catch him; he had a three-hour head start. She had to get the fastest horse the livery stable had available.

But it was dark outside.

I can't ride off into the night. She damned sure could! For Hawk, she would do anything. Anything!

Taking a quick look at her feminine attire, and knowing no riding clothes were in her room, she studied young Ted. *Hmm.*

"Ted, take off your clothes. "

A smile of astonishment burst upon his freckled face. "Why, Miss Margaret, you've answered my dreams."

"Dammit, I'm Charity! Now give me your clothes!"

Chapter Forty-five

Garbed in Ted's shirt and britches, Charity purchased a surefooted gelding from the livery stable and rode hell-bent out of San Antonio. The dark of night didn't frighten her—for once in her life. She was scared witless that she wouldn't be able to catch Hawk.

Despite her prowess as a horsewoman, her trail held no promise of her beloved. Not that night. Not as dawn approached. When the lathered gelding refused to go further, she rested the mount beside a gurgling creek, then took the saddle blanket and gave Firestorm II—as she had dubbed the gelding—a rubdown.

Herself exhausted, she sank to the ground, resting her back against a cottonwood's trunk. She gave way to tears. She couldn't catch Hawk. He was lost to her. Lost to her! Her past mistakes would haunt her all the rest of her days.

He might never know that it was her love that had spurred her to betrayal.

This was a price worse than hanging.

Firestorm II plodded over to nuzzle her shoulder. His tired eyes seemed to ask, "Where do we go from here, mistress?"

"I have no idea," she answered.

Maybe Hawk turned back.

Charity made the slow return to San Antonio. She learned that her mother and sister were consoling her Uncle Adolf, over the arrest of Antoinette. She also learned that Hawk hadn't turned back. No one had seen or heard from him.

"I'm sorry," her papa said.

The Menger reunion of father and daughter was brimming with sweet sorrow. "Thank you," she whispered, hugging him. "Without you and Hawk, not to mention Sam, my name wouldn't have been cleared."

Papa kissed her forehead. "I'd do anything for my baby."

"Have I ruined your career, Papa?"

"Absolutely not. What the Blyers did to us was pure evil. Folks have been rallying around. They're on our side."

"Thank God." Charity leaned against her father. "Hawk doesn't know about all the developments. Papa—If you see him in Washington, will you tell him the truth?"

"No, ma'am. That's for you to impart. Personally."

He was right, of course. "I tried to. I was too late."

Now it was too late for everything. By not putting her fate in Hawk's hands, she was dying a thousand deaths. Each more painful than the one before.

"May we come in?" Eleanor asked as she wheeled Maisie into the suite's sitting room.

Somehow Charity managed to receive them with a light heart. "Maiz, Eleanor, it's good to see you."

"Ye oughtn't t' be pleased to see me, ye whelp. I've a good mind t' take me cane t' ye!"

Eleanor skirted around the wheelchair and took Charity's cold hand. "Did your father tell you about the letter?"

"What letter?"

Reaching into her pocket, Eleanor extracted an envelope. "It's from Maria Sara. The landlord discovered it yesterday, when he was tidying up the place. Would you like for me to read it to you?"

"No. Just . . . just tell me what it says."

"She swore that you had no knowledge of Gonzáles's operation. She thanked you for your loyalty and friendship. She apologized for hurting you." Eleanor dabbed her nose with a handkerchief. "The poor thing said you were the only true friend she ever had."

Sinking into a chair, Charity squeezed her eyes closed. "She really was my friend."

"Yes."

The lump in her throat grew to hellish proportions. When she was finally able to speak, Charity glanced at Eleanor, then Maisie, then her papa. "I wish *amiga mia* could have been able to love Jaime."

"She didn't claim to be perfect." Her papa handed Charity a snifter of cognac. "Drink," he ordered. "You could use your mama's remedy right now."

"No, I deserve to suffer without any sedative." She shook her head. "Oh, Lord, I have made so many mistakes."

"Not a soul on this earth is perfect, lass." Maisie reached to tap her with the cane. "And I'm feeling awful sorry for ye. I know ye loved the lad."

"Love, Maiz. Love, not loved."

"How can I help you, Charity?" Eleanor asked.

"Actually, there is something."

She took a deep breath, deciding she would get away, travel to Spain, to Olga. There, she would try to put her life in order. *It'll never be in order, not without Hawk. He is what you need. Wherever he goes, you should be following.*

Wearily, she turned to Eleanor. "Do you know if the Narramore Line has a ship sailing for Europe anytime soon?"

"Ye won't be going nowhere without me!"

The steamship *Fallen Angel,* flagship of the Narramore Line, weighed anchor in Galveston on Christmas day. Its foghorn gave a mighty and forlorn bellow that rolled mournfully across the gray morning. Charity, alone on the swaying deck, watched land fade into the horizon. Clutching the lapels of her cloak to her chin, she shivered with despair.

Hawk. I'm so, so sorry about everything.

She had, before leaving San Antonio, posted a letter to him, sending it in care of the Indian Agency on the Osage reservation. Naturally there hadn't been any reply, and she expected there would be none.

"Merry Christmas, Miss McLoughlin."

She turned to the captain. Eleanor's son. She and Norman had two sons, Charity recalled. This one was Jeff Narramore, the younger one; Eleanor had called Jeff Davis Narramore the less handsome of the two. He had the look of the sea to him. He was tanned of face, lean of physique, confident of self. The breeze ruffled his dark brown hair, brought out the red of his mother's side of the family. Curiosity called out, *if this is the less handsome of the two, what does Beau Narramore look like?*

Not that Charity really cared. No man but Hawk was for her.

Jeff Narramore, nonetheless, had done his best to cheer her since she'd come aboard the previous evening. "Miss McLoughlin, I wondered if you might join me and my executive officers for a holiday breakfast. Your great-grandmother is in the dining room already. She's having an eggnog."

Maisie. She had been unusually tame this morning. Suspiciously so. And Maisie wasn't one to drink eggnog.

Not wishing to give Jeff Narramore any encouragement, Charity replied, "Thank you, but no thank you. I'd rather stay topside for a while."

"Oh, no. I'll have none of that. What I say goes on the *Fallen Angel.*"

He clasped her elbow and—there was no other way to describe it!—hustled her down the deck. Just before they reached the companionway leading to the executive dining hall, an arm reached out to grasp her from behind a bulkhead.

Fast as lightning, handcuffs were clamped around her wrists. *Handcuffs!* Her gaze traveled to the right. And she caught sight of Hawk.

Her heart soared!

Hawk!

Hawk . . . wearing the same sort of outfit that he'd worn on the night he abducted her in Laredo. Stetson and buckskins.

"Thank you, captain," he said, not looking at her.

"Do all your kidnappings require an accomplice?" she asked, her heart pounding in her chest.

"Well, you're quite a handful, little hellcat."

"Oh, Hawk, I have so much to explain to you. About Ian—"

"Don't spoil our reunion by bringing up that bastard."

Her gaze fell upon the sensuous curve of Hawk's lips. "All right."

"Good." Hawk nodded at Jeff Narramore, then fixed a stern look on Charity. "Two questions. Are you going to follow me willingly? Or do I need to risk both our necks by hauling you down those stairs?"

She surveyed him boldly. "You aren't planning to keelhaul me, are you?"

"That does it." As if she were a sack of flour, Hawk picked her up and tossed her over his shoulder. "I'll teach you to mess with me."

Jeff Narramore chuckled.

Once more she had been set against. But this time she was all for the treachery.

Laughing as Hawk negotiated the rocking steps, her hair swinging this way and that, she placed kiss after kiss on his arm. Once they reached the lower deck, she nipped his shoulder playfully.

"Hellcat."

"Savage." He set her to her feet, and she gazed up into his warm brown eyes. Raising her wrists, she said, "Unlock me. I'll do whatever you want."

"No way. Save your feminine wiles. Until later." He winked. "For now, I'm not taking any chances." Craning his neck toward Narramore, he said, "Lead the way, captain."

They followed Jeff Narramore into the dining area. It was decorated in holly and Christmas bells. Maisie and her wheelchair were parked next to a makeshift altar. Altar? Charity's eyes widened. Across Maisie's lap was a *shotgun.*

"What is going on? How long have you two been in collusion—*this* time?"

"Don't ye be making no never-mind. Ye won't be getting away, lass." Maisie patted the gun stock. "If ye don't behave, I'll be peppering your arse."

"You wouldn't dare."

"She would, angel. What's a shotgun wedding without a shotgun?"

"Sh-shotgun wedding?"

Hawk marched his captive forward. Jeff Narramore cut around them, going for a Bible. Several Indians filed in, as did a couple of the Four Aces's cowboys. And Charity caught sight of Sam Washburn, too. What on earth were they doing here?

The captain pointed to the area immediately in front of him. "Step right up."

Good gravy. This really was a wedding. Her wedding. Hawk's wedding. Their wedding! Once she wouldn't have been forced into anything. *Once.* Charity was now eager to comply.

As the captain read the solemn vows, she answered firmly in the affirmative.

"Will you, David Fierce Hawks take this woman to be your lawfully wedded wife?"

"It depends."

Oh, no! This was undoubtedly some sort of farce meant to pay her back for her misdeeds.

"It depends on whether she makes a few extra vows." Hawk leaned to plant a kiss on her cheek. "She must promise that she'll never lie to me again. And if she does, I have the right to beat her senseless, tie her to a stake, and lift her scalp."

"I will. And you'd better not!"

"Not good enough."

"Okay. You may scalp me if I ever concoct anything again."

"That's better." He raised her bound wrists to brush his lips across her hand. "Because I don't want *ever again* to know the hell of the past few days."

The captain cleared his throat. "David Fierce Hawk, will you love, honor, and cherish her for as long as you both shall live?"

Instead of another kiss, he swatted her backside. "Provided she doesn't give me any trouble about forming a Wild West show."

"Wild West show?" she repeated incredulously. "We can't do that. We've got to turn back. The Osage—Washington—"

"It's the Wild West show or nothing."

Maisie waved her cane. "Fierce Hawk, don't ye be forgetting about me. Ye promised I could make change at the ticket window."

Charity rolled her eyes. Stacking bills and making change—probably involving a bit of short-changing—would make Maisie happy as a pig in a trough. Maisie, though, was not the issue here.

"Hawk wouldn't be happy," Charity said. "His destiny is to help his people. It's not practical, the Wild West show. He'd be miserable in no time."

"I cannot bring peace to others if I do not have peace myself. Charity is my peace. She is my people." Hawk's strong, clear voice resonated within her. "Captain, she must also vow never to second-guess what I want out of life."

Charity looked deeply into his eyes. Not long ago he'd asked her to have faith in herself, in him. In *them*.

If he said he wanted to form the show, then that's what he wanted!

"Will I be needin' ta lift this shotgun, lass?"

"Don't you dare aim that thing at me, Maiz." Charity sighed. "Captain Narramore, there's no baby. There's no reason for a shotgun wedding."

"She's absolutely certain there's no baby?" Hawk asked. "Captain, perhaps you should remind the bride of a certain recent night she spent in my arms . . ."

"I don't need any reminders." She gazed up into Hawk's eyes. "And I'm not certain there isn't a baby. I hope there is."

"Ah, I may be seeing my great-great-grandbairns yet."

"Maiz, stay out of this. Hawk, we can't drag a baby around while we put on some Wild West show."

"Don't start getting sensible on me, Charity."

Once more Narramore cleared his throat and lifted the Bible. "Hawk, shall I repeat my question?"

"No need for that. By *Wah'Kon-Tah* and the Almighty, I will love, honor, and cherish Charity McLoughlin—forever and ever and ever."

"Good morning, Husband."

"Good morning, Wife."

They awoke, their bodies still joined. Amidst the tangled sheets of their marriage bed—in quarters borrowed from the captain—Charity nestled against Hawk's shoulder. She wore his totem. In the end it had brought her good luck.

Her lips opened on her husband's warm flesh, sweeping upward to his throat. His ankle wrapped around the back of her knee, bringing her even closer to him, if that was possible, that they could get any closer in body and spirit.

"Thank you," she murmured, repeating the words she had said the previous night, in the privacy of the luxurious cabin. "Thank you for believing in me. Tell me again how all this happened."

"I got to Waco before I had second thoughts about what you and Blyer were trying to accomplish. I realized I couldn't have been that wrong about you. I knew my angel wouldn't betray me, unless she had some higher motive than freeing herself."

A tear fell. *Gads!* She was becoming a veritable watering pot! "All I wanted was to make it easy for you. All I want—all I've wanted for a long time—is your happiness."

"Sweet angel . . ." Hawk's fingers combed through the hair at her temple. "I should have known there was no tarnish on your halo."

"I don't have a halo."

"Yes, you do."

Hawk got the last word. At last.

Author's Note

Writing about the McLoughlin family—first in *Caress of Fire,* and now in the love story of Charity and Hawk—has been a pleasure to me as a writer. I haven't had to put characters aside for ever and always! As I finish this novel, I look forward to the next McLoughlin daughter.

Charity needed a hero to understand her; triplet Margaret needs a hero who'll take the starch out of her britches. I have the perfect fellow in mind . . . and you've met him already. Margaret, being the brain she is, will much enjoy trying to take the starch out of *his* britches.

Brother Angus and triplet Olga make appearances in the next book, *Wild Sierra Rogue.* And I can't help but wonder if Maisie will get caught shortchanging one of those Europeans . . .

Martha Hix
San Antonio, Texas
March, 1992

PUT SOME PASSION INTO YOUR LIFE . . . WITH THIS STEAMY SELECTION OF ZEBRA *LOVEGRAMS!*

SEA FIRES (3899, $4.50/$5.50)
by Christine Dorsey
Spirited, impetuous Miranda Chadwick arrives in the untamed New World prepared for any peril. But when the notorious pirate Gentleman Jack Blackstone kidnaps her in order to fulfill his secret plans, she can't help but surrender—to the shameless desires and raging hunger that his bronzed, lean body and demanding caresses ignite within her!

TEXAS MAGIC (3898, $4.50/$5.50)
by Wanda Owen
After being ambushed by bandits and saved by a ranchhand, headstrong Texas belle Bianca Moreno hires her gorgeous rescuer as a protective escort. But Rick Larkin does more than guard her body—he kisses away her maidenly inhibitions, and teaches her the secrets of wild, reckless love!

SEDUCTIVE CARESS (3767, $4.50/$5.50)
by Carla Simpson
Determined to find her missing sister, brave beauty Jessamyn Forsythe disguises herself as a simple working girl and follows her only clues to Whitechapel's darkest alleys . . . and the disturbingly handsome Inspector Devlin Burke. Burke, on the trail of a killer, becomes intrigued with the ebon-haired lass and discovers the secrets of her silken lips and the hidden promise of her sweet flesh.

SILVER SURRENDER (3769, $4.50/$5.50)
by Vivian Vaughan
When Mexican beauty Aurelia Mazón saves a handsome stranger from death, she finds herself on the run from the Federales with the most dangerous man she's ever met. And when Texas Ranger Carson Jarrett steals her heart with his intimate kisses and seductive caresses, she yields to an all-consuming passion from which she hopes to never escape!

ENDLESS SEDUCTION (3793, $4.50/$5.50)
by Rosalyn Alsobrook
Caught in the middle of a dangerous shoot-out, lovely Leona Stegall falls unconscious and awakens to the gentle touch of a handsome doctor. When her rescuer's caresses turn passionate, Leona surrenders to his fiery embrace and savors a night of soaring ecstasy!

Available wherever paperbacks are sold, or order direct from the Publisher. Send cover price plus 50¢ per copy for mailing and handling to Zebra Books, Dept. 4029, 475 Park Avenue South, New York, N.Y. 10016. Residents of New York and Tennessee must include sales tax. DO NOT SEND CASH. For a free Zebra/Pinnacle catalog please write to the above address.